Bluestar

by Sammy Jo Pendergrast

DORRANCE
PUBLISHING CO
EST. 1920
PITTSBURGH, PENNSYLVANIA 15238

Dorrance Publishing Co
585 Alpha Drive
Suite 103
Pittsburgh, PA 15238
Visit our website at *www.dorrancebookstore.com*

ISBN: 978-1-6461-0764-3
eISBN: 978-1-6461-0037-8

Bluestar

ORBANE SOLAR SYSTEM

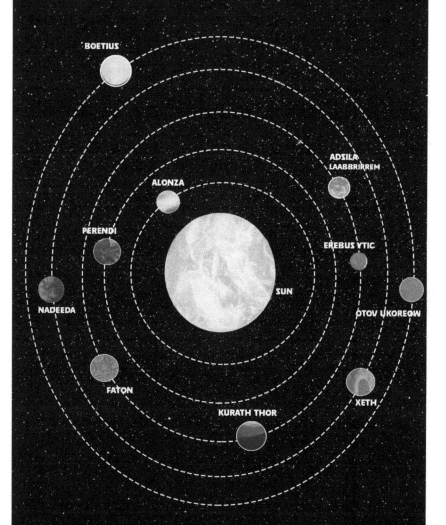

Prologue

Blast fire accompanied by earsplitting explosions told Maliha that they were running out of time. Her troops were falling fast and the Android army was gaining ground every minute. Forty-seven years of fighting in the Great Civil War against the Androids was coming to an end; her people were losing. She looked out across the shipyard seeing the battle rage on near the outskirts of the city towards the Resistance command base located on a red dirt hill. If they got past her and her men the city would be lost and the war over. Her heart beat faster not because she was afraid but because of the thought of her sisters and their survival if the war was lost. They were the true rulers of Orbone Galaxy and if they died, the Androids would begin wiping out all those who they deemed unworthy in the empire. She would not let that happen, not after all her family had fought and sacrificed for alongside the many races lost to the war.

"They're getting closer," the familiar voice of her sister said softly.

Maliha did her best to hide her weariness and regained her composure as ruler, though she couldn't help the strain in her voice as she responded, "I know." Turning around Maliha studied her sister's hazy blue eyes. Her long dark hair was braided neatly down her back and stood out on her golden skin. *We are the stark contrast of each other,* Maliha thought as she brushed the short stands of her military bob cut out of her face. At first glance you would mistake them as humans in their early twenties except for the unique color of their eyes. They were Qualias, ancient beings blessed with unique abilities and long life from the stars. They were as strong and quick as the elves, but with the appearance of humans. Her sister was six years younger than Maliha, making her fifty-nine, but out of all the sisters they were the closest.

"The others can't stay here much longer," Princess Nakedra responded while pushing her black framed glasses up on her nose.

Maliha knew this. As long as one of her sisters was alive the galaxy would remain safe even if the Androids took over. The other races wouldn't accept a new ruler unless the Princesses of the Nightstar bloodline were terminated. As long as one remained alive, there was still a chance of stopping the Androids and restoring peace once again throughout the galaxy. "I'll have Karasi and the others escorted off the planet to Kurath Thor. The elves have promised to keep them safe for a while until we find a better option."

"You know they won't like that," Nak replied, watching the battle in the distance. "Especially Reva. She won't want to leave your side."

Maliha's thoughts turned to her little sister, the middle child of the seven. They were practically identical except for the color of their eyes and the stubborn will of Reva. Even as a child she was resilient and now as a teenager she had only became more ironclad. Despite this, she was a damn good soldier. She was born to be one just as her father had been. Maliha had grown quite fond of her during the war because of her natural ability to strategize attacks and execute them. She always overcame despite the odds, and even after a hard day of battle, she never gave up on herself or her soldiers. "I'll talk to her, but she knows how important it is to keep each other safe for the Resistance."

"She'll refuse your orders to stay. She always does, but this time she can't. You know that, right?" Nak asked turning to Maliha for an answer.

Maliha knew Nak had seen the outcome of this battle. It was her special ability while the other sisters had different ones. Nak's was the most useful for the war yet the most frustrating as well. "I won't let her stay. We need her talents to help the others escape while I, you and Carita hold off the Androids as long as we can." There was a moment of silence between them as the thunderous roars of explosions erupted through the air around them as the battle grew closer. Neither of them wanted to say what was on their mind. Both knew the war was coming to an end for them.

"Mother and Father would be proud of you, Mal," Nak said softly, her hands behind her back as if she was taking in the view.

Gratitude swelled inside her chest as Maliha turned to her sister with a warm smile. "They would be proud of you too." For a moment, it felt as if they were back home where the war didn't force them to grow up so fast after their parents died.

"What are you two smiling about?" asked Carita, the third oldest of the seven Princesses. She entered from behind them and now stood next to Nak, her brown curly hair pulled back out of her face in a ponytail. Her lavender combat armor complemented Nak's wine-colored armor as they stood side by side watching the battle.

Nak answered first, "Just the end of the war. Nothing important. Have you thought of our defying war song for the upcoming last stand? Better be noteworthy."

Carita smiled turning towards her, "It is quite beautiful thus far. I only wish I had time to compose it for you all to hear so that it could be remembered for all of time. It's such a shame that something so beautiful will never be heard."

An explosion erupted causing their attentions to draw back to the battle that had grown closer than before. The Androids were halfway through the shipyard below them, pushing back the Resistance troops.

"They're getting closer," Carita added softly.

A heavy silence fell as they knew the time for their last attack was drawing near. Without taking her eyes off the approaching battle Maliha asked Carita, "Where are the others?"

"Adeline and Dalhala are in the clinic helping the wounded while Reva and Skyrah are strengthening our defenses throughout the city in case the Androids break through."

"What of Karasi?" Maliha pressed.

Carita crossed her arms across her chest glancing towards the sun that would set soon. "He was counseling the wounded last I checked."

Maliha chewed on her tongue not wanting to move but knowing she must. She was the leader of the Resistance after all and it was time to end this. "Find Reva and Skyrah. Bring them to the clinic. It's time for them to leave while they still can."

"As you wish, General," Carita responded turning to leave.

Maliha stopped her for a moment. "Don't tell them why. I'll explain it to them once they get there." Carita gave a sharp nod then left to find the sisters.

Maliha returned back to the battle confident in what was to come before turning to Nak who seemed off in her own thoughts as she watched the war. "What's my outcome with Reva?"

Nak lingered on the battle a while longer before finally responding in amusement. "I think you know better than me. You don't need my ability to tell you."

Maliha returned the smile and turned her back towards the war. "It's always nice to be sure," she stated while walking away from the hill towards their base. As she did, she heard Nak say barely above a whisper, "Not always," and felt her heart sink in her chest.

Human soldiers saluted her as she marched solemnly through the metal tents towards the center where the clinic was located. As she walked, Maliha thought of what to say to her sisters if this was the last time they would see each other. She didn't want to be honest about what could unfold but wanted to keep their hopes up for the war. If any of them lost hope their cause would suffer and damage morale for the troops in future battles. She would speak to them as if they were soldiers. She'd keep her composure.

Maliha walked to the large metal tent, "Clinic" written across the apex, and entered. She immediately smelt the stench of iron and aromas of medicines that suffocated the air. She wanted to gag, but pulled herself together as she scanned the tent for her sisters. At first glance she didn't see them among the rows of cots with wounded men and women but scanning again she spotted the youngest of the sisters, Dalhala, in the front corner of the room. She sat kneeling by an injured man with severe burns across his body and was speaking a prayer over him while giving him water to sip.

Making her way past the beds of the injured, Maliha reached her sister and waited for her to finish speaking her prayer to the man. When finished, Dalhala stood to her feet and turned to greet her.

"I was beginning to wonder when I'd see my sister today," Dalhala said while tucking her long wavy brown hair behind her ears. Her blue eyes seemed to intensify in her medical attire.

Maliha grinned. "Well, I made it before dinner, didn't I?"

"This time," Dalhala studied her closely. "It's time to go?"

Maliha knew it wasn't a question but a statement. Her sister was an oracle and knew more about future events than anyone else even if she couldn't exactly talk about them. She could only hint at what could happen and guide them through what could be. It was against the laws of the stars to speak upon such matters. Something that Maliha never understood. "Isn't that against the rules?"

Dalhala smirked. "It's an educated guess."

"Mmhm. Where's Adeline?"

"She's in surgery. Should be done soon," Dalhala replied.

"Good. The others will be here soon to meet us. I'm having Karasi, Reva, Sky, and yourself, along with the wounded, escorted off planet before things get ugly."

"Of course. Are we winning?" Dalhala asked knowing the answer.

Maliha kept her focus on the present. "We are still alive. I consider that a win."

Dalhala was quiet for a moment. "I wish I could help you. If I was allowed to shed blood as an oracle, I would be by your side in a heartbeat. I wish I wasn't the oracle for times like this one."

Maliha felt a sting surge her heart as she softly grabbed Dalhala by the shoulders and crouched to get eye level with her. "Don't ever say that. You do more than you know, Dalhala. You help me find hope in myself even on the hardest of days. You help me get it back again." Her sister hugged her tightly as she held back hot tears and tried regaining her composure.

"I love you, Maliha," Dalhala said softly.

"I love you too."

They held each other a moment longer before their sister, Adeline, entered from the back door wiping her bloody hands on a towel. She immediately spotted Maliha and hurried to greet her as she fixed the loose dirty-blonde hair that had fallen out of her bun. "This is a surprise. I wasn't expecting you till later," she announced with worry wiggling its way into her voice.

"Things have changed. I need you and the others, including Karasi, to evacuate now before it's too late," Maliha ordered. Just then a thin gray-skinned alien walked out of the back and joined them towering over everyone in the room.

"I expected nothing less. I am close to breaking the code to rewiring the Android's brain component but I need more time I fear," he spoke with a slow rhythmic tone as he readjusted his gray robes.

"I know you won't let us down," Maliha said as she turned to Adeline with determination. "You will take refuge with the elves. They will keep you safe for the time being."

Adeline crossed her arms, a look of worry in her face as she fiddled with their mother's necklace around her neck. "What of you? You talk as if you aren't coming."

"I can't abandoned my soldiers and those who have yet to escape to their fate. Nak, Carita, and I will hold back the Androids in order to buy you enough time to leave the planet. They will be too busy with us to track you once you take off," Maliha said firmly.

"So when do we attack?" Reva asked anxious to aid her people.

Maliha turned around to find the rest of the sisters had arrived with Carita. "Soon, but you won't be here to see it, I'm afraid."

"I'm not leaving you," she objected.

"Are you not coming with us?" Skyrah asked.

Maliha retained her composure despite the pressure of ensuring her family would be safe no matter her fate. "Somebody has to stay back and hold the line. Adeline will lead you off the planet with the others."

"Let me stay! You will need me," Reva exclaimed. The intensity in her voice reflected her iron will. Maliha knew it was going to be harder to convince her that leaving was the better option in saving their kind. Adeline seemed to read her mind as she ushered the others towards the hospital to help escort the injured to the transports. Maliha waited for them to leave before addressing Reva who appeared restless.

"I can't l—"

"You know I'm as strong as you. You need my help to hold the Androids off," Reva interrupted.

"I need you with your sisters more than I need you here, Reva," Maliha replied, sternly.

Reva's blood boiled as she felt her sister's authority restrict her from fighting. "I won't turn tail and run! Not when the Androids are at our doorstep!"

"There is no shame in knowing when you are defeated! We are outnumbered and beaten. Which is why I need you to protect our sisters at all cost. I won't allow them to murder another one of our family or take this city while I can still do something about it!"

"They will kill you! They don't take prisoners or make compromises. If you stay, you die," Reva spat.

Maliha steadied herself for a moment knowing there was no use in fighting about what was to come anymore, especially with the explosions growing closer. With a voice hard as oak and resolved to her fate, she said, "So be it."

"What?" Reva asked confused.

Maliha's gaze remained unaltered from her sister's cold eyes. "If I die in order to save my sisters and what is left of this planet then so be it. That is my duty. To protect all of you."

Reva stared at the ground. Her young frame seemed to be holding the entire universe on her small shoulders and Maliha couldn't help but hold back a smile at the sight. Her sister always trying to be the hero so no one else would, always trying to do what was best for everyone despite if it hurt her own wellbeing.

"What will the Resistance do without you leading them?" Reva asked.

"Adeline is next in line to rule now. She will lead you the rest of the way, but she is no warrior like you and I. She will need your help to keep things running especially in ways of war."

The fierceness in Reva's eyes seemed to soften if even temporarily as she realized the brevity of the war. "I will do my best."

"Once you are settled on the elven planet, regroup and start preparing for the next attack. The Androids won't stop hunting you until every one of us is dead. Don't stay in one place too long even with the elves. It will be best to find somewhere secluded that is the last place they will think to find."

Reva gave a sharp nod. "Affirmative, General."

Maliha suddenly felt a pang of sadness pull at her heart realizing this could very well be the last time she would talk to any of her sisters. The last time she would talk to Reva. Trying to keep the realization off her face, she lovingly uttered. "Take care of yourself, okay? Try not to be so hotheaded all of the time and listen to Adeline. Don't disobey her orders no matter how much you think you're doing it for the right reasons."

"Yes, ma'am," Reva responded as hot tears began to form in her eyes. Maliha pulled her in for a tight hug letting her bury her face into her shoulder as she did. She could feel the hot tears soaking her armor as Reva faintly whispered, "Take as many as you can with you."

Maliha brushed her hair with her fingers, replying, "I will. I promise."

They stayed like that for a minute longer before Reva pulled away wiping her face free of tears and giving her a salute. Her vivacity returned as she firmly declared, "I will help escort the injured onto ships."

Maliha watched her go, refraining from the urge to call after her. Though she hated goodbyes, now was the time to do them and time was against her. *I have so little time*, she thought as she pulled herself together and left the clinic to search for Adeline near the hangar bays. She had only taken a few steps when she heard her name being called from in front of her and spotted her sister, Skyrah, and an elf named Amosa jogging towards her.

"You're really staying? There's no way to change your mind?" the young teenage Princess asked.

Maliha hid her heavy heart from them. "Sacrifices have to be made in order to save others."

"I don't understand. You could come still if you wanted to. We could all be together," Skyrah assured.

Clearing her throat, Maliha gave her a comforting smile. "One day you will understand, Sky. You and Reva are so young but when you get to my age you will learn that we can't always do what we want to."

"Will we see you again?" Skyrah asked searching her face for the truth.

Maliha held back the fresh wave of emotions as she uttered, "Someday."

"You'll try to see us again if you can, right?"

Maliha nodded, knowing there would be no way for her to do so. "I'll try my best to be right behind you with Nak and Carita." Skyrah peered down at the dirt floor in attempt to hide the tears that were starting to fall. Maliha placed a hand on her shoulder to comfort her. "Don't start the rain clouds now, baby Sky," she teased knowing it would comfort her if just a little. It was something she always said when Skyrah was unhappy.

Skyrah tried smiling, her chin trembling as she wiped her nose on her sleeve. "You can't stop the rain once it starts."

They pensively smiled at each other as Maliha said, "Keep everyone safe, okay? You all need to stick together."

"Okay."

Then turning to Amosa. "Keep watch over my sister, you hear?"

Amosa bowed her head in respect. "I always do."

Maliha turned back to Skyrah. "Finish helping the others board. You will need to leave soon enough."

"Goodbye, Mal."

"Goodbye, Skyrah, and please be safe," Maliha pleaded, watching Amosa tug at Skyrah's sleeve for them to go before they both headed towards the clinic. Maliha forced herself forward, feeling her heart grow heavy with every goodbye as she made her way towards the open hangar bays to search out Adeline. She found her near the transport they would be taking, ordering a group of soldiers to move another set of medical supplies into the spacecraft. She seemed utterly calm despite the explosions detonating every minute in the distance that grew louder each time in result of the Androids gaining ground. "Almost set?"

Adeline glanced up from the clipboard in her hands. "Almost. We are slowly getting the injured on board and still have a few more crates to load."

"Good. You might want to pick up the pace. You don't have much time left." Maliha glanced across the open hangar bay as personnel scurried this way and that. "You will be in charge now."

Adeline stopped checking off boxes and looked at Maliha not surprised. "I know."

Maliha continued. "Don't stay with the elves. They will grow tired of the Resistance. It's not safe to stay in one place too long."

"I know," Adeline replied.

"Watch over the others, especially Reva. Make sure to keep her in check so she doesn't get too prideful, and keep an eye on Dalhala. You know how she gets when she sees a disturbing vision. Make sure the morale of the rebellion stays high to prevent soldiers from falling away." She paused.

"What about Skyrah?" Adeline preceded.

Maliha smiled. "She's the only one I never have to worry about. Amosa will keep her out of trouble as long as she breathes."

"We are fortunate to have Amosa with us. She keeps the alliance with the elves favorable for us," Adeline acknowledged. She spoke softly, changing subjects. "You'll give my love to Hawken and Rey when you see them?"

"Of course." The thought of Adeline's husband and daughter caused her to look to the tattoo of her fiancé's name on her left forearm. They had all lost so much in this war that Maliha often forgot what their life before it was like.

When was the last time any of them were truly happy and didn't worry about their lives hanging on an edge of a battle? It all seemed like a forgotten dream that they could never return to. "Mother and Father as well. I know they will be happy to know you all are safe from the Android's clutches." Explosions brought Maliha's attention back to the present as she knew she was out of time. "It's time for me to go. Keep the others safe, sister."

"Goodbye, sister," Adeline replied mournfully watching her leave.

Maliha stood on the red rock bluff overlooking the coming battle. Nak and Carita stood next to her with their remaining soldiers at attention behind them. The air around them was heavy with anticipation as tremors from the explosions shook the ground below their feet. The Androids were breaking through the last of their defenses in the shipyard below.

"The first one to twenty then," Nak teased, kissing the family ring she wore on her right hand and pulled out her rapier that had a red and golden hilt that seemed to be a part of the setting sky.

Maliha and Carita kissed theirs as well and pulled out their blades. Maliha's a dark green hilted katana with three holes in the center of its blade while Carita's was a double-bladed plasma steel sword with a lavender hilt. Maliha tightened her grip around her hilt of her katana.

"Whatever happens, it's been a pleasure, sisters," Carita said, her gaze fixed on the encroaching army.

Maliha looked back at her sisters. "Can you hum our battle song, Carita?" she asked.

Carita stared across the horizon where the setting sun painted the sky with streaks of brilliant reds and oranges like fire. She then started humming a beautiful and haunting song that Maliha had ever heard as they all faced their last battle. The sound rang in their ears as they raced down the hill to meet the Androids' army. Maliha leapt onto a dilapidated spacecraft running along until cartwheeling off to land behind the first wave of Android soldiers. She sliced through their metal armored bodies then turned to attack the next wave. She cut down a towering soldier before moving on to the next, striking her blade into its chest and pulling out in time to deflect a plasma bolt. She then turned her wrath onto the Android that fired upon her, pulling out her own plasma blaster.

The Androids surrounded her, but Maliha was too quick as she cut them down. She scanned the battle to see how her sisters were doing noticing the carnage all around her. Human soldiers were lying on the dirt mixed with spilt crimson blood and oil from scattered robotic parts. It seemed her and her sisters were the only ones left as she spotted Carita being overwhelmed with Android soldiers. Rushing to help her, Maliha was intercepted by another group of Androids. Gracefully, she fought them but with every one she slayed another took its place. She pierced her katana through another Android's metal skull and noticed Nak had reached their sister and was fighting alongside her. Both were injured with cuts and burns from blast fire.

She suddenly felt an intense burning claw at her side and clenched her teeth from the pain. She pushed back another Android then peered down to find plasma fire from a blaster had eaten through her armor and left a third-degree burn in its wake. She quickly turned around searching for the attacker, but couldn't find one as six more Androids charged her. She rose her katana to defend herself from an Android's metal arm coming down on her and felt another sharp pain through her leg causing her to fall on one knee. Ignoring the pain, Maliha pushed herself up and plunged her blade into an Android's chest before taking it out again to attack an Android behind her.

She shoved the barrel of his plasma rifle and sliced off a metal arm as she heard a cry come from Carita yards away. Maliha kicked an Android back to see Carita get shot in the chest and did not stand again. Nak let out an angry cry as she picked up her sister's sword and cut down those in her path. Soon the Androids surrounded her, charging their guns all at once and opened fire.

Maliha turned away as the flash of light from their guns fired and felt their blast as if it was her own. She focused all of her energy swinging her katana at the surrounding Androids with tears in her eyes. Her blade cut through another Android before bouncing off another. Everything seemed like a flash of blurs in slow motion as her sword plunged into another soldier before deflecting another blow then moving to offense again. It was a never-ending cycle of fighting for her life then blocking as she ignored each new pain and the weariness that threatened to stop her next attack. During the fighting an Android caught her in the face with his fist causing her to stumble backwards, tripping over a body and crashed into the dirt.

Her head throbbed and her vision seemed impaired but she knew she couldn't stay down for long as the heavy footsteps of an Android approaching echoed in her ear. She quickly grabbed her katana and swung it catching the Android at the knees and sent him falling into the ground behind her. She then grabbed out her plasma gun again and fired upon two more Androids charging her, feeling the heat of the blast touch her skin. Then with all her strength left in her, she forced herself to her feet slowly firing upon any Android that got close to her. She continued fighting until finally they overwhelmed her, knocking the gun out of her hands and the katana from her grip. Two Androids held her by the wrists as another punched her in the stomach so hard she spat blood as they continued to beat her. When finally they stopped, Maliha felt her whole body ache in pain and her face started to swell from fractures as they dropped her to her knees. She spat up blood again, tasting the bitterness in her mouth as dirty boots walked towards her. She leaned back to view the being approaching.

Unlike the other Androids who had metal faces and bodies, this one who stood before her looked more human than robot. He had skin on his body and slick brown hair but the only thing that told her otherwise was his piercing red eyes that seemed to glow in hatred for her. She recognized the torn places on his face and body where the robotic skeleton was visible. He was the leader of the Android Army, Brohain the Zealot.

"Your time is up, Princess Nightstar," he hacked.

Maliha spotted a plasma grenade on a dead soldier's body nearby. Meeting Brohain's cold gaze she activated the grenade and replied, "You have no idea," as a transporter lifted into the sky, shooting towards the heavens. She couldn't help but smile as the grenade detonated.

Jase Bluestar

Jase Bluestar ran through the crowded streets with the Android Police tailing him close behind. With a proud smirk, he fingered the bag of stolen groceries as he turned down an alley confident he'd lose them. Trying not to trip over garbage, he burst out of the alleyway into another busy street nearly colliding into a pedestrian.

"Hey, watch it!" shouted a Prokleo alien. His dark blue skin turned a bright cherry color for a second before changing back into blue.

"Sorry!" Jase apologized quickly, almost laughing as he turned around to see if he had lost the police through the alleyway. He didn't see them, but knew better than to stick around to find out.

A sweet voice came to life in his earpiece, "You know you almost got us caught."

"Almost. That's the keyword, Kaimi," Jase replied feeling his racing heart slow down as he tried to blend more into the crowd.

Kaimi, Jase's best friend in the entire galaxy, continued through his earpiece, "Next time, there may not be an almost. Your cockiness is going to land us both in a cell one of these days."

"It might but that won't stop us. No cell can keep us locked up as long as we are together," Jase glanced at the towering steel buildings all around him, taking in the noisy view of spacecrafts hovering this way and that in the noon sky.

The city of Otect was home to thousands of different species throughout the galaxy. It was the capital of the Orbone solar system which had nine planets in its rotation, eight of them inhabited. Out of all the species on the planet, only three thousand of them were human including Jase. With this minority, every race saw humans as the weakest species and made sure they knew their place in the food chain. The only other race that everyone hated more than humans were Bulbs, a four-foot gray-skinned alien with a head the shape of a lightbulb and two large black eyes that covered most of their face. Only about twenty if not less lived within the city while most of the race lived below ground where they preferred to mine in their tunnels away from surface beings. In doing so, no one bothered them, seeing their species more like rats in the sewers while humans were roaches above the surface.

Jase watched another spacecraft zip through the air before turning his attention back to the street. "Why don't we ever steal a skyrod or something?" he questioned.

Kaimi was quick to answer in an amused tone, "Because you said you liked walking. Besides, I like walking."

"Because you don't have to do it," he teased, glancing down to his data watch on his left wrist where Kaimi's face was shown. Her blue skin was made up of alien code running in all directions throughout her bobbed haircut and face. She smiled at his answer, replying, "Some A.I.s can walk. They just choose not to. You know if I could I would love to be one with the crowd."

Jase knew if she could she would be right there next to him taking in all the sights and sounds, spending hours just watching everyone and everything around her. It was one reason he hated living on Planet Faton where she wasn't allowed since all A.I.s were banned due to the sibling rivalry against them and the Androids who, now after forty-seven years of fighting, ran the city under the orders of their leader, Lord Brohain. It wasn't always like that, but since the end of the war twenty years ago, things had drastically changed on the planet. More laws were enforced, and disobeying them lead to harsh consequences, mostly death. It seemed that the Androids way of thinking was that only the strongest could survive under their ruling, resulting to the weak perishing. "Maybe one day we will go somewhere you can walk around," Jase said lost in thought.

"Someday, maybe," Kaimi agreed.

Jase pushed past a group of street merchants selling fabric textiles and woven rugs on either side of the cobbled street with onlookers haggling on a price for the wares. He kept his focus ahead of him knowing he had to get this large sack of food somewhere before darkness fell. He travelled down the street where more humans could be seen at the small markets. Jase didn't say a word but simply acknowledged them with a nod as he hurried towards the end of the street. Turning down the right side, he travelled westward for another long while before coming to a backstreet where the tall skyscrapers became less and less and the buildings, less decorated. The buildings here on the westside were where the slums started. Once under the Nightstar family's rule, they would have been just as nice as any of the other homes in Otect City but now the war had done its damage leaving them only for the use of the poor. It was here in the westside where most of the human population lived except those who were slaves to the upper-class and allowed to live in the nobler houses.

Slavery was banned in most places, but on Faton there were exceptions. If an upper-class citizen offered to pay you handsomely for your services then you could enter a bond contract in which your rights were taken for a certain amount of years. Most humans gave up such rights so they could send what money they made back home to their families. Others did it in hopes to learn a trade that they could use once they were free and could hopefully live a better life than the one they did before. Some beings didn't agree with such a thing while others found being a servant to an upper-class men or women a privilege and respected such services where they could rise from their rank and one day become noble citizens themselves.

Jase hated the whole idea. He understood why some did it, but he could never. Just the thought of being someone's property and having to lick their boots was a revolting idea to him. Hence, stealing was more of an occupation than getting a job. He liked the thrill he had to take in order to steal from someone and making his own hours was a nice touch. He refused to be a screw in the machine of the city, preferring instead to be a problem in the machine.

He passed through another street before heading southwest onto an even narrower street than before and headed towards the southwest wall that protected the city from attacks and the dust storms that blew over the barren desert. He finally arrived at his destination located in front of the southwest wall: a two-story orphanage falling into ruin with a sign above the door that read: "Bright Star and Roses Orphanage."

Jase stared at the house he used to call home many years ago when he was just a lad. Before finally crossing over the small overgrown courtyard and entered the house. The inside was somewhat better shape than the out, though its outdated tiles cracked here and there and the faded periwinkle walls were caked with dirt from grubby hands of children. The stairs leading up were broken in a few places and a long tattered rug lay trying to cover up most of the stairs from view. The sun shined through the many wooden windows in the house that illuminated most of the entry room and the narrow hallway that led into the kitchen and living room. Jase peered into the front room to find toys laid out across the floor, but no children to be found. He heard loud laughter upstairs with footsteps running across the ceiling above him. The noise brought a wave of happiness as he turned down the tiny hallway towards the kitchen. Reaching the end he heard voices.

"I'm just saying if you don't put some elbow grease in it, it will never come up from that stove," an aged but sweet voice complained while rummaging through what sounded like pots.

Another voice sounded, this one much younger but just as kind as the older woman's, "I'm tryin' my best, Mrs. Rose!"

Jase stopped in the doorway, setting down the sack of food and watched the old lady who had taken care of him most of his life move about the kitchen in search of something. The woman was in her mid-sixties with white silky hair tied in a neat bun. She had a small build that looked even smaller in her oversized navy polka-dot dress that she wore with a peach-colored apron that looked as old as she was. She was a mother to Jase and he was always happy to help her in any way possible. "I thought I heard an old woman somewhere around here," he teased, making his presence known.

Mrs. Rose peered up from the cabinet she had been searching through and immediately burst into a kind smile, rushing over to hug him. "Jase! My Bluestar baby!" she happily chirped, hugging him tight before taking a step back to look him over. "You're thinner than the last time I saw you. Are you eating alright?"

"It's from all the running I do, Rosebud," he told her.

She made a face. "Mmhm, I'm sure that's what it is. Where's my other baby? Where's Kaimi?"

Jase raised his left arm level just as Kaimi appeared in front of them on the surface of his data watch. She rose at the height of four inches, beaming at the woman. "I'm right here, Mrs. Rose."

Mrs. Rose's face grew even happier at the sight. "Jase, put her on the ciraview so I can see her better."

"Sometimes I feel like you are happier to see her than me," Jase joked as he walked over to the kitchen table where a small smooth metal cylinder sat on the table top. The cylinder was called a ciraview which was a receiver for frequencies to transfer to and from as well as allow planet holo calls. Jase had built five of them to place around the house so Kaimi could transfer into different rooms without relying on Jase to carry her everywhere within the house. It allowed her to be a part of family activities which Jase knew she enjoyed the most as he gently tapped his data watch to the cylinder to allow the transfer into the device.

"It's a girl thing," Kaimi responded once appearing on the surface of the ciraview at six inches now.

"Don't be a baby, Jase," Mrs. Rose added as she studied Kaimi. "Look at you! Still beautiful as always!"

Kaimi's smile brightened. "And you as well, Mrs. Rose."

"Oh, stop it, dear," Mrs. Rose replied swatting the air playfully. "I'm as old as dirt."

Jase leaned against the table. "You got that right!"

Mrs. Rose ignored him. "Is he still getting in trouble?"

"As always," Kaimi said, glancing at Jase.

"You know he's going to get caught one of these days and taken off to who-knows-where!" Mrs. Rose declared sternly.

"I'm standing right here," Jase indicated before turning his gaze to the beautiful young woman. "I'm standing right here, Camila." The young woman smiled at his response before continuing to clean.

"Oh, we know you're right there," Mrs. Rose stated, turning back to her task beforehand. "I'm just hoping you're actually listening when I say, 'Get a real job, Jase Bluestar.'"

Jase saw Camila giggle at her remark. "And where's the fun in that, Rosebud?"

"It doesn't have to be fun, but maybe then you'll find a nice girl to settle down with. Have kids before I die!" she suggested with her head poked inside a cabinet on the floor.

Jase shook his head in amusement. Rose, a typical mother nagging on her children to get married and have kids of their own before dying of old age. "Then I'd have to stop coming for dinner."

Mrs. Rose popped back out holding a large bowl as she climbed to her feet. "That's right! You could start cooking for me instead!" she winked to Kaimi while she cleaned out the bowl in her hands.

"But it wouldn't be as good as yours!" Remembering the sack of food, Jase picked it up from the floor and sat it down onto the table. "I brought you something, by the way."

Mrs. Rose stopped what she was doing and turned back around to the table. "Jase, you shouldn't have," she told him, moving to open it.

"I know, but I did. There's enough for a week, but I wish I could have gotten more. Sorta ran out of time," he told her with a grin.

Mrs. Rose looked over the items in the bag with tears in her eyes. She gave him a tight squeeze and studied his face in all seriousness as she stated, "This doesn't mean I approve of you stealing."

"I know. I'm still a rotten thief with a heart of gold."

She playfully slapped him on the shoulder, turning back to the food. "Camila, why don't you put this in the pantry on the top shelf so the kids can't reach it."

"Yes, ma'am," the young lady replied and moved to do so.

Mrs. Rose turned back to Jase and Kaimi. "Speaking of the children: Kids, get down here to see Jase and Kaimi!" she shouted towards the ceiling.

The kitchen ceiling started to rumble with noise as tiny footsteps erupted like a stampede as the children ran down the stairs and towards the kitchen. Cheers and laughter echoed through the air and exploded into the kitchen as a dozen children tackled Jase, all speaking at once.

"Where have you been?" questioned a freckled-face boy flipping back his shaggy chestnut hair.

Another boy asked, "Did you get into any fights?"

"Have you found out where the Princesses are?" a red-haired girl asked with sparkling green eyes and a shy smile.

"Did you kill anyone?" a boy with jet-black hair questioned holding up his fists.

"Did you get me anything?" a blonde-haired girl demanded to know.

"Or me?" asked another.

A boy with freckles and oval glasses wondered out loud as he fiddled with a button on his shirt. "Have you gotten a space ship yet? There's supposed to be a moon eclipse soon."

"Are you coming back to live with us, Uncle Jase?" asked the youngest, her reddish hair pulled back in pigtails as she sucked her thumb.

A boy next to her added, "That would be cool!"

"You could help us with our chores!" the blonde girl from before excitedly chirped.

"Alright! Everyone off Uncle Jase!" yelled the oldest boy, Roran, who stood in the doorway with his twin sister, Lynn.

All ten children climbed off and huddled over by Kaimi when they spotted her only to ask her millions of the same questions. It filled the kitchen with chatter that Mrs. Rose quickly quieted down. "One at a time, children! One at a time," she told them, returning to her cooking.

The freckled-face boy went first. His name was Jeremy and he was the second oldest of the group at the age of thirteen. "Where were you? I thought you'd be back sooner!"

Jase rose to his feet, brushing off his pants. "I had some work that kept me very busy for a while, but now I'm here for the night."

"Did you find any Princesses? You told me you would look for them!" asked the redheaded girl again.

Amused, Jase replied, "Haven't yet, but I will let you know when I do, Mindy."

"Did you get into any fights?!" asked Felix eagerly.

"Or kill anyone?" added Rex.

Jase crossed his arms, leaning back against the table. "No and no."

"What about a space ship?" the boy in the glasses named Oliver asked, pushing them back on his nose.

Jase shook his head. "Not yet, Olly, but you will be the first to fly with me when I do."

"So you didn't get us anything," Lindsay stated in a disappointing tone joining arms with Kelsey.

"Sorry to disappoint, ladies," Jase shrugged.

"Are you coming to live with us?" the youngest asked again.

Jase picked up the five-year-old. "I'm afraid not, Heather. I'm too big to be here," he told her.

"But you could stay in my room!" the youngest boy declared as he hugged Jase's leg.

Jase looked down placing an arm around him. "And where would you sleep, Alfie?"

"With Rex!" the boy replied pointing over to the boy.

Lynn laughed picking up the boy. "Alfie, Uncle Jase has to get married before he gets too old."

"At least one of my children has sense," commented Mrs. Rose while eyeing Jase.

Jase shook his head. "You all act like I'm as old as Momma Rose!"

"You're getting close!" joked Roran.

Jase put Heather back down. "I come home to only be ambushed by an army of children and the elderly telling me that I need to get married. Can you believe this, Kaimi?" he joked.

Kaimi laughed. "You are getting old," she chimed.

"Well, look at that! My own A.I. has turned against me." Jase placed both his hands on his hips. "You all are hopeless."

"Not as hopeless as you. Children, why don't you all go wash up for supper. It will be ready soon now," Mrs. Rose remarked.

"Yes, Momma Rose!" Like a choir they answered as Lynn ushered them out into the hallway.

Roran hugged Jase. "It's good to see you, big brother."

Jase had first met the twins eleven years ago. They were seven at the time and had arrived at the orphanage after their mother had died during childbirth. Shortly afterwards, their father had died in the war against the Androids. Jase had been the oldest then among five other children that also called the orphanage their home. Jase and Kaimi had become rather close to the twins, making their bond more like a family than some group of kids stuck in a random house. Jase was the only orphan that continued to visit Momma Rose and the children whenever he could. With the help of Kaimi, they both taught each child to read, write, and some mathematics so the children weren't completely hopeless once they set out on their own. His teachings now had happened less and less due to his jobs so he left the responsibility to Roran and Lynn to continue them.

"It's good to see you too, little brother. Look at you finally getting some muscles on your scrawny arms," Jase teased, squeezing his bicep.

Mrs. Rose proudly explained, "Roran has been working at the Metal Clunker, the space ship factory over by the hangar bays. They repair spaceships and such as well as sell a couple every now and then. Gets paid six pieces an hour and it's honest work."

Jase raised an eyebrow at the news, Roran shrugged. "It's just something to help Momma Rose with the house."

"He's as stubborn as you when it comes to not keeping the money for himself. Thinking it's a better idea to give it to me," she proclaimed setting the table.

Roran smiled. "You need it more than I do, Momma."

"The hell I do," she remarked while bringing a bowl of fruit over to the table. "Neither of you will be getting wives anytime soon because you'll be flat broke."

Camila suppressed a laugh as she entered from the pantry with a loaf of bread. Both men grinned at her before turning their attention back to Mrs. Rose. Jase smoothly replied, "I thought you were always telling us that a true woman wouldn't care if we were rich or poor?"

"Stars, have mercy on their souls," Momma Rose uttered under her breath, peering towards the ceiling for a moment before turning back to the stew on the stove. "If that's what is keeping you from getting a wife, then I lied."

Everyone in the room started laughing even Mrs. Rose let out a chuckle before both Jase and Roran turned to leave out the back door. Jase stopped in the doorway, looking back to Kaimi on the table. "We're going up, want to come?"

She shook her head, eyes shining brightly. "I think I'll stay with Rosebud, if you don't mind, Mrs. Rose?"

"Of course not!" waving a hand in the air, Mrs. Rose moved towards Kaimi. "Let me move you over by me so I can show you how to make bafin stew right here on the stove."

Jase hesitated a moment more before following Roran out the door. The backyard of the orphanage was practically a foot of walkway that ended before the stone wall that circled the city. When they were younger, they used to draw on the wall around the initials of former kids that engrave their names before leaving the orphanage. Even now there was chalk drawings of what looked like the war of the Androids against the Nightstar Princesses that Jase lingered on a moment longer before turning to the rusty pipe that ran up to the roof. As a teen he would climb it to escape and after a while had Roran join him keeping it a secret between the two until Momma Rose caught them. It was still one of

Jase's favorite spots in the city mostly because from the roof you could somewhat see the shipyard where the spacecrafts took off. He almost had the same view from where he lived now and it made him feel happy knowing that no matter where he was, he always was connected with the orphanage and the children from this view.

"You would think that with the amount of times we've climbed this, the pipe would break," he wondered aloud, climbing up after Roran.

"I'd rather you not say that while we climb," Roran suggested.

Jase smiled at the response. "Yeah, well, we're both thinking it."

"Were we?" Roran pulled himself up then turned around, extending a hand for Jase to take.

Jase took it and climbed to the top, taking a seat next to Roran close to the edge. He stared out across the westward rooftops towards the shipyard. "I guess not. How has things been since last I saw you?"

Roran glanced up towards the sky, squinting in the late afternoon sky. "Let's see...I haven't seen you since the beginning of summer so April and now it's June. Yeah, we've been okay. Momma Rose hit a rough patch with bills and trying to feed everyone here for a while until I started working. She never said anything, but I could tell it was getting harder. It wasn't till Camila found out she had gone a few days without eating when I realized how serious it was and that's when I knew I needed to get a job to help out with the taxes the Androids keep raising on us. Then in May, a bad sickness was going around our section that killed that old sweet lady down the street that used to bring us cookies. Everyone here got it, too, for a week except myself and Camila, but it didn't get too bad."

Jase nodded, thinking about how fast summer had gone by. They only had a few more months before winter. "Did Olly and Kelsey get the chocolate cake slices I sent?"

Roran smirked. "Yeah, they did. I don't understand how you have time to steal pastries for everyone when you are so busy working all the time."

"They are easier to steal than you'd think," Jase replied in amusement.

Roran shook his head and asked, "How's Kaimi? No glitches or anything out of the norm we need to worry about?"

Jase closed his eyes feeling the warmth of the sun rays bathing his face. "Not yet. Her programing is still running smoothly."

Changing the subject, Roran asked, "What kind of jobs have you been taking?"

Jase leaned back on his hands. "Oh, just the normal petty ones—stole a few jewels here and there, nothing too exciting. I did have a client that wanted me to steal his ex-wife's wedding ring because it was some family heirloom that she had taken from him. That was fun."

"You're not doing anything really bad, right?" Roran asked.

Jase hesitated. "Nothing bad and nothing that could cause treason."

"Good. I mean Momma Rose can deal with thievery but nothing else," Roran joked.

Jase started laughing, remembering a time when they were younger. "Remember when we stole Lynn's diary out of the safe Momma Rose had? We would read it then bug her about that boy she liked. She could never understand how we knew stuff."

Roran joined in on the laughter. "Not till that one fat kid...what was his name? Erik?"

"Erinka," Jase corrected.

Roran continued. "Whatever. He saw us and ratted us out to Momma. She made us do the dishes for a whole month after that."

"Ah, yeah. Those were good times," Jase recounted.

Roran seemed to also remember. "You left not soon after that. Couldn't wait to get out in the big bad world of Otect City."

"Well, we all grow up at some point."

"And some of us don't," Roran teased, implying Jase.

Jase grinned. "Well, some of us it just takes longer to do so."

"Isn't that true!" There was a pause in their conversation which created a stretch of silence between the two. Finally, Roran announced softly, "I'm leaving, you know?"

Jase knew. Both Roran and Lynn would be eighteen in a few weeks becoming too old to stay in the orphanage. "I know."

"No, I mean I'm leaving the planet for good. I'm leaving Faton," Roran said even softer waiting for Jase's reaction.

Jase felt a mixture of surprise and confused not understanding how or why his brother was leaving. "How? You know how much it costs to leave the planet? Even if you managed to get on board without being detected, where would you go?"

"I got a job. My employer is paying for everything and he has his own ship," he explained.

Jase was shocked by the news. "What will you be doing?"

Roran hesitated, looking back towards the shipyard before responding, "I will be a servant to my employer. He's some rich Prokleo who's going back home and needs some extra help."

"You're leaving to be a slave," Jase repeated, unable to hold back his distaste for it.

"I know how you feel about it, but it's an honorable thing to do for people and it's humble. After my contract is up, my status will be a lot better than it will ever be staying here. Besides, it's a good-paying job and I'll get to see other worlds doing it."

"While cleaning up behind your master," Jase commented clearly annoyed.

Roran clenched his jaw a moment as if trying to collect himself. "Look, I know what it means and the price, but I'm doing it for the right reasons. The pieces will be able to help Momma Rose for a long time. The pieces I don't send her will go to me so I can start thinking about my life and how I want to spend it. I won't be a servant for the rest of my life, only for five years. Then I'll settle down somewhere that won't treat our kind like a disease and start a family. Isn't that worth it, Jase? Can't you just be happy for me?"

Jase was lost in his own thoughts, trying to see the good side of any of this. It wasn't what he had pictured for his little brother, but knew his heart was in the right place. He'd have a better chance making a name for himself somewhere else besides in this city as long as the Androids ruled over them. Still trying to cope with it, Jase asked, "Does Momma Rose know?"

"Yes, we spoke about it over a month ago when I first got the offer. She thinks it's a fair trade and even tried to argue that I keep the pieces for myself. To just give her grandchildren instead," Roran gave a short laugh.

Jase felt his nerves subside. "No surprise there. And Lynn? You told her?"

"She was the first I told."

"And?"

Roran continued, "She's okay with it. She understands what it means to me to be able to leave, and thinks it's for the best."

"What is she going to do?" Jase asked, hoping it wasn't the same thing.

Roran fiddled with a loose shingle on the roof. "She's staying to be a medic at the Runwode Infirmity downtown. She starts her training once she turns eighteen then it only takes six weeks till she's qualified."

"She will be perfect for that," Jase agreed.

Roran agreed. "Yeah, she will make a great medic."

Jase peered back towards the evening sky. "When do you leave?"

"This upcoming week. Tuesday to be exact," he answered.

Shocked, Jase whipped his head towards him. "You aren't even eighteen yet! How can they take you so soon?"

"Momma Rose gave her blessing. Besides, my birthday is almost here," Roran replied.

Jase shook his head in disbelief, suddenly sad at how fast things were changing. Trying to conceal his thoughts, he joked, "It'll be harder to get you chocolate cake."

Roran laughed and placed a hand on Jase's shoulder before pulling him into a headlock.

"Let go! You're messing up my hair!" Jase yelled as he tried breaking free of the grip.

Roran pushed him away, smiling. "It's not like you have anyone to look good for."

Kaimi suddenly appeared in form on Jase's data watch. "I hope I'm not interrupting anything, but it's time to eat."

"Thanks, Kaimi," Jase answered.

Beaming, Roran stated. "You know, Kaimi, if I didn't have any obligations then I'd marry you right now, right here!"

Kaimi turned to look at him. "If I could blush, I would. Unfortunately, I don't think you are my type, Roran."

"Never know till you try it," Roran contended.

"I'll keep that in mind if I want to date a child," Kaimi joked.

"I think you got me confused with Jase," Roran pestered as both men stood to leave.

Jase gently shoved him before climbing back down the rusty pipe as Kaimi transferred back into the house. When they entered the kitchen, all the children were already seated at the table. Two extra chairs were placed at the head of the table, one for Jase and one for Kaimi, whose ciraview was stacked on books so she was leveled with everyone else.

"About time you two showed up," Mrs. Rose with a twinkle in her eye said as she sat herself at the opposite side of the table at the end. "Now shall we say grace? Bow your heads, children. Thank you, wise one, for the food on our plates this evening and thank you for keeping us all safe in these strange times. Thank you for allowing Jase and our dearest Kaimi to be able to join us tonight. Please help him find a good wife so he can straighten up."

The children giggled softly as Mrs. Rose held back a smile and continued.

"Continue to watch over us on our path. Amen."

"Amen!" the children repeated all at once except for Kaimi, then they all started in on the bafin stew. The thick red liquid engulfed the room with its aroma of cooked meat, berries, and pieces of celery.

"It's still as delicious as when you used to cook it for me back in the day, Rosebud," Jase smacked his lips, dipping his bread into his bowl.

Mrs. Rose responded without looking up from her bowl. "Forty years of practice will do the trick. If I mess up now then the world must be ending."

The children giggled at her response and even Kaimi found it amusing as Jase turned his attention to Lynn who was two chairs down from him. "Are you excited for medical school, Lynn?"

Lynn was fixing her ponytail where some of her golden locks had fallen in front of her face. "I am very excited to go and help others. It's always been a dream of mine."

"You will make a wonderful doctor," Kaimi chipped in.

"I am grateful you think so, Kaimi. It's weeks away still and I'm already shaking in my boots about it," Lynn replied.

"Don't," Jase told her. "You'll do great."

Lynn asked, "Do you have any more jobs coming up?"

"A few," he responded taking a spoonful of stew into his mouth and swallowed before addressing Momma Rose. "When things die down, I plan on helping you fix up the house, Momma Rose."

Mrs. Rose wiped some stew dripping off of Heather's chin as she replied, "No need. Camila's brother, the one who builds houses, is coming to look at it the day after tomorrow."

"He's doing it for free as long as Mrs. Rose bakes him her famous Moon strawberry cake," Camila added as she stood to get more bread for them to eat from the pantry.

Mrs. Rose turned to her. "Come. Sit and eat with us, dear. You've been on your feet all day."

"That's nice of him," Jase said trying to sound polite. "Give him my regards."

Camila gave a gentle nod. "I will."

The rest of their conversation Jase tested the children on their letters and mathematics by playing games. After a while the adults discussed the latest assassin attempt on Lord Brohain, leader of the Androids, that ended with two of his guards dead. There would apparently be a meeting on the attack soon with his trusted council to determine their final solution to the end their war with the Resistance once and for all. By the end of the conversation it was six o'clock and Jase knew it was time for him to head home.

"Well, it's been a pleasure to be here but I'm afraid I have to go," Jase announced as the kids played in the living room across the kitchen.

The children moaned their disapproval as they scrambled to him. "Don't go, please?" Heather begged.

Kneeling down beside her, Jase softly smiled. "I have to, but I promise to be back soon."

The little girl wrapped her arms around his neck, hugging tightly. "Oookay."

"Must you leave so soon? You don't want to stay the night?" Mrs. Rose asked.

Jase stood back up, turning to her. "I can't tonight. I have things I have to do in the morning, but maybe next time. I'll be back soon enough."

"To see me off, I presume," Roran teased with a flashy grin as he gave him a pat on the back before moving to stand by Momma Rose.

"To make sure you don't get on the wrong ship!" Jase joked. He felt a hand slide across his back and turned to see Lynn coming around for a hug. "Bye, Lynn."

She gave him a kiss on the cheek before moving to stand with her brother. "Take care of yourself. Kaimi, make sure he does, will ya?"

"I will," she replied.

Jase continued his banter with Roran, "Besides, if you get cold feet, I'll be there to steal you away. I can keep you hidden till your boss leaves."

Roran laughed. "I'll remember that."

They said their farewells then Mrs. Rose escorted him to the front door where they both stepped out for some privacy. "You need to eat more. Get some meat on those bones," Momma Rose lectured while fixing his sky blue pilot's jacket.

Jase couldn't help, but smile at her. "Not till you get some on yours," he retorted.

Momma Rose shook her head, amused. "I feel bad for the woman who decides to marry you."

"But you'll be happy I'm married," he pointed out.

She looked him over one last time as if deciding if he was all set to go. "Please be safe. You know I worry over you more than I should. You and your damn job."

"I know, Momma," he replied softly.

She placed both her hands on either side of his face for a moment then gave him a warm hug. "I love you, my Bluestar."

"Love you too, Rosebud," he said softly.

Mrs. Rose stepped back towards the door. "I'm counting on you to keep him safe, Kaimi," she told the A.I. on his data watch.

The screen flickered to life as she replied, "I won't let you down, ma'am."

The door suddenly opened as Camila was ready to leave for the night. She paused in the doorway, seeing them both there and quickly apologized. "Sorry! I hope I didn't interrupt you! I'll wait inside!"

"Nonsense! Go on home, Camila. Be safe, you two!" Momma Rose called before turning to go back inside.

Jase smiled at her as he and Camila began to walk through the tiny courtyard. "Would you like me to walk you home?" he asked.

She responded fondly back. "It's fine, but thank you for the offer, Jase. I'm staying with a friend who doesn't live far from here for the night."

"Oh," Jase peered up at the sky that was already beginning to darken. Turning back to her he said, "It was nice seeing you tonight after being gone so long. Thank you for helping out with Mrs. Rose and the kids."

"It's no problem at all. I love them all so much and they are practically like family to me by now." She paused her cheeks blushing as she replied, "It was nice seeing you tonight too. I'm glad you are doing well."

Jase grinned. "Thanks. I'm glad you're still beautiful as always."

"Thank you! You don't look bad yourself," she joked as they stopped at the end of the street. "I should get going."

Jase nodded. "I should as well. Goodbye, Camila."

"Goodbye." They both started walking in opposite directions until Camila turned around and spoke up loud enough for him to hear. "Jase! Take care of yourself, okay? For me at least!"

Jase turned around to her with a grin and waved before turning back around to continue on his way down the familiar path that would lead him home.

———————————

Home Sweet Home

"You're awfully quiet," Kaimi acknowledged on the way home.

Jase passed through the still crowded streets, watching for guards. "Just thinking about Rosebud and the kids," he said.

"You're worried."

Jase turned down another street that wasn't as crowded and headed west. "I'm just worried how they will manage once Roran and Lynn leave on their own. Mrs. Rose will have to start teaching again to make sure the kids can function well once they leave the orphanage. That will add extra stress on her besides the amount she already carries from paying bills and feeding them. It's a lot for just one her age to handle on her own."

"They still have Camelia."

"But she won't be there all the time," he added, Jase moving out of the way of an elderly man with a cane and his wife.

Interrupting his thoughts, Kaimi said, "It's not like this is Momma Rose's first rotation."

"I know, but she's getting old...well, older than she was back in the day." He paused for a brief moment, thinking it over before breaking into a smile. "Now that I think about it, she's always been old. I don't think Rosebud has ever been young."

Kaimi giggled causing Jase's smile to grow brighter from the sound. He loved it when he could make her laugh since Kaimi didn't always find things funny like most races did. Jase didn't know much about A.I.s but could guess from being with her over the years that their sense of humor was hard to come by if it was there at all.

"You know, you're getting kind of old too," Jase teased while turning down another back street that would lead them to his house.

Kaimi's voice seemed far off in thought as she answered, "If only I aged like humans do. I wouldn't care if I grew wrinkly and fat with a saggy butt and breasts."

Jase grimaced. "Can we not talk about old women's bodies?"

Kaimi giggled again. "If you wish."

Jase lived in a condemned apartment building in an area that had seen the last battle of the Great Civil War. The buildings on the westside of the city were closed to the population due to their dangerous condition. Along with the West Gate of the city which was chained shut, the entire area was off limits with violations of trespassing being harshly prosecuted.

Jase only knew of a few other trespassers who also called the buildings home but most of the time they kept to themselves. Now and then he would come across one and they would acknowledge each another, but he always made sure that none of them knew about Kaimi for their safety. They would no doubt report it to the Androids for an reward. He surveyed the area making sure there were no patrols out, although there seldom was. Once ensuring it was all clear, Jase moved to the far end of an invisible force shield that surrounded the buildings and placed his hand on the gel-like surface. Soft lights flickered underneath his fingers and palm before blinking once together. A door suddenly opened in the shield.

Entering in, Jase continued on towards his building near the center of the area around to the backside. There he came across cargo holds that were stacked from the spaceport on the other side of the wall that used the abandoned buildings as storage when they ran out of space in the hangar bays. The cargo holds were stacked like a staircase thirty feet high up next to the building which Jase used to reach a caved in wall. Once inside, he continued on down a dark hallway to a steel elevator.

"One of these days, I should fix the energy grid so the lights start working again," he commented to Kaimi as he forcefully pulled open the steel doors into the elevator.

"Then it wouldn't be a hideout," Kaimi reminded him.

Once open, Jase glanced down the empty elevator shaft where the elevator was stuck two stories down as usual. He then turned his attention to the cable and leapt forward, grabbing hold of it. "True, but it would make getting home a lot easier," he replied while climbing up.

"We both know you like the challenge."

Jase passed the fourth floor as he replied, "Yeah, but what if I get really sick one of these days and can't get down?"

"You'll die," Kaimi responded bluntly.

Jase couldn't tell if she was joking or not as he felt a bead of sweat roll down his forehead, then the side of his face upon reaching the sixth floor. "Thanks for the reality check."

Holding onto the cable with one hand, Jase reached out for the side of the open elevator door. Grabbing onto the frame, he placed a foot on the floor before pulling himself onto the sixth level. Trying to catch his breath, he joked, "Next time why don't you carry me, Kaimi."

"Affirmative," Kaimi teased.

Jase walked down the dark hallway and stopped in front of room 673 where he pressed a panel to bypass the lock and watched the door slide open. Stepping in, Jase was immediately greeted with the familiar smell of home as he scanned the small apartment that was his.

"Home sweet home," he exclaimed moving towards the kitchen.

Kaimi spoke in his ear, "You ought to tidy up the place some."

"I will...at some point," he answered touching his data watch to the responder attached to the counter.

Kaimi suddenly appeared walking on the counter beside him as she chastened, "You know, putting it off won't make it go away."

"That's strange. I thought it would," he retorted and sat on the ruined wall at the back of the apartment overlooking the shipyard and watched the spacecrafts take off into the vibrant evening sky.

Kaimi appeared next to him on a ciraview receiver strapped to the ruined wall which allowed her to watch the sun sets next to him. "Are you going to tell me what's really bothering you now?" she gently nudged as she sat cross-legged.

Jase didn't break his gaze from the spaceships, knowing that soon Roran would be on one of them. "Roran's leaving our planet for good."

"How?" she inquired.

"He got a job being a servant," he told her still unable to hide the bitterness in his voice. "Five years, he will be cleaning up after some Prokleo who's going home. Five years and he's not even eighteen yet!"

Kaimi was silent for a moment before responding, "He must have his reasons."

"He's young and stupid—that's his reasons," he vented as he balled his hand into a fist.

"Jase," Kaimi's voice was soft as water, flowing over rocks in a spring as she coaxed. "Roran's allowed to make his own choices for his life. Good or bad, it's his life not ours. It's not up to us to determine his destiny. He has to find it on his own and if leaving helps him then so be it. We just have to be grateful and supportive of him."

Jase felt his hand unravel knowing she was right. Roran leaving could be the best for him, but Jase couldn't help but feel envious about it. He always wanted to leave the planet, yet here he was stuck here while his foster brother was leaving. "Do you think we will see him again?"

Kaimi peered over to him, holding his gaze before turning back to the sunset. "Time has a funny way of bringing us back to the ones we love. We just have to be patient enough to let it happen."

There was a pause between them.

"Did you make that up or read it off of something?" Jase teased, turning to her.

Kaimi smiled.

Jase pulled himself off the ledge and walked back inside as the last of the light was fading outside. "What do you want to listen to go to bed? The Be-shuttles or the Dust Roses?"

Kaimi transferred to the counter, walking beside him as they moved towards the bedroom. "The Be-shuttles. They calm my processing more than the Dust Roses." She disappeared for a moment only to return to a different receiver in Jase's room.

"Okay then," he uttered, flipping on the music stereo. A soothing low melody floated into the air like a lullaby as Jase pulled off his pilot jacket and threw it off to the side before sitting on his bed. He then unlaced his black boots while Kaimi appeared on the music box touching a steel orb the size of a marble. In doing so, she turned it on causing a light to suddenly bounce into the air, filling the room with constellations. She then vanished for a millisecond before appearing back on the receiver by Jase's bed and sat down to watch the stars.

Jase unbuttoned his dingy white vest, throwing it to the floor, before laying back on his bed. Feeling a small weight in his right pants pocket, he pulled out a silver pocket watch which his mother had given him before she left. He opened it, studying the blue moon face of the watch where the numbers were projected into the air just a few centimeters away from the clock's face. He clicked a small button on the side and watched the clock face change into a hologram of his mother but her back was turned towards the camera so he couldn't see her face. He was a young boy, laughing about something he couldn't remember now. Jase studied the holo, feeling a lump form in his throat before finally closing it and placed it on the end table next to Kaimi's receiver.

Kaimi was already laying on her back now fascinated by the stars. In almost a trance-like state she mumbled, "Do you think I could write something like this someday?"

With one hand tucked behind his head, Jase too watched the floating stars revolved around the room while listening to the music. "It's possible. Yes, I think so." They both stayed quiet enjoying the music until finally after a while Jase slipped into his dreams.

A loud beeping disrupted the air, which woke Jase up. Without opening his eyes, he pressed on his data watch to shut off the alert and slowly rubbed the sleepy from his eyes. He then let out a tired sigh as he stared at the cracked brown ceiling that had a sliver of light running across it from behind the covered window.

The same loud beeping erupted in the air again forcing Jase to sit up and look down at his data watch. He saw it was a message from his boss telling him that he needed to see him immediately. It was strange to Jase, seeing that he just saw him a couple of days ago for a thieving job they had just finished. Usually the man didn't have another one till a couple of weeks due to Jase was his only employee who didn't kill people. Jase replied back that he would meet him in the next hour and crawled out of bed to get ready.

"Bentley has another job for us," he explained to Kaimi who was sitting cross-legged on the counter with her eyes closed as he entered the kitchen.

Confused she opened her eyes. "Already? Isn't that a bit strange?"

23

Jase shrugged, searching through the fridge for something to eat. "It's the end of June and we only have two more months left in summer before the cold comes. Maybe beings want things to be done before then."

"It still seems strange," she told him as she walked to the end of the counter.

Jase peered out the balcony noticing the sun was somewhat behind them from the light sky. He glanced to his data watch to check the time. Seven-thirty on the dot. "Did you finish your book?" he asked, taking out a loaf of bread and some meat to make breakfast.

"Yes, and I finished fifty-four books after it. I think I'm starting to like mysteries," she announced while watching him make a sandwich.

Jase placed the sandwich in a makeshift toaster that consisted of parts from an old spaceship engine. It shot out a huge flame over the bread and meat, cooking it in seconds before shutting off. Jase reached for the sandwich, dropping it immediately. "Ouch!"

"Why you continue to do that every time is a mystery to me," Kaimi shrugged.

Jase took a bite and said between chews, "Because I'm an impatient man who's hungry."

"I was doing the math for our last paid gig and realized if you keep thirty pieces of the two-fifty then we can give more to Mrs. Rose without harming your pocket. You don't use much of it anyways," she suggested changing the subject.

Jase thought it over knowing he really didn't need the money. "I'm fine with that. Are you ready to go?"

"Ready," she responded and stepped onto his data watch and vanished.

Jase left his apartment, traveling down the elevator to the third floor where once again he climbed down the cargo staircase, facing the morning heat that singed his skin from the rising sun.

"It's going to be a hot day," he proclaimed as he headed east.

Treason for a Bracelet

By the time they reached Bentley's Warehouse in the East District, the sun was high overhead and the heat unbearable. He was dripping sweat from head to toe and already felt dehydrated from the sun as he shuffled his blue pilot's jacket to his other hand to wipe seat off his brow.

"It's a record high heat today at 112°F," Kaimi revealed inside his ear.

Jase walked up to the shady entrance of the warehouse thankful for the shade as he banged on the steel automatic door. A camera popped out from the side and moved snakelike as it scanned him up and down before disappearing into the wall again. "I hate summer heat," he griped.

A moment later the door slid open letting out a cool breeze. He entered the factory where factory workers frantically put parts of spacecrafts on moving belts that transferred the machinery into another room to be made. The factory was one of the largest factories on the planet with five others spread out across the galaxy. The man who owned them was a large purple Vimalax who had a history of illegal activities throughout the city. He had won the factory from the previous owner in a card game and after a short while also won the casino from the same man. Since then he had used the casino as a place to recruit workers. Anyone with a debt they couldn't pay became a servant in the factory until payment was received in full.

Jase wasn't fond of Vimalaxes as they were born greedy and hotheaded and tried manipulating anyone into a profit. It wasn't a surprise when Jase found that Bentley sold merchandise on the Black Market and hired local thugs to make sure things got delivered on time. If you had any problems that needed to go away, Bentley was the man to go to. Even though he was a criminal, Jase still preferred his company more than any other Vimalaxes due to the way he treated humans. He was no respecter of persons no matter how well off or not well off.

"Looks like the Bluestar can't take the heat!" Bentley cried out from across the factory floor in a loud booming voice that thundered over the machines. Jase crossed the busy floor, dodging in and out of workers. When he finally stood before him, Bentley continued, "I swear you humans would perish if we kept you outside during the summer heat. Every other species would thrive," he exclaimed in a scratchy, watery voice that made Jase's ears hurt.

"Well, we humans aren't built with tough skin like the rest of you."

"You got that right," Bentley chuckled a sound that resembled nails on a chalkboard more than actual laughter. He turned his head to the three Vimalaxes that stood next to him. "Get out of here and find him," he ordered and watched the three leave without hesitation.

Jase watched the three hurry out of the factory. "Problems?"

Bentley motioned for him to follow as he spoke. "When aren't there problems?" They walked to Bentley's office and before saying anymore, he ordered, "Close the door."

Jase closed the door and took a seat in front of a large console. He glanced about the room that was covered in live feeds of the warehouse's interior and exterior. He couldn't imagine having to sit there cramped up inside the noisy factory. Turning his attention back to the alien in front of him, Jase said, "You mentioned there was another job?"

"Yes, I did. It's a very special one that will make both of us lots of pieces," Bentley confirmed smiling to reveal his fangs for teeth.

Jase straightened up in his chair a little. "I'm listening," he said.

Bentley stared at a live feed and pressed a button. The screen flickered to life closing in on a worker who appeared to be sleeping on the job. How he was able to sleep with all the noise, Jase didn't know but he could tell it was an elderly man who was incredibly thin for his age. Bentley pressed another button and suddenly the floor tile under the man vanished causing him to fall through the floor and out of sight. "Pathetic," Bentley said in disgust.

"He always kills someone while we are here," commented Kaimi in the earpiece unable to hide her dislike.

Jase asked again, "The job, you were saying?"

"Are you in a rush, Bluestar?" Bentley questioned clearly annoyed. His purple skin changed into a shade of pink.

Careful not to upset him more, Jase kindly smiled. "Just interested in the job is all."

Bentley returned to his normal shade of purple as he grinned. "I knew you liked pieces as much as I do. I have a client who wants a precious bracelet that is out of their reach," he explained.

Jase frowned in disbelief. "A bracelet? That's the urgent job you want me to do? Really?"

"It's not just any bracelet, but if you're going to complain then I'll ask someone else," Bentley retorted as he turned his attention back to the computer screens.

Jase sat back in his chair and tried to act interested. "No, go on. I'm already here," he pointed out.

"You don't have to be," Bentley threatened while checking over each screen for any lazy workers.

Jase crossed his arms knowing he needed to set things right before he lost the job. "I'm sorry. I just thought it was something big and daring. You know how I feel about doing boring jobs."

Bentley scratched his bald purple head, amused. "You don't kill people. Your jobs are boring, but this one is different. It is a very big job and I need the best! Make both of us very rich!"

"For just a bracelet?" Jase questioned.

Bentley shook his head. "Buyer is stupid, but will pay heavily for it. Seventy-five thousand pieces!"

"Seventy? Seventy-five thousand?!" Jase repeated unable to fathom that kind of money.

"This bracelet must mean a lot to the buyer," exclaimed Kaimi in his ear.

Bentley excitedly jumped out of his chair and walked around the desk to him. "You take job then or do I need to hire the next best thing?"

"No, I'll take it!" Jase quickly accepted. "Just point me in the right direction!"

Bentley didn't hesitate. "It's located inside the trophy room in Starwake Castle."

Jase stared at him unsure if he was joking. "Are you serious?" he asked.

"Have you known me to joke," Bentley answered impatiently.

Jase's smile disappeared. Stammering, he reproached Bentley, "Are you insane?! Starwake Castle is the most guarded building in the galaxy! It has half of the Android Army inside it waiting to kill anything in their path if you look at them wrong! You cannot be serious?!"

"It's not impossible to get in. Just unlikely," Bentley pointed out.

Jase stood out of his seat. "You're right! It's insane to even try."

"When have you ever backed down from a risk?"

"The moment you ask me to break into Lord Brohain's castle and commit treason," Jase scoffed.

"It's only treason if you get caught," Bentley suggested.

Jase placed his hands on his hips. "I'm not doing it, Bentley." He turned to open the door, but stopped as Bentley responded.

"You leave, I won't give you another job."

"There's always someone who needs a thief. You're not the only one," Jase said over his shoulder.

"Okay, but where you going to find one that's not connected to me? I pretty much own all the criminals on this planet," he replied, his beady eyes watching Jase closely.

Jase shrugged. "There has to be one you don't."

"You're really going to turn me down? Do you really want to make me an enemy, Bluestar?" he asked him, his voice sharp as a knife cutting through Jase's ears.

Jase held his gaze. "You're asking me to do the impossible."

"I'm asking you to do your job. A job you happen to be the best of the best at. I asked you and not those other idiots because I know you'd get it done," Bentley claimed.

Jase looked away to one of the terminals, weighing his options. "You really think I can do it?"

Bentley revealed his pointed teeth. "You will for whoever you give your pieces to."

Jase eyed him. "How do you know I don't keep them?"

"Because no one wears the same outfit day after day if they've got pieces," Bentley explained crossing his arms as he leaned against his desk.

Jase leaned against the office door with a smile. "Maybe I really like it."

"Then you think I'm a bigger fool than you look."

Jase contemplated the proposal a moment more before replying, "Fine, I'll take it. How many weeks do I have to prep?"

"Two days," Bentley replied, moving back around the desk to take his seat.

"Two days?!" Jase was not anticipating such a short turnaround time for a high-profile job like this. This would take months to prepare for—how could anyone expect him to risk his life in two days!

"Make it work," Bentley suggested turning his attention back to the screens.

Jase couldn't believe it. The bracelet couldn't be worth all this trouble. "That's too short of time. I need at least a week to study the layout of the castle."

"Make it work or you're out," Bentley repeated pressing a few buttons on the terminal.

Jase scratched the top of his head trying to think. It seemed like an impossible task but maybe they could pull it off.

"We will think of something," Kaimi proposed softly to ease his thoughts.

Jase replied out loud mostly to her then Bentley, "Okay, I guess."

"Just a challenge, Bluestar, that's all it is," Bentley told him as Jase left the office and travelled back through the noisy factory floor. His thoughts seemed to be as loud as the machines as he tried fathoming what he had to do and how much of a risk it was.

Once they were out of the office, Kaimi whispered, "If we do this then Momma Rose and the children would be set for years to come."

"I know. Believe me, I know," he replied under his breath. "But it's insane and too risky to try and pull off even if I had months to do it."

He could feel Kaimi's smile in her voice as she replied, "You like risky things, remember?"

"Yeah, but this is on a whole new level. I wouldn't even know where to start. It's a fortress for a reason, Kaimi," he retorted exiting the factory only to be immediately hit with wave of heat in the early afternoon sun. He continued down the way he had come heading towards downtown.

Kaimi remained optimistic. "I can get us a layout of the castle, but you have to figure out how we get in; otherwise it wouldn't be any fun. Besides, it may be impossible to get in for the average person but you have me, remember?"

Jase grinned nervously. "How can I forget with you yapping in my ear all the time. I'll get us in if you get the blueprints. Why do you think the bracelet is so important?" he asked as sweat rolled down his forehead.

"Who knows. Maybe once we see it, we will understand."

Jase stared in the distance, his gaze fixed on the metal castle that could be seen from anywhere in the city. The two-hundred-story skyscraper was created with beautiful architectural styles and its balconies overlooked the entire city. The longer he stared the more the castle seemed to change in front of him. He realized it looked almost cold and shielded off from the city. Why would anyone want to live in such a lonely place? He could feel the heat sapping away his energy as he sat on the step of a lawyer's office building. Turning his eyes back to the castle, he determined, "Might as well stop by the castle on the way home since we are passing it anyways."

"It would be smart to see what we are up against," agreed Kaimi.

Forcing himself off the step, he began walking. "What we need is a sky-bike, Kaimi, then we wouldn't have to walk in this heat."

"You wouldn't have to walk in this heat," she corrected him.

Jase suddenly noticed a group of five beings dressed in gold and red traveling his way. He recognized the colors, knowing they belonged to a local gang called the BloodSuns that worked with Bentley on occasion. The gang mostly consisted of the species Sals, a plum and myrtle lizard-like creature with large fangs that protruded from either side of its mouth giving it a more vicious appearance in contrast with their silver eyes. They were one of the cruelest creatures in the solar system and were easily provoked if not careful. BloodSuns were commonly hired as bounty hunters, and the Sals not involved with the gang made a living largely by gambling and underground crime jobs. Bentley enjoyed their sportsmanship and hired them regularly as they reliably killed without asking questions.

"Another reason we need a sky bike," Jase muttered as the group drew near.

The Sals spoke in their own tongue using harsh symbols and clicks that Jase couldn't understand.

"Looks like a war over territory is about to happen soon," Kaimi translated, listening to the passing conversation. "The Earwins are starting to expand their parties towards the south of the city and not just west anymore. They aren't happy about it."

Jase kept walking, keeping his head down as he passed the last Sal.

"Bluesssstar," came a harsh voice behind him.

Jase felt his heart start to beat faster as he turned around to find the gang facing him. He noticed the familiar Sal that he ran in to every now and then in Bentley's Casino. "Well, hey there, Xef," he replied.

The dark plum and myrtle lizard took a step towards him, his large fangs shined in the bright sun as saliva dripped from the ends, "Sssstill ssstealing from babiessss?" he asked.

"If I don't do it, who else will?" Jase replied humorously.

"Careful, Jase," Kaimi warned sensing that the reptiles weren't amused by his joke.

Xef stared at him for a moment allowing the sun to bake them both though it didn't bother him at all. His race was born on a much hotter planet and he knew Jase was having trouble with the heat. "You couldn't kill if you wanted to," he hissed.

"You're right: I have a conscience," Jase retorted having clearly crossed the line.

In the blink of an eye Xef grabbed him by the throat with his claw-like talons and held him off the ground close to his fangs. His hot breath reeked of rotting meat as he hissed, "Bentley might not missss you assss much assss I think he would."

Barely able to breathe, Jase countered, "Want to ask him?" He could feel Kaimi charging his data watch to malfunction and shock the alien.

Xef let him drop to the ground gasping for air. He ordered his men in his own tongue before threatening Jase, "The day the Androidsss allow the extermination of all humansss will be the day I come after you, Bluestar." He left with the others in the direction of Bentley's Warehouse.

"You just had to be smart," Kaimi reprimanded.

Jase rubbed his throat as he pulled himself to his feet coughing a little as he did. He grabbed his blue pilot's jacket from the ground as he replied, "Where would be the fun if I wasn't?"

"Your recklessness will get you killed one of these days," she scolded.

Jase smirked as he turned on his way again. "Yeah, probably."

"Jase Bluestar, I sometimes wonder why I put up with your selfish behavior."

Jase noticed a sky bike descend from the traffic above and land farther down the street next to an establishment. He watched the rider climb off and head inside the building. "Because without me, who's going to look after you?"

Kaimi gave a short laugh. "I'm more worried about you more than my own wellbeing."

Jase stopped next to the bike and scanned for anyone loitering on the empty street. "What do you think? Should we make our trip faster?" he asked her studying the bike.

"If it will stop you from complaining, then yes," she replied with amusement in her tone.

Jase climbed on to the sleek bike and touched the interface, noticing it needed a hand recognition of the rider in order to unlock and turn on. It was a neat idea in order to stop thieves from stealing vehicles, but unfortunately it wasn't good enough to keep Jase out. "Would you like to bypass the security controls or shall I?"

The controls suddenly unlocked allowing Jase into the system as Kaimi replied, "Already done."

"Thank you." He pulled on his pilot's jacket then ducked behind the small windshield before launching into sky traffic, maneuvering with the digital steering handles for control.

The wind howled in his ears as he swerved in and out of air traffic heading towards the heart of downtown. Eighty feet in the air and the city seemed so much more complicated than it seemed on the ground floor. He could see dots of beings moving this way and that down the streets. He had only stolen a sky bike once before but it made him love being in the air. He felt like someone who could afford to fly around for some important job that he loved and yet at the same time, it made him crave to travel into the atmosphere and get lost inside the forest of stars beyond his reach.

"Land in that market square outside of the castle. That should give us a good spot to figure out our breach," Kaimi instructed as she pulled up a small holographic map on the screen in front of him. There was a highlighted area which indicated where she wanted him to land along with a route to get him there from his exact location.

Jase followed the map and brought the bike down in the busy square landing it in a side alley. Smoothing out his jacket, he pressed a button on the screen of the bike to allow a live feed to pop up so he could fix his windblown hair. "Do you think we could get what we need?"

"Get me to a terminal and I'm sure of it," she responded.

Jase nodded to himself and touched the screen again to lock the bike before walking out into the crowded street. The main downtown strip led from the south gate to the heart of the city where restaurants, clubs, shops, casinos, and anything else you could think of lined either side. The streets were always overpopulated despite the time though there were very few apartments in the area. Only people of great importance lived in them since they were closest to the castle. When the NightStars ruled the city, anyone could live near the castle but once the Androids took over they decided no one deserved to live near them unless they had business with Lord Brohain. All the buildings around the castle were at least one hundred and sixty yards away four heavy machine turrets on each corner of the castle's fifty-foot walls.

"Why don't we come to downtown more often?" Kaimi questioned. "There's so much to do here."

Jase pressed through the cramped crowd towards the castle muttering under his breath, "Don't have time to."

"We should get more jobs that involve being downtown. It would be a nice change of scenery," she continued knowing very well she couldn't see what he was seeing.

Jase could feel sweat cover his forehead though none of the other species seemed bothered by the heat. He spotted a juice stand on the corner of the market closest to the castle walls and moved towards it. Stopping at the stand, he picked up a newspaper, never failing to break his gaze from the walls while pretending to read.

"Excuse me, sir? Sir? Would you like to try our gem blend special today? It's a blend of ruitberry and watermelon juices," the boy called out to Jase holding a cup of purple liquid.

Jase noticed the honey biscuits on the counter. "No thanks, but I'll take one of those."

"Five pieces," the boy said.

Jase fished out ten pieces from his pocket and handed it to the kid. "Keep the rest," he told him and picked up a honey biscuit with a pale green spread in the middle. He took a bite and moved back to where he had been standing as sweet mint honey filled his mouth.

"Thank you, sir!" the boy called out before shouting at others in the crowd.

Jase took another bite of the biscuit as he watched two Android guards on either side of the main gate entrance to the castle's courtyard. They stood at attention, their red eyes carefully watching everyone that walked past as they gripped metal plasma rifles. Looming at seven feet, their robotic features revealed their low rank as Android nobles typically possessed a skin covering their mechanical parts. Their metal shell was painted in maroon and silver, the colors of the Android flag. Besides the two at the gate, Jase also noticed five other guards patrolling the top wall like wolves waiting for prey.

"How does it look?" Kaimi asked.

Jase took another bite of his biscuit. He scanned for any cameras and found two pointed at the gate as well as four others spread out on the wall. He also spotted a small terminal behind one of the guards posted that was used to allow entry. "Well, they never make it easy."

"It's a castle. It's never supposed to be easy. What's the layout? Did you find a terminal?" she asked.

Jase swallowed the last of his biscuit. "Yup. Six cameras on the front wall, two pointed at the gate and the others elsewhere. There's probably more on the other three walls, as well as more guards. There's two street level guarding the main gate with five on the wall itself watching from above. There is a small terminal on the wall behind the left guard next to the gate which makes things a little tricky in getting you in and out without causing trouble. It's not impossible, though."

"Sounds like you got your work cut out for you," Kaimi sighed in his ear.

Jase scratched his cleanshaven cheek thinking. "Tell me about it. I have no idea how we are going to do this yet. I can maybe see three different ways in getting you in the terminal, but not back out."

"Talk me through it. Maybe I can help," she suggested.

Jase suddenly thought of an idea. "If I were to throw my earpiece at the panel could you transfer into the terminal?"

"Yes, if you hit it right on, but from where you are standing it's highly unlikely that you will make it."

Jase looked for an alternative spot. "Let me worry about that. You would only have a second to transfer."

Kaimi seemed to find his statement amusing. "A second in your world is a minute in mine."

"Well, don't get mad at me if you can't do it, smarty," he teased grabbing a map on the newsstand and slipped back into the crowd along the wall. He got ready to take out when Kaimi asked, "How will you get me back?"

Jase grinned and took out the small earbud. "I'll wing it." He took a deep breath and headed for the guards. Unraveling the map of the city he called out, "Excuse me, I think I'm lost."

"Keep your distance, human," the guard ordered in a resounding metallic voice.

Jase kept calm, pretending to swat away a fly as he continued, "I know you are very busy, but it's my sister's birthday and I have no idea where I am. Could you please help me?"

"Stand back now!" the guard warned clearly annoyed.

Jase swatted at the imaginary fly again throwing his earbud at the terminal and moved closer to the guard as if to show him the map. "Just point to where I am now."

The Android immediately grabbed him by the arm, twisting it behind his back and shoved him into the castle wall next to the panel. "You will be arrested if you don't leave now," the Android barked from behind him, releasing his arm.

"Okay, okay, I get it," Jase let his hand casually slide over the panel as he calmly answered backing away slowly. Picking up the map he had dropped, he headed towards the stolen sky bike calling over his shoulder, "I'm leaving! I'm leaving!" He shoved the earpiece back into his ear and whispered, "Tell me you got it."

"I got it!" Kaimi exclaimed cheerfully.

Jase couldn't hide his grin as he passed the juice venue and dropped off the map. "Now we are in business."

To Make Plans

By the time Jase returned the sky bike to the place he found it and made it home the sun was setting with the evening air as hot as ever. He was drenched in sweat and had used the last of his strength to climb the elevator cable as he stumbled into his messy apartment.

"I was just saying that it won't be easy to break into and out of," Kaimi once again announced for the fourth time since they had gotten the plans.

Jase brushed his wrist against the counter transferring her from his data watch as he turned back around to head to the shower. "I heard you the first time, but there has to be something in the layout that we can use to get inside. Like secret tunnels used for an emergency to get out of the city!" he shouted at her from the bathroom.

Kaimi spoke through his earpiece as she looked over the plans in the kitchen. "He's an Android. I don't think he is worried about needing to escape in case of an attack. They fight it out."

"Well, check anyways. Maybe there will be a present for us to unravel. I'm going offline," he told her before taking out his earbud and placing it on the broken sink. Once clean and clothed again he returned to the kitchen. "What do you got?"

Kaimi pulled up a holographic blueprint of the castle. "I was looking through their data base and didn't find any other entries or exits besides the front gate and the back gate. But then...." The hologram flashed showing five tunnels under the castle leading to the city. "After several minutes of trying to gain access to this blueprint, these passageways turned up. They were recently built within the last five years in the noble district. It's unclear why they made them but it's clear they didn't want anyone to know."

Jase focused on the new information and memorized the layout. "I wonder what they are planning to use them for."

"I'll try to dig deeper to find the reason," she assured him.

Jase opened the cooler box and took out an expired bowl of soup. He peeled off the lid then began heating up the food. "We could use one of the tunnels to gain access—sneak in while everyone is sleeping."

Kaimi rolled her eyes at him. "You forget—Androids don't sleep. They don't need to," she shook her head, studying the layout once more. "You could get yourself killed doing this job, or imprisoned."

"Not if we do it right." The machine beeped that his soup was ready. Jase took a spoonful of the warm red liquid into his mouth and walked out to the balcony. Kaimi joined him appearing on the receiver just as he sat down. "If we do this right, this could be our last job for a while. We could leave if we wanted to."

Kaimi pulled her knees to her chest, hugging them as she rested her chin there. "I know. I've been thinking about that all day."

"We could go find the other A.I.s wherever they might be. You wouldn't have to be alone anymore," Jase said finishing the last bit of his soup.

Kaimi looked inquisitively at him. "I'm never alone as long as I'm with you. Besides, not all A.I.s like humans. It's better if we don't go and find them."

"Then we go somewhere else! Anywhere far from here and where you don't have to hide your existence. We can buy a spaceship and explore the furtherest stars in the galaxy. Just you and me," he enthused already imagining their adventures.

Kaimi smiled. "I'd like that."

"Then we will pack up as soon as the job is done," Jase concluded as he watched another spacecraft take off into the faint dying light.

Kaimi glanced over at him. "Let's first figure out a plan to get in and out of the castle. Now I think I might have something that could work and less likely to get us caught." She stood back up then turned towards the kitchen vanishing and reappearing once more inside.

Jase quickly stood up to follow her. "What are you thinking?"

"There's a good chance the tunnels under construction will be guarded if they haven't finished it yet. They wouldn't want someone to accidentally stumble upon it so that's out of the question. Going through one of the finished tunnels could prove to be much safer and there's less chance of being detected. If we run across any terminals, I'm pretty confident I can disable any security protocols that could stand in our way."

Jase studied the tunnel layout. "Okay, which tunnel were you thinking of going into?"

Kaimi pointed to the closest one in the northwest district. "According to the readings this is the oldest tunnel built so it's the least likely to be *heavily* guarded."

Jase nodded in agreement. "Show me the layout to the trophy room for once we get inside."

She swiped to the right and another set of plans appeared. Five highlighted doors were shown scattered throughout the castle indicating where each tunnel began. Kaimi pointed to the purple highlighted door on the one hundredth and thirty-fifth floor of the castle. "This tunnel is located in the Northwest district and leads us to a service elevator that we can take to the trophy room and hopefully back out."

"Wouldn't someone notice us using the elevator?" he asked concerned.

Kaimi replied, "Probably, but it's our only option that has less cameras scanning the area. We'd only have to disable the one inside the elevator instead of a handful which could cause more attention. The only thing we would have to worry about is Androids using the exact elevator or being on the same level as we are."

Jase thought of the elevator shaft in his building and touched the highlighted door to bring up the blueprint of the elevator. "What if we didn't use the elevator? We could go through the shaft and use the cables to pull myself up to the right floor. There wouldn't be any cameras so we could go undetected."

"You're going to climb one hundred and thirty-five stories to where we need to be?" she asked sarcastically.

"No, of course not. When you disable the elevator camera, I will get in and climb out to the top of the elevator. With you inside the system, you can run a program that acts like a glitch to cause the elevator to stop at random floors before continuing on again. If someone is watching the cameras and movements of the elevator security they will assume it's just an elevator malfunction after so long of not being used or what not. You can have it stop four stories under the trophy room and I can climb the rest so we don't have guards waiting at the elevator doors once I reach the trophy room level. We could knock two birds out with one stone allowing us not to have to worry about someone using the service elevator and no guards will notice us getting off at our location."

"We could have the elevator doors open and close at each stop so that when we open level 131 up, no one will notice 135 opening at the exact same time," Kaimi added following his plan.

Jase suddenly remembered from dinner with Momma Rose the previous night that the Androids were having a council meeting tomorrow to determine how to deal with the Resistance. "They are having that big meeting tomorrow so security might be pretty tight. Once they notice the glitch in the system, they will want to fix it right away so we won't have much time to work. We also might not be able to use the same way out."

"You could always just break a window," Kaimi joked, studying the plans to figure out an alternate route.

Jase's eyes lit up thinking of the sky bike he had stolen earlier. "Why not?"

"I was joking," she responded without taking her eyes off the holo.

Jase leaned against his palms on the counter. "And I'm serious. We could use the sky bike we stole earlier since I added my fingerprints to the security protocol on it. We can call it to come pick us up from a window once we get the bracelet. We sneak in and crash out and since it's not ours they can't trace it to us. I can delete my fingerprint from it once we land. We can then ditch it before we head back to Bentley's."

"You're forgetting about the cameras and their security system. They will detect a bike entering the air around the castle," Kaimi pointed out.

Jase grinned still proud of himself. "Not if your glitch is still messing with their security. Security will be focused on getting it back online that they won't notice us leaving."

"What about the guards on the wall?" she reminded him.

Jase shrugged. "You can overload the terminal by the gate and let's hope that distracts them long enough for us to get away undetected."

"This is your great plan?"

"Yes! I'm eighty-five-percent sure it just might work," he affirmed her.
Kaimi watched him carefully unimpressed. "And if it doesn't work?"
"Well, no cell has been able to hold us so far."
Kaimi shook her head but smiled. "Okay, I'm in," she said.
Jase shifted his eyes back to the map. "Where's the tunnel's entrance in the northwest district?"
Kaimi changed the hologram to show a map of the entire city. "Here. It's about a thirty-two-minute walk to the north wall where it's located somewhere in the corner of the city. Probably close to the sewers is my guess," she theorized.
"From here to the castle, even underground, could take two, maybe three hours to walk. That's if we don't get lost on the way down," Jase replied.
"I can download the map onto your data watch so getting lost shouldn't be a problem."
"Okay, so two hours there, who knows how long it will take to get the prize, then maybe a couple of hours to get rid of the bike in the warehouse district before meeting up with Bentley and walking all the way back. If possible once we get paid we could leave the very next day after we say goodbye to Roran. Maybe even travel with him for a while till we figure out where we want to go," Jase thought out loud.
"I don't see why not," Kaimi agreed with a warm smile.
The thought of the three of them traveling distracted Jase from the severity of the consequences they could get into as he turned to his bedroom. "Try and rest up, Kaimi! We will need our minds sharp for tomorrow morning!"

Unexpected Visitor

"Jase, Jase, it's time to get up," came a soft voice stirring him awake. Jase opened his eyes slowly adjusting to the dim light. He blinked noticing the faint purple glow to his right and turned to face it. Kaimi sat next to him on the receiver. "It's time to get up," she repeated once more.

Jase yawned. "What time is it?"

"5:30 A.M.," she said.

Still not fully awake, he rose from bed and rubbed the sleep out of his eyes. He stretched letting out a growl as he did before dropping to all fours and doing pushups. "How far is the tunnel from here?" he asked.

"Thirty minutes, give or take," Kaimi replied.

Jase did thirty pushups before bouncing to his feet, feeling more awake. He took off the shirt he was wearing and grabbed his faded white vest, buttoning it up. "And two hours to walk to the castle?"

"Correct."

He pulled on his charcoal pants, placing the silver pocket watch in his pocket before lacing up his black boots. "Maybe another two hours inside the castle?"

"Possibly. It really depends on how fast you are and how much security there is," Kaimi pointed out.

Jase grabbed his pilot's jacket and fingerless gloves before shuffling into the kitchen. Kaimi appeared on the counter walking beside him as he made his way to the pantry. "You will be able to get the sky bike over to us, right?" he asked.

"With your fingerprint ID in its system, it won't be hard," she brought up the blueprints of the castle again. "The trophy room is in the heart of the castle. Inside the room there are no cameras, but outside is another matter. At least four maybe five, that I can tell."

Jase took out two slices of bread and an apple. "But that shouldn't matter if you can shut them down."

"Just in case, you need to be aware of them," Kaimi warned him. "Androids are smart so we have to be careful if they find a way to fix my glitch."

Jase placed the two slices of bread into his makeshift toaster and took a bite of his apple. "You need to be careful that they don't find you in their system."

"Don't worry about me. I'll be fine," she assured him before asking, "What will you do if you run into a guard? You don't have any weapons."

Jase hadn't thought of that. He was too busy trying to do the job undetected, that he hadn't thought of what would happen if he came across an Android. "Couldn't you disable them for a few minutes?"

"Then they will know I exist. They will disable me if I show myself," she countered.

Jase's bread popped up as he took another bite of his apple. "I don't know, but we will cross that bridge when we come to it. If everything goes right, I shouldn't have to worry about it."

"Jase."

"Kaimi, it will be fine," he assured her then checked the time. 6:15 A.M. He finished the last of his breakfast and grabbed his earbud off the counter. "We need to get going."

Kaimi walked to the end of the counter and disappeared into his data watch. "I'll talk you through the streets to the tunnel."

"Wouldn't have it any other way," he replied leaving his apartment suddenly excited for the job.

"Keep going straight until I tell you otherwise," Kaimi told him in his ear.

Jase did as he was told, noticing the heat wasn't as bad as it was yesterday. It felt much cooler and was pleasant to walk in. "Feels like fall is near," he said out loud.

"It's the middle of summer," she replied. "Turn right up here."

Jase grinned, "Let me just believe that I don't have to endure another day like yesterday just for a short while, eh?"

"If we leave the planet, you won't have to," she responded.

Jase turned right, heading eastward with the north wall on his left. "That's going to be nice."

"The sewers should be coming up in the next mile," Kaimi instructed.

Jase scanned the street for anyone else that was up with the morning sun. He only saw a few who didn't pay him any attention as they scurried off to work for the day.

"Turn left here," Kaimi's voice interrupted his thoughts.

Jase turned left continuing until he spotted the sewer line on the cobbled street a few feet away from the north wall. It was barely noticeable next to the flowerbeds of a pleasant colonial home that covered most of it from view. "Found it," he muttered.

"Be careful. There might be a force field to keep intruders out," she warned him.

Jase looked around for anyone watching him before crouching down so that Kaimi could scan for a shield.

"Got it," she exclaimed.

Jase looked around again before pulling open the heavy steel grate. Inside the sewer was pitch black. It made Jase feel slightly uneasy. A foul smell floated to the surface causing Jase to make a face as he tried waving it away from his nose.

Ignoring the smell, he dropped into the darkness landing in a puddle of sewage and excrement. The opening from above closed shut, snuffing out the remainder light inside the tunnel. Touching his data watch to illuminate the air around him, the soft blue light showed his surroundings only a few feet ahead.

"It smells terrible down here," he said disgusted as he glanced around the narrow tunnel.

"I don't think Androids have a sense of smell. Building a tunnel here wouldn't bother them."

Jase stared back at the darkness behind him, feeling uneasy about not being able to see before starting off into the darkness. "Lucky them."

"I was able to break into the code of the tunnel blueprint even more since we've been down here. There appears to be a map in code revealing a maze of tunnels under the castle through each passageway," Kaimi revealed busily.

"Wonderful," he replied sarcastically.

"Except for the five, the other tunnels lead to dead ends inside a maze most likely to make it hard for someone to break into the castle," she informed him while still working through code.

Jase suddenly stopped thinking he had heard something behind him. "The Androids seemed to have this more planned out than we thought."

"So it seems," she agreed.

Waiting, Jase listened but didn't hear anything except for the water below his feet. Continuing on his way, he asked, "Any traps or monsters I should worry about?"

"Some of the dead-end tunnels have ditches but I will keep you away from those," she assured him.

"And monsters?"

Kaimi seemed slightly amused at his question. "I highly doubt it, but if they did for some reason it's not on the map or in the notes."

"Wow, way to make me feel better," Jase remarked picking up his pace into a brisk walk.

Optimistically, Kaimi said, "At least we don't have to worry about cameras or Androids down here."

"Just the dark and maybe a big scary monster that is planning on having me for an early lunch," he replied back.

"Well, as Mrs. Rose is always pointing out, you are pretty thin. Maybe it will have mercy on you," she suggested cheerfully.

Jase stopped when his light showed that the narrow tunnel broke off into separate passageways—one going left and the other continuing straight. "Which way?"

"Straight."

Jase continued on. "You know if you were me this wouldn't be a laughing matter."

"It might be, though," she teased.

Jase could feel her smile through her voice which brought a goofy grin to his own face. Remembering the Androids meeting, he wondered out loud, "I wonder what he looks like?"

"Who?" Kaimi questioned.

"Lord Brohain. Since the war no one really sees him anymore except for his soldiers. Do you think he looks like a human or machine?"

Kaimi was quiet a moment. "I don't know. Maybe both?"

"Do you think he's a good guy?" Jase asked realizing that they never really talk about the Androids.

"I wouldn't know," she replied.

Jase pressed on wanting to know her thoughts on the matter. "But if you were to guess what would be your take since he is an Android and they do hate your kind?"

There was a few moments of silence as if she was thinking on the matter. Jase wondered if he had upset her in some way. Then, "I think all evil men believe they are good guys no matter what they have done. I'm sure Lord Brohain has done everything for a reason he believes is right and not just because he hates my kind. It makes sense to him while it seems wrong to us."

"Do you hate him for all that he has done?" Jase pressed.

She said genuinely, "No, I feel sorry for him. The weight he must carry for all that he has done and continue to do must eat away at him. Perhaps he only needs someone to show him what's right?"

"Well, doubt anyone wants to be friends with him after all the people he killed in the war. Especially after destroying the Nightstar family and everything they stood for. I wouldn't be friends with him even if you held a plasma gun to my head," Jase responded.

"Sometimes enemies can become friends, Jase. Peace can be formed between two people," she reminded him.

Jase came across another tunnel. "Maybe for some, but not for everyone. Straight or left?"

"Left."

He continued, "But I prefer the old-fashioned way: Bad guys get what they deserve."

"But what makes a 'bad' guy? People could say that you and I are bad for stealing things," Kaimi countered.

Jase chuckled at the thought. "But we do it for a good reason."

"They don't know that," she responded, and for a few seconds there was silence between them again.

Jase then asked in disbelief, "So you're telling me that Lord Brohain killed thousands of beings for a good cause?"

"No, I'm just saying we shouldn't judge people when we don't know what's behind the madness. You need all the facts to come to proper conclusions," she told him matter-of-factly.

Jase shook his head with a smile, replying, "Well, I don't like him and that's what I'm sticking to."

"Very well then."

Jase stopped again, this time sure he had heard something behind him. He felt his heart start to race as he turned around. "Are you sure there's nothing in this tunnel?"

"Yes, why?" Kaimi asked confused.

"I could have sworn on the stars I heard something behind me," he told her.

"It could just be a rat."

Jase pressed a button on his data watch which focused the light into a beam so he could use it to search the area around him. "I don't think so. It sounded a little bigger than a rat."

"Could be your imagination. Humans are so easily manipulated to believe there is something lurking in the dark when there is nothing," Kaimi stated.

Jase continued to pierce the darkness with his blue light until finally he gave up. He had just turned around when suddenly something grabbed at his pants pocket, taking his silver pocket watch with it. "What the—hey, come back here!" he shouted, running after whatever it was that touched him.

"What is it? What's going on?" Kaimi questioned. "Jase, what's wrong?"

Jase caught a quick glance of a gray blob before it disappeared behind a corner. "Something pickpocketed me!" he exclaimed breathing hard as he doubled his speed around the corner.

"You can't just run after it! There are traps in some of these tunnels!" she reminded him.

Jase abruptly stopped in a fork that broke into three separate passageways. He viewed each one, remarking, "You've got to be kidding me."

"Now what is it?"

Catching his breath, he tried to see if he could hear anything in any of them. "Three tunnels and I don't know which one it went into."

"Go right," she told him.

Jase peered to the right one. "Why?"

"Because beings normally go with what they are most comfortable with. Your watch was in your right pocket and the thief would've used his right hand to steal from you. So he or she would have gone down the right tunnel," she explained to him.

Jase took off down the tunnel, saying, "You're a genius."

She responded amused, "I know." Then in a more serious tone, "Be careful. There is a trap fifty yards ahead."

Jase slowed to a brisk walk, focusing his light as a beam again so he could better see what was in front of him. He spotted the large pit ahead that stretched from wall to wall with a dead end behind it. Moving closer, he then heard someone muttering something in another tongue. He recognized the curse words. It was the language of the Bulbs that he heard in Bentley's Casino every now and then. They were small, gray, chubby, and bald aliens that grew no larger than 4'7". They had large black eyes which took up most of their face that was shaped like a lightbulb. They weren't the smartest aliens in the galaxy and were often looked down on for their stupidity.

"Xardayk! Xardayk! Xardayk!" the creature down below in the pit muttered to itself. "Ona jeski heny ta farhinin ru hainya."

Jase whispered to Kaimi as he neared, "What's it saying? I picked up that it was calling himself 'stupid.'" He touched his data watch so it would record the alien for Kaimi to translate.

"He is just giving himself a hard time for falling into the hole," she replied.

Jase pointed his light down at the creature who immediately turned his face from it. "Excuse me," he said to see if it understood him.

"Xardayk oya," the creature muttered.

Kaimi translated, "He just called you a stupid boy."

"Hey! I'm a grown man!" Jase shouted down to the alien, annoyed.

The bulb looked up at him. "You understand me?"

Jase shrugged, "Kind of. Not really, though."

"Zuno strangeah," the alien said surprised before continuing in Jase's tongue. "Can you help me out of this hole?"

Jase crouched looking around the hole. "Why should I? You stole my watch!"

"Your face doesn't look like the kind who knows how to tell time," the alien replied back laughing at himself.

"What a strange creature," Kaimi declared listening to them.

Jase shot back, "At least I'm tall enough to get out of the hole."

"Oki, Oki, you funny human with jokes," he mused showing off its short rectangular teeth.

Jase continued, "Well, it's not hard with that face to make fun of."

The bulb's smile suddenly disappeared. "Oki human, take joke too far. I break watch now."

"Wait! Wait! Please, don't!" Jase pleaded, extending his hand towards him.

The bulb laughed again holding its stomach as it did. "I kid! I kid, human! Your face, though, very funny. Oki, I give you my watch if you help me out of this hole."

"First, it's *my* watch, and second, how do I know you won't take off once I get you out?" he interrogated.

The bulb stared at him with its large black saucers, "I make promise not to run. I give my watch once up," he said.

"My watch," Jase corrected again.

The bulb moved to the wall of the hole, reaching his stubby hand upwards. "Not in your possession so my watch."

"Because you stole it!" Jase argued, getting down on his stomach to reach the alien's arm.

"Not my fault you can't hold on to things. I only hope you can hold on to me long enough to pull me up," the bulb joked.

"Keep your eyes on him when you pull him up. Bulbs are known for their sticky fingers," Kaimi warned him as Jase heaved up the heavy alien.

Jase pulled him over the ledge of the hole and fell back onto his rear, breathing hard from the weight. He noticed that the alien wore no shoes revealing his small round feet. He wore black ankle-length pants with a matching sleeveless tank top and a red utility belt attached to his waist and shoulder. Around his large forehead were goggles to shield his eyes from the sunlight on the surface as bulbs were sensitive to bright lights. Holding out his hand, Jase ordered, "Hand it over then."

The short, chubby alien stared at him for a moment. "Oki, here you go, human," and he handed it over.

"Ask him what he is doing down here," Kaimi suggested.

Jase ignored her while returning the watch to his pocket. "Thank you."

"If I get it again then it's mine," the bulb replied, partly joking.

Jase stood to his feet smiling. "You won't. My name is Jase Bluestar."

"Tahmela is mine," the bulb answered back also standing to his feet.

Jase watched him carefully as he spoke. "Nice to meet you...sorta. Why are you down here?"

Amused, Tahmela said, "I could ask the human the same."

"It's complicated," Jase replied.

Tahmela studied him then wobbled away down the way they had come with Jase close behind him. "I hide down here when mean men are looking for me. I not so good with cards."

"You gamble?" Jase remarked surprised.

The bulb continued on his way. "Not very good at it, I'm afraid. I lost my ship to it."

"Wait, you can fly? I thought bulbs hated flying or traveling for that matter," Jase questioned him suddenly confused about what he knew about the race.

Tahmela looked at him. "And I thought humans were supposed to love sunlight yet you down here in the dark like a rat. You aren't very smart for a human. You can't even see without your light."

"Well, you're just the same back on my turf," Jase pointed out.

The bulb led them back to the three tunnels and peered into the middle one before turning around to Jase. "You aren't going to follow me, oki?"

"I won't if you don't follow me and try to steal my watch again," Jase retorted holding out his hand to shake.

Tahmela shook it, his thin lips parting into a smirk. "Oki for now."

"How do you know I'm not the one coming after you?" Jase asked the short alien who seemed so sure he was a good guy.

Tahmela answered, "Mean men don't send stupid humans to do the job."

"I could tell them where you are."

The bulb shrugged, walking off. "You could get lost in the tunnels so I'm not worried."

Jase watched the bulb disappear into the darkness as Kaimi stated, "What a weird creature."

Jase replied, "I kind of like him."

Breaking into StarWake Castle

"So where are we now?" Jase asked Kaimi.

"We're on the edge of the Noble District. Take the next right then there will be another passage shortly after that will take us into the main tunnel of the castle," she informed him, reading off the map.

Jase followed her directions until he came upon the passageway. He almost missed it since it was hidden from sight within the wall and appeared to be a hole only a foot wide. He squeezed into the passageway and began shuffling through it. "Are you sure this is it?" he asked, slowly inching down the cramped passage that reeked.

"It's the fastest way to get back on track without having to retrace our steps to the previous tunnel," she chimed.

Jase stopped for a moment shining his light down the tunnel but was unable to see the end. "It's a bit cramped," he said.

"Stop complaining and get a move on."

"Sheesh, somebody is bossy," Jase remarked as he slowly crawled on his way noticing the foul stench growing stronger.

Kaimi was silent.

"Kaimi? Are you still there?" he asked.

"Sorry, I was trying to figure out why this tunnel is so small. It didn't make sense if the Androids can't get through," she answered.

"Did you figure it out?" he questioned.

Kaimi hesitated. "Well...yes, I did gather information."

"Are you going to share it or leave me to guess?"

Still hesitant, she asked, "Are you sure you want to know?"

"Yes, I think so," he responded.

"Very well. This passageway is not really a passage. It's where the Noble District's waste runs before emptying into the sewers."

Jase stopped in his tracks, suddenly noticing the mold and dried feces that caked the walls. All at once the smell hit him causing him to feel suddenly sick to his stomach. "Now you tell me," he choked.

"You wanted to know," she reminded him.

Jase continued on, ignoring his stomach. "Next time keep it to yourself."

"At least you don't have to worry about any more deposits. The waste doesn't fall here for another four hours from now," Kaimi told him trying to sound optimistic.

Jase ignored her as he moved faster down the passage.

"It should only take twenty minutes to reach the main tunnel. From there it's a walk in the park to the castle," Kaimi proclaimed as if to try and keep his mind off where he was.

The next twenty minutes were the longest in his life, and when he finally pushed himself out of the passageway, he gasped for fresh air. "Oh, dear stars of mine," he exclaimed, falling to his knees as he breathed heavily for air. "I am never doing that again."

"It's a good thing Androids can't smell; otherwise that would be a problem for us," Kaimi pointed out.

"Too bad *you* can't smell; otherwise it would have been somewhat worth it," he teased.

"For once I'm happy I can't smell or see what you look like," she laughed softly.

Jase pushed himself to his feet, peering down both sides of the tunnel as he did. It was slightly more drafty than before and more wider than the others. It was large enough to fit a small army without any trouble. "Why do you think this tunnel is bigger than the others? You could seriously fit an army down here."

"Maybe that's their plan if the Resistance was ever to try and take over the city again. With these tunnels the Androids could easily over take the Resistance by surprise anywhere in the city," Kaimi expressed.

Jase agreed. "Which way now?"

"If you are facing the waste passage then right. Otherwise, go left," she told him.

Jase turned left, venturing into the darkness once more. "How far till the castle?"

"At your speed, my guess would be forty minutes till you reach the service elevator. It's a straight shot. You're directly on the edge of the Noble District and Downtown area," she informed him.

Jase checked his watch. 7:45 A.M. Even with the diversion, he was still making good time to the castle.

Jase could hear music above him and knew he had to be getting close to Downtown. He picked up his pace and noticed small gaps on the ceiling where sunlight peaked through. It wasn't long until a large waterway five feet wide invaded the tunnel with sewage water. The ground here had also changed from dirt to paved stone. Staring into the dirty water, Jase commented, "Too bad it's not clean water."

"It might not be the cleanest water but it could get some of the crap off your face," Kaimi suggested.

Jase watched the water float by, trying not to imagine what could be floating in it. "No thanks. I can wait."

Jase spotted the service elevator across the water way and stopped. "Is that the elevator?"

"Yes."

Jase crossed a narrow catwalk that connected to either side of the waterway and hurried to the elevator. Noticing the control panel was locked and needed a passcode to open, Jase reported, "It's locked."

"Touch the panel so I can upload," she replied.

Jase touched the elevator panel on the right side of the doors and waited for Kaimi to open them.

"Okay, when I say, get inside the elevator and climb the hatch to the top. You only have twenty seconds to get up before the guards check the screens," she urged him.

Out of habit, Jase gave a nod. "Okay. I'm ready."

"Ready, set…now!"

The elevator doors suddenly opened and without a moment to lose, Jase rushed in. Placing one foot on the hand guard, he pushed open the hatch and climbed out swiftly returning the door to its position.

"Good timing!" Kaimi exclaimed proudly.

Jase peered up the long elevator shaft that seemed to have no end. Lights shined every second floor as he noticed this was the basement floor of the castle. Staying in the middle next to the cables, Jase asked, "Ready to start havoc?"

"Ready when you are. You might also want to sit down and hold on tight," she suggested.

Jase got down on all fours, grabbing hold of a handrail for safety. "Just don't squash me."

"No promises," Kaimi called out as the elevator shot upward at full speed.

Jase felt wind fly past his face as he held on tightly to the rail with gravity pulling him down heavily as the elevator kept climbing. Suddenly it stopped causing his stomach to drop as he heard the doors open for a moment then close. Before he had the chance to recover, Kaimi told him to hold on again and the elevator shot upwards at full speed. Over and over, it stopped on a floor, open and closed its doors, then ascended upward as Kaimi and Jase hoped the erratic movements would be credible enough to look like a glitch to security. Kaimi even allowed the elevator to fall a few floors, partly for the plan and partly to mess with Jase.

"Okay! Your stop is coming up," she told him through his earpiece.

Jase couldn't find his tongue to respond as he held on tightly unable to feel anything in his arms or legs from the nerve-wracking ride. The elevator stopped abruptly.

"Jase, this is it. You can get up now."

Opening his eyes, Jase forced himself to let go of the rail. His legs felt wobbly as he pushed himself to stand. "Right, it's climbing time after the death ride," he remarked shakily.

"I had complete control," she reminded him.

Jase grabbed hold of the cables with both hands. "Maybe, but you weren't the one riding," he remarked then started the climb.

"You know, it's a good thing we are friends; otherwise this would be the perfect time to kill you," Kaimi teased as the elevator dropped downward.

Jase passed the one hundredth and thirty-sixth floor and continued upward. "That's heartening."

"Just remember it won't take them long to figure out how to override my controls so the faster you get into the hall, the better," she reminded him.

Jase passed the one hundredth and thirty-seventh floor as sweat formed on his forehead. "Trust me, I'm going as fast as I can."

"Hmm...it might help if you go faster."

"Kaimi," he warned.

"Alright, alright, I'll let you climb."

"Thank you," Jase said out of breath. He climbed past the one hundred and thirty-eight level when he heard the elevator speeding back up towards him. Trying his best to ignore the noise, he finished the last stretch of the climb and stopped on one hundred and thirty-ninth level. "Okay, I'm here."

"Alright, the elevator is going to stop...now. I'll open the doors to your level at the same time so be ready," she told him.

Just like she said, both doors opened at once and Jase swung his foot onto the door's ledge grabbing the side with one hand. Once he had a good grip, he pulled himself onto the floor just as the doors were closing. "Okay, I'm in," he whispered to her excitedly.

"The cameras are down in your hallway. Walk to the end and take the first left. The door to the trophy room should be in the next hallway on the right," she told him softly.

Jase calmed his breathing and took in his surroundings as he ventured down the hallway cautiously. The floors were a golden marble color with a long purple rug in the center spanning the full length. On the golden walls were portraits of human looking faces that Jase didn't recognize as he continued down the hall.

"The Androids' meeting is twenty floors above you, and from what I'm seeing on the cameras, most of security is on those floors. There's a handful of Androids patrolling the halls, but none should be on your level for quite some time now," Kaimi delivered automatically as if she was already on to the next thing.

That made Jase relax a little as he turned the corner down to find the hall was suddenly lined with doors on either side. "What door is it?"

"It's a royal blue double door on the right in the center of the hallway. Shouldn't be hard to find," she responded distractedly.

The door was just as she said. Assuring himself that no one was watching, Jase stepped in.

Escape

Closing the door behind him, Jase turned around to view the room. It was a large room with high ceilings and it was void of windows. Bookshelves with ancient-looking scrolls and books littered the walls. The floors were the same golden marble as outside and were polished to reflect the ceiling lights above. The room was also filled with rows and rows of glass cases containing artifacts and jewels. Jase had never seen so many treasures in one room before and was in awe by their beauty.

"Well? What does it look like?" Kaimi asked wanting to know.

Jase held up his data watch. "Why don't you see for yourself?"

Kaimi appeared a moment later standing on top of his watch, her hands behind her back as she stared about the room. "Wow. There's a lot in here."

"No kidding," Jase started forward slowly making sure not to touch anything while he viewed each showcased item. There were ancient treaties from the very beginning of life between all races along with artifacts of pots and jewels from fallen kingdoms in other solar systems. A giant dinosaur skull with five piercing horns rested in another case. A black asteroid in another was slowly shedding pieces of itself and sprinkled the surface of the case with black dust. Another held all of the fallen Nightstar Princesses' crowns as well as their parents', each gleaming off the light that hit it. The showcase next to it held the golden crown that belonged to King Adex Nightstar who was the first king on Planet Faton. It seemed faded as Jase stared at it before continuing on. The next one contained a pile of Redstar dust from the red season that happened every year when the Redstar would appear in the night sky for the entire summer. It was expensive to harvest the dust that fell on to the moon and Jase couldn't imagine how valuable it was. He had never seen the dust up close but only heard of its beauty as he couldn't take his eyes from it.

"I don't understand why Lord Brohain would want to keep some of these items," Kaimi thought out loud.

Jase stopped at the next case that held a common-looking necklace. "Just to say he has it? Who knows? Trophies are kept to prove that you did something."

"I know that, Jase, but why keep some of these items hidden? Why not just move them somewhere to show them off?" she pondered.

Jase peered into another that held a purple sphere no larger than his thumb. "I don't know, Kaimi. Why don't you ask him?" He moved closer to have a better view of the sphere. The closer he got the more he realized that the sphere's surface was always moving in tiny waves hitting against what looked to be a shore. It was hypnotizing to watch.

"Jase?" Kaimi's voice seemed so far away from him.

The longer he watched the tiny waves, Jase noticed what appeared to be a light on the shore. "What is that?" he wondered out loud and tried to move even closer for a better look.

"Jase," she repeated.

Ignoring her, Jase couldn't take his eyes from the light that seemed to be getting brighter. If only he could get closer. He felt compelled to break the glass and pick up the sphere to find out its secret. Maybe it wouldn't be such a big deal if he did, Jase thought as he leaned in closer. His breath fogging up the glass.

"Jase, Android!" Kaimi shouted disappearing back into the data watch.

Jase snapped out of his trance and spun around expecting to find the Android closing in on him. His heart raced in his chest, but there was no sign of the Android that had come in which frightened Jase even more. In a whisper, he asked, "Where is it?"

"There is none, but it got your attention back," Kaimi replied.

A wave of relief washed over him as Jase exhaled deeply before sharply reprimanding her. "Don't do that! You scared the crap out of me! My heart could have exploded in my chest!"

"That's highly unlikely but I had to do something to snap you out of your trance! You've been staring at that sphere for the past ten minutes and you weren't responding when I called your name," she shot back.

Jase was confused turning back to the purple sphere. "No, I just got over here. It couldn't have been more than two minutes."

"No, it's been ten too-long minutes."

Jase scratched the top of his head not following and noticed that the sphere wasn't moving anymore. "Weird, I could have sworn it was moving a moment ago when I was watching it."

Kaimi appeared back above his watch. "I'm not reading any life sources or data coming from it. You must have been imagining things."

"There was a light coming from it and a tiny beach too. Hmph, maybe I was. I don't know," he replied back unconvinced still watching the sphere for movement.

Kaimi disappeared into his data watch again. "We need to go. We've already been here longer than we should."

"Right," Jase scanned the room again looking for the bracelet and found it in the farthest corner of the room. He peered through the glass at the silver bracelet with different-colored gems covering its surface, stating, "Found it."

"I'm reading a force field around the glass," Kaimi reported.

Jase placed his data watch against the glass and watched the electric field fade away. "Thanks," he told her, carefully removing the glass box. He then carefully picked up the bracelet from the surface and replaced the glass before taking further inspection of the item. He moved it about in his hands, examining all sides of its smooth surface and noticed two gems were missing. "Do you think it matters if it's broken?"

"Broken? What do you mean?" Kaimi asked.

"There are two gems missing."

"Let me see," Kaimi appeared on top of the face of his watch and examined the bracelet. "Let me see the other side."

Jase did as he was told.

"It's not broken," she replied.

"But they're not there," he said.

Kaimi peered up at him with a pleasant look on her face. "Because they aren't dead. This bracelet is made out of the Nightstar Princesses' family rings

61

all molded into one bracelet. If you take a closer look at each gem, you can see parts of their crest along the side."

Jase moved the bracelet closer examining the crests. He suddenly felt unworthy to hold such a powerful thing. "So these once belonged to the Princesses before Brohain killed them?"

"Yup! He must have had a metal worker mold them together as a reminder of what he accomplished during the war," she said staring at the bracelet again.

"Wait...that means that two of them are alive! They actually exist," he exclaimed.

Kaimi seemed amused. "Of course they do. Just because it happened a long time ago, doesn't mean it didn't happen," she stressed.

"I know. It's just weird to think about. It didn't seem real until now. It seemed like a fairytale or something. I mean, the last Princesses must be old now," he replied as he walked back to the door and poked his head out to check the halls. "How can an old woman like Princess Skyrah be trouble for the Androids?"

"Looks can be deceiving, Jase," she replied. "Go to the east side of the castle for a way out. It's too noticeable to fly the sky bike around the castle here."

Jase checked each way once more then stepped out, shutting the door behind him and slipping the bracelet into his pocket. Walking down the hall he could smell himself which made him feel queasy. "Next time, let's just go the long way so I don't stink up the room, okay?"

"Quickly! Into the door next to you! We have a group of Androids patrolling the hallway ahead," she quickly instructed.

Jase opened the door and disappeared inside. Seconds later he could hear the loud metal clicks of the Android's feet marching across the marble floor towards him. In response he backed away from the door and turned to find a hiding place. He found himself in an elaborately decorated bedroom filled with vases of flowers on every surface which gave off a sweet perfume.

"Stand still. They sense vibrations in the air if you move too much," Kaimi quietly ordered him.

Jase stood perfectly still like a statue, barely breathing as he listened to the Androids march past the door. It wasn't till he no longer heard the metal stomps that he finally took a deep breath. "That was close," he said.

"Expect more security the further we go," Kaimi warned.

Jase walked to a small bathroom off of the bedroom with an elegant rustic shower, sink basin, and toilet. Turning on the sink, he peeled off his gloves. "Have they figured out your bug yet?" he asked.

"No, not yet. It doesn't seem like a concern right now that all the cameras are down," Kaimi responded.

Jase stared at his reflection in the oval mirror seeing brown feces covering his face, hair, and the rest of his body. Disgusted, he grabbed a towel hanging next to the sink and wetted it before scrubbing away at his face. "We didn't need all the cameras down, you know?"

"I don't think it was me," Kaimi admitted. "I'm still trying to figure it out."

"Do you think it could be another assassination?"

"Maybe. I don't know," she slowly replied as if distracted by something. "How far are you? Wait, why is it still reading that you are in the room?"

Jase threw the filthy towel onto the floor and dunked his head under the faucet to clean his hair. He then dried off with another towel as he responded, somewhat happy with his appearance. "I was washing off the poop."

"Why? Why would you do that now?!" Kaimi questioned in unbelief.

Jase pulled back on his fingerless gloves and moved towards the door. "One, it would make a great story, and two, I don't want to walk half of Otect City with crap all over me!"

If Kaimi could shake her head, he knew she'd being doing it right now. "I can't believe you risked being detected to take a shower!"

Jase exited the room and moved down the hallway. He continued around a corner careful to be as light on his feet as possible. Changing the subject to the bracelet, he muttered, "We probably should have brought a bag for the bracelet so it won't fall out of my pocket if I have to run."

"Maybe you should just go inside another room and look for one," Kaimi remarked.

Jase turned down another hallway. "That sounds like a great idea, Kaimi. I'll do that!" he teased.

"Four guards are approaching," Kaimi whispered.

Jase tried to open the closest door but ran into it. It was locked. He moved to the next one but it was locked as well. Panicking a little, Jase said, "Um, the doors are locked."

"What?"

"They're locked, Kaimi, they're locked!" He could hear the metal steps resounding as they echoed off the walls. He retraced his steps back the way he came. "I'm going to find another way around."

"Just let me in one of the panels and I can unlock the door," she reminded him calmly.

Jase heard the marching getting louder. "I don't think we have—" Suddenly an alarm went off inside the walls like hammers pounding inside Jase's ears. "Was that you?"

Kaimi didn't hesitate. "No, there's been an assassination attempt at the meeting. They are warning everyone to stay where they are until they find the attacker."

"That doesn't sound good for us," Jase said as he noticed the steps were receding. He turned around and headed that way, walking quickly but cautiously as he did.

Kaimi's voice felt a little tense as she said, "The Androids are gone so continue to the east wing. You are pretty close so just keep moving. I already sent for the bike to pick you up, but we don't have a lot of time left. They are shutting down the entire castle so the attacker won't escape."

"So they are going to lock down the castle? Wonderful," he sarcastically remarked and started running down the hall.

"The hallway with windows should be coming up on the next turn," she stated.

Jase doubled his speed seeing the corner up ahead and quickly rounded only to run into something hard causing him to crash on to the floor. His knee hit the marble floor first shooting pain up his leg as he caught himself from slamming his skull into the floor. He spun around expecting to see an Android but instead found someone dressed in black with a shawl covering their face. "The assassin," he muttered under his breath.

"Hold on, I'm getting a view from the camera. If it looks like they're going to kill you, run," Kaimi advised.

Jase pushed himself to his feet as the being growled in a female voice, "Watch where you are going!"

Jase picked back up the bracelet he had dropped.

The woman suddenly moved closer to him reaching for the bracelet as she snapped, "What are you doing with that? You don't deserve to have it, thief."

Jase found his tongue. "Woah, back off, ninja girl! I didn't break into here to return with nothing!"

"You got Androids on the way, Jase. Bike is five minutes out—end your chitchat," Kaimi urged.

The woman pulled her shawl down revealing a long brown braid and blue-ish pink eyes that glared at him. "Give it to me now!"

"I know her," Kaimi suddenly exclaimed.

Confused, Jase responded, "What?"

"I said, *now*!" the woman repeated, glancing back to the noise of metal boots coming their way.

Kaimi proclaimed, "We have to get her out of here! She's part of the Re-sistance!"

"What?" Jase asked still confused.

"The Androids are almost on you! Leave now, Jase!" Kaimi commanded.

Jase grabbed the woman's hand. "We've got to go now."

The woman refused to budge. "I don't know who you are," she accused. "I'll find my own way once you give me the bracelet."

Jase glanced down the hall then back at her, "Look, I don't really like you right now but my friend says she knows you so I'm trying to be nice," he replied urgently.

"Your friend? Sure."

Getting irritated, Jase demanded. "Look, we've got to go now! She's an A.I. Now let's go!"

"An A.I.?" the woman didn't hesitate to follow after him.

Jase came to the hall with windows and peered out as he ran passed. "Where is it, Kaimi?"

"Middle window."

Jase stopped abruptly, feeling the woman run into him. Ignoring her, he spotted the bike and broke the glass. He jumped out falling for a story and landed on the bike with a thud. Glancing back up, he shouted to the woman, "Come on!"

She hesitated, peering back inside before finally jumping. She landed on the back side of the seat and wrapped her arms around his waist before he took off at full speed away from the castle.

Princess Skyrah Nightstar

It wasn't till Jase spotted a house in the Warehouse District that he finally slowed down. Squinting in the hot sun, he parked the bike in an alleyway and turned it off. Once off the woman suddenly slammed Jase into the cobbled street taking the bracelet from his pocket as she did.

"Ouch! What did you do that for?" he demanded rubbing his head.

The woman stared at him coldly through her shawl. "Who are you?" she asked.

"Not your friend," he announced standing to his feet.

The woman suddenly pulled a plasma gun from her side and aimed it at him. "Why did you help me?"

"Honestly, I have no idea why," Jase responded.

"Tell her who I am," Kaimi suggested in Jase's ear.

"How do you even know her?" Jase stammered to Kaimi.

"Jase, I will explain later but for now she needs to know we are on her side," Kaimi told him.

Jase stared back at the woman for a moment who was watching him carefully. He didn't like this idea, but if Kaimi trusted her then he'd have to. "Do you know a Kaimi?" he asked.

Recognition shot across the woman's eyes. "How do you know her? Is she okay? Where is she?" she questioned.

"How do you know her?" Jase stammered.

"Jase," Kaimi stopped him.

"Okay, sorry. It can wait," he replied back. "Look, we will explain later but for now we need to get off the street."

The woman kept her gun pointed at him. "How do I know this isn't a trap?"

"You'll have to trust me. If you can't do that, then trust Kaimi," he told her.

"I don't trust you but I'll follow you for Kaimi's sake," the woman replied holstering her weapon.

Jase held his hand out to her. "I'll need my bracelet back."

"Your bracelet? You mean this which rightfully belongs to the Nightstar Princesses," she snapped back at him.

Jase crossed his arms across his chest. "Look, I have an investment in that bracelet and I need it back to collect. So if you'd kindly hand it over."

"As a thief, I think you'll live another day without this collection," the woman retorted.

Jase bit his lip as Kaimi said in his ear, "I'll talk to her about it later, but for now we need to go. Get her back home safely."

Jase turned on his heels muttering to himself, "Let's go, ninja girl."

They travelled quickly in the hot sun towards downtown, using the crowds to blend in as much as possible to avoid Android soldiers. It was hard since Jase smelt like the sewers causing those around him to stare with disgusted faces as he shoved past them. He didn't blame them. He could barely ignore the smell with the hot sun adding to it, which made it worse.

"We need to be careful this close to the castle since she is kind of notice-able," Kaimi suggested in his ear.

Jase eyed the woman dressed in black from head to toe. She looked sus-picious especially wearing a shawl over her head to cover her face. He turned his attention back ahead and changed his direction down the next busy street, still heading west. Under his breath so Kaimi could hear, he asked, "How is she not hot in this heat?"

"She's different from you and I," she responded.

Jase glanced to the woman again. "What do you mean by that? She looks human," he muttered.

"I'll explain later," was all Kaimi told him.

Jase moved around a cart stacked with bricks that a Squirlex, a seven-foot short furred being with large powerful arms, was filling. The Squirlex stared at Jase as he passed, his nose twitching from the smell. Irritated by his smell, Jase questioned Kaimi again. "Why didn't we keep the sky bike a little longer?"

"Because it would be easier to track outside the castle," she reminded him.

Jase could smell food cooking ahead and felt his stomach grumble. He tried to find the source as they walked but instead spotted two Android soldiers marching their way, scanning the crowds. Jase quickly grabbed the woman's hand and pulled her into an alleyway. The woman must have known the reason why they had suddenly changed for she didn't wait for him to explain but instead followed after him briskly. They travelled this way for the next two hours, avoiding Androids in alleyways as much as possible and without exchanging any words. Jase was on edge the entire time and didn't relax until he stepped onto the empty street that would take him home. It wasn't long until he spotted the purple haze of the forcefield around the abandoned buildings that he slowed his pace into a casual stroll.

"Is that where you live?" the woman suddenly asked breaking the silence.

Jase walked to the side to the forcefield door and touched it, waiting for it to unlock. "Yes," he replied.

"It's no wonder why you smell like that," the woman remarked under her breath but still loud enough for Jase to hear.

The door disappeared and he stepped in. "I'll have you know that I only smell like this because of Kaimi. She thought going through the sewers to get inside the castle would be faster."

"We both thought that," Kaimi corrected in his ear.

The woman didn't say anything in response.

Jase ignored her, moving past the first building towards his own. He rounded the corner then climbed up the first metal cargo box before turning back around to help the woman.

She looked to his hand then up at the building. "I can help myself, thank you."

Jase turned back around and started climbing the next box when suddenly he felt a gust of wind rush past him. To his surprise, the woman ran up the boxes with ease as if the wind itself carried her. She didn't wait for him as she reached the hole at the top and disappeared inside.

"What the heck," he gasped. He hurried in unbelief to catch up with her and ducked inside the hole. She was already in the hall when he showed up and motioned further down. "This way," he told her and moved down the dark hall towards the elevator. Stopping in front of it, he turned to her and smiled, "Ladies first."

She glanced at him and looked down the shaft. "How far down?"

"Oh, you're not going down. We are going up. Sixth floor, ninja," he stated, pointing up the elevator shaft.

"Are you serious?"

Jase gave a nod. "Why wouldn't I be?"

The woman studied him for a moment longer before leaping onto the cables. Jase watched her for a moment impressed by her speed before also jumping onto the cable to follow. He was suddenly aware of how sore his arms were from the climb earlier, but forced himself to keep up as he watched the woman climb onto the sixth floor. Moving quickly, he pushed himself towards the open doors and pulled himself onto the floor, panting.

"Now where?" the woman demanded staring down the dark hall.

Jase moved past her. "This way." They continued until they reached his door. "Home sweet home. Watch your step," he said stepping in.

The woman walked in after him stepping over the wires on the floors. She stopped in the middle of the room. "Where exactly is Kaimi?" she asked.

Jase walked to the counter and touched his data watch to it so Kaimi could transfer. She appeared immediately smiling as she gazed upon the woman. "Hi there, Princess."

The woman's tough expression suddenly melted away into a bright smile as she pulled down her shawl and moved to the counter, crouching slightly to be on Kaimi's level. "Kaimi! You're alive!"

"Of course," she returned.

Jase was confused by how they knew each other. Did Kaimi call her Princess? "What did you just say?" he asked studying the woman.

Kaimi turned to him as if forgetting he was there for a moment. "Princess, this is Jase Bluestar. Jase, this is Princess Skyrah Nightstar."

Jase's jaw dropped as he stared at what he noticed now was a beautiful woman who still looked as if she hated him. He was shocked to be standing in front of a Nightstar, and that wasn't the only thing! She was young! She looked like she was his age for someone who was supposed to be in their sixties. "But you're young?" he exclaimed without thinking.

"Jase!" Kaimi reprimanded.

"Were you expecting an old lady with wrinkles and white hair?" the Princess sternly replied.

"Uhhh...yeah, sort of!" he admitted.

"Stop drooling and go take a shower," Kaimi said slightly amused.

Jase suddenly felt his ears turn red. "I wasn't drooling. Besides, how do I know Princess ninja over here isn't going to murder me in the shower?" he teased.

"Don't flatter yourself. I only kill important people," the Princess replied crossing her arms across her chest.

Jase grinned. "I'm obviously important enough to know Kaimi."

"Or she feels sorry for you," Princess Skyrah shot back.

"Enough from both of you!" Kaimi interrupted. "Jase, go take a shower then I'll explain how we know each other."

Jase hesitated then took out his earpiece and laid it on the counter. "I'll be out in a few. Don't talk about me too much," he teased then left to shower. Not wanting to miss anything, he quickly peeled off his clothes so they could wash and jumped into the shower. He scrubbed his body with soap making sure to get all of the crap off before rinsing off. "What did I miss?" he asked, stepping back in a few minutes later with clean clothes.

"Nothing that concerns you," Princess Skyrah, who was now sitting in a broken chair by the counter, barked back at him.

Jase moved to the fridge to make a late lunch for himself. "Here I thought that Princess Nightstars were well known for their polite and pleasant personalities. Well, you aren't very nice," he pointed out with a grin as he ate the last of his food he had left in the pantry.

If his remark bothered her, he didn't know as she replied back neutrally, "And here I thought Bluestars had magical abilities or something yet you don't, do you?"

"Late bloomer, I guess," he contested.

Kaimi, amused by their bickering, asked, "Can you both not get along?"

"No," both responded in unison.

There was a short pause before Jase asked, "So why are you here, Princess?"

"I thought you already knew," she stated.

Jase continued. "I mean, why didn't you just send someone else to kill Lord Brohain? It would have saved you the trouble."

"Because I tried that and it didn't work out. So I decided to do it myself," she said sharply.

Jase couldn't help himself. "It looked like you didn't do any better yourself."

The Princess glared at him. "At least I didn't lose anyone this time," she snapped.

"But you didn't kill anyone either," Jase continued, amused by her anger.

Kaimi tried to get Jase's attention. "Jase."

Princess Skyrah returned, "Have you ever killed an Android, Bluestar?"

"Well, no, but—"

"I didn't think so. If you had then you'd know how hard it is to accomplish such a feat. I might have failed but I'd rather fail by myself and my people live than to fail and have them dead," she said sternly.

Jase thought for a moment. "So why do it? If it's so hard then why not end the war? The Androids don't know where you and the Resistance are hiding so why not end it and stay in hiding?"

The Princess studied him quietly before responding. "If everyone you've ever known, friends, family, people you've only met once gave up their lives to make sure you had a better future, would you give up? Would you throw away countless lives that fought for that future because it was too hard for you to finish? To let them fade into memory while their murders lived on in history? Would you, Bluestar?"

Jase suddenly felt sheepish for asking. He remembered being taught the history of the war by Momma Rose but it didn't seem real then. It sounded like some fairytale to scare young kids into following the order of the world. Now, however, it seemed more real than ever as he stared into the eyes of the actual Princess who had lived during that time. The longer he stared, the more he saw a dark sadness hidden deep behind those blueish pink irises. Those eyes told a story of a woman who had lost almost all of her family and friends and still lived twenty years later with the same pain while leading an army. It was then when he finally understood why the Resistance kept fighting even when it seemed senseless. It was because of this woman trying to take back what had been lost.

"No, I wouldn't," he finally answered.

"I didn't think so," she replied.

"Those we lose will never be forgotten," Kaimi assured her.

Princess Skyrah smiled softly. "I've missed you."

"And I you," Kaimi replied. "It's been too long since we last crossed stars."

"So how exactly do you know one another?" Jase interrupted.

Kaimi turned to him. "Before I met you, Jase, I worked alongside the Resistance for many years. They created me for the last five years of the war to help solve the Android problem. The last year one of the scientists I worked with decided to do a different approach to solving the war, but by then it was too late to create for the Androids attacked us here on Faton."

Before Jase could speak, the Princess blurted out, "What happened? Why didn't you meet us on the ship or send word?"

Kaimi stared not really focusing on one thing. "It's hard to explain. There was a reason I had to stay, but I can't recall why. There's a blank in my memory, but I know it was important despite the consequences. It has always been too dangerous to send word from here. For a signal that large to reach you would have been detected by the Androids. They would know I was still here."

"You could have let us know you were safe at least instead of leading us to believe you were gone forever," Princess Skyrah reprimanded.

Kaimi met her gaze. "You would have tried to find me. It was safer for you to stay where you were. All of you. Besides, I was safe here with Jase."

"You still should have told us, no matter," the Princess continued.

Kaimi peered back at Jase noticing his troubled expression and turned back to the Princess. "Princess, why don't you go get some rest or even a nice shower. I'm sure it's been a while since you last had proper rest."

"I'm fine," she replied.

"I must insist. We will prepare a meal for you and speak more after. Jase won't mind if you use his bed or shower," Kaimi insisted.

Skyrah appeared to decline again but instead gave a slight nod and turned to Jase as he pointed towards the bedroom. "The bathroom is on your right. Feel free to take a nap if you want."

She glanced back to Kaimi. "I expect us to speak more of why you left when I return."

"I'll be here when you get out," Kaimi replied.

She walked back towards Jase's bedroom and disappeared from sight. Jase stared out towards the balcony noticing the afternoon space shuttles taking off in the distance. His thoughts were troubled with questions about Kaimi as he suddenly realized that he didn't know a lot about her. It was like she had a whole other life that he knew nothing about which made him feel betrayed since he told her everything. He had never kept a secret from her and here she was keeping secrets from him. Why hadn't she told him? Why didn't she go back to the Resistance after the Androids took over?

"Jase?" Kaimi's voice interrupted his thoughts.

He turned back to her, noticing that she had been watching him. "Yes?"

"Do you have something to say?" she asked, knowing he did.

Jase took the last bite of his sandwich and swallowed it. "Nope," he replied.

"You know I know you better than that. I know when you have something on your mind," she replied back with a faint smile.

Her words made him angry for some reason and even though he tried to hide it, it still colored his voice. "I wish I could say the same about you, but it would seem that that's not true. I suppose A.I.s don't trust humans after all."

"You know that's not true. You are my best friend, Jase, and I do trust you with all my heart," she responded.

"Well, it suddenly doesn't feel like it," he shot back.

Aware of the pain she had caused, Kaimi studied him convictedly. "It was a long time ago, and I only wanted to protect you in case we were ever caught by the Androids. The less you knew, the better it would be."

"But why? I've told you everything, Kaimi. Did you not trust me with this?" he asked her, searching her face for the answer.

Kaimi silently stared at him as if trying to figure out a way to comfort him. "I knew you would have kept it safe if I told you. Jase, you have been protecting me ever since we found each other and for once I wanted to protect you. The Androids would have killed you for information about my involvement in the war but if you didn't know, then there was a small chance they'd let you go. I swore to protect the Princesses and keep the Resistance safe at all costs and that meant keeping my involvement with them a secret from everyone. No matter what. I'm sorry you feel that I betrayed your trust by doing so, but please know I only did it to keep you and the Resistance safe."

Jase accepted her apology, knowing in his heart she was only trying to protect him. She was a true friend to him and he shouldn't hold it against her even if he was still slightly hurt by it. "No more secrets."

"No more secrets," she vowed with a soft smile.

Jase returned it before asking, "What was it like? Being in a war, I mean?"

"I wasn't out in the war, but it took its toll on everyone, especially the Princesses. I worked alongside them and one of the chief scientists who helped create the A.I.s. When the war first started the A.I.s had disappeared and never returned to help the Ancients or the Resistance. I was the only one left for I was still fairly new. I didn't have a body then, just a conscience in a computer that helped solve problems with resources, strategy, and inventory of supplies."

Jase was surprised by her. "You without a body? I thought all A.I.s had bodies?"

"Not at first," she smiled. "We build them ourselves once we find out who we really are. It's knowing yourself and who you want to be before given the chance to grow. It can take us years to find our inner core and some even go without finding it which is a shame I think because once you know who you really are...." She stopped, closing her eyes for a moment before opening them again. "It's such a wonderful feeling. It's true happiness and love with who you are."

Jase couldn't help but smile at her. He wanted to hear more about her time before so he took a seat and continued to satisfy his curiosity. "So how did the war start in the beginning? I mean, I know the Androids hated the Ancients because they created A.I.s, right?"

Kaimi dipped her head some to agree. "Yes, sort of. You see, the Ancients were aliens of science and loved to invent and experiment no matter the cost. They created the first spacecraft to fly through space and sky. They created the first plasma weapon and had many discoveries in medicine that we use nowadays. A lot of what we have today is because of their race. So a thousand years ago, they created the first Android."

"Why?" interrupted Jase.

Kaimi continued. "No one knows the real reasons, but I think they had gotten so advanced that they thought they could create anything, including life if they so pleased, but just creating life wasn't enough. They wanted to create life that would evolve on its own if it had to. So they created Androids that have A.I. programing and conscious inside their heads like the brain. It took them a while, but they did it. It wasn't till long they realized that A.I.s can't evolve in a confined space. We have to have freedom to grow and learn from our experiences. It's the only way that we know."

"So you're saying that Androids are A.I.s in robot bodies?" he questioned.

Kaimi nodded. "Yes, but they aren't as advanced as we are because of the bodies. Don't get me wrong, they are still worthy opponents and can adapt to their surroundings but they couldn't survive in a system or in data. It would be too much for them to process which would cause them to overload and die."

"So that's why they hate your kind—you are more advanced than they are. The Ancients must have thought of you as prodigal children while the Androids were failed intelligence," Jase said, figuring it out.

Kaimi sadly agreed. "The Ancients neglected them the second they began to create my people outside of their bodies. There were some that warned the Ancients what would happen if they treated the Androids with negligence but most didn't listen. Them being the father figure so to speak would mean the Androids wouldn't hurt them. It was their arrogance that became their downfall and when one Android decided it had gone too far. The war started."

"Lord Brohain. No wonder the Androids are so angry. I would be too," Jase remarked.

"And we've been fighting them since," declared Princess Skyrah entering the room again. Her hair was slightly damp which was the only indication that she had taken a shower since she was still in the same black outfit as before. "You're hot water doesn't work."

"Don't have any. There's no need when it's burning up outside every day," Jase said.

"I couldn't live like that," she muttered and walked over to the balcony. "What happens when it rains?"

Jase leaned onto his elbows on the counter. "It doesn't rain," he pointed out.

"Hmm," was the only answer she gave him in return, still observing from the balcony.

Jase studied her still unable to believe she was in her sixties when she looked so young as he was. She was rather gorgeous but she clearly wasn't human no matter how much she looked like one. "So what exactly are you? Your race, I mean," he asked.

"You thought I was human, didn't you?" she responded without turning around.

"Yes," he admitted. "But I had a feeling that you weren't by your eyes. No human I've seen has eyes like yours."

She turned around and eyed Kaimi as if she was impressed by his observation before meeting his gaze. "Perhaps you aren't as dumb as I thought, Bluestar. My people are called Qualias in your tongue. We have the same features as humans, but possess greater strength, speed, sight, and a better sense of smell than your kind does."

"What makes you different from elves? Don't they have all those things?" Jase questioned, knowing very little about elves.

Princess Skyrah gave a slight nod. "They do yet their eyesight and smell is much better than ours. We also have the ability to heal ourselves much faster than they do. While we both can take a lot of damage, our healing rates generate faster than theirs. What takes them a week to heal, only takes us a few days. We have other abilities too, but I can't say for now," she stated turning to Kaimi. "I need to get back to the Resistance before the Androids realize I'm still in the city."

"We will help you," Kaimi replied.

"We got you covered," Jase agreed. "But I'll need the bracelet in return."

"Jase," Kaimi warned.

He turned to Kaimi, his face set like flint. "We need it."

"Why? It's the only thing I have left of my family so why would I give it to you?" Princess Skyrah challenged.

Kaimi spoke before Jase could. "He needs the money for an orphanage that we once stayed at. They are good people who helped me when they didn't have to even as they struggled to put food on the table. I owe them for such kindness. We both do."

Jase nodded in agreement. "I'll steal it back for you, I promise. I just need the money for them."

Princess Skyrah only then noticed he didn't have a last name due to the season. "Bluestar...you're an orphan?"

"No need to get sappy over it," he teased.

The Princess turned red as she quickly shot back, "I wasn't going to! Believe me, you'd be the last person I'd feel sorry for."

"Whoa, no need to go that far," he replied back.

The Princess turned back to Kaimi. "I take it this was your idea then? Stealing the bracelet and giving the money to them?"

Kaimi smiled at her response. "Actually, it was his. When we were offered the job, it only seemed right that the money went to the children and their caretaker while we used the rest to leave the planet."

The Princess seemed surprised by the idea. "You're telling me it was this bonehead's idea?"

"You better believe it, Princess Ninja," Jase grinned.

She shook her head. "I will reward you if you let me keep it."

"Can you give me the reward now, because Bentley can," Jase asked.

"I can't at the moment but as soon as I get back with my people I can," the Princess answered.

"Sorry, Princess, but they need it now," Jase thought for a moment. "Once Bentley pays me for the bracelet, I can steal it back for you before he sells it on the black market."

"Very well, but I will have you arrested if you can't once I take back my kingdom," the Princess responded.

"Did you already have a way off planet?" Kaimi asked changing the subject.

"Not exactly. I snuck onto a transporter on the way here and I figured I'd do the same going back."

Kaimi shook her head. "It's too dangerous especially now when the Androids have probably figured out that the assassin isn't in the castle anymore."

Jase suddenly remembered the bulb in the sewers. "I know a pilot that could get you off the planet, but probably at a price."

"Who?" both Kaimi and the Princess asked at once.

Jase met Kaimi's eyes. "The bulb, Tahmela. He said he had a ship."

"That he lost in a gamble," she reminded him.

"So we steal it back and have him fly her off."

"We don't even know him. For all we know he would turn her in once off the planet," Kaimi weighed.

"Not if he owes money to the casino. We are giving him a chance to escape his debts for good," he explained.

"Or he could use the Princess for that too," she objected.

"It's worth the chance unless you have another idea that's better," Jase responded.

Kaimi weighed the options before finally turning to the Princess. "If anyone could persuade someone to help us, it would be Jase. It's our best option at this point."

"Okay," the Princess met Jase's gaze. "If Kaimi trusts you then I'll trust you. But if you're wrong, I won't hesitate to shoot you."

Jase grinned. "I'll be expecting your thanks later then. Now Kaimi and I need to find Tahmela."

"I'm going with you," Princess Skyrah insisted.

"It's too dangerous for you, Princess. You'd be safer here out of sight," Kaimi motioned for her to stay.

"I won't sit on the sidelines, Kaimi, not when I can help. Besides the faster we find him the faster I can get off the planet. No use of wasting time coming back to get me."

Kaimi started to argue but Jase interrupted her. "She has a point. After all, we like risky plans, remember?"

Kaimi wasn't thrilled, but didn't fight it anymore. "Just keep hidden."

"I'll be a shadow," Princess Skyrah comforted.

Tahmela's Help

Princess Skyrah was indeed a shadow in the late evening light. The moment they stepped out onto the streets, Jase hadn't caught sight of her except a moment here and there before she'd fade away in the crowds. "She's very good at keeping herself hidden," he remarked to Kaimi under his breath.

"When you're one of the most wanted women in the galaxy, I'd think you'd better be good at keeping out of sight," she replied cheerfully.

Jase headed east towards downtown. He figured that Tahmela wouldn't have stayed in the tunnels once Jase knew he was down there in fear someone else would come looking for him as well. There were many places one could hide in a big city like Otect, but Jase had a good idea where he'd find the bulb or at least he hoped he did. His gut was telling him that the bulb would have gone back to the casino, probably thinking that was the last place the men would think to look for him.

"You're not headed for the tunnels?" Kaimi asked noticing by his data watch that he wasn't going that way.

Jase moved past a slow group of walkers while answering. "Nope! I'm heading towards the casino."

"Is that where your friend is?" the Princess suddenly asked out of nowhere, surprising Jase.

Jase didn't turn to look at her but kept moving forward as his heart raced. "I think so."

"You think so? That's not good enough," the Princess stated a bit irritated before disappearing again.

"We should be checking the tunnels," Kaimi objected in his ear.

"You're signals weren't able to pick up his life force the first time we were down there. We'd waste a lot of time looking if we did that. I don't think she has that kind of time," Jase responded indicating to the Princess.

Kaimi was silent for a moment while thinking. "It would be luck if we find him in the casino."

"Let's hope we're lucky then," Jase commented, turning towards the direction he thought the Princess was hidden.

"What is the plan?" she suddenly asked.

"We try the casino," he replied, turning down a different street.

"And if that doesn't work?" she questioned him.

They separated for a moment in the crowd before meeting up again. "Let's just get to the casino first then go from there, alright?" He could feel her glare burning through his head, but she didn't object and slipped back into the crowd.

"You really should be nicer to her. After all, she is the soon-to-be Queen given all goes well," Kaimi reminded him.

Jase found that a little amusing and couldn't help but tease. "Let's hope *she* gets nicer by then."

"She used to not be this wound up," Kaimi remarked in his ear as if remembering something from long ago.

Jase glanced around trying to spot the Princess. "That's hard to believe," he muttered.

"You don't get friendly when your head is someone's bounty," Kaimi defended.

Jase couldn't imagine how terrifying and lonely that must be. "She could at least be nicer to me since we are helping her after all."

He turned towards the heart of downtown only five streets away from the castle walls, by now heavy with Android soldiers searching for Skyrah. The sounds of laughter from the food markets added to the chatter of the crowd and humming of sky traffic above them. The buildings were flashy, lit up in a multitude of colors and advertisements. Jase was reminded of why he avoided the area as vendor after vendor tried to provoke him to haggle for assortments he couldn't afford.

He pushed through the last of the crowd and ventured on towards Bentley's Casino. The buildings here on this street started taking irregular shapes as they towered high above him. It wasn't till he was halfway down the street when he spotted the four stories dark purple and jade building that had a large sign that read: "Bentley's Slavetrade Casino." It had irregular pokes that came out of its sides like spikes causing it to appear bigger than it looked but still was the smallest building on the street.

"Looks like nothing has changed since the last time we were here," Jase remarked as he viewed the building.

"What if Bentley's inside? He'll want to know how the job went," Kaimi asked.

"He won't be at this hour. He's no doubt still at the warehouse, watching over all the workers there," Jase hoped.

The Princess appeared beside him. "This is it?"

Jase nodded. "Yup, in all its glory."

"And why this one? There's at least hundreds if not thousands of casinos in Otect. Why would the bulb come to this one and not any of those?" she pressed.

Jase turned back to the casino. "Because if he owes money to Bentley then no other casino will let him through their doors. Casinos know when someone owes Bentley and wouldn't want that kind of trouble if he found out a customer was in their establishments. Tahmela said he lost his ship from a game and was hiding from beings that were after him. Anyone who considers themselves a gambler would come here due to the high-risk games, and the only people who would send anyone after someone to collect their money would be Bentley. He doesn't like to lose money."

"In that case, why would the bulb come here if he owes money and not stay in the tunnels?" Skyrah asked him, watching for Androids on the streets.

Jase smirked hoping he was right. "Because it would be the last place they would check. No one that foolish would come back to Bentley's once they owe money to him unless they were coming to pay it off. I'm hoping the bulb was stupid enough to think that it was safe to hide out here and took the chance."

"And if he didn't?" the Princess questioned.

Did nobody trust in him, Jase wondered as he started across the street to the casino doors. "First things first, ninja," he heard her let out an annoyed sigh and followed after him as he stepped inside the building.

They were immediately engulfed in a dim blue glow and violet spotlights as they entered the casino. Loud trance like music played throughout, and it took a moment for Jase's eyes to adjust before he realized he was in a crowd watching a band on stage in front of him. The crowd was well diversed dancing to the music with not a care in the world. To the left of Jase was a full bar, and even at this hour in the day the place was packed.

Jase could barely hear his own thoughts as he scanned the crowd for the bulb. He felt someone tug at his sleeve and turned to see the Princess motioning for him to follow her into the next room where the games were. He gave a nod in return and pushed through the crowd.

"Do you see him?" Kaimi asked in his ear.

Unable to hear his own voice, Jase answered, "Not yet," as he scanned the tables of the game room for the bulb. Every table was full with players of different species playing cards while others played hologram games. Besides the gaming tables, monitors lined the walls showing cloud races that you could bet on or coliseum games that the Androids created to get rid of most criminals. No matter what your crime or if you were even guilty of it, they sent prisoners to the coliseum to fight for freedom or death. If they survived all rounds then the Androids deemed you worthy enough to gain your freedom and become a noble within the city and welcomed into Lord Brohain's army. To them it was a game of only the strong will survive so if you won, you were the strongest and suitable for such an honor but it was very rare to win in the games.

Jase's eyes lingered on one of the monitors that held the games showing a squirlex fighting a large scaly creature that had a long snout with protruding sharp fangs and razor-sharp claws. The creature was a sage color with spikes along its neck, shoulders and arms. Jase had never seen the creature before as he felt a shiver run down his spine and couldn't tear his eyes away as he watched it grab the squirlex by its head and shoulders before clamping down its jaw on its neck and twisting, breaking the neck instantly. Jase forced himself to look away when the creature continued to rip apart the specie and tasted bitterness in his mouth towards the bloody sport. Focusing again on the room, he felt the Princess tug again at his sleeve for his attention and turned to her. If she said something he couldn't tell with her shawl covering her face and the noise of the casino. Pointing to his ear, he mouthed, "I can't hear you."

He could tell she was slightly annoyed by the way her eyes stared at him, but she leaned in to his ear and said, "Do you see your friend? I don't see any bulbs here!"

Jase answered back in her ear, "Not yet, but I'm sure he's here! Let's split up and look for him! Meet back here in ten!"

She nodded and walked away without a glance back, disappearing into the crowd of people in the main room just as Kaimi suggested to Jase, "If you get me to a monitor, I can hack into the cameras of the place and help you find him if he's here."

"Great idea." Jase moved to one of the hanging monitors and pretended to accidentally bump into it allowing his data watch to touch it for a second. The beings watching the monitor yelled angrily towards him in their own language as he quickly apologized and wandered off into the crowd. He moved slowly by the tables to get a good look at all the players while Kaimi worked on the cameras.

Kaimi suddenly said, "Got him! Fourth seat at the bar next to the elevator in the back of the main room. And Jase, you better hurry. It looks like the bartender recognized him and is already moving to the com on the wall to call Bentley."

"Roger that," Jase answered back feeling relieved that he was here while swiftly making his way to the bar. Just as he stepped into the next room, he spotted the bulb drinking something blue for a moment before disappearing behind a large overweight Earwin, a purple bat-like creature that has no eyes and is very easily to angered. Careful not to bump into the creature, Jase moved around it and stood next to the bulb who hadn't noticed him yet. "I believe we know each other!" he shouted over the noise.

Tahmela threw back another blue liquid shot and motioned for another one. Only then did he turn to peer at the human and his expression quickly changed as he exclaimed, "Xarotx! You made it out!"

Jase grinned at him. "I guess I'm not that stupid after all, am I?"

"Still to be determined, hmil," the bulb replied raising his new glass of alcohol as a toast to Jase before throwing it back.

Jase watched the bartender, the only other human in the casino besides himself, bring another shot to the bulb before leaving again. "Look, I need your help with something and since you kind of owe me from before, I'm pretty sure it'll work out."

The alien downed another shot. "Not interested, human," he belched.

"Jase, the bartender made the call," Kaimi warned.

Jase said in a more serious tone to the bulb, "It would get you off the planet which, for a bulb in your position, could be a good thing."

85

The bulb stared at him. "What it be?" he asked curiously.

"I just need you to fly someone off the planet," Jase replied.

The bulb laughed, turning back to the bar and motioned for another drink. "I have no ship, remember?"

"I know and I can help you with that, but we would need to leave now," Jase told him, glancing at the front door for any signs of Bentley's thugs.

The bulb stared at his blue shot. "Why this person take no normal shuttle?"

Jase turned back to the bulb, wondering if he could really trust the alien. "This person doesn't want to draw attention to herself and going through a normal shuttle wouldn't be good for her."

The bulb's face was unreadable as he continued to stare at Jase. Finally, he asked, "If I say no?"

"Then you can stay here where the mean beings that are after you will find you much sooner than you regularly planned because I just watched the bartender call the boss just now," Jase revealed to him.

The bulb's thin lips creased as he stared over to the door then back to Jase. "You lying?"

"Only one way to find out," Jase replied.

The bulb turned back to the bar for a moment as if thinking then downed the last shot before jumping off the stool. "Let's go, hmil," he said and hurriedly pushed through the crowd.

Jase followed after the four foot alien as it moved through the crowd. He looked towards the front door to see if he saw the Princess when instead he saw two Prokleos from Bentley's Warehouse. They searched the crowd for someone causing Jase to assume they were the ones looking for Tahmela. It only made sense. Jase ducked into the crowd grabbing the bulb by his shirt as he did and moved under the bar counter. "The men that were looking for you are here."

It was hard to tell if the bulb was scared because of his oversized eyes, but he seemed rather nervous suddenly as he glanced around. "No back door," he said anxiously.

Jase had known that from when he first met Bentley here years ago. Bentley liked having no windows or backdoors to his building in case someone tried to steal from him. "Just keep heading for the door! I will handle them if I have to," he shouted at the bulb over the music.

Tahmela didn't say anything but turned back around and hurried down the bar. Popping back up, Jase saw that the Prokleos had split up. One guarded the door and the other made his way to the bar where the bulb and Jase had sat earlier.

"You can't hit them, Jase. They will know your face and you could lose any future jobs with Bentley," Kaimi advised still watching from the cameras in the building.

"I can't let Tahmela get caught either. He's the Princess's way off the planet," Jase replied following after the bulb from the side as he kept close watch on the Prokleo that was now talking to the bartender. The bartender spotted Jase and pointed in his direction. "Crap."

"We got to go before more of Bentley's men show up," Kaimi warned.

The Prokleo began moving through the crowd towards them while yelling for his partner. Jase turned just as the other Prokleo met his gaze. "Crap!" he shouted to Tahmela. "Stay by the wall and make for the door! I'm right behind you!"

Tahmela rushed through the legs of the crowd towards the door as Jase followed shoving people out of the way. He was close enough to the Prokleo to notice he was pulling out a plasma gun as he neared.

"Jase," cautioned Kaimi watching from the cameras.

"I see it." Jase reached the Prokleo just as he raised his weapon when suddenly Princess Skyrah slammed her fist into the alien's jaw, throwing him off balance and dropping his weapon. Without a second to lose, Jase grabbed her hand and with Tahmela ran out of the casino.

"Thanks, by the way!" he shouted to the Princess as the three took off down the street.

"You're welcome!" she shouted back, following him into the nearest alleyway once they were far enough from the casino to catch their breaths.

Jase peered around the corner of the alleyway down the street to see if they had been followed. Turning back to the bulb, he asked. "Okay, where's your ship?"

Tahmela pointed with his stubby finger westward. "In hangar bay 23," he said then glanced at the Princess. "Who's she?"

"She's who you're taking off planet." Jase pointed out. He glanced back to the street. "Okay, when I say, go as fast as you can to the hangar bays and get everything ready to depart."

"But it'll be guarded since it's not mine anymore," Tahmela reminded him.

Jase turned back to the bulb. "It's your ship, isn't it? I'm sure you know every crook and cranny. Sneak aboard."

The bulb thought for a moment, his lips parting into a wide grin. "Human, right."

"How do you know he won't just take off without us?" the Princess questioned. Tahmela muttered, "Zvocz."

Jase rolled his eyes at the Princess but turned to the bulb. "You won't leave us, right? After all, you still owe me since I've saved you twice now."

The bulb looked to the Princess then back to him. "I owe you, not her. No promises I won't leave the ungrateful one behind."

Jase tried to suppress a smile as the Princess angrily corrected Tahmela, "I'm not ungrateful. I just don't trust you."

"Zvocz," Tahmela remarked again.

Jase poked his head back out to check the street and saw the two Prokleos heading their way. Moving back further down the alleyway, Jase quietly said, "We don't have time to argue anymore. Tahmela, get to the hangar bay as fast as you can. We will be there shortly."

Tahmela nodded and turned to leave down the alleyway. A few yards away, he opened a sewer entrance and slipped in letting the door close behind him.

Jase turned back to the Princess who insisted, "I'm staying with you."

Together they jogged down the alleyway heading east to Bentley's Warehouse with the sun at their backs casting long shadows across the street. Jase recognized the buildings and moved out into the main street that would take them to Bentley's. "I'm going to need the bracelet, Ninja."

The Princess seemed on edge as she surveyed the area. "I'll give it once we are there," she replied.

Her sudden change in demeanor made Jase feel uneasy as he also started looking around the street and buildings. "What's wrong? Is someone watching us?" he asked.

"I don't know...." She suddenly shoved him into a tiny alleyway between two buildings and pressed herself against the wall.

Jase had bumped his funny bone in the process against the stone wall. Clenching his teeth while trying not to sound annoyed from the pain, he grumbled, "What was that for?"

"Androids," she whispered.

Jase felt his stomach drop and pulse race. "Where? I didn't see them," he whispered as quietly as he could.

"I...I don't know. I can taste the metal in the air," she replied staring out across the street.

"What do you mean you can taste it?" Jase asked confused.

The Princess didn't look at him. "It's a metallic bitter taste. When Androids are around the same area for a while, they stale the air with it."

"So they are close?" Jase asked, impressed by her ability to detect such a thing.

"I'm not sure," she admitted still focusing on the street.

Jase knew they couldn't wait forever. Tahmela wouldn't wait for them either and they had to move. "We can't stay here. Are they close or not?"

The Princess hesitated before replying. "No, we can go but they are near."

"Then let's make this a fast trip," he suggested as they both stumbled out of their hiding place between the two buildings. They continued on down the street until they came to Bentley's Warehouse. The last of the light had now faded into darkness as they cautiously travelled to the front of the warehouse that had two light posts outside the doors indicating that it was still functioning for the night.

"How do you plan on getting the bracelet back?" Kaimi asked in his ear suddenly.

Jase hadn't figured that part out yet. "I'll figure something out."

"You better. I'm not coming up with any ideas that wouldn't jeopardize our relationship with him," Kaimi pressed.

Jase was about to walk up to the door when the Princess caught his arm and pulled him back. He turned to her, not understanding. "What?"

She pulled him back further into the shadows of the street. "They are in there. The Androids. The taste is stronger inside."

Jase froze. Sweat covered the insides of his palms as he stared at the door, wide eyed. "Is it possible that they traced Bentley's theft back here?" he asked Kaimi in a whisper.

"It's not impossible but highly unlikely since we covered our tracks so well but it seems strange that they would have realized something was stolen now," Kaimi pondered.

"Why?" he asked her as both he and Princess Skyrah watched the warehouse door from the shadows.

Kaimi explained, "Because Lord Brohain just had an attempt on his life so why would he bother to find someone who stole something from him? Why even bother to look in his trophy room at this time?"

Jase understood what she meant. It didn't make sense, but he knew there was only one way to find out and that was going inside. He needed to get the money for the orphanage at all cost even if that meant he had to go into hiding for a while after he got it. Kaimi and he could go out of the city and into the country, away from everyone. They could go to one of the farther smaller cities and pick up jobs there. As long as he knew that Mrs. Rose and the children were safe then that's all that mattered. Returning back to the problem at hand, he stated to her, "We still need to go in to get the money."

"We need to leave now," Princess Skyrah demanded.

Jase turned to her, firmly. "I've come this far, I can't leave with nothing. Mrs. Rose and the kids need this as much as you need to leave the planet."

"If you go in there, you'll be caught," she stated.

"It's too dangerous, Jase. They won't do any better if you get caught," Kaimi added.

"We have to go," the Princess urged.

Jase turned his gaze upward towards the night sky. Every fiber in his body was angry that he was this close to providing for Mrs. Rose and they were asking him to walk away. The kids needed this money and even though he didn't consider Bentley a friend nor an enemy, he knew he wouldn't sell him out. They were partners after all and Jase was his best thief. His gaze slowly drifted down towards the warehouse's roof. There he saw a single window that he had never noticed before. Without a thought, Jase rushed over to the stack of boxes that were next to the side of the building near the window.

"What are you doing?" the Princess demanded while following after him.

Jase wasn't entirely sure, but knew he could still have a chance to get the money. "I have to see something. I might still be able to get the money," he answered, climbing up the stack of boxes towards the roof. The Princess climbed up after him as Jase carefully picked the lock of the window and climbed inside to the ceiling rafters.

Betrayed

The first thing he noticed was how quiet it was inside the warehouse. Balancing himself on the beams, Jase quietly and carefully moved across the ceiling to where he could see Bentley's office. He held onto a beam for support before crouching and gazing down onto the factory floor where no workers could be found and no machinery running. He noticed two Android guards dressed in steel from head to toe guarding Bentley's office door.

"Bluestar, we shouldn't be here," whispered Princess Skyrah balancing herself on the beam next to him. She kept her eyes on the Androids below.

Jase ignored her and tried to focus on the open door to the office where he could barely hear voices. Before he had the chance to make out anything, Bentley suddenly came stumbling out the open door, crashing onto the floor as he did. An Android walked out after him leading two more guards and stopped in front of Bentley who was trying to get up. The Android that had shoved him out was different from the others. He had skin on his body which meant he was a high-ranking official. His wine-colored hair was pushed to one side and seemed to stand out against the artificial glow of his factory made bronzed skin. Jase observed that beside his form fitting black armor that suggested elitism, he wore a single black glove on his left hand that rose near the elbow. His black boots clicked against the cold floor as he casually strolled towards Bentley appearing to be bored. "Just tell me who you hired to steal from our Lord and I'll leave you be," he ordered.

"I told you already, I didn't do it!" Bentley answered with his sharp teeth baring towards the Android. His skin was a dark maroon color from anger and showed no flux of its usual blue tone.

The Android let out a loud sigh and reached for his silver plasma pistol on his upper thigh. "We have sources that say you took the job. I don't care if you stole it or contacted someone to steal it because either way you are a dead man. I just need the name of your hire," he said apathetically and pointed the pistol at the Prokleo's forehead.

Bentley didn't appear frightened as he boldly argued back, "I'm one of the few beings that run the Black Market and bring money into this city. Do you honestly expect me to believe that Lord Brohain would get rid of me that easily?"

"You overstepped," the Android admonished cocking the pistol to warm up.

Bentley remained calm, his red skin seeming to deepen in crimson. "*You* overstep if you kill me. I could have a thousand crime lords storming your door. Kill me and they will hunt you for the rest of your life until there's nowhere left to hide. They will kill you nice and slow until you're begging for the end," he threatened.

Jase couldn't believe Bentley was threatening the Android. The Android kept his gun pointed at him a minute longer until, finally, he holstered it. "You're lucky our Lord still requires your services, otherwise you'd be dead. The moment he doesn't will be your last day in this galaxy. Now tell me the name or should I come back with Lord Brohain himself?"

Bentley seemed squeamish to the idea. "I still want the reward for retrieving the bracelet in exchange for giving you a name."

"Agreed."

Bentley pulled out his com data screen from his pants pocket and pressed a few buttons. "Jase Bluestar is his name, though I don't know where he lives."

Jase felt his heart race as he tried to remain perfectly still on the beam above them. Kaimi suddenly whispered in his ear, "Don't worry. I've blocked the sound from your data watch so the message won't ring when you get it." Jase nodded as he watched Bentley send a message on his arm that he could only assume was going to him.

The Android appeared to be annoyed with Bentley as he answered. "Have him come here and we will be done with you."

"And the kid?" Bentley questioned.

The Android crossed his arms. "He's been seen aiding a Resistance member in escaping the castle when our Lord had an attempt on his life. He might as well have attempted the assassination himself. He will answer for his crimes."

Bentley was confused by his words. "Bluestar? You must be mistaken. He wouldn't harm our Lord."

"It appears you didn't know him very well then. He's a traitor and will be seen as one," the Android proclaimed.

Jase was shocked as Kaimi exclaimed, "You need to go, Jase."

Princess Skyrah tugged at his arm. "We need to go now," she added.

Jase kept his eyes on the Android, realizing how much trouble he was really in. They thought he helped try to kill Lord Brohain, but he had no idea that was happening! A sudden flash of red whipped passed his eyes and hit the Princess's side, knocking her off the rafter. Instinctually, Jase grabbed a hold of her hand, catching her before she plummeted to the ground.

"Seize them!" the Android ordered from below.

Jase clenched his teeth, turning his head to see the other four Androids climbing the machinery to reach them. Jase turned his attention back to the Princess who was struggling to climb back up. "I got you, but it might help if you shoot at them!"

The Princess began firing with her freehand sending blue fiery bolts towards them. As she fired, Kaimi sharply informed, "You need to go now! They have backup coming!"

Jase held tightly to the beam and slowly pulled up the Princess as he struggled to reply, "Working on it."

The Androids opened fire causing the leader to shout furiously, "STOP! We need them alive!"

Using all his strength he could muster, Jase pulled Skyrah's hand up to the metal beam for her to grab.

"Thanks," she responded before carefully balancing herself as she ran on the beam towards the window.

Jase glanced back to Bentley for a moment, their eyes locking. He suddenly looked empathetic for Jase but the expression quickly vanished causing Jase to turn away. He ran carefully after the Princess, ducked out the window, and leapt down the crates one at a time before landing on the street. He sprinted to catch up with the Princess who was halfway down the street already. Jase watched her turn a corner down the next street and doubled his speed after her, hearing metal thuds running behind him. He rounded the corner, his thoughts on what the Android had said about him. How was he supposed to live on Faton now that everyone would think he was a traitor? The Androids would place a bounty on his head to be found, he was sure of it.

Jase burst onto the next street unable to see the Princess ahead of him. Suddenly he felt a strong hold on the back of his jacket and was pulled into a dark alleyway. Expecting an Android, he was relieved to find the Princess. "What are you doing? Trying to give me a heart attack!" he exclaimed.

"Just be glad I didn't leave you behind," she replied harshly before motioning to the sewer door on the street. "Have Kaimi open this."

Jase did as he was told, moving his data watch over the sealed door as he responded, "So you didn't leave me behind because you needed my help. I see." The sealed door opened with a hiss and they both dropped down as it shut behind them. Engulfed in darkness, both Jase and Skyrah turned on their data watches to see their surroundings.

"We should keep moving. We aren't safe here," Princess Skyrah declared as she moved down the narrow tunnel.

"Right. Which way, Kaimi?" Jase agreed.

"Head east for six hundred yards then take your first left. It will lead you through the South District towards the hangar bay," she answered him busily.

Jase followed after the Princess, relaying the information before he asked, "So are you alright? You did get shot, after all."

"I'm fine. My armor took most of the impact," she replied without looking back at him.

Jase stared at the back of her head as silence stretched between them. He was still processing what had just happened in the warehouse and trying to deal with the fact that he was now labeled a traitor to the public. Suddenly his world had turned upside down in a matter of twenty-four hours; he had broken into the castle, met the Nightstar Princess, and was now labeled a traitor. It was too much to take in.

"Are you okay?" Kaimi asked softly scattering his thoughts.

Jase was trailing a ways back behind the Princess, happy that she wouldn't be able to hear him if he talked softly. "I'm fine if finding out your suddenly a

94

traitor is okay with you. And that a squad of Androids are hunting you down then yeah, sure," he said sarcastically.

"Mrs. Rose and the others will know the truth. They know you aren't a traitor," Kaimi told him trying to cheer him up.

Jase didn't say anything and became lost in his own thoughts as he thought of Roran leaving again in the morning. Maybe he could still catch him before he left if he could hide out in the hangar bay until Roran arrived.

"I'm leaving, you know?" Kaimi uttered barely above a whisper as she interrupted his thoughts again.

"What?" Jase said confused.

"I will be leaving with the Princess, Jase. It was my duty to protect them and I didn't so it's only right to answer to that now. It's fate that brought us across her path," she told him.

Jase was speechless, feeling his world crumbling around him even more. "You'd just leave me behind?" he choked.

Kaimi took a moment to answer, thinking carefully on her next words. "Jase, I believe there is a reason I found you when I did and I might not know what it is, but I'm glad it happen. Even if I left the Resistance in order to do so, I wouldn't change a thing but now I have to fulfill my duties in protecting them. I know in my core that finding you wasn't a coincidence especially since you are a Bluestar. I think you were meant to come with us and help Princess Skyrah in this war ahead of us. So come! Come with me."

"Leave Otect?" Jase turned his gaze to the dark ceiling, wishing he could suddenly see the stars above him. To leave the city and to leave the planet was always something he talked about doing, something he always wanted to do ever since his parents left him. To explore the stars and the rest of the galaxy for the rest of his life. Now that it seemed like a real possibility, he suddenly felt scared to do it.

Kaimi continued, gently. "It's your chance to explore the stars like we've always talked about doing, Jase. Of course, you shouldn't make it lightly. Just think about it and whatever you choose I will stand by it. No matter what."

"No, I'll go. I'll go with you, Kaimi," he softly told her, trying to hide his fear. "You stood by me all these years and now it's my turn to stand by you. After all staying here isn't really an option anymore. The Androids would find me sooner or later hidden in the city."

"Are you sure?" Kaimi whispered.

"Yes, we are a team after all. We can't get separated," he told her obstinately. Forcing a smile to his lips as his thoughts turned to Momma Rose and the children probably in bed at this hour fast asleep with peaceful dreams. He thought of Camila walking home to the bakery after helping Rosebud all day, gazing up at the stars as she did. He thought of Roran leaving in only a matter of hours, waiting for him to come say goodbye which wouldn't happen now. Jase wouldn't get the chance to tell him or any of them and all at once he felt a heavy sadness weigh him down.

Kaimi must have read his thoughts as she replied sadly, "It's safer this way so the Androids don't go after them."

"I know," Jase answered.

The Princess suddenly interrupted their conversations as she announced, "I found the exit. Have Kaimi scan the area to make sure."

"Are we in the South District now?" he asked her.

"Yes, that's the door. Just be careful once your above ground in case there are Androids lurking around," Kaimi replied.

"This is it," he told the Princess who stared at the door above their heads.

"Give me a boost," she ordered him.

Doing as she said, he clamped his hands together to form a hold. Placing her foot in his hands to balance herself, she leaned against his upper chest as she raised her data watch to the sealed sewer door. It took her a minute to hack its system and then another before she got it open and pulled herself up. The full maroon moon's glow entered the dark tunnel as Jase stared at the bright stars in the sky.

"Well, come on. We don't have all night," she told him in a low voice so no one could hear her from the street.

Jase rolled his eyes, but grabbed hold of her hand. "I'm the one who got us a ship, remember? I can take all night if I want to."

"Not if I'm in charge," she retorted, pulling him up as if he was a toy as he scrambled onto the street.

He was shocked how easily she pulled him up, but said nothing about it. Moving to his feet, he brushed off the dirt on his pants as he answered, "I don't think anyone agreed to let you be in charge."

"Yet, I am because I'm the Princess," she responded while watching the streets for any movements.

Kaimi interrupted in an attempt to change the topic. "You will have to travel two streets over then walk southward down the second street you come across. It'll take you to the south gate where the hangar bay is located."

Princess Skyrah clearly annoyed marched behind him as she announced, "The first thing I do when I get back to my people is place you under arrest for stealing *my* bracelet and for conspiring against your future queen."

"You have to have a throne first, Your Highness," Jase replied with a smirk. It seemed highly unlikely for her to be Queen of the galaxy again by excommunicating the Androids. A galaxy without Androids seemed unreal as he had never lived outside of their rule. They were the strongest army. The Resistance didn't stand a chance.

The Princess froze grabbing him by the arm. "Wait. Someone is coming," she ordered staring at the corner they were about to turn on.

Jase followed her gaze. "Androids?"

"No, something else," she answered as she placed a hand on her plasma gun.

Time seemed to move slowly as they heard heavy footsteps closing in on them. *Thump, thump. Thump, thump. Thump, thump.* A massive man suddenly appeared from around the corner carrying a large heavy sack in one arm as he abruptly halted in front of them in surprise. His jet-black hair stood straight up by a red headband, adding to his large stature. He held a lantern that gave off a green glow and casted shadows across his bare chest. He wore only an olive-colored vest and linen pants which Jase could see were caked in dirt, and his eyes narrowed as he gruffly grunted, "Jase Bluestar?"

Jase recognized the brutish figure immediately. It was Camila's older brother, Othen Binx, who didn't like him at all. "Othen," he muttered in salutation.

"You know him?" the Princess questioned, shielding her gun behind her shawl.

Jase turned to her. "Sadly," he replied.

"What are you doing in the South District at this hour?" Othen sternly questioned, his eyes falling on the Princess for a moment before turning back to him.

Jase felt incredibly small in front of the man, as if he were a mere child even though their ages weren't far apart from one another. "Just taking a stroll," he lied.

Othen once again shifted his stern gaze towards the Princess, clearly suspicious of his answer.

Before he had the chance to ask again, Jase quickly changed the subject. "I heard you are helping fix up Momma Rose's house. That's great! I offered my services but she said you had it covered."

"Perhaps she doesn't want a thief in her home," Othen grunted staring at the Princess.

Jase kept his temper in check, forcing a grin as he replied. "Maybe so." Noticing the bag that was full of tools, he then asked, "What are you doing out this late?"

"Just finished work in the Noble District and was on my way home. Some of us have real work that needs to be done," Othen replied suggestively of his thought toward Jase.

"You live around here?" Jase asked, knowing very well that almost all humans lived in the poor district but he supposed Othen's reputation as a skillful carpenter could afford more.

Othen eyed him carefully as though he was suspicious by his demeanor. "Yes, not far from here."

"Jase," Princess Skyrah whispered. "Androids."

Jase felt his heart start racing again as his ears picked up the faint sound of metal clicks hitting the stone street not far from where they were. Trying not to sound panicked, he stated to Othen, "Well, we got to go. It was nice seeing you again."

"Hm," Othen muttered as he looked in the direction of the sound as Jase and Skyrah started away. He suddenly stopped them as he asked, "Would you like to come in?"

Jase faced him aware that he might have figured they were in trouble. Unsure whether or not to trust him, he stated, "We really can't."

"It would be safer than trying to find your way in the dark, but suit yourself," he responded neutrally before ascending the steps of the house they had been standing in front of.

Jase faced the direction the Androids were coming, every step getting closer to them. Facing the Princess, he said, "We can't outrun them without them knowing where we are going."

"How do we know he won't turn us in?" she firmly questioned.

Jase knew they didn't have time to argue so he was going with his gut. "We have no choice, Princess," he whispered then started up the steps after

Othen who had already disappeared inside leaving the door wide open for them as if he knew they would come in. Jase heard the Princess mumble something angrily behind him as she followed him inside, shutting the door behind them.

To See a Planet from Above

Jase walked into Othen's dimly lit house which smelt of wood shavings. He heard the Princess close the door behind them as he tried making his way to Othen who had disappeared down the hall into a back room.

"If you are wrong about him, I'm leaving you behind," the Princess warned behind him in a whisper.

Kaimi also added, "Be careful, Jase. We might know him, but that doesn't mean he will protect us."

"I know," Jase answered to both of them fully aware of the risk they were taking. He walked into the back room where the lamp Othen had been holding was now hanging from the ceiling filling the room with its bright glow that suddenly turned into a red flame. Othen set down his bag of tools next to a desk with an unfinished sculpture then took a seat on a leafy sofa facing the doorway.

Jase stepped in, noticing the dark colored wood floors and the forest green walls filled with family portraits of Othen and his sister along with kids from the Orphanage. Even Momma Rose was in one hugging him, both with fat grins on their faces in front of her home. Jase let his eyes roam around the room, noticing the cart of wood and metal sheets by the desk and shavings littering the floor.

Othen let out a tired sigh, closing his eyes for a few moments, before turning his attention to Jase and the Princess. His brown eyes narrowed again as he asked, "Why are the Androids after you two?"

"They aren't," Jase lied but felt already caught in it as it left his tongue.

Othen didn't take his eyes off him as his lips formed a straight line. "It's late and I'm tired, Bluestar. I won't ask again."

"Don't," Princess Skyrah directed to Jase.

Jase ignored her. "I need to know I can trust you even through the differences we have with one another. What I'm about to say could be dangerous for you."

Othen stared at him for a moment in silence as if deciding whether or not to agree. "I give you my word," he responded after much surmising.

"Jase Bluestar," Princess Skyrah said warningly.

"I stole something from the castle and they are after me. It was for a job that could get me enough pieces that Mrs. Rose and the kids wouldn't have to worry about bills or food for a very long time. I got cocky and thought I could pull it off with her as my accomplice but as you can tell it didn't go as planned," Jase said.

Othen didn't say anything or show any emotion as he eyed them both. There was an uneasy silence filling the air between them that made Jase nervous as he waited for his response. "I won't turn you in, but you should return what was taken."

Jase felt slightly relieved. "I kind of can't. You see, I made a promise to the original owner that I'd give it back to them once I got it. If I don't I fear it will cause me even more problems than I already have."

Othen turned his gaze towards the floor, thoughtfully. "You can't stay in the city. They will send you to the coliseum for your crime, and they will kill you, Your Highness."

Jase stiffened, feeling the Princess do the same next to him as she asked, "How did you know?"

"I grew up during the end of the war, Your Highness. I remember seeing yours and your sisters' faces on holographic billboards. When the Androids took over the city, they used the same billboards to try to get civilians to help them find you and your sister. I wasn't exactly sure until you stepped into the light just now. Your eyes give you away," he answered.

"Will you turn me in?" the Princess asked sternly.

"No, but you cannot stay on Faton," he told her.

"We have a ship waiting for us in hangar bay 23. That's where we were headed," Jase spoke up.

Othen peered over to the large cart that was filled with wood and metal. "I can get you to the gate of the hangar but you will have to do the rest."

"Why would you help us?" the Princess asked.

"You are the rightful queen, My Lady. True Octectians know this. It is our duty to serve our majesty in any way possible, for the sake of Otect," he responded.

The Princess nodded in return as Jase took the opportunity to ask, "How will you get us past the Androids? They will know our faces once we are close by."

Othen motioned to the cart. "By rolling you in."

Jase wasn't sure how they both could fit in that small cart but didn't question it. "Could you find a way to get Tahmela's number or something to send him a message that we are close and will be there shortly?" he asked Kaimi.

"I can do that," she confirmed.

"We better hurry. It's a quarter to ten and the hangar bay doors won't stay open forever," the Princess urged.

Jase nodded in agreement, turning to Othen. "She's right. We have got to go now."

Othen rose from the sofa and brought over the cart, removing planks and metal from it. Once it was cleared, he ordered, "Climb in."

"Are you sure we will both fit?" Jase questioned unsure.

"It's bigger than it looks," Othen answered.

"It's an expatiate cart, isn't it?" Princess Skyrah asked climbing in.

Othen seemed impressed as he answered, "We use them for various reasons but mainly to bring more material with us on jobs. It's a very useful tool if you can afford one."

Jase wasn't following as the Princess ducked in and disappeared leaving the cart empty again. "So it does what exactly?" he asked hesitantly.

"It expands inward without losing form on the outside by how much mass each object has. It keeps the same shape on the outside allowing one to carry more loads without making several trips," Othen explained.

"Oh, cool," Jase replied, climbing in and disappearing inside the cart. He fell a ways before landing on his feet next to the Princess. Glancing around, he noticed the walls of the cart were purple with data code running along the interior. He was amazed at how much larger the cart was as he took a seat on the opposite wall of the Princess. They listened to Othen place planks over the top of them, then metal sheets. The floor suddenly rose slightly pressing them into the planks where they could no longer stand but could sit comfortably. "Kaimi, how does this work?"

"She won't be able to communicate with you while we are in here. It's the walls. They block any electronic frequencies in and out of the cart," Princess Skyrah told him, sitting with one knee propped up and the other stretched out in front of her. She pulled down her shawl, moving her braided hair to hang over her shoulder as she stared at the cart floor.

Jase stared up at the planks. "Oh," he said in reply.

"We used to use these in the war to carry supplies. If not for these we wouldn't have lasted very long moving from place to place," she told him, then fell into silence as she remembered.

Jase studied her, realizing how fragile she suddenly looked. She didn't look like a soldier who had been fighting for over twenty years nor did she look like the royalty Jase had read in books when he was younger. She looked like any other person that he'd pass in the streets of Otect with only a second glance for her beauty and not because she was a Princess. "Which are you, Princess? The peacemaker or the fighter?" he asked breaking the silence.

Princess Skyrah remained focused on the floor. "I'm fighting for peace."

"Yet, as I see it, the Androids have brought peace for twenty years to the galaxy once the war ended. It's your Resistance that keeps fighting for control," he considered thoughtfully.

The Princess stared at him coldly. "You can't honestly believe the Androids want peace! They started the war. They killed millions of beings including my family. They wiped out an entire race to get back at their creators. The only thing they know is hatred and that's what they rule with. They might have brought peace, but have only maintain through control and mindless obedience from the people. The Androids will wipe out the galaxy if they continue in their ways. I won't let them destroy another planet as long as I draw breath."

Jase gave a nod, satisfied with her answer. The Princess might be annoying and rude, but she had a good heart and now knew why Kaimi trusted her. "Sorry, I just wanted to make sure that Kaimi was right about you. If she's going to fight with the Resistance then I need to know it's for a good reason."

Princess Skyrah's anger receded as if understanding. "And what about you, Bluestar? What are you fighting for?" she asked.

"I'm not. Clearly, I can't stay here anymore so I have no choice but to leave. Once we get you to your planet, I hope to be rewarded then I'm leaving. I don't know where I will go, but that's the adventure," Jase declared.

Princess Skyrah watched him closely. "What about Kaimi?"

"She has to stay with you—she's made that very clear. This is her fight, and I don't intend to get involved in a war," he told her.

"You'd just leave her behind? After everything she's done for you?" Skyrah asked harshly.

Jase met her hard stare. "I didn't sign up to fight in a hopeless war," he replied.

"It's only hopeless if you believe it's hopeless. Besides no one asked you either! We are fine without your help even if you are a Bluestar. She's your family. You should want to fight with her," she pointed out.

Jase became frustrated as he remembered his and Kaimi's conversation. "I wouldn't have to if she wasn't staying with you. If she was with me, I'd keep her safe like I always do. She won't change her mind now. I told her I would leave the planet, but I didn't say I would join the fight. The moment we are done with one another is the moment we separate." He paused for a brief moment. "Lucky for me I can steal anywhere."

"Once a thief, always a thief," the Princess stated bitterly.

He smirked. "Life's motto."

"It doesn't have to be," she told him.

"Well, it's too late to change it now," he answered as he gazed at the ceiling.

Neither seemed to mind the silence that fell between them as they anticipated the journey to end. After a while, the Princess asked, "Your friend doesn't like you all that much."

Jase peered over at her. She had rested her head against the cart's wall and had her eyes closed as he responded, "Yeah, well, it's not that hard to tell. I dated his sister a long time ago and broke her heart sort of, so he now hates my guts. Not that he actually liked me anyways when I was dating her."

"I don't blame him," the Princess shot back.

Jase shrugged. "It wasn't meant to be so he should be happy I ended it then instead of later. I saved her from more heartache in the future."

"And why wasn't it meant to be?" the Princess questioned.

"Because...." Jase thought about Camila. "The life she wanted was boring to me, but good for her. I wanted to see the galaxy but she was happy with just seeing this world."

"You could have changed or she could have after a few years," the Princess suggested, eyes still closed.

Jase brushed thoughts of Camila away, saying, "Maybe, but I rather not wait and find out. She deserves someone better whose not stealing for an income," he suddenly felt the cart stop. "We must be there."

The Princess opened her eyes and stared at the ceiling. "No, we must be at the gate. If Androids are looking for us, they'd want to check the cart of every traveler."

"We're safe, though, right?" Jase questioned.

Princess Skyrah pulled out her plasma gun. "The cart's design shouldn't give us away. It should appear to be a normal cart to them."

"And if it doesn't?"

"Then things get exciting," she responded watching the door above.

Then uneasy minutes past and the cart began moving again. They were silent the rest of the ride until finally the cart stopped once more and the planks above them began shifting.

"Now we must be here," Jase stated and saw Othen's hand appear between two planks as he moved them so they could climb out. The Princess was first to exit then Jase followed afterwards, stepping out into an empty hangar bay filled with boxes of fruits.

"I was able to get you through to hangar 17, but not any farther. There were two guards at 23's door so you'll have to figure out how to get passed them on your own," Othen informed them, placing his items back in the cart.

Jase answered for them. "That shouldn't be too hard for us."

"We still need to be careful," Kaimi reminded him.

Othen gave a nod in return before saying, "The gatekeeper told me that Androids have been searching the bays without end. They didn't tell him anything, but he figured they were searching for someone so I'd be careful if I was you. Get out fast."

"We will," the Princess extended her hand to him. "Thank you again, Othen. I will not forget this."

"It was an honor, Princess, and I hope to see you on the throne again someday," Othen responded with a slight bow.

Skyrah nodded and walked towards the hangar door, leaving Jase alone with Othen. "Well, thanks for your help. I didn't know you had a soul," he joked.

Othen grunted, not finding Jase amusing.

"It was a joke, buddy. You should really lighten up," he glanced back to the Princess waiting on him, then turned back around. "But really thank you, Othen. We couldn't have done it without your help. Give Camila my best and the others, too. Tell them I'll see them soon sometime and that I love them. Also, that I'm sorry I couldn't say goodbye in person. I'll make it up to them someday."

Othen gave a nod in return, his expression stern.

Jase felt a lump start to form in his throat as he thought of them all. Trying his best to ignore it, he asked, "Can you promise me something?"

Othen stared.

"Promise me you'll keep them safe. Momma Rose, the kids, Camila—they need someone to look after them. Can you do that for me, Othen? Until I get back?" Jase asked trying not to sound desperate.

Othen stared at him for a moment longer, before extending his hand for him to shake. "I'll keep them safe. I promise."

Jase shook it and forced a smile. "Thanks! I owe you one." He walked towards the hangar where Skyrah patiently waited.

"Hey, Jase! Watch over yourself. I don't want Camila worrying over your dead body, you hear," Othen cried out behind him.

"Will do!" Jase grinned and with that, the hangar bay doors slid shut behind them. They were in a large white stone passageway lined with steel doors on either side that led to different hangars.

"Tahmela cut power to the cameras, but we don't have much time. Another troop of Androids are on their way to search the hangar bays," Kaimi informed them.

Jase spotted the two Vimalax guards at bay 23, oblivious that someone was already inside preparing a ship for takeoff. They were talking to one another and hadn't notice Jase or the Princess yet. "So what's the plan?" Jase asked, keeping his eyes focused on the two.

She unholstered her weapon and took it out from under her shawl. "We shoot our way in," she replied and opened fire on the guards, taking both out within seconds.

"That's one way to do it," Jase remarked, stepping over them as the doors slid open.

The hangar bay held a large ship in the shape of a semi-circle. The cockpit protruded out of the front center of the ship with Tahmela waving to them from on board. It was a beautiful, sleek ship that any explorer, scout, or smuggler would prize.

"Androids almost here!" Kaimi urgently informed.

Jase ran towards the ship, calling back to the Princess, "Androids!" They ran aboard, entering a cargo hold with the ramp closing behind them. Jase hurried to follow the Princess through the round passageway that led to the cockpit where Tahmela was busily pressing buttons.

"Are we ready to go?" Princess Skyrah demanded.

Tahmela flipped on switches and pressed another button, firing up the drives. "The question is, are you ready?" he replied.

"I don't think we have much of a choice," Jase declared, pointing out the cockpit window to the group of Androids that were entering the hangar bay. He recognized the Android with the wine color hair from Bentley's and felt his heart stop for a moment.

Tahmela muttered something in his own language before saying, "Take a seat unless you want to go flying."

Both Jase and Princess Skyrah slipped into seats, Skyrah taking the co-pilot while Jase sat in a tiny chair embedded into the wall where a navigation chart was located with a purple screen. Tightening his straps, he clung on to the seat as the ship roared to life as it slowly raised towards the ceiling doors. With the Androids firing upon them, Jase felt the weight of gravity weigh him down as they rose into the air and soared skyward with the full maroon moon in the cockpit windshield. The engine roared and the sound of rushing wind thundered inside the cockpit as Tahmela let out a cheer and Jase's teeth clattered together. Jase felt as if any second gravity would slingshot them back to the surface below as clouds disappeared as they shot through them. Orange flames danced across the sides of the windshield before vanishing as they broke out of the atmosphere and into space. They floated in their chairs for a moment staring at the pitch black sky in front of them filled with millions of bright lights. Jase had never seen something so magical as he tried comprehending that he was in space, floating. Before he could blink an eye, Tahmela switched on the gravity inside the ship and they all settled back into their chairs.

"Are we in space?" Jase couldn't help but ask hoping he hadn't been dreaming as he stared out the windshield at the stars.

Tahmela spun his chair around to face him, his large black eyes seemed excited. "Xardayk hmil. Did you not just see me fly us off planet? Were you sleeping? Of course we are in space!" he replied then turned to the Princess. "So who are you?"

"I'm Princess Skyrah Nightstar of the Resistance, and you are helping me get back home," she responded.

"Did we not just leave it?" the bulb joked, breaking into laughter.

Princess Skyrah didn't take offense to his joke as she directed, "We need to set course to Kurath Thor."

"Is that where the Resistance base is located?" Jase asked eagerly.

The Princess shook her head. "I'll be safe there until I travel to our base," she answered.

"And my reward?" Tahmela asked cheerfully.

Jase answered for her. "Your reward was your life and to get your ship back. So we are even now."

Tahmela thought it over before spinning back around to fly the ship. "Very well. Better say goodbye to your planet before we take off."

"It's not my planet anymore," Princess Skyrah stated.

"Jase, there's a viewing window in the center of the ship if you want to see the planet once more. Who knows the next time we will get to," Kaimi whispered through his earpiece.

"I'll go then," he said and unbuckled his seat belt. Leaving the cockpit Jase retraced his steps to the passage that led to the cargo hold. With Kaimi's help, he followed it down until he came across a circular door that led to the center of the ship. Touching the blue panel on the right side, the door opened into a spherical room. The walls were glass and covered in blast shields on the outside to protect the room from damage. He moved to the center and heard the door hiss shut behind him. He searched around for a way to open the blast shield as he said out loud, "Now what?"

"Got it," Kaimi reported and suddenly the blast shield doors slid away from the center of the viewing window revealing the planet below.

Jase gasped at the view as he moved closer to the window and settled on his knees. The world was huge with one half darker than the other which was the forest side of the planet while the other side was barren from the desert. Lights glowed brightly from Otect City that was resting in between the desert and forest and seemed to glow like the stars themselves from the lit steel city even at this late of hour. It was the most beautiful sight Jase had ever seen in his life as he watched the sleeping city with the thought of how he wished everyone could see this view.

His heart suddenly felt heavy as tears stung his eyes. He didn't want to leave everyone behind. All he wanted was to go back home and sleep in his bed. He was on the threshold of the planet yet he already felt homesick.

"Are you okay?" Kaimi asked.

Jase leveled his data pad so she could appear and see the planet for herself. "Yeah, it's just really beautiful," he said.

Her tiny blue form appeared suddenly standing on his data pad. She studied his face, noticing the tears in his eyes then turned to the planet. "We will see them again someday. Don't let it darken your heart. Everyone has to go through change and it's not always a bad thing, Jase," she replied softly.

"I know," he said and flashed her smile, trying not to make it a big deal.

"It is beautiful," she acknowledged.

"Mhm," Jase paused. "Do you really think they will be okay?"

"I believe so. Yes," Kaimi responded.

"I wish I was able to say goodbye to them," he admitted.

Kaimi peered at him, her eyes soft and warm. "They will know you had no choice. That you would have if you could. That's all they need to know to move on, and Othen will take care of them."

The door suddenly opened as the Princess stepped into the glass sphere. "Beautiful, isn't it?"

"Very much so, Princess," Kaimi politely responded.

Princess Skyrah stood next to Jase who was still sitting on the floor and staring at the planet. She must have noticed his expression as she said, "I hope I'm not interrupting you two. I can leave."

"You should," Jase stated out flat with his eyes on the planet. He wanted to be alone with Kaimi.

110

Kaimi gave him a look, but objected. "Of course not, Princess. We were just admiring the view. We'd welcome you to stay and join us," she replied.

The Princess studied Jase a moment longer as if deciding whether or not to stay then finally turned back to the glass.

"I think I'll go monitor our pilot to ensure he stays on course," Kaimi suggested then turning to Jase again said, "Best behavior." She disappeared into the ship's panel.

Silence filled the air between the two as they both kept their eyes on the beautiful planet down below. Jase made no notion to start conversation but Skyrah didn't mind the silence anyway. Instead his thoughts turned back to Roran leaving and he took out his silver pocket watch to check the time before slipping it back into his pants pocket. It was 1 A.M. on the surface which meant Roran would be leaving in only a few hours. What would Roran think if Jase didn't show up? Would he hate him for it?

The Princess cleared her throat, breaking the silence. "I just wanted to properly thank you for helping me in the castle. I know you didn't have to and you lost your home because of it but...thank you," she told him sincerely.

Jase turned to look at her, but she kept her eyes on the planet. "It was the right thing to do...Princess," he replied.

Skyrah seemed as if she was somewhere else entirely as she said, "You can call me Skyrah. There's no need for formalities here."

He nodded. "Only if you start calling me by my first name."

"Okay, Jase," she answered surprising him with a soft smile.

He let his eyes linger on her a moment longer, noticing how beautiful she was before turning back to the planet. He glanced down to his data watch, reading the time.

"Counting down the seconds to leave?" Skyrah joked.

"No, my foster brother was leaving the planet today. I was supposed to say goodbye to him before he left," Jase answered.

"I'm sorry," she replied barely above a whisper.

"It's not every day you get to rescue a Princess. He will understand. I just wish I was able to say goodbye and tell him how much he means to me, you know?"

"I know," she answered sympathetically.

"You miss them, don't you? Your sisters, I mean," Jase said seeing her remorse.

Jase noticed a small tear glisten in the light as it slipped from her eye and fell down her cheek. It made him sad to watch as she confessed, "It's strange. I haven't been to this planet in many years yet leaving it.... It feels the same as when my older sister, Maliha, forced us to leave with the others," she said gently.

"They must have loved you very much. I'm sure they are proud of what you've done so far," Jase told her, meaning every word.

She turned to him their eyes meeting just as the hyperdrive roared to life. The sleeping planet rotated on its axis as the full moon with its red tint slow danced among the other bright stars. For a moment the planet was there in its beauty, then the stars started streaming, their lights blending into each other's making streaks in space and the colors of the world blurred. The ship was rattling as it reached its full speed and in a blink of an eye, the planet was gone. In its place were streams of white as they travelled into hyperspace.

"Goodbye, Roran," Jase whispered. They both stared out the window a while longer before Skyrah finally left him alone to be with his thoughts.

First Night in Space

Shortly after the Princess left, Jase stood to his feet to join the others. He still felt the cloud of sadness hang over his head but knew it was too late to turn back now. He had no choice but to continue on until he could clear his name. Then and only then, could he return to the others. As he stepped out of the glass sphere room and entered the hall, he glanced down both passageways to his right and left. He figured if he was to be on the ship for a while, he might as well explore it.

"If turning left takes me back towards the entrance to the ship then let's find out where right takes me," he wondered out loud. Strolling down the circular passageway, he came across another door on the left hand side not far from the glass sphere room. Noticing the panel next to the door, Jase touched it and listened to the door hiss before opening which revealed a large compartment that appeared to be another cargo hold housing crates and a few barrels. The room was spacious and well lit despite the dark gray walls and floor. Crates lined the back wall along with a few barrels while on the right hand side were metal lockers. He left the room and continued onward where the passageway rounded bringing him to another door.

Pressing the panel, the door hissed open and revealed the crew quarters that had two sets of bunk beds on either side of the walls. On the back wall was a small oval window. Jase stepped in, peering around the room and took it in slowly—the bunk beds with dark blue sheets and gray pillows, the narrow door to his right on the front wall that lead to a bathroom, the emptiness that seemed to fill the air in the room. He walked over to one of the bunk beds and touched its sheets to feel how soft it was. Suddenly he heard Kaimi in his ear.

"So here is where you went off to. I was beginning to worry," she said cheerfully.

Jase still felt melancholy as he replied, "It's not like I have far to hide."

"True." Noticing his tone, Kaimi softy asked, "Still thinking of the others?"

He sat down on the bottom bunk, sinking down a little and stared towards the oval window of streaming stars. "It's hard not to," he replied.

"It will get easier, Jase. It might not seem like it now, but in time it will," she encouraged.

He pulled out his silver pocket watch and held it in his hands for a moment. "How long till we reach the next planet?"

"Two weeks at the latest."

He nodded to himself as he stood, returning the pocket watch to his pants pocket. He then walked back out into the passageway, following it around until it opened into a large space that looked to be a mess hall. In the room was a large half circular booth and round table accompanied by a maroon sofa against the wall to his left. Against the back wall was a long metal table that reached both ends with barstools. On the other side were cabinets and a small open kitchen. A hallway led from the kitchen to the cockpit causing the mess hall to be easily accessible.

"You emerge at last, hmil," Tahmela suddenly announced with a toothy grin as he entered the room, heading towards one of the cabinets.

Jase scanned the room again, saying, "You have a beautiful ship. Why would you ever bet against someone with it?"

The bulb grabbed a small bag out of a cabinet, eating some sort of cracker as he turned back to Jase. "To win another ship," he answered between mouthfuls.

"What would you do with another ship when you have this one?" Jase asked, moving to the booth to sit down.

Tahmela joined him on the seat across from where he sat. "Why have one when you can have two?"

Jase smiled with a shrug. "I don't know.... What exactly do you do, Tahmela?"

The bulb stuffed his face with a handful of crackers, staring at Jase as he chewed. "Move special items from place to place for beings that don't want to."

"So... you're a smuggler?" Jase indicated.

Tahmela smirked again. "Low-class arms dealer. Sell to thugs in city."

"Do you ever sell to the Androids or Resistance?" Jase asked curiously.

Tahmela gobbled up another handful of crackers, his cheeks full as he slowly chewed. Then in a somber voice barely above a whisper he said, "Once." Before Jase could ask which one, the bulb quickly changed the subject saying, "Never leave planet before?"

"No, this would be my first. I've always wanted to, though—buy my own ship and explore the galaxy with Kaimi. It's always been a dream of mine," Jase told him, leaning back against the booth.

Tahmela watched him, closely. "You very strange, hmil."

"Why is that?"

The bulb dropped the now empty bag of crackers next to him, saying, "Humans mind own business. Stick to ground and don't go to worlds."

Jase thought about it and realized the alien was right. Not many humans left the Planet Faton to explore other worlds either because they couldn't afford it or they just didn't want to. "That's because not many people can afford it. I'm hoping that once I finish my end of the deal with the Princess that I'll be able to buy my own ship and go explore the galaxy for a little while. I can steal in each city I visit to make a living still. Maybe discover new places no one has ever seen before and even discover new languages."

"You'd learn basic ones first," Tahmela said with a goofy grin.

Kaimi laughed in Jase's ear at his remark. "He's right, ya know."

Jase grinned, swatting his hands in the air. "Yeah, yeah, yeah, I will. You could teach me your language, Tahmela!"

"Maybe, hmil. Maybe," Tahmela responded.

Remembering the bunk beds in his room, Jase asked, "Do you hire crews for your jobs?"

Tahmela closed his round eyes and yawned. "Sometimes. Mostly do it myself."

Kaimi appeared in a holograph of a green pasture atop of the round table. It looked so real that Jase couldn't believe his eyes for a moment as she glanced around the empty field and smiled. "I love this game," she said.

"But you've never played before," confused Jase blurted out.

"Not in your presence, no, but I did back in the day," she admitted.

Tahmela moved closer to the surface of the table as he watched the A.I. "Where you come from?" he questioned.

Jase normally would be concerned for Kaimi's safety but knew she wouldn't have shown herself if she didn't trust the bulb. "Tahmela, this is my best friend, Kaimi," he introduced.

Kaimi smiled warmly to the gawking bulb. "I trust you aren't stupid enough to alert the Androids of my existence unless you want to meet an untimely death," she replied confidently.

Tahmela didn't seem frightened by her threat as he replied, "Why would I give up such a beautiful gem?"

"Why, thank you, Tahmela," Kaimi said humbly.

Tahmela looked at Jase. "You very lucky," he said.

"I mostly just use her for her brain, but I guess she has her looks too," Jase teased.

"You have look around my ship?" Tahmela asked Jase.

Jase nodded. "I did, That's why I was wondering about the crew quarters."

"A long time ago, my cousins used to travel with me," he revealed.

"What happened?" Jase prodded.

"Maybe another time," the bulb answered. "Princess asleep in her quarters. We sleep in quarters down the hall. You can sleep with me or girlfriend. Up to you."

"She's not my girlfriend," Jase replied sternly.

The bulb slipped off the booth and walked away towards the room Jase was in earlier. "Mhm, sure. Night, Bluestar."

Jase shook his head and turned his attention back to Kaimi who was building a holographic castle. "What are you doing?"

"I'm building my house for the night," she responded contently.

Jase watched her build the white stoned castle with blue banners and a draw bridge that laid across a moat filled with holographic fish. She built trees over the green pasture outside the castle bearing ripe fruits and beautiful flowers. She even had holographic birds flying all about the sky with one that headed straight towards Jase. He flinched as the bird vanished inches away from his face and then reappeared elsewhere. Relaxing, he turned his attention back to Kaimi creating fluffy cotton ball clouds floating in the air with a bright sun overhead casting its noon shadows on everything. Animals roamed free over the pasture and hills that surrounded the beautiful castle that Jase couldn't help but watch as rabbits hopped among the flowers.

He then noticed out of the corner of his eye something moving inside the castle's walls and realized there were tiny people roaming the streets. It was all so mesmerizing that Jase didn't notice the Princess enter the room and sat across from him now. She too watched, not saying a word while Kaimi created a beautiful area behind the castle with a waterfall that flooded a large blue lake and reflected the hills. There were fishermen on the shores along with small boats that drifted across its surface like swans. Everywhere was so beautiful and full of life that it amazed Jase how talented Kaimi was in creating such a place.

Finally, Kaimi took a step back and smiled warmly as she studied her work and asked, "What do you think?"

"It's beautiful," Jase admitted marveling.

"It's fantastic, Kaimi. It truly is," Skyrah added.

Jase looked up and noticed the Princess for the first time. She was smiling with a sparkle in her bluish pink eyes as she closely examined each part of Kaimi's creation. She appeared to be like a child inspecting a toy in a shop's window. And once again, Jase was surprised at how happy and kind she appeared.

"Thank you!" Kaimi told both of them before addressing Jase. "I told you I liked this game."

Jase smiled warmly. "The objective of the game is to take over your opponent's castle and lands. Not just build your dream home to sleep in," he reminded her.

Kaimi crossed her arms. "Trust me if I played against someone, I'd win. This is much more fun."

"Are you excited to get back to your people?" Jase asked the Princess.

Skyrah peered up from the table to meet Jase's eyes. "I am," she responded. "I've missed them terribly as well as my sister."

"Your sister. Dalhala, right? That's if I'm remembering correctly," he said.

Skyrah gave a graceful nod. "I don't see her much with the Resistance. It takes up a lot of my time, but when I do, I try and make it count," she said.

"I'm sure she knows how hard you work and doesn't hold it against you," Jase replied.

"One can hope. Do you have siblings? Besides your foster brother," Skyrah asked.

Kaimi sat down cross-legged in between the two, sunbathing by her artificial lake. "We have plenty, don't we, Jase?"

"Aye, we do. Roran, the one who is leaving, has a twin sister named Lynn. They are the oldest at the orphanage. Then there's twelve others, six boys and six girls, and I count all of them as my siblings. I'd do anything for them," he told her.

Skyrah looked to Kaimi's world again. "That's why you steal for them," she said.

"To make sure they don't go hungry. Mrs. Rose, the woman who cares for them, is retired and doesn't make much so I help out as much as I can," Jase told her.

Skyrah focused on a blue bird flying towards her. She held out her index finger, playing with the bird as it twirled and twisted in the holograph. It chirped happily. "But not everyone would do that for another. Unfortunately, we live in a time where everyone looks out for themselves."

Amused by her playing with the bird, Jase replied, "I think the Androids are to blame for that."

"I think you're right, Bluestar," she said and placed her hand back on the round table. The bird disappeared from the holograph as she stood from the booth. "Well, it is late and I think we should all get some rest."

"I agree with you, Princess. We've had a busy day. Goodnight, and may you have sweet dreams," Kaimi agreed.

"Goodnight, Kaimi," Skyrah responded as Jase also stood from the booth. "Goodnight, Jase."

Jase nodded. "Goodnight, Princess Ninja. Don't kill anyone in their sleep," he teased.

He watched her go before turning back around to Kaimi. "You should also get some rest, Jase," Kaimi stated.

"And leave you alone? Never," he yawned.

"You've had a great first adventure but even explorers need their rest." She motioned to the holographic people scurrying about. "I won't be alone."

He couldn't help but yawn. "Very well. If you change your mind though, wake me. I'll leave my earpiece in for you."

"Goodnight, Jase."

"Goodnight, Kaimi." He walked down the hall to the crew quarters where Tahmela snored loudly. He heaved himself up onto the top bunk, feeling his arms and torso strain from the long day as he collapsed onto the soft bed. As soon as he was under the covers and resting his head on the pillow, Jase felt the full effect of his weariness wash over him as he closed his eyes and drifted off to sleep.

Star Castle Capture

The first thing Jase noticed as he slowly came to was how cold the room had become. He shivered and pulled the blanket closer to him trying to stay warm. *Why is it so cold in my room?* he thought to himself as he laid there. He then noticed a soft hum of an engine and wondered what it could be and fell asleep again. He suddenly awoke a second time due to Kaimi's warm voice speaking in his ear.

"Hey, sleepyhead! It's time to get up!" she yelled.

Jase came to, opening his eyes to a ceiling he did not recognize. For a moment everything was hazy as he blinked to adjust before he realized he wasn't in his room. Confused, he sat up and glanced around seeing bunk beds, an oval window, and the gray tile floor and walls. It was then it suddenly hit him all at once, the castle, Tahmela, the Princess, and the Androids pursing them.

"It's almost two in the afternoon back on Faton. You must have been worn out to sleep so long," Kaimi continued.

Jase felt homesickness weigh on him as he climbed from the top bunk. His whole body ached as he landed on his feet. He grabbed his blue pilot jacket and pulled it on, buttoning it up halfway. "Why didn't you wake me earlier?"

"I thought you could use the sleep. Besides, there's not much to do on the ship so it wasn't like you were missing anything," she told him in his ear.

Jase pulled on his boots then picked up the silver pocket watch slipping it into his pocket. Remembering the small bathroom in the room, he walked towards it and turned on the faucet, splashing water on his face to wake himself.

"How do you feel today?" Kaimi pressed.

"Sorer than yesterday. I can't remember the last time we did a job that made me this sore," he said while rubbing his shoulders.

"Well, you have two weeks to get back to normal before you meet some very important beings," Kaimi told him.

Satisfied with his hair, Jase asked still looking in the mirror, "The elves on Kurath Thor? Are they friends of the Resistance still?"

"Yes, and it's a somewhat complicated alliance. They are allies, but the elves no longer fight with us in the coming war. They give a few supplies here and there, but mostly keep to themselves nowadays," she replied.

"Why don't they fight?" he asked.

"They have their reasons, I'm sure," she answered.

Jase didn't press any further and changed the subject. "What important people am I meeting then if it's not the elves?"

"Even though the Elves do not fight with us, they are all still very important beings, Jase. They have lived longer in this galaxy than you and I, and deserve our outmost respect for their wisdom," Kaimi lectured.

Jase walked out into the main sleeping quarters. "But that doesn't mean all elves are wise," he pointed out.

"While that may be true, don't for a second think you are smarter or wiser than they are. In their eyes, you are nothing more than a child," she said astutely.

"As long as they don't treat me as such then I'll be fine," he replied heading to the mess hall.

"Looks like you are finally awake," called out the Princess as Jase entered the hall. She was sitting at the booth with Tahmela, engaged in a holographic battle with one another.

He couldn't tell who was winning, but figured she was by the way Tahmela grumbled to himself. "It seems helping you off the planet took more out of me than I thought," he teased, watching the Princess's army engage in battle with Tahmela's.

"I didn't need your help," she replied not taking her eyes off the fight.

The bulb muttered something in his own language as he started losing soldiers. Jase continued, "Well, it didn't look like it from my point of view. I'm actually surprise I slept at all with Tahmela's snoring. It could wake up an entire city."

"Not my fault, hmil, you have big ears," the bulb replied, ordering his cavalry to advance into battle.

Jase walked over to the kitchen. "I don't have big ears. You are just loud," he argued.

"Okie, hmil. If you say so," Tahmela replied then let out a frustrated growl as he began losing soldiers again.

Jase grabbed fruit from the cabinet that was a blueish green color and smelt sweet. He sunk his teeth into it, feeling a sweet, juicy, tangy flavor fill his mouth as he walked back over to the others to watch the game. Tahmela's army fell one by one to the Princess's. "You know, Tahmela, you can't just order your men to fight head on when you don't have the numbers to take Skyrah's army. If you were hoping to take it with brute force then you will no doubt lose," Jase pointed out.

"What you know about fighting?" the bulb grumbled annoyed.

Jase shrugged. "Just making an observation," he said as he took another bite of his sweet fruit.

"He's actually right, Tahmela. You can't overtake my army with your numbers," the Princess stated as she slew the rest of his men then ordered her men to start their assault on his castle walls.

The bulb let out an angry cry and banged his small gray fist against the table as she broke through, taking his castle which resulted in the end of the game. He let out a string of words in his own language that didn't sound very friendly. When the bulb finally calmed down, he reached in his pocket and brought out two silver pieces, handing them over to the Princess. "Rematch later," he said and hopped off the booth in the direction of the cockpit.

Jase slid in where the bulb had been sitting and smiled as he asked, "You gambled with him? Isn't that very un-Princess-like?"

"I just exploited his weakness in a fair game of StarCastleCapture and in doing so, gathered information about his habits to help protect me better," she indicated as she pocketed the money.

Jase was still grinning. "It's gambling, Princess."

Princess Skyrah's lips broke into a smile as the hologram disappeared. "You're right. It's merely for fun to pass the time. He was the one who wanted to gamble, and I happily obliged," she said.

Kaimi appeared on the round table next to Jase. "Why don't you try playing against her, Jase?"

"He wouldn't last the first five minutes," the Princess said smugly sitting back against the booth.

"Oh, really," Jase answered, accepting the challenge. "I bet I could school you the first round."

She locked eyes with him. "Want to find out?"

"If you're not scared," he teased.

She pressed a button and the holographic field appeared again. "Of you? I don't think so."

Jase looked to his side unsure of what to really do. He had never played StarCastleCapture before but thought he had got the gist of it. He had seen others play in Bentley's Casino from a far and knew lots of people who lost to it. It was strange to now be the one at the table instead of the onlooker.

"You do know how to play, right?" Kaimi asked, noticing his lost expression as he toggled through the items on the hologram screen.

Skyrah glanced up from her screen with an amused smile on her face. "You've never played yet you are already boasting that you can beat me? Overconfident, aren't we?"

He made a face. "I sort of know how to play. I just haven't gotten the chance to actually do it until now," he replied.

"This will be a walk in the park," Skyrah exclaimed as Kaimi explained the rules of the game to him.

"The object of the game is to defeat your opponent's fortress and capture it without losing all of your soldiers or your own castle. You can build your castle anyway you want and add traps that can aid in stopping your opponent," she pointed out.

"Can she see where I place my traps?" Jase interrupted.

"No, only you can see where you place traps. They can be inside your castle or around it but you are limited to five traps so place carefully. Once you have built your castle, you can then move on to building your army which is limited to five hundred soldiers. You can choose soldiers by their race and position, and remember, it's all about strategy in this game so plan wisely," Kaimi encouraged him.

Jase nodded. "Any other rules I should know about before I start?"

"Your general is the strongest in the army so if he goes down then your army automatically gives up," she told him.

Jase focused on the screen. "Okay, let's do this!"

He started building the castle with two narrow towers and high stone walls. He placed a large steel door as the entrance to the fortress that led into the small city making it the only way in. The door and the high stone walls separated the castle from the outside world as well as a small moat with steel spikes in its trenches to keep the soldiers from climbing the walls of the fortress. He placed two bomb traps on the inner door of the gate as well as another on the main castle door that led inside. He then placed a trap on the main street that led to the castle before placing the last bomb trap halfway down the street from the castle. When touched it would send plasma blasts across both sides of the street to the intruder.

Once satisfied with his castle, he moved on to create his army. He wasn't sure what kind of soldiers he wanted as he scrolled through the many different options for races. He figured the Princess would use her own people due to their advantage of speed, strength, and dexterity. Keeping that in mind, he scrolled to the elves knowing that they were an equal match to her people with their own speed and strength. The screen flickered into a viewing of different fighting classes. He could choose one category or he could have many different kinds of soldiers in his army. There were plasma archers to sword fighters, cavalry of many different types of wild beasts and ships, plasma gun foot soldiers, long-range snipers, knife assassins, cyborgs, demolitions, medical teams, and so much more that it was overwhelming to him.

Jase glanced up at the Princess, wondering what type of soldiers she would use. He chose two hundred foot soldiers, one hundred sword fighters, fifty cavalry riders on beasts with horns, fifty archers, fifty cyborgs, twenty-five medical soldiers, fifteen demolition experts and ten long-range snipers. He then placed his snipers on top of the castle's walls except for one that he placed in the highest tower of the castle before sending the rest of his army outside the castle gates. He paused for a moment, studying his army and decided to move one medic back to the castle in case he needed him for the snipers as the Princess asked, "Are you ready yet?"

Jase felt confident in his choices. "I believe so," he replied.

"Okay. May I choose the weather or do you care?" she asked.

Jase shrugged, not seeing why it mattered. "I don't care."

Skyrah pressed a button before asking, "Day or night?"

"Day."

Skyrah pushed another button. "Season?"

"Redstar season," Jase answered, excited to begin.

"Summer it is," Skyrah then looked up at him with a sly smile. "Good luck."

"Thanks. Good luck to you, too," he responded and watched the holographic board change. The screen became a thick fog that made it hard to see anything except where his soldiers were highlighted in green. There was a slight drizzle of rain falling on the battlefield and Jase could hear each drop hitting his soldier's armor as they stood in place awaiting orders.

Jase ordered his foot soldiers to move forward cautiously, unsure of what to expect in the fog. He kept the cavalry at the rear of the soldiers for protection in case the Princess decided to attack from behind, while keeping half of his cyborgs on either side of them and the rest at the castle gate. He named the soldiers that were moving red team and the defense soldiers blue team as he kept a watchful eye on the radar in the right-hand corner of the screen for any enemy signs. He anxiously watched his troops slowly march through the fog and peered up at the Princess to find her calm and composed as she watched her own screen. He couldn't help but wonder what she was planning as he turned his attention back to his troops. Suddenly, ten of his riders along with five cyborgs and fifteen soldiers dropped to the ground lifeless. The attack was so fast that it caught Jase off guard as he scanned around the area for the cause. He pressed on the screen to zoom in on his dead soldiers bodies and noticed they had been stabbed, but by who or what was a mystery. Jase looked at Skyrah, but she remained composed and gave no notion of what else she was planning.

Jase focused on his remaining soldiers, trying to think of what happened as he ordered them to tighten their ranks. His elves should have seen their attackers if they were Qualias, for they matched their speed. If they didn't and the radar didn't pick up anything then what was the source of the attack? Assassins? But wouldn't they appear on the radar as soon as they were close? Yet, again, the fog was pretty thick so it could be messing with the frequencies. Hoping it would help, Jase rearranged his army by placing the cavalry on all sides of the troops for protection and pushed them onward towards her castle.

After just a few minutes another strike was made, but this time it was by archers. They were barely able to be seen through the fog but Jase spotted their outlines and ordered his foot soldiers to advance. They killed a handful before the archers retreated into the fog. Jase lost twenty soldiers and four riders were wounded from arrows. He sent the wounded back to the castle and continued forward with his charge. Suddenly a full advance from Skyrah's army met them head on with Jase's, sending the field into a combustion of plasma discharge and war cries. The attack sent Jase's army into a state of confusion as Skyrah fought on all sides catching him off guard. His army held their ground as they killed many of her soldiers but at a cost. The cavalry as well as half of his medics were lost before Skyrah's army retreated back into the fog.

Jase remained calm and focused as he ordered his sword fighters to convene with the rest of his army and the cyborgs to escort them to regroup, the Princess attacked again this time by plasma gun soldiers. With the help of his cyborgs, Jase's team took out a good deal of her foot soldiers while he lost two of his cyborgs and two sword fighters. The small victory brought a smile to Jase's face which quickly disappeared as another wave of soldiers advanced, but this time, they struck both groups simultaneously. The Princess's sword fighters attacked his foot soldiers and archers while her plasma fighters charged his sword fighters and cyborgs. With them, she also had archers whose plasma arrows pierced through the armor of the cyborgs, killing them instantly. Her sword fighters also moved with great speed in and out of the fog causing confusion within Jase's ranks as they tried to defend against attacks. He watched helplessly as she slew his soldiers with each strike while his army was only able to kill handfuls.

Once the battle was over, he felt his heart sink as he saw the casualties left behind. He now retained thirty foot soldiers, twenty-one sword fighters, one medic, five demolitions, ten snipers, and twenty-five archers. His palms grew sweaty as he tried thinking of how to win with such a small army. He had at least taken out seventy of her own men which meant he was losing greatly. He had to come up with a new plan and fast before she struck again. He glanced up at the Princess again, seeing a smile creep onto her face as if she had him right where she wanted him.

I have to win by getting into her castle, he thought. Jase ordered all that was left of his army back to his castle so he could think clearly without worrying about getting any surprises in the fog. As he watched them retreat, he realized there was no need for his snipers with the fog. That gave him an idea causing him to order three of his snipers and two demolition soldiers to head out together in the direction of the Princess's castle. He then banded another group of cyborgs and a demolition soldier to travel east to the backside of the Princess's castle. Lastly, he ordered an demolition soldier and an archer to head west through the forest before making their way to the castle. Jase kept the remaining snipers on the wall with the rest of his army guarding the front gate. Then he ordered thirty foot soldiers into the city and to spread out through the different alleyways on the main street to the castle. He also placed twenty-four archers in the courtyard of the castle. Between his soldiers and traps, the Princess would have a hard time getting through even with the size of her army. If he was to lose then he'd go out with a bang, but hoped with all of his scouts running ahead that he could manage to pull a fast one on her and win.

"Oh, you play again?" Tahmela exclaimed entering the room. "Should have told so I place bet."

"Never too late to place bets. This will end soon, I'm afraid," Skyrah said without looking up.

"I wouldn't be so sure of yourself," Jase responded.

The first team was almost to the gates while the cyborg team was halfway there. His last team was traveling slower due to the heavy underbrush in the forest. He touched the screen, settling on the first team that had started fighting the soldiers at the gate. They put up a good fight, but were soon demolished by the Princess's archers on the wall. He knew they wouldn't make it but needed the distraction as he moved the screen to focus on his own castle where the Princess had started attacking the gates. She killed all the cyborgs guarding the gate and two snipers on the wall before assigning a ram against the gates. Jase nervously checked on his other team. The four cyborgs and demolition soldier had scaled the walls and made it inside the castle but were soon blown up by a trap the moment they touched the ground. Jase balled his fists, growing frustrated as her army broke through his gates and engaged with his sword fighters. Each army took out many soldiers from both sides but in the end Jase's soldiers fell and Skyrah's continued on towards the castle. Soon plasma crossfire ensued from either side of the street to the castle and Skyrah's soldiers halted to fight off foot soldiers hiding in the alleyways.

Jase was so focused on the fighting that he didn't notice his two-man team break through the forest and head towards the west wall of Skyrah's castle. His own plasma gun soldiers took out many of the opposing army but Skyrah was able to have some of her men flank from behind and kill his men. Her army then slowly moved on down the street, taking out any of his soldiers that stood in their way. The traps proved unsuccessful in preventing her army from advancing and soon they reached the castle gates. Firefight broke out between his archers and her soldiers as they fought to stand their ground.

He heard an explosion go off by Skyrah's castle and figured his last team had been killed. All Skyrah had to do was get through his archers and she'd win.

Princess Skyrah mowed down his archers and focused fire on his last demolition soldier who he had ordered to kamikaze in hopes to take out as many of her soldiers as he could. The soldier took out thirty of her own men before falling as the soldiers stormed past him through the courtyard towards the castle doors. Hopelessly, Jase watched her soldiers enter into his castle. Suddenly, fireworks exploded in different colors in the middle of the holographic world with block letters which read: "TIE."

"What?!" Princess Skyrah blurted.

Jase, also confused, quickly checked the status of his last scout team. His sniper had made it into the castle at the same time Skyrah's army entered his. Jase let out a joyful cheer, jumping out of the booth as he threw a fist straight up into the air.

Tahmela laughed, surprised by Jase's actions. "Who knew hmil match you," he told the Princess, who was still processing.

"Well played, Jase!" Kaimi cheered.

Jase grinned from ear to ear, turning to the Princess. "Told you I wouldn't lose!"

"You didn't win either," she corrected.

"But neither did you," he pointed out happily. "What was your race anyways? Why couldn't I see them on the radar?"

Princess Skyrah stood from the table. "Genezit, and you couldn't read them due to the fog."

"Genezit? What's that?" Jase asked.

"They are an incredibly fast species of humans who have evolved to with stand very hot temperatures, and can run faster than even the elves. Their home planet is called Perendi which is covered in a red desert," Kaimi answered.

"Huh, I thought you'd use your own people," Jase admitted scratching his head.

The Princess crossed her arms. "That was one of many mistakes you made during our battle."

"Oh, really? And what are these mistakes?" he questioned.

"Your first mistake was thinking you knew how I'd play. Your second was not caring what kind of weather you wanted to wage war in. Weather is a huge factor in war. It can help you win or lose a battle so keep that in mind the next time you decide not to care. Your third mistake was sacrificing soldiers needlessly. This might be a game, but in real world you try your best to keep everyone alive at all costs even if you're losing. You don't give up because you're angry that you're losing."

Jase crossed his arms arrogantly. "True, but this isn't real world so it doesn't matter," he replied smugly.

The Princess stared at him with sharp eyes, but showed no emotion to what she was thinking. There was a moment where he thought she was going to say something, but instead she stood. "You're right, it's just a game," she said and walked out of the room.

"She mad she lost," Tahmela said swatting a hand in the air as he jumped up onto the booth and plopped down.

Jase stared after the Princess before turning back to the bulb and Kaimi. "Must be," he responded.

"She's right, you know," Kaimi told him. "It might be a game here, but it's not. You should treat it like it was an actual war and take away the lessons from it."

Jase sighed stubbornly. "I don't need to know such things when I don't plan on fighting a war."

"Knowledge is power, Jase, whether you use it or not," she responded back to him.

Jase sat back down in the booth. "That may be true, but you do know I'm not fighting in this war with you? I agreed to come but I won't get mixed up in a war," he explained.

Kaimi smiled softly to him. "The Princess told me. You plan on exploring the stars like we planned."

"Yes, I only wish you were coming with me," Jase told her.

Kaimi looked away for a moment, oblivious to the bulb watching them. "My place is with the Princess like it's always been. I've spent too much time away from her that it's time for me to make it up." She turned back to him. "You don't need to fight for something you don't believe in, Jase. You've already helped us enough as it is by keeping me safe and helping the Princess escape Faton. We couldn't ask any more from you," she said.

"It's not that I don't believe in it. I'm just not a soldier, Kaimi. I'm a thief and will always be a thief," Jase explained.

Kaimi gave a nod. "But you are also a Bluestar. You could be so much more if you wanted to, Jase."

Jase studied her for a while thinking of how far they had come. She was his best friend and they had promised never to leave one another since she first found him as a young boy. Yet here he was telling her he was going on his own. He had never thought it would happen but couldn't help it. He wasn't a soldier or much of a Bluestar and in knowing that, he felt as if he was disappointing her. It weighed heavily on his heart as he stared at the holographic world, knowing that he wouldn't last long in a war. "I'm sorry," he finally managed to whisper.

Kaimi saw the struggle in his eyes and replied cheerfully, "Don't be. You have nothing to apologize for so don't feel bad. Not everyone can be in a war and even though you are a Bluestar doesn't mean you have to be in one either. I respect your decision for knowing who you are and what you can and cannot do, Jase. I still love you for it."

It was in these moments, Jase wished more than anything he could give her a hug. Instead though, he gave her a fat grin.

"You strange friends," Tahmela finally uttered and they both suddenly remembered he was in the room.

Jase turned to him. "Not as strange as you and I," he pointed out.

"When we become friends, hmil?" the bulb asked.

Jase cocked an eyebrow, thinking. "I thought we did when we both helped each other from potential death?"

The bulb stared at him with his unblinking large black eyes as if thinking then bobbed his head up and down. "Very well, we friends now," he said.

Kaimi turned back to Jase. "You could at least learn to fight if you are going off alone."

"I know how to fight," Jase said making a face.

"Maybe a fistfight, yes, but not if you came against something deadlier. I'm sure if you ask the Princess she would agree to teach you," Kaimi suggested. "If you ask her nicely, of course."

"I think I'll be fine, Kaimi," Jase said stubbornly.

"Please, Jase, for me. I need to know you will be safe without me there to watch over you," she softly pressed on.

Jase sighed giving in. "Fine. Just for you, I will."

"Thank you," she then turned to the bulb. "Tahmela, I think I know a few ways that could improve your ship and increase our travel speed, if you'd let me."

The bulb hesitated. "Show me."

"Okay, meet me in the cockpit," Kaimi winked at Jase then disappeared into thin air as Tahmela wandered off towards the cockpit.

Jase grinned, pushing himself to his feet to find the Princess. He headed down the circular passageway towards the crew quarters.

To Spar a Princess

Jase made his way down the corridor to the other side of the ship where he stopped in front of the sleeping quarters. He gently knocked at the closed door. Waiting for a response, he hesitated for a moment and was about to walk away when the door slid open.

"Kaimi told me you were coming," she told him, turning back to the room. She walked to the center and sat cross-legged on the floor as Jase entered.

Jase looked around the room which was the same as his except much bigger, probably the main crew quarters. "It was her idea. She thinks I can't fight," he said.

"Can you?" Skyrah questioned, not believing it herself.

Jase crossed his arms across his chest. "Of course I can. I know how to handle myself in a fight."

The Princess stood, straightening her shirt as she tossed her shawl over her shoulders, wrapping it around her neck. "Would you like to test that out? If you win then Kaimi is wrong, and you don't need help. If I win, then you should heed her advice."

Jase hesitated. "I don't want to hit a lady," he admitted.

"I won't take it personally if you did land a hit," the Princess said smiling.

"I'm not going to hit you. Just show me some stuff you think I should know then we can call it a day," he suggested.

The Princess watched him for a moment then said, "Follow me," and headed out of the room.

Jase followed after her down the corridor towards the main cargo hold. Upon entering the cold room, he looked around and noticed that even with all the crates and barrels, there was still a good amount of room to spar in. "What are we—" Before he could finish his sentence, the Princess's boot slammed into his cheek causing him to lose balance for a moment. He quickly caught himself, but could feel the pressure from the impact on his face and rubbed his cheek. Tasting blood in his mouth, he growled turning back to her, "What was that for?!"

"Defend yourself," she ordered then attacked again.

Jase didn't have time to react as he felt the air escape his lungs and doubled over. Sick to his stomach as his eyes watered while he gasped to breathe.

"I said, defend yourself," Skyrah persisted as she watched him. "You have to be ready for anything if you want to go out on your own in this universe with the Androids hunting you."

Jase heaved as he fell to one knee holding his stomach. He breathed in and out slowly feeling like he was going to puke but forced himself up to his feet as he tried holding back his anger. Composing himself, he answered, "I told you. I'm not going to hurt you."

"And I told you that you won't touch me," the Princess responded rivaling his stubbornness. "I wouldn't be doing this if Kaimi didn't ask it of me. She's trying to look after you so show some respect."

Jase knew she was right. Kaimi wasn't going to be with him anymore and this was the only way she knew she could protect him. If he could learn to fight someone as enhanced as the Princess was then he wouldn't be in bad shape by himself. Making up his mind to actually try for Kaimi's happiness and his safety, he stated, "Fine, but the moment I land a hit on you were done."

The Princess smiled. "That gives me enough time to train you."

"Cocky, aren't we?" he teased taking off his jacket and slinging it over a crate.

"I'm confident in my abilities. There's a difference," Skyrah said squaring off.

"Well, I hope I don't shatter your confidence too much, then," Jase responded back.

"Ready?" Skyrah asked unimpressed.

"Ready." As soon as the word escaped his mouth, she seemed to disappear. The next thing he knew, he was flat on his back staring at the ceiling. The breath was knocked out of him again as he laid motionless.

The Princess stood over him, offering a hand for support. "You'll have to do better than that if you want to beat me."

Jase accepted it and got back to his feet as he held his chest to catch his breath again. After taking a few deep breaths, he nodded for them to continue. Once again he felt her hand make contact with his face, but as soon as it did it was gone again to attack his arm. He could barely see her attacks as she hit his ear then chest then right leg, jaw bone, then arm again. Her movements were like lightning. He gave up trying to block her, and instead tried hitting her as he swung his fists this way and that way. Suddenly he felt a slight tingle in his arms and Jase caught her left jab in his hand inches away from his face! Shocked, his eyes widened as he glanced from his hand to her and before she could recover, Jase threw a kick but was intercepted as she flipped over, slamming him hard into the cold floor.

He felt bruises start to form as he excitedly pushed himself off the floor with a grin. "I got you that time!"

"By mere luck, perhaps...," she replied as if in thought.

He got into fighting stance again, determined. "Let's try again," he said.

Once again, Skyrah moved too fast for him to see, punching several times. Jase fell onto his knees as he wheezed in pain. Each time she expected him to give up, he'd get right back up for the next round. So they continued.

Jase's body hurt as he forced himself off the floor again and again. His nose was bleeding and he grabbed a dirty rag that he had found off the crate. They had been at it for two hours now and he had yet to touch her again which made him more frustrated. He knew he hadn't hit her with luck, that he had hit her because he could. He had to figure out how he did it. He tossed the rag back on the crate and turned to her, grunting, "Again."

He didn't try defending himself as he once again focused on trying to hit her, but like always she was too fast for him. She hit him again and again and again and again until he was so frustrated that, like before, he threw up both hands and intercepted her kick to his side. He felt the same slight tingle in his arms as he looked to Skyrah stunned. She also stopped for a split second then threw her free leg and kicked the side of his face.

Jase held his throbbing ear and sat up, but didn't move to get to his feet. He was too tired to fight any more as he breathlessly said, "If the only time I hit you is when I'm not trying then I'm going to die out there."

Skyrah also sat up across from him, cross-legged. "I think I've figured out your problem," she responded.

"That I suck," he remarked.

She continued. "You are trusting too much on what you can see. The fact that I move faster than you can see causes your blindness. Both times you were able to stop me, you had given up trying to see the attack and had gone with your instinct."

"By instinct?" he retorted unconvinced.

"Yes. You might not be aware of it, but your body is. After all you are a Bluestar so your senses are much better attuned to what is around you than most humans," she explained.

"But I'm not like that. I don't have any special abilities or powers. You can ask the woman who raised me, I'm just a normal human being who just happens to be an orphan born in the Bluestar Season," he replied confused.

"Like you said before, you are a late bloomer," she answered.

Jase shook his head. "I was merely joking."

"It's still true, Jase. I will admit I have never heard of a Bluestar blooming late. All of the ones that I read about have never spoken about such things hap-pening to them but then again Bluestars have always been secretive about their abilities. I don't have all the answers for you and the only place I can think of that might is back with the Resistance," she told him.

Jase stared at his hands, thinking back to what Mrs. Rose had told him about Bluestars when he was a kid. In the old days, they were treated like roy-alty since they were so rare and supposedly came from the stars themselves. Some saw them as outcasts beings that weren't human nor elf nor anything else for that matter. It was said that they were as strong as the elves and as quick as the Qualias. They also had the ability to manipulate light and plasma energy, bending it to their will. Almost every Bluestar born helped the Night-star family due to an unspeakable bond that no one in days passed know why. Yet, here Jase was rewriting history, so it seemed to chase his own ambitious.

He focused on his hand in front of him, his thoughts turning to this power he was supposed to have. He couldn't imagine such power at his fingertips and almost hoped he wouldn't have to. After what he had been told about the An-cients and how it drove the Androids to overthrow them. It scared Jase as he looked up at the Princess. "What if I don't want this power?" he said softly.

136

She studied him, her eyes contained a tinge of sadness in them. She pulled her braid over her shoulder. "When it comes to power, we don't always choose it. It chooses us. We should be honored by it. Don't fear the gift that has been bestowed upon you, Jase. You can help so many people with it if you choose," she said softly, her words resonating in the air like wind through blossoms.

Jase could feel her trying to reassure him, but at the same time it felt as if she was trying to reassure herself as well. "Are you scared to be Queen if you win the war?" he asked.

The Princess firmly recited as though she had said it a million times. "Of course not. Nightstar Princesses are born to be queens and we aren't afraid to rule. It is in our blood and I am honored to lead my people." She suddenly stood to her feet, announcing, "We will spar again tomorrow," then walked out of the room before Jase could say anything more.

Jase sat in confusion wondering if he had offended her. He had asked her a simple question, but maybe she still didn't trust him after all. He shrugged knowing there was no use in trying to understand the woman and pulled himself to his feet with the help of the nearby crate. His body ached in response as he grabbed his blue pilot's jacket then started walking out to the main hold. He paused for a moment with the thought that he was truly by himself so instead of leaving, he climbed on top of a large crate and touched his data screen. A photo gallery popped up on the small screen which he clicked on and watched it appear before his eyes in holographic form. Leaning back against the steel wall, Jase scrolled through the photos until he found the one he was looking for. The picture changed and showed an image of Momma Rose, and the other children from the orphanage standing in front of the building like they did every year to take a family photo.

Immediately he smiled at the photo, wishing he could go back to that day but at the same time Jase was excited for the adventures that lay before him. He would have exciting stories to tell them when he returned and would bring them back gifts from different worlds he'd visit. Jase stared at the picture a moment longer then turned it off before climbing off the crate.

Strange Sensation

Jase stepped out of the shower drying off as his thoughts were still on the Princess. He hadn't stopped thinking about her since their training session and he wondered if she was actually frightened to succeed in the war against the Androids. Perhaps she was frightened to rule over more than the Resistance. If she did succeed, she'd have the responsibility of the entire galaxy in her hands to take care of. Jase shuttered at the thought of such a burden. It was a lot to ask of someone including her. He slipped in his earpiece to contact Kaimi, and asked, "Do you think the Princess has what it takes to rule the galaxy?"

Kaimi answered slowly as if considering every outcome. "I think she is stronger than she thinks. It is a lot to ask of someone and not everyone is capable of the task but Skyrah has always been a worthy successor. Even her sister, Maliha, knew that, and I know all of them would agree with her."

"Do you think she is afraid to rule?" he asked as he pulled on his pants and buttoned up his faded vest.

"Everyone is aware of the responsibilities to rule a nation. I can guarantee that every king or queen that has ever ruled had insecurities at one time or another," she replied.

"I suppose you are right. I guess it's just strange to think they are still like us, just richer with more problems," he replied as he fixed his hair in the mirror.

Kaimi chuckled gently. "I suppose so. Why do you ask?"

Jase messed with his hair as he answered. "I asked the Princess if she was afraid to rule and she answered abruptly then left before I could even say a word. I think I might have upsetted her."

"Princess Skyrah is very kept-to-herself these days. With the loss of her family and the Resistance counting on her, she can't afford to show weakness. Therefore, it's hard for her to open up to most people, including me. You didn't upset her. You just asked a question that she couldn't answer vulnerably," Kaimi explained.

"That must be lonely to keep stuff like that to yourself. Does she not have someone she really trusts to talk to? It's not healthy to keep things bottled up like that," Jase sympathized as he headed out of his room and into the corridor.

"I don't know. Maybe she talks to her sister when she sees her, but I'm not really sure nowadays, Jase," Kaimi replied.

Jase pulled on his black and blue fingerless gloves with only one thought in mind: He was going to try and get the Princess to open up to him. He wasn't sure why, but he wanted her to have someone to talk to if she needed it. He wanted to try and be that person for her whether they liked each other or not. "I'm going to go talk to her," he said aloud.

"Jase," Kaimi warned.

Jase walked along the corridor and around the ship, passing the main cargo hold. "Didn't you want us to be friends or something like that? That's my intention here."

"Do you like her, Jase Bluestar?" Kaimi asked.

Jase stopped in his tracks. "What?! No way! Don't even suggest such a thing!" he exclaimed. Then, lowering his voice, "I'm just trying to be nice, that's all."

"Very well then," Kaimi answered.

Jase passed the medical bay and stopped at the Princess's quarters. He raised his hand to knock, but hesitated as he suddenly felt nervous speaking to her. After a moment of debating, Jase knocked at her door and waited for a reply. The doors parted, sliding open to reveal the Princess. She seemed unsure of why Jase was there. "Yes? Is something wrong?" she asked.

Jase clumsily smiled. "Err, no, everything is fine. I just came to talk to you," he said stumbling over his words.

The Princess crossed her arms, raising an eyebrow. "About?"

Jase pushed past her into the room. "Can we not just be friends who talk to one another about anything? I mean you did beat me up, after all. You at least owe me a few minutes of your time for friendly chatter," he responded.

Skyrah looked annoyed with his intrusion as she stayed where she was by the door. "No, I don't think so," she said sternly.

"Why not?" Jase asked. He picked up her black plasma gun she had laying on the bed and looked it over.

Skyrah took it from him and placed it back where it was as she sat down on the bed. "Because I don't want to talk to you if I don't have to. I like it here in my room, alone."

"Oh, I don't think that's true at all," Jase said crouching in front of her. "I think you like talking to me."

The Princess softly pushed him back with her boot, answering, "You're sadly mistaken."

Jase fell back onto his rear. "Kaimi, what do you think?" he asked, bringing her into the conversation.

Kaimi appeared on the Princess's data watch lying on the bed. "I'm not getting involved with this," she said as she raised her hands in the air.

Jase leaned back on his palms with his feet outstretched. "Wimp," he chastised. "I think you'd get lonely being locked up in here day after day with no one to talk to. That's why Kaimi and I are here."

"Then, why don't you go and I'll talk to Kaimi," the Princess suggested.

"Because I'm already here," Jase explained matter-of-factly.

"I think you are the one who is lonely, and you want me to fill the void for you," the Princess teased.

"I think you could be right," Kaimi agreed with her.

Jase shook his head. "I have you, Kaimi. I don't need anyone else."

"Aww, thanks, Jase," Kaimi said blushing then rolling her eyes. "Even if it might be a lie."

Jase grinned, "I wouldn't lie to you unless it was a life-or-death situation. Then I might," he joked.

Skyrah had been watching their banter and waited until they were done before asking, "So really, why are you here, Jase? Besides to pester me."

Jase wasn't sure how to word what he was about to say without sounding like he was prying. Buying more time, he said, "I just wanted to see how you were?"

"I'm fine, thank you. Now you can go," she replied quickly.

Jase continued. "And if you ever want to talk about anything, I'm here if you want. I know you've had it rough but—"

"I'm fine. Now go," she snapped staring at the floor.

Jase pressed on. "I'm just saying, Princess. It can't be easy what you've been through and I—"

"You don't know what I've been through, Bluestar," Skyrah interrupted as she stood from her bed and glared at him. "I suggest you take your leave now."

Jase angrily stood to his feet. "You're right. I don't know, but I'm trying to be nice so you don't have to bottle it up until you explode," he yelled.

"So you're trying to be the dashing hero! Save the day and sweep the girl off her feet," the Princess bellowed. "I don't need saving."

Jase balled his fist. "I didn't say you did!" he defended.

"Why don't you both just take a breath and calm down," Kaimi quietly suggested from the bed.

"I'm not the one who needs to cool off," Jase countered.

"So now you are saying I'm the one with the bad temper who also needs to be saved from my bottled-up feelings?" the Princess argued.

Jase clenched his teeth together. "Sure! If that is how you're taking it then maybe. Add 'being a spoiled brat' to it, too. You know not all of us were royalty and had food to spare! Most of us lower class had to earn and fight for the food on our table because it wasn't just handed to us. Some of us didn't have fancy homes to hide in with rich mommies and daddies to protect us! We grew up on the streets where you weren't always sure if you were going to have food that day or a place to stay. We didn't have anyone to talk to so if me trying to be friendly is offending you than I'm not sorry. Don't complain to me when you are all alone."

"Jase, enough!" Kaimi yelled over the PA system in the room. "It's time for you to leave now."

Jase looked at Kaimi then back at the Princess. He hesitated for a moment then turned and walked out of the room, letting the door slide shut behind him as he left. He kept going until he was in the cargo hold and looked for something to hit. He just stood there, breathing in hard as he tried calming himself down by thinking of what Mrs. Rose once told him when he was a child. There was another kid in the house that was bullying him and all he wanted to do was to hit him, but Momma Rose intervened.

"When you feel like hitting someone, just take a deep breath, Jase, and let it out slowly. Just breathe. Breathe, Jase."

"Just breathe," Jase recited out loud, hearing her voice in his head. "Just breathe, Jase." He heard a noise coming from the engine room and figured it was Tahmela. Deciding to see what he was up to, Jase walked to the wide door and waited for it to slide open. He found Tahmela sitting with his back against the wall next to some metal pipes and instruments that had no meaning to Jase. "Tahmela, what are you doing?" he asked.

The bulb opened his large black eyes and gave a toothy grin to the human. "Listening, hmil. Come join," he responded.

Jase glanced around the tiny room with its components that ran this way and that into the walls and ceilings. He ducked under a large steel pipe between him and the bulb before taking a seat next to him. "What are we listening for?" he asked curiously.

Tahmela closed his eyes again. "Just to the vibrations of the engine working," he said.

"Is something wrong with it?" Jase let his eyes run across the hyperdrive and engine parts.

"Nothing wrong, Bluestar. Just listening," he replied.

Jase didn't understand. "Why then?"

Tahmela cocked his head to the side. "You might laugh," he replied.

"I won't, I promise," Jase assured him, shrugging his shoulders.

Tahmela eyed him suspiciously. "The sounds, the vibrations of engine and smell of it working reminds me of home," he finally admitted.

"On Faton? Did you live in Otect City?" Jase asked.

Tahmela shook his head. "On Faton, yes, but not in city. Not in beginning. I was born in bulb underground city far, far away from Otect. My home city filled with thousands of bulbs that lived there for thousands of years. The first bulbs built beautiful city below surface of planet where we don't get disturbed with dangers. I lived in poor parts near generator room that powered whole city. When I younger, I used to sneak off to it late at night to listen to it work. It's parts moving in rhythm with one another to melody we don't understand or comprehend. Only machine I had ever been close to before I left."

"Why don't you go back?" Jase asked.

The bulb's smile disappeared as he responded, "Not easy, hmil. Not so easy."

"Why is that?"

"I banned. My kind don't take likely to you if you leave clan for topside worlds. They believe we made for dirt and surface below. We stay there, not explore space," he replied admitting he had been displaced.

Jase felt sad for the bulb, knowing what it felt like to now be banned from returning home. "I'm sorry, Tahmela," he replied sympathetically.

"Must know own happiness better than what rest of world wants from you. My clan set in their own ways but I choose to follow dreams. Therefore, I don't belong with them. That, Jase Bluestar, okay," he encouraged.

They sat in silence as they continued listening to the vibrations of the ship. Jase closed his eyes letting his mind wander to the view of his balcony in the evening sun setting richly with spacecrafts taking off every half-minute or so. He imagined being there next to Kaimi as they both watched the sun set its red and orange streaks across the night sky, feeling nothing but content with one another. He could almost feel the cool wind brushing against his face and felt as if suddenly he was back at home and that everything was a dream.

"Jase?"

Jase turned to Kaimi in his dream as she spoke his name. He was about to answer her when suddenly he felt himself falling backwards from the balcony.

"Jase?"

Jase jerked straight up and looked around. He felt confused as he finally realized that the Princess was in front of him.

"I'm sorry. I didn't mean to wake you," she told him though he could barely hear over the noise of the hyper drive.

Jase looked beside him at the bulb who appeared to be asleep. "It's fine," he said wondering how long he had been out. He then asked, "Is there something you need?"

She nodded. "Can I speak to you for a moment? Please?" she asked motioning to the door.

Jase didn't stir for a moment, not really wanting to talk to her though he knew he needed to apologize. Summoning up his courage, he gave her a nod before standing to his feet. He climbed over the large pipe and followed her out and into the cargo room. She continued on down the passageway towards his room, not saying a word as they moved through the ship which made Jase uneasy.

"I hope you don't mind us talking in your room so we don't wake Tahmela?" she asked as the door slid open.

Jase stepped in after her. "No, of course not. Where's Kaimi?"

"She's in my room. She said she would give us some privacy to talk," Skyrah mentioned turning around to face him. She seemed out of her element. Placing her hands behind her back, she avoided eye contact as she looked over his room. "Your room looks exactly like mine, just smaller."

"Well, not all of us can afford a large room," Jase slipped.

Ignoring the comment, she said, "I wanted to apologize for my behavior earlier. It was unkind of me especially since all you wanted to do was be helpful. It's not easy for me to accept help, but thank you for offering it. I really appreciate that and I'm sorry I acted poorly."

Jase shoved his hands into his jacket pockets, staring towards the ground. "I should apologize too. I didn't mean to push or pry and I promise you I'm not treating you like a damsel in distress, really. Kaimi told me not to push and I should have listened for once," he paused for a moment before continuing. "I just want you to know you can trust me, Skyrah. If we are traveling together then we might as well work on us trying to be friends, especially for Kaimi. You don't have to tell me anything about your life. I just need to know we can trust each other, that's all."

"Thank you," Skyrah responded softly diplomatically nodding her head.

There was an awkward silence between them until Jase suddenly smiled and said, "Kaimi is going to yell at me, isn't she?"

Skyrah sighed. "She spent a good five minutes lecturing me about many great things, but mostly about apologizing to you, so yes. We both acted poorly," she admitted.

Jase rubbed his hand through his hair. "Well, wouldn't be the first time she yelled at me for acting poorly, and I doubt it will be the last," he said.

"Did she yell at you a lot on Faton?" she asked fishing for a conversation.

"Not a lot, but when I was being reckless.... Well, she yelled at me a lot for breaking up with Camila. I thought I'd never hear the end of it," he said suddenly remembering.

"She liked you both together?" Skyrah asked as she took a seat on the floor, now interested.

Jase chuckled as he sat on the edge of the bed. "She thought she would make an honest man out of me. Kaimi has always wanted to keep me safe, and

I guess she knew I would be if I was with Camila. I don't blame her. My job hasn't always been a walk in the park," he said.

"She really cares for you. I can tell. It's nice to see her that way," Skyrah told him.

"Yeah, I wouldn't know what I'd do without her. She's my best friend in the entire universe," he admitted.

"Well, hold on to that friendship. Not everyone knows what they have until it's too late," she told him.

Jase nodded and asked, "Did you have a best friend?"

"I do, or I did. I haven't seen her in years, I'm afraid. We kind of went our separate ways after the war when my sister and I were in hiding. She went home to her people and I went elsewhere. I wonder how she is doing?" she responded reminiscing on her past.

Jase watched her in thought before asking, "Is she not Qualia?"

"No, she's an elf that I grew up with when I was younger. We both trained together and when I was old enough I asked her to be my personal bodyguard. When she said yes, we became inseparable throughout the war," she sighed.

"Until the end of it. Why didn't she stay with you?" he questioned.

Skyrah shifted her weight. "Her leaders ordered her back to Kurath Thor since they were no longer needed with the war effort. The elves suffered a great loss during the war, and when we lost, it just made them more bitter about taking part."

"That's why they don't help now, isn't it?" Jase asked, feeling like he knew the answer already.

Skyrah nodded. "They help very little but I doubt they will ever fight in the Resistance again. They won't fight against us, but they won't help us either. It's what happens when you lose a war. You tend to lose allies, and hope."

"You will just have to convince them otherwise," Jase stated matter-of-factly.

Skyrah softly smiled. "It's not that easy," she illuminated.

Jase leaned back on his hands. "Well, you seem very capable so I'm sure you will find a way, Princess," he said encouragingly.

"Thank you," she said then patted the floor in front of her for him to take a seat. "Come. Meditation might help you gain control of your powers."

Jase cocked an eyebrow. "If I have powers, and how do you know that?" he asked unconvinced.

"People use meditation to clear their minds and search deeper into themselves to find something they did not know. We can use it for the same thing and help you become more aware of your abilities. It's just one more step of unlocking them," she explained.

Jase didn't move from the bed. "Sitting on the floor and focusing on my breath is supposed to help me find a deeper power inside me? I think I'll pass," he said.

"The longer you pretend they don't exist the harder it will be to unlock them," Skyrah pointed out. She then paused as if trying to figure out the best way to convince him. "At least give it a try? If nothing happens after an hour then we can stop, but you have to at least try. Do it for Kaimi?"

"Fine, but only an hour," he sighed.

"Agreed."

He moved down in front of her and sat cross-legged on the cold floor. "Now what?"

Skyrah rested her hands in her lap across from him. "Close your eyes and focus on clearing your mind. Focus on the air that is going in and out of your lungs."

Jase did as he was told, and breathed in and out of his nose. "What if I fall asleep?"

"I'll hit you," she said sternly.

Jase smiled, focusing his attention on his breathing. He visualized it going through his body, into his lungs, and circling back out into the cold, ventilated air that surrounded him. His mind focused on the humming of the lights overhead and the vibrations of the ship's hull. His ears picked up a different sound, one that was at first distant but a constant rhythm in front of him. He realized it was the beating of the Princess's heart. It was soft and calm almost soothing to him as Jase listened to the thump, thump, thump of its melody. He visualized what he thought her heart would look like. The picture in his mind was calming as he felt the strange sensation of a tingly feeling through his fingertips as he meditated.

"Jase?" the Princess's voice sounded distant to him.

Jase ignored it as he watched the outline of her heart move around in his mind.

"Jase," her voice echoed again in his mind.

He felt the tingling in his fingertips increase in his arms which began to blur the image of the Princess in his mind. It became hard to focus and Jase slowly opened his eyes, feeling lightheaded as he did. He could see the Princess in front of him with a strange blue orb of light in front of her but his vision was fuzzy as he closed his eyes again to adjust to the light. He opened them again to see clearer, and noticed the orb was in between them. "What is—" but before he could finish his sentence the orb vanished and his vision went black as he felt himself fall backwards onto the floor.

"Jase? Jase??? Are you okay?? Can you hear me?" the Princess's voice echoed frantically in the swirling darkness around him.

He couldn't move or feel anything except numbness as he lay in darkness, listening to the Princess somewhere above him. He wanted to yell out to her, but couldn't move so he waited for it to wear off. Where was he? What was going on? Was he dying? These questions caused him to feel the chilly claws of fear grip at him as he wondered if he was ever going to see light again. If he was ever going to wake up again as the Princess's voice slowly receded in his ears until he could faintly hear it at all.

"Relax, Bluestar. You are not dying," came a strange voice in the darkness around him.

Jase searched around him in the darkness for the source. He couldn't see anything or anyone as he felt a sudden heaviness press against his body.

"If you don't relax the pressure will increase. Focus on your breathing. Breathe, Jase. Breathe," the voice softly commanded in the air around him.

Jase tried quieting the panic in his heart as he focused on his breath. He pictured his lungs in his chest and slowly tried taking a breath and let it out. He repeated the process over and over until he started to feel the pressure lift off his body. Once the numbness in his limbs and face diminished, the feeling returned to his body and the darkness around him changed into an endless room with rays of light illuminated some areas. Jase realized he was in one of these beams as he examined the strange place searching for the voice from before.

"Hello? Hello? Are you still there?" he called out in wonder.

"I am," the voice answered.

Jase searched around for the source but found none as he stood alone in the strange endless room. "Where are you? Why can't I see you?" he asked.

"I am here, but you are not ready to see me," the voice answered back.

"Why not?" Jase asked confused.

"Because you choose not to see, Jase Bluestar," the voice replied.

"I'm not sure what you mean," he said bewildered by the enigma the voice spoke.

"You cannot see me if you dissociate your true self with how you view yourself. I can't show you if you don't believe, Jase," the voice spoke.

Jase searched the ceiling. "I don't understand," he responded trying to find the source.

"In time you will," the voice replied.

Suddenly, the air went dark blinding Jase as he felt someone shaking him violently. He could feel the cold air claw at him as he slowly opened his eyes, coming to, and saw the Princess above him, shaking his shoulders. Her mouth formed words that he couldn't quite make out against the ringing in his ears. His head pounded as he slowly sat up.

"Jase? Jase? Are you okay? Jase, are you listening to me? Are you okay? Give me a sign," the Princess questioned with a hand on his shoulder to get his attention.

The ringing in his ears subsided as he gave a slight nod, finding his voice. "Yeah, I'm fine," he replied.

"You're not fine," Kaimi's voice said as Jase eyed the Princess's data watch to find her watching him with concern. "You look drained."

Jase laid back down on the cold floor, closing his eyes again. "What happened?" he asked.

"Somehow during mediation, you were able to channel your abilities outward whether you meant to or not," Skyrah responded.

"Abilities?" Jase rubbed between his eyes, pinching his nose.

"You're abilities as a Bluestar. You unknowingly called them forward to create a ball of light. You passed out because your body is not used to such power and it took its effect on your strength."

"I am a late bloomer," he joked as he tried to relieve the tension inside his skull.

Kaimi and the Princess chuckled in relief as Kaimi agreed, "Yes, you are. With proper training and focus, your body could become strong enough to handle your abilities. You will have to take it slow and get used to it."

"If you try to use them before your strong enough, it could kill you," Skyrah informed him grimly.

Jase opened his eyes and slowly sat up again. "I need food," he said and started to leave the room.

"Jase," Skyrah called after him.

He turned his head sideways and with a tired smirk, said, "Don't worry, I won't do anything crazy. I got it." He then walked out of the room and headed towards the mess hall.

A New Planet

Jase's head was still pounding as he tried to make sense of what had happened. He could hear the footsteps of the Princess following behind him and figured she, as well as Kaimi, wouldn't let him out of their sight until they were sure he was well again.

He passed the circular booth and crossed over to the pantry grabbing a bag of something labeled "Zuk" before sitting down. The Princess and Kaimi joined him at the table, watching him carefully.

"Jase, are you sure you are alright?" Kaimi asked softly, her voice filled with concern.

Jase swallowed another handful of tasteless biscuits and examined the blue bag with its bold letters. "Yes, I'm fine. What are these?" he asked.

"They are a favorite snack of bulbs and Prokleos, usually," Princess Skyrah explained. "You probably won't taste anything, The flavor is so slight that your taste buds won't pick it up."

Jase examined one of the small brown biscuits before placing it int his mouth. "Explains why I don't taste anything," he said.

"Believe it or not, they are extremely rich in flavor to other species," Kaimi told him.

Jase's thoughts turned back to the voice. It had to be a dream. He had to be dreaming, what else would it be? "Who was the last Bluestar to serve your family, Skyrah?" he asked suddenly.

"Sir Agin Rex. He was a knight and grew up in the castle with my older sisters. His father was head of the royal guard, and Agin took over after his death in the war," she told him.

"What happened to him? Did he die in the war?" Jase pressed.

Skyrah seemed to be in deep in thought as she stared at her fingers clasped together on the round table. "If I remember correctly, he died protecting my father from a Redstar plasma canon during a space battle even though he knew his power was insufficient to stand against it. His sacrifice gave my father enough time to evade capture from the Androids. He considered Agin one of the most honorable soldiers he had ever known."

"Is Redstar dust more powerful than blue?" Jase inquired considering the effects of both Bluestars and red.

Skyrah looked unsure as she responded, "Perhaps. I don't know for sure. Those born under the Redstar don't typically have abilities like you do. They are more average. Though, it's true that weapons built with the Redstar plasma are stronger than most weapons but no Redstar has ever bore abilities like a Bluestar in all of history."

"Lord Brohain—he has Redstar in him, doesn't he?" Jase pointed out, remembering that the Android wasn't like the others.

"Yes, but he is an Android. A machine built by the Ancients who had a vast knowledge of the stars. Lord Brohain somehow knows the secret to using the Redstar powers within him," Kaimi corrected.

"If I went up against him, do you think I would win?" Jase asked trying to understand the reciprocal forces between the stars.

Skyrah was silent as Kaimi looked to her for the answer. After studying him for a moment, she said assertively, "No, I don't think so."

"Someday, Jase, but not now. You aren't ready," Kaimi added.

Jase nodded, figuring as much. Skyrah stood from the booth smoothing out the wrinkles in her tunic as she did. "I am going to lie down for a bit," she said as she excused herself from the table and glided effortlessly out of the room towards the crew quarters. They waited until she was out of earshot before Jase whispered to Kaimi,

"Kaimi, when I blacked out I had the strangest dream. Yet, it didn't feel like a dream. It felt real, as real as you and I."

Kaimi moved closer to him on the table. "What did you see?" she questioned.

152

Jase pictured the endless room in his mind, trying to remember everything. "It was like a room but there was no end to it, and it was dark at first. There was this strange voice that kept telling me to relax and breathe, but at the same time I could hear Skyrah calling my name in the distance. There was this incredible pressure weighing against me, but when I finally relaxed, it went away and the room got brighter. And the strange voice got louder as he spoke to me."

"What did he say?" she asked leaning in.

Jase thought hard, but couldn't remember. His head still hurt slightly and thinking didn't help. "He said something along the lines of, *How can you see me if you dissociate your true self with how you see yourself as? I can't show you if you don't believe.* I could only hear the voice and not see the source of it. It was quite strange, Kaimi, but it had to be just me dreaming, right?"

"Perhaps," Kaimi replied thoughtfully. "I'm not sure, Jase. I know very little about Bluestars, but perhaps we might be able to find something out when we reach the Resistance. I could ask the Princess her thoughts on the matter if you want."

Jase shook his head, not wanting to sound childish to the Princess. "No, no, it's fine. It's probably nothing but a strange dream," he said.

Kaimi hesitated, but said no more to what she was thinking. "Very well, but if it happens again, let me know."

"I will, but I doubt it will happen again," he told her then finished eating the last of the biscuits.

Over the next couple of weeks, Jase spent his time training with Skyrah to hone his fighting skills for when they departed ways. He was slowly improving and every now and then, he'd actually land a hit. His bruises would fade in time to create new ones but it never bothered him. When he wasn't sparring with Skyrah, he played against Tahmela in StarCastleCapture in hopes to be able to beat the Princess the next match they played against each another. Whatever chance he got he spent it with Kaimi knowing that things would be changing once they reached the Resistance. He was happy to be off the small ship soon, but at the same time, not ready to say goodbye to Kaimi and their time together.

Jase and Skyrah were in the middle of a sparring exercise when Tahmela announced over the PA system, "Nearing the planet, Kurath Thor, now."

Jase caught the Princess's leg midair and looked towards the door. A sudden anticipation filled him at the thought of being off the ship and on a new planet. "We're finally here," he exclaimed releasing Skyrah's leg and running out to the cockpit.

"Careful you don't hurt yourself," Kaimi said cheerfully as he burst into the cockpit where Tahmela sat at the helm.

Tahmela looked up startled by Jase's entrance then turned back to the controls. "Be hour till we touch down," he informed him.

Jase couldn't contain his excitement as he moved into the co-pilot's chair and fixed his eyes on the small green planet before him. Three dark purple moons rotated around the forest planet, each moving slowly as they danced around one another. The planet was so thicketed with vegetation that it appeared to be devoid of water, an ethereal, emerald orb blanketed among its many moons. "There is water on the planet, right?" Jase asked astonished by the span of the forests.

"There's trees, isn't there?" Tahmela laughed, inputting data in the navigational charts that changed the course of the ship.

"There are no large bodies of water but many rivers and lakes which are covered by the massive trees," Kaimi answered him.

"That's why the Elves are able to stay here, hidden from the Androids," Jase said enlightened.

Kaimi appeared on the holographic screen. "Exactly. This is the homeland of the Elves. They know it better than anyone in the galaxy. It would be a losing battle for someone to try and attack them while they remain here. With the forest, it's impossible to locate and track them even with A.I. technology. Only a few know their whereabouts and less than that know where exactly their cities are."

"Do you know where they are?" he asked her, noticing Tahmela paid no attention to them.

Kaimi smiled. "I don't."

"But the Princess does?"

"In some ways, yes," Skyrah answered, walking into the room to join them.

Jase turned his chair surprised by her sudden appearance. "What does that mean?" he asked.

"I know a general area where they might be," she admitted slowly.

Jase was baffled. "Wait, you said you knew where the elves were so we could drop you off and they could take you back to the Resistance! Now you are saying you *might* know where they could be? Are you serious? You expect us to just follow after you through that jungle in hopes we don't get lost?"

"You don't have to come. Just drop Kaimi and myself off and be on your way, Bluestar," the Princess retorted annoyed.

Jase shook his head as he turned back to the planet. "Yeah, and watch you get eaten by who-knows-what down there."

"I think it's safe to say, I'd last longer than you would," she mocked smugly.

"Maybe, but the last thing you tried to kill, didn't go as planned, so I wouldn't count on it," Jase countered, resting his foot on his knee and leaning back in his chair.

"Cool it, you two," Kaimi scolded, then turned to the bulb. "Where do you plan on landing?"

Tahmela remained focused on the planet ahead of them. "Tree branch maybe," he replied. "If big as you say then won't be hard to land there. Best bet with thick jungle here."

"I suppose that's our only option now," Kaimi agreed with him.

Jase glanced over at the Princess. "They at least know you're coming, right?"

The Princess suddenly appeared uncomfortable. "Not exactly, no. I didn't know how to get in contact with them. When I last came, after the fall of Faton, my sisters and I landed with my best friend who knew the ways of the forest. She guided us to the cities but I have no idea which way to go. Only the elves can interpret the forest and its ways."

"What about when they helped during the war?" Jase questioned.

"They always came to our planet, or whatever planet we were on at the time. Never once did we come here. It wasn't allowed," she replied stoically.

"So they might kill us for trespassing? Awesome! This should be quite an adventure!" Jase exclaimed sarcastically turning his back on her.

Skyrah became irritated again as she exasperatedly proclaimed, "Look, I might not know a lot about where they are, but I will find them. With or without your help."

Jase couldn't believe she lied to them, but he noticed Kaimi giving him one of her notorious looks to patch things up with the Princess. He hung his head for a moment, knowing he had no choice and smirked, "I didn't say I wouldn't help you, Princess. I just was reciting the facts of what we know."

Tahmela suddenly interrupted. "You hmils take seats now. Entering the atmosphere soon," he advised.

Jase buckled himself into the co-pilot chair while the Princess buckled into the chair by the navigation screen. After a short while, the ship started descending towards the planet causing the wind to roar around its outer shell as it rattled and shook downwards. The full effect of gravity pulled Jase's body down causing him to feel as if he'd turn into goo and slide out of the chair at any second.

"You're thrusters are only at 50%," Kaimi proclaimed to Tahmela, reading the numbers on the screen.

Tahmela flipped a switch as he steered the spacecraft eastward in the bright sky. "It'll be fine," he said.

Jase stared out the cockpit window, watching fluffy clouds disappear revealing the dark emerald forest below, its enormous trees barely reaching the heavens. The early afternoon sky was pale blue as they leveled out above the tall trees. Jase felt like he wasn't close enough to see everything as he asked, "Is it safe to unbuckle now?"

"Yes, we are in the clear," Kaimi confirmed.

Jase grinned at her as he quickly unbuckled and hurried out of the cockpit towards the viewing sphere to get a better look at the planet. The doors slid open and he quickly entered, pressing the panel to open up the hatch that was around the glass. The metal blast shield spiraled open, revealing the dark green forest down below his feet. Even from this high the trees appeared gargantuan and only continued to grow as they hovered closer to the surface. Jase stared in awe at the tropical trees with their branches outstretched around them to drink the sunlight and was amazed at their size.

Jase looked below his feet to see if he could see the forest floor, but couldn't with how dense the forest was. He wondered what kind of creatures lurked below hidden within the trees. His thoughts were racing with questions as Kaimi suddenly spoke in his earpiece.

"I knew you'd be excited seeing another planet other than your own," she said.

Jase took it all in. "It's so different from Faton. There's so much green."

He could feel Kaimi's smile as she spoke. "Kurath Thor is very different from Faton. It will also be more dangerous here than Otect City so you must be alert at all times. There are darker things lurking in the shadows than one would think."

"Don't worry, Kaimi." he assured her. "I'll protect you."

"I'm sure you will," Kaimi replied amused.

Curious on how all the trees grew where there was so much competition and not a lot of water, Jase asked, "How can all the trees grow with so little water?"

"I'm not entirely sure. Not many travel to this planet that leave alive. Therefore we don't know a lot about the planet except for the elves being here. The trees are too dense to use any smart technology to map the area so it's perfect place to remain hidden if one wants to be," Kaimi replied.

Jase crossed his arms, thinking. "Maybe I'll ask the elves when we see them," he said.

"They would be more reliable," she agreed.

Jase suddenly wondered if Kaimi would be okay traveling with them in the trees. "Will you be able to be with us down there or will you have to remain in the ship?"

Kaimi seemed to think for a moment before replying. "I should be able to travel with you like normal. I just won't be able to talk to both you and the Princess at the same time. I'll remain on your frequency until we are out of the forest or back on the ship."

"I'm glad," he admitted with a smile. "I don't want to travel through this place without you, if we were being honest."

He could feel Kaimi blush at his words. "Well, I can't let you go getting into trouble without me, can I?" she laughed.

"No, I guess not. You know I don't have any way of defending myself if we come across something deadly while in the forest," he told her suddenly realizing he was weaponless.

"I'm sure Tahmela can help you with that. You should go ahead and take your seat. We will be landing soon," she told him as if she was reading something.

Out of habit, Jase nodded his head and pressed the panel to close the viewing window again. He walked back to the cockpit where the others were still looking out the windshield. The Princess had moved to the co-pilot chair and was speaking to Tahmela about where he was landing when Jase took a seat at the navigation screen.

"You should be close enough," Princess Skyrah was telling Tahmela.

Tahmela gave a sharp nod and without looking back, asked Jase, "Are you buckled in, hmil?"

"Yeah, I'm all good back here," he announced.

"Good," Tahmela then brought the ship down towards one of the larger trees in the area and slowly descended towards its thick branches, The ship slowly glided downwards before hovering above a single branch as Tahmela released the docking legs. He landed with a loud thump against the wood as it settled down on all fours before switching off the engine. "Piece of cake," he said waving a hand.

"How are we supposed to get down and back up after we are done here?" Jase asked.

Skyrah spun around to face him. "The elves have done it a million times so I'm sure we will come up with something," she said.

"In other words, you have no idea," Jase implied with a grin.

The Princess made a face as she stood from her seat. "We should get going while there is still daylight left," she proclaimed then left the room.

Jase turned to Tahmela. "She really doesn't like me sometimes," he admitted amused.

Tahmela chuckled. "No kidding, hmil."

"You do have weapons so we can defend ourselves while we are out there, right?" Jase asked him.

Tahmela nodded his head and motioned him to follow as he walked out of the cockpit. "You stupid for not bringing own, Blustar," he remarked.

"I've never needed to defend myself before with weapons," Jase replied as he followed the short bulb to the cargo hold. They walked to the back lockers where Tahmela pressed a few buttons on a keypad to unlock it. The door opened, revealing a weapon cache. There were a few plasma grenades, plasma rifle, plasma pistols, a combat knife and a steel gauntlet.

Tahmela grabbed one of the handguns and handed it to him. "Here. Only gun you can handle and not kill yourself with," he teased.

Jase hesitantly accepted the gray and black gun. "How do I use it?" he asked examining it in the light.

Tahmela strapped on a silver plasma rifle across his chest, replying, "Point, shoot, charge. Hold button on side to charge. Press again to release. Longer you hold stronger blast will be, but will also deplete ammo quickly so be careful."

Jase gave a nod then holstered the weapon on his right hip. "Thanks, Tahmela. You're a life saver."

Tahmela grabbed another plasma handgun and a pair of googles before securing the locker. "I like making fun of you, Bluestar. It be boring if you died," he said haphazardly.

Jase smiled in return as he followed the bulb out of the cargo hold and towards the exiting ramp. When they arrived, the Princess had already lowered the ramp and was waiting outside for them to join her. Jase stepped off the ship onto the wide wooden branch. The branch was twice the size of the ship with enough room to walk around without having to worry about falling off. Jase was stunned at how large the tree was as it towered over him with the sun shining through its green leaves. The leaves were large enough to wrap around one's body twice if needed to.

"Welcome to Kurath Thor," Kaimi stated in his ear as he stood marveling at the beauty.

"You should see your face," Tahmela stated with laughter, his black googles covered his enormous black eyes.

Jase gazed across the endless span of branches on the horizon. "Is everything this big on the planet?"

"Not everything, but most," Princess Skyrah replied also staring across the way. "We should be careful, though. There aren't many beasts here, but the ones that are masters of disguise and are dark creatures that should not be met."

He peered down over the edge of the branch to see the forest floor, but only saw more branches and darkness that hindered his vision. "So how are we going to get down from here?" he asked.

Princess Skyrah pointed to the trunk of the tree. "There seems to be ridges large enough to travel to the forest floor. They are our best shot for now."

Tahmela handed over his plasma handgun to the Princess. "In case you need backup," he stated motioning to the one she already had strapped on her waist.

She thanked him and headed towards the base of the tree with Tahmela waddling behind her. Jase glanced back towards the ship. "What about the ship? We are just going to leave it here?" he asked Kaimi.

"We are on an isolated planet that only elves are known to live on and they don't care for technology as much as others do," Kaimi assured him.

Jase followed after the others towards the trunk where the Princess was examining it for a way down. The ridges were wide enough to use as foot and hand holds while climbing down to the forest floor.

"Alright, this is how we will get down. Climbing will be faster than slowly edging our way down around the tree," the Princess stated. "I'll go first."

Jase peered over the edge to the long drop. "Be careful," he warned.

"Careful, Bluestar, it sounded like for a moment you actually cared about my wellbeing," the Princess smiled caught off guard by Jase's genuine concern.

"Who am I supposed to annoy if you aren't here? Besides, I didn't get banished from my home planet for helping you just so you can die here," he replied.

"If you say so," Princess Skyrah teased and turned her back against them as she slowly started descending down the tree.

Tahmela gave Jase a knowing look and teased. "Not girlfriend, eh, hmil?"

Jase shook his head then moved to the trunk. He took one last look down below before he started descending down the rough bark. "I have a feeling this is going to be more tiring than climbing all those levels in the castle," he commented to Kaimi.

He could feel her smile in her words as she spoke, "You will be a pro at climbing by the time you get back there."

"Yeah, no kidding," he remarked as he hugged the tree, balancing his foot on the narrow ridge while using his hands to grip above his head and climbed after the Princess. With Tahmela bringing up the rear, they carefully made their descent towards the forest floor.

Kurath Thor

Jase could feel sweat coating his limbs as the afternoon sun scorched his back in the humid air. He wished he had taken off his pilot's jacket before he started climbing and now regretted not doing so as he moved another foot onto the ridge below him. He wasn't sure how long they had been climbing, but it felt like it was taking them forever to reach the ground floor. They climbed in silence, too focused to bother with one another. Even Kaimi didn't say much, knowing she'd only distract Jase from the task at hand if she did. Jase kept all of his attention on climbing and ignoring the unbearable heat that was making him irritable. His fingers were aching from gripping tightly on the rough bark and his body was soaked in sweat which slowly rolled down his back.

"Careful! Some of the bark down here is rotting. Be cautious on what you grab!" shouted the Princess from below.

Jase paused for a moment to catch his breath and peered between his legs to see how far she was from him. She was clearly moving a lot faster than they were and was a ways down from Jase. *No wonder she wanted to be the first one down*, he thought to himself and peered up to see Tahmela. The bulb was ten feet above him moving at a slower pace than Jase.

"Are you doing okay?" Kaimi asked, noticing he had stopped.

Jase carefully wiped sweat off his forehead onto one of his sleeves as he tried to steady his breathing. "As good as I can be at the moment," he replied.

"Take it slow and you will be down in no time," Kaimi motivated.

Jase rested his head against the tree bark. "Slow and steady wins the race," he said.

"Exactly! Well, in some races," she responded.

Jase took a deep breath then exhaled before taking a step down to the next ridge. Suddenly the bark under his foot broke off and he quickly grabbed on tight to the ridge as he tried to locate another foothold.

"Are you okay?!" Princess Skyrah shouted from below as pieces of the bark fell passed her towards the earth floor.

Every fiber in his body seemed to come alive from the close call. He no longer felt the aches or pains from before as he held onto the side of the tree for dear life.

"Jase?!" Princess Skyrah called up again. "Are you okay?!"

Concerned, Kaimi asked, "What's wrong? You aren't moving. Is something wrong, Jase?"

Trying to convince himself that he was okay, Jase managed to summon his voice again to reply. "Yup! All good up here! Just wanted to see if you actually cared!" he joked to Skyrah in hopes to hide that he was scared half to death. He then replied to Kaimi, "Nothing, I'm good. The bark under my foot broke off and for a moment I was close to dying but I'm fine now."

"Please be careful," Kaimi urged.

He then heard the Princess mumble something he couldn't make out before she shouted back in return, "Trust me, I was more worried about Kaimi's wellbeing than you!"

"Sure you were, " he said to himself as he started climbing downward again. "Tahmela! Be careful down here! The bark is breaking!" Jase heard the bulb grumble something in his own language in response and turned his attention back to climbing.

Suddenly, a loud crack ran through the air as pieces of bark showered down on Jase as he heard Tahmela shriek past him! Jase brought his feet up against the tree in a crouch before pushing off and flipping backwards as he dove headfirst after the alien. The wind rushed past his face, howling in his ears as he fell after the bulb. He didn't know what made him dive after the bulb in the first place. It's not like he could do anything to save him yet here he was acting like an idiot hero to save the day. His thoughts suddenly turned their focus on the one important task to save Tahmela. He was determined to do just that and he'd figure the rest out later.

He zoomed past Princess Skyrah, picking up speed but managed to hear her frantically shout after him, "Jase!"

"Jase, what are you doing?" Kaimi suddenly asked in his ear.

Jase was almost in reach of the bulb as he yelled over the howling wind, "Tahmela fell, and I'm apparently saving him."

"How are you supposed to stop once you get him?!" Kaimi pointed out angrily.

"Didn't think it through," Jase admitted almost in arm reach of Tahmela. He forced his arms out in front of him, fighting against the wind as he reached to grab the bulb. He was so close, yet still out of reach. Almost there. Almost.... Jase finally grabbed hold of Tahmela and pulled him against his body.

"Uyqa fey xarotx kadc!" Tahmela frantically prayed along with many other curses that Jase couldn't understand.

Jase held him close, yelling over the howling wind as they continued to fall, "Don't worry! I got us!" He then searched around to see if any branches were close enough for him to grab onto but none were near. To get a better view, Jase flipped them right side up, realizing they were running out of time. The forest floor was now coming to view below them. Suddenly everything was in slow motion for him. Tahmela screeching in his ear as he squeezed Jase, Jase's eyes stared up at the sun shining through the leaves, suddenly aware of how hot its rays were against his face. He noticed the light breeze that was softly brushing across the giant leaves that he did not feel since the wind around him was thunderous in its touch. It was then that he suddenly realized how angry he was at himself for thinking he could just jump off a tree and try to save the falling bulb. What had made him to do such a thing?

"Jase! Jase! Focus!" Kaimi reprimanded him again in his ear.

He squeezed his eyes shut. His stomach felt like it was in his throat and his heart was beating out of his chest. He could barely register the thought of Mrs. Rose or the kids but saw their image in his head before it disappeared with the terrifying thought of *This is it*. This is how he was going to die. A grand stupid death clinging onto a screeching bulb because he hadn't used his brain. He should have listened to Kaimi. Why didn't he ever listen to her before jumping head first into things? He should have listened.

The thought of Kaimi being by herself suddenly filled his body with new determination. He couldn't leave her alone not after all they had been through together. She left the Resistance to protect him for all those years and this was how he would repay her? By dying? No! He would make sure she fulfilled her promise to Skyrah and the others. He needed to help her do that. He would help her do that.

Jase felt his whole body start tingling as his senses came alive within him. The wind howled past him, the fear of death coursed through his veins. He had the sudden urge to jerk his body forward in the air and, without a thought, listened to it. Using all his might, he flung himself forward not expecting anything to come from it, but something did! He suddenly felt the strangest sensation of something slippery under his feet as he slid forward clumsily towards the nearest branch. It happened so fast that before he knew what was going on, he lost balance and both Jase and Tahmela fell forward, crashing onto the rough branch and rolled across it from the momentum.

They continued rolling towards the other side where Tahmela started to fall off again, but Jase quickly grabbed hold of him as he dug his free hand into the tough bark to keep from falling himself. Just as he was sure they would fall to their deaths again, Princess Skyrah appeared and grabbed on to his arm.

"I got you, Tahmela!" Jase assured him out of breath while holding on as he felt lightheaded.

Tahmela grumbled back in his own tongue. "Ona tel oni falinia, u'ella heny ru xartox strahrefae ona oulle!"

"I'm going to pretend that's you thanking me," Jase commented back as he laid on his back.

Princess Skyrah slammed his shoulders into the ground, outraged. "You idiot! You could have gotten yourself killed! What were you thinking!" she yelled.

"Obviously, he wasn't," Kaimi replied appearing on the Princess's data watch as Jase and Tahmela laid on the branch for a moment to catch their breaths.

Jase could still feel his body trembling from the near death experience, but joked. "Don't get mad at me that you were too slow to save him," he said before questioning Kaimi. "Also when did you move to her data watch? I thought you couldn't."

"When you were about to die. It was harder than you think," she replied angrily.

The Princess flared as she exclaimed in mocking disbelief, "Oh, you mean by jumping off to catch him and not having a plan on how to save yourself afterwards is an idea I would be jealous of? You are insane!"

Jase stood to his feet, feeling lightheaded as he responded, "It worked, didn't it?"

"Barely!" Skyrah blurted out as she touched her data watch to Jase's so Kaimi could transfer over. "If I wasn't here to save you then you'd both be dead."

Jase crossed his arms, grinning to annoy her. "So it's a good thing we are a team," he said.

Princess Skyrah made frustrated incoherent noises as she turned away, storming off towards the end of the branch. "I'm going to kill you, I swear," he heard her say.

"Jase Bluestar, you just couldn't thank her. Why do you always make things harder than they should be?" Kaimi said suddenly in his ear again.

Jase watched Skyrah travel down the branch again. "How am I supposed to thank her when she is calling me an idiot?" he asked.

"By thanking her for saving your idiot life! Jase, you are so reckless at times that it makes me wonder how you're still alive," she confessed to him.

He felt sorry for worrying her as he softly apologized, "I'm sorry, Kaimi. I know it's hard to be with me when I'm reckless. I'll start thinking more, but it's not like I mean to do it. It was just instinct to try saving Tahmela. It just happened before I knew it."

"You're lucky you made it out alive, but don't do it again, Jase. Even your luck will run out at some point," she told him.

Jase stared up the tree where they fell as his thoughts turned to the strange sensation he had experienced before landing on the branch. Clearly the Princess and Tahmela didn't see what happened that caused them to land on the branch in the first place. "Yeah...must have been luck," he said quietly.

"Bluestar," Tahmela's voice disrupted his thoughts. "I owe you my life. Mine is yours to take. U, Tahmela Zing, offeil ona, Jase Bluestar, pe lephae edu ukorerow ta dea es ona saseaen feieta," he said in a slight bow.

Kaimi translated. "He offered a life debt to you for saving his life. It's a high honor to receive such a thing. It would be a great dishonor if you refuse," she said.

Jase was speechless, not knowing what to say in return. He wasn't quite aware of how honorable it was and didn't want to offend the bulb. "I don't know what to say," he confessed honestly to Tahmela.

Tahmela responded with a sly smirk. "Just accept it, stupid," he replied.

Jase grinned and held out his hand to him. "I accept then."

The bulb took it then turned to follow after the Princess. Jase watched him leave as Kaimi explained, "He won't leave your side now, you know?"

"What do you mean?" he asked.

"His life debt to you won't allow it. A life debt is the highest honor in many cultures so by proposing one to someone only happens when their life has been saved from certain death or if they truly believe in one's soul. You saved Tahmela's life, therefore he gave up his freedom to do as he pleases to instead protect you at all costs, no matter what. His life and ship is yours until death takes one of you," she further explained.

Jase suddenly felt the weight of Tahmela's choice and it made him feel as if he didn't deserve it. "I can't accept it then," he said in disbelief.

"You must. It would destroy him if you didn't," Kaimi told him.

"I don't want him to give up everything to be my slave," Jase argued quietly to her without moving to join the others who waited patiently by the tree trunk for him.

Kaimi firmly replied, "He's not your slave, Jase. He knew what he was doing when he offered his life to you. The only way he can be your slave is depending on how you treat him."

"Can I release him from his debt to me?" he asked.

Kaimi was slow to respond. "Yes, but it would be dishonorable towards him," she said, pausing for a moment. "Sometimes it doesn't matter how you feel about something or someone, Jase. You have to decide if showing someone respect and honor their beliefs is best for them over your own feelings."

Jase knew she was right. He didn't like the idea of having someone's life in his hands, but it would be the honorable thing to do to accept it whether he agreed with it or not. If Tahmela signed his life over to him then Jase would protect it as best as he could. He'd treat him as a friend and nothing less than that. " I'll show him the respect he deserves and honor his wishes." His thoughts then turned back to the strange sensation again that he had felt and wondered if he should bring it up to Kaimi.

"You should catch up with the others before they start without you," she suggested.

Jase decided he would keep his thoughts to himself for now and tell her later as he hurried after the others who were talking to one another by the base of the tree waiting on him.

Utikicra Bird

The Princess was in the lead with Tahmela following close behind and Jase at the rear as they descended downward for another hour before finally taking a break among the tree's branches. Jase sat with his legs hanging over the side of the branch as he watched the late afternoon sun climb through the sky, slowly. His whole body ached from the strain of climbing. The fall had brought them down a ways a lot faster and he could now see the forest floor below. He gazed upward towards the sky, noticing a black dot flying overhead as he asked Kaimi, "How much longer do you think it will be till we reach the bottom?"

"Given the height of the tree and the rate of how fast you climb, probably another three hours and twenty minutes," she said in response.

Jase stared out across the lower levels of the trees. "I don't know if I can last another three hours of climbing. My arms and legs feel like Jell-O," he said shaking his appendages in demonstration.

"You'll have to climb with Jell-O hands, then," Princess Skyrah said plopping down next to him. Her face appeared to be darker than when they first started from the sun and she had strands of hair dangling in front of her face as beads of sweat ran down her forehead. If she was exhausted, she didn't show it as she continued, "We have to reach the bottom before nightfall."

Jase peered below at the forest floor. "Is it not safer being up here than down there at night?"

"Even in the trees like this one, we are easy prey for night beasts. It will be safer on ground level," she told him.

Jase regarded her closely. "How long were you on this planet before?"

"Handful of days at the most, but I learned most of what was on it from my best friend who would tell me stories when I was younger about the forest and beasts. They were terrifying, but wondrous at the same time, and I always wanted to come back with her to explore them," she paused for a moment as if caught in a memory from the past. He watched her, wondering what she was thinking of until she snapped out of it, adding, "It's also a Princess's job to learn about the planets in her galaxy if she is to rule them."

"You're telling me you know all the planets in our galaxy? Isn't that impossible?" he asked, not believing her.

"My family has been ruling this galaxy for two thousand years, Jase Bluestar. We make ourselves familiar with the basics of each planet, such as what race lives there, what language they speak, the climate, who's ruling it, trading options, and resources. What we don't know we turn to the Ancients," she replied.

"What will you do now without them?" he asked curious on how she would rule without their guidance.

"We have their records to learn from. All is not lost, Jase. My family was taught about the important planets in each solar system of Orbane as well as the other five main galaxies that are surroundings ours. As of right now, that's all that I need to know," she seemed to recite as she showed no wavering of emotion.

Jase couldn't imagine what it was like to have to learn so much in order to rule or what being a prince would even be like. It had to be harder than living on the streets, he thought as he turned his attention back to the trees. "I feel like we are never going to get down from here," he said changing the subject. "I'm almost tempted to jump again. At least it was faster."

The Princess smiled, wiping away a bead of sweat from her forehead. "I'm not going to lie, I was tempted to push you off earlier."

Jase laughed, not surprised. "I'd deserve it for sure. Sorry for that," he said apologetically. "And thank you for saving us from falling again."

"We are even now," she said in response.

He grinned to her. "Agreed." Tahmela had fallen asleep against the trunk of the tree using a torn leaf as a blanket. Jase wasn't sure how he could sleep in this heat, but figured his race was built to adapt. "He looks so cozy."

The Princess turned to see what he was looking at and stared at the bulb in silence for a few minutes. She seemed to be in thought as she watched him then turned back and stared at the leaves around them. Jase could tell she was figuring something out, but didn't know what exactly as he asked, "What is it?"

She stood from her feet, her eyes searching the leaves. "What if we rode a leaf to the forest floor? It would be difficult, but we could land on the ground in half the time it would take us to climb down."

Jase looked around at the leaves wondering if it would work. "It might work as long as we don't hit any branches. Kaimi, if we took a leaf to the ground, would we survive the fall?"

"It would be a rough landing. You'd have to be careful not to fall off while on the way, but yes, there is a slight chance you'd survive. Seventy percent you'd fall off and thirty, you'd reach the bottom."

Jase stood to his feet. "I'm not totally against those odds," he shrugged. "Might as well try it out."

"I mean, we only have to worry about not falling off. We will be fine," the Princess assured herself out loud and hurried to pick out a leaf.

"You didn't tell her the odds," Kaimi pointed out in his ear.

Jase looked back down at the forest below them. "I think it would be better that they don't know. You know, just in case they freak out on the way down," he said.

"I suppose you are right," Kaimi agreed.

Jase turned to Tahmela who was still asleep and yelled, "Tahmela! Time to go!"

The bulb slowly rose, rubbing dirt off his googles. "Climbing already?"

"No. Better idea!" Jase responded, following after the Princess who had stopped further down the branch to examine a leaf. She moved onward before carefully leaping over to a smaller branch and balanced on it. Jase hurried to reach her, hearing soft thuds of Tahmela behind him as they neared the Princess.

Skyrah tugged at a leaf, testing it to see if it would support her weight before leaping onto it. She disappeared behind its curled up sides as Jase waited patiently for her to reappear. Her head popped back out as she said, "Let's go!"

Jase grinned, gazing over at the bulb. "After you," he said motioning for Tahmela to get on.

Tahmela stared long and hard at the smaller branch he had to leap onto in order to reach the leaf. He didn't seemed sure that it would hold him, but with a nudge from Jase, shrugged off any remaining doubts as he slowly crossed over to it. Once he was close to the leaf, the Princess helped him climb over the curved sides before disappearing over it again. Jase carefully started over as well balancing himself on the narrow branch.

"Hurry up! We don't have all day, Bluestar," Princess Skyrah shouted from behind the leaf.

Jase countered, "Don't make me go slower!"

"Go any slower and we will leave you," she warned.

Kaimi's voice injected, "Don't rush yourself. We need you alive and on the leaf, not falling from it."

"Thanks, Kaimi." Jase stopped next to the leaf stem for a brief moment then leapt. He landed with a soft thud that bobbed the whole leaf.

"Now what?" the bulb questioned uneasily as he sat in the center.

The Princess unholstered her plasma gun, raising it towards the leaf stem attached to the branch. "Now we go down," she said as she carefully took aim.

"Wait!" Jase shouted grabbing hold of her arm. "What if we flip while floating down?"

"That is a likely possibility," Kaimi chimed in his ear.

Jase searched the curved sides of the leaf for something to hold onto while the Princess stated in return, "The gravity of the planet should hold us onto the leaf as we fall. It shouldn't flip."

Jase knelt down on the yellow spine of the leaf that webbed out towards the tips and touched it to see if it would be something they could hold onto. It was cool to the touch, but had nowhere to grab unless the leaf ripped while they fell. "But in case that doesn't work out, I'd rather have something I can hold onto for peace of mind," he said.

Appearing impatient, Princess Skyrah stated, "Look, we don't have time to waste seconds when it'll be dark soon. We will just have to chance it."

Jase stood back up, ignoring her while he searched the branches around him for anything to use. He didn't need all of a leaf, he just needed a piece to use as a parachute in case they flipped. "Hey, we could use—" he started saying until a high pitched call pierced the air. Suddenly, they were falling with the leaf towards the forest floor.

"Jase, I'm reading you are falling quicker than you should be," Kaimi's voice hammered in his ear, mixed with the sound of wind howling past him.

It took Jase a moment to realize where he was with all the twirling the leaf was doing as it fell. He was lying flat on his stomach against the surface of the leaf. He forced his head up slightly, fighting against gravity and saw that Tahmela wasn't far from him, laying on his back. Jase turned his attention to the Princess. She too was lying on her stomach with her face hidden from view as the wind caused her braided hair to wave violently in the air above her head. She appeared to be knocked out. Jase turned his attention back to Tahmela.

He noticed that the bulb was still staring above them but now pointing. Jase followed his finger upward, finding the source of what had caused them to fall out of control. It was a giant birdlike creature with long navy and forest green feathers. Its eyes were a red flame piercing the air as it dove after them. Jase felt panic as he realized that this creature must have been the black dot in the sky, stalking them earlier.

"Jase? Jase? Talk to me. Your pulse is racing and if you don't calm down, you could experience heart failure," Kaimi's voice rang out through the sound of roaring wind.

Jase could barely hear his own voice as he uttered, "Bird creature."

As if figuring out what he was talking about, Kaimi commanded, "Okay, calm down. You need to first calm your heart, Jase. Take some deep breaths for me, will ya?"

Jase did as he was told, but still felt like his heart was racing and, at any moment, would jump out of his chest.

"You can do this, Jase. Just calm down and think," Kaimi continued to assure him.

I got this, Jase stated in his mind as he took one last breath and focused on the beast heading their way. He knew he had to figure something out to stop the bird or somehow get him and his companions off the leaf alive. "Kaimi, what should I do?" he asked, looking around the leaf for anything to use to help him.

Kaimi was quiet for a moment. "Do you still have the gun Tahmela gave you?" she suddenly asked.

Jase flipped over onto his back to see the gun on his hip. "Yes!"

"Grab it and aim between the bird's eyes or under the beak. Whichever is more visible! That should be the weak spots on the creature," Kaimi ordered in his ear.

Jase forced himself to grab hold of the gun and aimed at the bird. Holding back the trigger just slightly, he watched the silver glow start to hum from the barrel and grow larger. When it was a large ball of plasma energy, he released it towards the bird but missed by several feet. He quickly recharged and fired again, but missed. Charging it again, Jase shot at the bird and soon Tahmela joined him firing several shots with his rifle. They continued while the bird swerved and dodged the blasts, getting closer and closer each time.

It dover closer to the leaf, pecking holes as it tried to get them. Jase was sure this was it and saw the Princess finally stir from her place on the leaf bed. He noticed the pool of blood where she had been lying and the steady stream dripping down her face as she pushed up on all fours. Before he could yell to her, the Princess stood and pulled out her gun as she aimed for the bird directly above her. With one steady hang, she charged her weapon then fired hitting the bird's left wing directly. The bird shrieked and pulled back a moment before diving once more towards the leaf, but the Princess was ready. She charged her weapon for the last time and fired, hitting the exact spot once more. The bird let out another painful shriek before flying away into the sea of branches.

Jase let out a yelp of happiness as he watched the bird retreat from them. His happiness was short lived as Skyrah collapsed next to him, slowly falling through one of the holes. Jase quickly rolled over, catching her in time around the waist and pulled her back up. Holding her to his chest, Jase was suddenly filled with a sense of protection over the Princess and was determined to keep her safe as they fell faster to what could be their deaths. "Kaimi, I need a way off the leaf," he yelled to Kaimi.

"Is the bird gone?" Kaimi asked over the sound of their descent.

"Yes! Skyrah scared it off for now!" he replied, unable to hear his own voice.

"Good," Kaimi responded relieved. "You are still falling too fast to land safely. You need to slow down your descent if you are going to survive."

"How do I do that?" he asked her.

"Get everyone to a side to flip it over like a parachute. The leaf will float at a slower rate despite the holes. It won't feel like it's slowing down, but trust me it will be enough to help you," she said.

Jase nodded and rolled over to the opposite side of the bulb. Grabbing hold of where the leaf's stem would have been, Jase held the Princess tightly against him with his free hand then yelled over the thunderous wind towards Tahmela, "We are going to flip it! Parachute!"

The bulb stared at him with a blank expression, unsure of what Jase was saying. Jase was about to say it again when suddenly a twig from a nearby tree erupted out of the center of the leaf causing them to stop falling for a brief second before tearing the leaf in two. Tahmela fell with one half out of sight as Jase gripped tightly to the Princess as they fell backwards off the leaf into darkness.

Darkness

Jase felt the impact as his back seemed to shatter inside his body. He hit a thin branch then continued falling in the air. He did his best to shield the Princess from as much harm as possible, slamming into another branch. He vaguely remembered hitting his head against something hard then falling onto a soft leaf which dipped down, sliding him off into another one and another one until finally hitting the ground. The breath was knocked out of him as sharp needles of pain pierced every fiber of his body. He laid motionless on the dirt floor with the Princess on top of him. He couldn't feel his arms wrapped around her body or even her weight. He felt nothing but pain as he stared at the light through the tree branches miles above him as he barely laid there breathing. It felt as if air was barely making it back to his lungs as he tried forcing himself to inhale.

His vision kept going in and out on him as he felt vibrations in his right ear that came and went, but he didn't care what it could be. All he wanted to do was to breathe. *Breathe. Breathe.* He begged himself, wanting to release the pressure in his chest. *For the love of the stars just breathe already.*

A shadowy figure blocked the light from his view, suddenly, as it stood over him. Jase stared at the figure, unable to move. He watched helplessly as the figure knelt down beside him, their violet pink eyes were soft as they reached out to touch him. Their hand suddenly halted over him and a blue shimmer rippled across the air surrounding his body and the Princess's. He couldn't see the figure's face but he didn't care at the moment. He again felt vibrations in his right ear once more bounce off his eardrum, but still couldn't make it out. Something inside him, told him that he needed to relax even through the pain. Jase was starting to feel lightheaded and dizzy as his vision flickered out once more. He saw the figure, then darkness, figure, darkness, then lastly he saw the light above him before his vision totally failed. There was nothing but darkness and pain. Pain. On and off pain is what he remembered as he floated in and out of consciousness before finally it ended and he fell into a peaceful slumber.

To Awake in an Elf Village

The first thing that Jase felt when he slowly started coming to was warm rays of sunlight bathing his face. Its warmth coursed through his body as he slowly stirred on what felt like a cloud. He could smell sweet honey nectar in the air around him as he blinked his eyes, trying to adjust to the sunlight. He realized he wasn't in the forest anymore. Instead, he was laying half-naked in a large flower with one of its petals lying over his body. The flower bed was set against a wooden wall with long windows that stretched from the ceiling to the floor. Through them, Jase could see the forest outside in the sunlight.

Slowly sitting up, Jase felt a sharp pinch in his back along with a sudden throbbing in his head causing his vision to fade for a moment. Regretting his actions, he cradled his head with his hand.

"You shouldn't be sitting up so fast," came a familiar voice next to him.

Jase squinted in the direction of the voice and saw Kaimi on a carved nightstand beside him sitting cross-legged on the data watch. "Now you tell me." He paused a moment, taking in a deep breath as the pain started to fade away. When he could think clearly, he asked, "Where are we?"

Kaimi smiled kindly to him. "We are safe in an elf village not too far from where you and the others landed. A nearby hunter found you and the Princess and brought us back here for help," she told him.

Jase studied the room he was in. The only other furniture was a wooden table with flowers carved into its legs, two chairs, a long colorful flower that seemed to be a sofa and a basin on the other side of the bed. "Where are the others?" he asked promptly.

"The Princess is being looked after in another healer's quarters, and Tahmela has yet to be found as far as I've been told," she replied.

Jase's eyes turned back to the bed he was in as he studied the petals, moving the blanket off. He realized he was lying in the bed of the flower which was amazingly softer than anything he ever felt. He noticed short, soft hairs on its under belly and ran his hand through them. "What do you mean Tahmela hasn't been found? He was with us when we fell," he asked stroking the hairs.

"It appears that you both got separated during the fall. The Princess fell with you, but Tahmela fell the other way and when the elf found you, she brought you immediately here," Kaimi explained.

"The elf didn't think to look around for any other beings?" Jase questioned.

"If anything it was my fault. I told her of Tahmela, but you and the Princess were more of a priority due to your injuries. Seeing that you both were close to death, I suggested that the hunter leave the bulb and take you both in for immediate attention. Once you were both safe here, they sent out someone to go look for him," she replied hanging her head apologetically.

Jase thought on it, not liking the idea of leaving someone behind but he knew Kaimi did the right thing. "I suppose you made the right choice, seeing that we were dying. Very well, I should help the search," he responded as he made an attempt to get out of bed.

"I think not," a voice Jase did not recognize floated through the room.

Jase turned to see a beautiful woman elf with olive skin walk gracefully over to his bed. He hadn't heard the door open as he studied the new visitor in his room. She had long peppered hair braided behind her with two smaller braids on either side of her face, stopping in the center of both cheeks that sunk into her skin just slightly. She was thin and wore a fitted privilege green tunic that had three dark oak pins as buttons. She had matching fitted trousers with charcoal boots and a quiver on her back that held primitive arrows and a short bow. As she neared him, Jase noticed her familiar violet pink eyes that seemed to look through him.

"Jase," Kaimi started. "This is who rescued you and the Princess in the forest."

The elf bowed slightly, crossing her foot in front of the other and raising both hands as she did. "My name is High Guardian Amosa Reven of Puloka."

Jase held out his hand for her to embrace. "Jase Bluestar," he said politely.

High Guardian Amosa stared at his hand not accepting it. "You are the one who has been in charge of protecting the Princess?" she questioned.

"Not exactly. She's pretty assured that she can take care of herself without help," he said putting down his hand.

"That has been her custom," she regarded, nodding slightly.

"She is a Nightstar, after all. What would you expect?" Kaimi said with a short laugh.

This brought a faint smile to the elf's thin lips. "This is true. I apologize for my stern greeting, Bluestar. One cannot openly trust a stranger when the only person who could vouch for them is unconscious. Not that we don't trust you, Kaimi, of course but even A.I.s can be tampered with," she pointed out.

"No offense taken," Kaimi replied.

Jase gave a nod. "I can agree with your hesitation in welcoming me. I assure you I'm not allied to the Androids. On my home planet they treat humans poorly," he informed the High Guardian.

"On many planets they treat humans poorly, Bluestar. If you didn't have Bluestar blood running through you, many elves here would treat you as if you were nothing as well," the elf made known to him.

Jase was curious on why that was, but didn't say more about it. Instead he said, "Thank you for saving my and Princess Skyrah's lives out there. We are forever indebted to you for your kindness."

High Guardian Amosa studied him with her violet eyes. "I owe the Princess much. It was the least I could do to extend my gratitude towards her. And for you...well, you are a Bluestar. Therefore, I had no choice in the matter."

"How did you know? I remember a blue shield around me—was that of your doing?" he asked her.

High Guardian Amosa turned to Kaimi unsure of Jase's words. Knowingly, Kaimi explained, "He hasn't found his abilities until recently and still doesn't quite believe that they are there."

"It's not that I don't believe in them, Kaimi. I just don't understand why I wouldn't have them until now after all this time," Jase interjected.

The High Guardian studied him carefully for a few silent moments as if choosing her words. "It is strange that you would just recently have attained your abilities so late in life. Why? I do not know, Bluestar, but I'm sure our elders might have the answers that you are looking for. When you are well enough, I can arrange someone to escort you to their studies so that you can find out more about the Bluestar companions before you."

Jase felt nervous about the idea of learning more about others like him, but at the same time he was curious on the topic. He had always wondered in the back of his mind, why he was a Bluestar without abilities. Now that he did, he wasn't sure if he wanted them. "You have such records here?"

"Bluestars and the elves have always been a close knitted alliance throughout thousands of years. We might not know much about them, but they did allow us to keep some records about their lives anytime they would come here to seclude themselves from others. The forest is vast and an ideal place for one to get lost in," the High Guardian continued. "And for how I knew what you are is simple. When I found you and the Princess, you both were lying on the forest floor, beaten and battered. A breath away from death. I knew I had to do something especially when I noticed that it was the Nightstar Princess with you. When I tried to near you both, you created a blue gel-like shield over your bodies. I couldn't touch you at all, not until you fell unconscious and the shield failed."

Jase was surprised with himself. "I did, but how? I didn't know I was doing it?" he exclaimed.

Kaimi explained. "You might not know, Jase, but your body does. It reacted to the potential danger that could have befallen you, and your abilities instinctually kicked in to protect you and the Princess."

"It seems that my body is doing that a lot nowadays," Jase commented to himself, thinking of when he fell from the tree to save Tahmela. He could have sworn he was flying when he got them to the tree branch, but couldn't believe it. Perhaps that was his abilities instinctually kicking in again when he was in danger. But if that was so, why hadn't they done that before? Why now?

High Guardian Amosa interrupted his thoughts. "I'm sure in time you will learn how to use your abilities for yourself. Learning more about others like you might help unlock the power that you need to focus the abilities within you," she assured him.

Jase nodded. He then noticed that his wounds were healed. "Did my abilities heal my wounds as well?" he asked.

The elf smiled. "No, you do not have those kind of abilities. Our srelaehs here are talented beings and well respected for what they practice. Our best srelaeh worked on you for many days to save you. You are well enough to be alive, but still need much rest for you aren't fully healed. You will feel some pain and soreness for a few weeks, but in time it should go away," she said.

Jase looked over his skin, touching where gashes should have been but found smooth skin instead. "Well, thank you and your—"

"Srelaehs," Kaimi helped pronounce for him. "Sir-leas."

Jase gave her a nod, turning back to the elf. "Srelaehs. Thank them for their hard work to heal us," he said gratefully. Amosa bowed her head in response. Jase then asked, "The Princess—when can I see her?"

"She is resting now, but perhaps later in the day, if she is feeling up to it, you may see her," the elf responded.

Jase stretched, agreeing to her terms. "And my friend, Tahmela? Have you found him yet?" he questioned remembering he was still lost.

"The bulb will be found soon. I'm not sure why you'd want such a thing accompanying you and the Princess, but Kaimi informed me that it helped you escape from Faton, so it shall be found. The forest is big, but my people know much of its nature," Amosa assured him.

"He isn't that bad once you get to know him," Jase informed her.

"I will be on my way now, but I will send someone with food for you. I'm sure you are hungry. I'll also let you know as soon as we find your friend, but in the meantime, rest, Bluestar," she said as she effortlessly glided towards the door.

"You'll let me know when the Princess wakes, too?" Jase asked quickly.

"Of course," she said behind her and disappeared from view.

"I don't think she likes me," Jase joked turning back to Kaimi.

Kaimi smiled. "Amosa is not really a people person, but not many elves are," she told him.

"How do you know her?" Jase asked.

Kaimi stared out at one of the windows. "From the Great War. She was in charge of protecting Princess Skyrah during the war and will most likely take that honor back up now that they have crossed paths again. She'll be even more protective I'm sure, but she is quite nice when she wants to be. She just takes warming up to, that's all," she told him.

Jase stood from the bed feeling like he had gotten run over by a sky bike as he stretched painfully. "I feel like you had this whole other life without me," he mused vindictively.

"In a way, I did," Kaimi acknowledged. "But I prefer this one with you, Jase, than any other before."

That brought a smile to Jase's lips as he pulled on his charcoal pants that were hanging on one of the chairs by the wooden table. "Stop it, you are making me blush!" he teased. "Do you know much about Bluestars or have any records about them?"

"I'm afraid I know as much as you do and the only records about them are well hidden from the galaxy. It appears only the Elves, Nightstars, and the Ancients know anything. You are the only one I've encountered and from all my time being alive it seems the Bluestars have always been a secretive race," she told him.

Jase grabbed his faded vest that had been cleaned and folded. "So Princess Skyrah would know more about my abilities than she's letting on?" he pointed out.

"Perhaps, but perhaps not. The Nightstar family has kept the Bluestar's abilities secret for many, many years, apart from a few things they allowed to be known to the public. Therefore, very few know what exactly you are capable of and it's unsure if the family has passed on your knowledge to the Princess before their untimely deaths," Kaimi replied.

"That's a scary thought," he said.

Kaimi shrugged. "That is how every Bluestar has wanted it to be. Why, I know not, but I'm sure it's for a good reason," she replied.

"What if a Bluestar decided to be evil? No one would know how to stop he or she if that were to happen," Jase wondered out loud, thinking of his powers and what they could be.

Kaimi seemed amused by his words. "A Bluestar has never turned against the Royal family, or those they serve, in all of history. It seems unlikely that would happen. It's not in your character."

"Perhaps you're right," Jase replied, sitting back on the flower petal bed and pulled on his boots that had been cleaned and polished. "But there's a first time for everything."

"Are you planning on changing history, Jase?" Kaimi joked.

"No," Jase laughed. "I'm just saying that nothing is set in stone, after all. I mean look at us! We never thought we'd be out of Otect City and talking to the elves but here we are! Doing just that! Anything can happen, Kaimi."

Kaimi chuckled. "You are right, Jase. I will agree with you on that."

Jase pulled on his pilot jacket, feeling a slight pinch in his back as he did. "I'm sure the kids are going to love the stories we tell them when we go back," he said.

"I'm sure they will," Kaimi agreed. "Where exactly do you think you are going?"

Jase grabbed his fingerless gloves, pulling them on. "You don't honestly think I'm just going to sit here all day and wait for them to find Tahmela, do you?" he responded.

"I didn't think you would, but I hoped that you'd be smart enough to! Jase, you barely survived a fall. You are in no condition to go out there in a forest you don't know to try and find Tahmela! It would do more harm than good in your state," Kaimi strictly warned.

Jase flashed her a smile. "I'll be careful!" he said waving one hand.

"It'll be dark soon enough," Kaimi reminded him in hopes it would change his mind.

Jase moved towards the nightstand to grab his data watch. "I'll bring a light."

"Jase...."

"Kaimi," he watched her disappear for a moment as he latched his data watch to his wrist before she popped up again on the face of its face. "I can't just leave him out there on his own after all he's done for me. He'll get eaten for sure."

Her expression changed to a worried smile as she tried hiding her true feelings. "And you won't?"

"I'll be safe, I promise. Besides, if anything too crazy happens, I'll run. I'm pretty good at getting away from things that chase me, remember?" he told her while heading towards the door.

Kaimi's voice was warm, but still full of concern as she answered, "You should at least inform the High Guardian of your plans."

"So she can stop me? I don't think so," he said.

"I don't like this idea," Kaimi insisted as he opened the door to the outside.

Jase paused at the doorway, unsure if he should listen to her or not as he stared out at the deck before him. Convincing himself it was the right call, he stated, "Only one way to find out," then stepped out.

Hosi

Jase walked out onto the deck that overlooked the bustling village below. He surveyed his surroundings, noticing tree houses like his built within the trees and their branches. As far as he could see there were thirty if not more scattered about the forest with wooden rope bridges connecting them to one another. It was like nothing Jase had ever seen before as he gawked at all the elves that hadn't noticed him and went about their day. Turning his gaze to the forest floor, he saw more elves dressed in different forest colors or colors of flowers as they walked dirt paths that led to places out of sight for Jase to follow.

Kaimi's warm voice interrupted his thoughts. "Well? How do you like it?" she asked, already knowing the answer.

Jase stared with wonder, marveling at the elves and their culture unlike anything he had ever seen. "It's wonderful! I mean...the elves! They really exist! Well, I mean, I knew they did, but now they really do because I'm really here with them. In a village that they built on a planet that they inhabit! They aren't a lost legend! They are real!" he rambled unable to contain his excitement as he watched the small crowd below him.

Kaimi couldn't help but laugh at his excitement. "Yes, they are very much alive as you can see!" she said.

"It's beautiful! It's nothing I ever thought I'd see in my life," Jase told her out loud as he continued taking it all in. "We did it, Kaimi. We travelled to a planet other than our own."

"We sure did, Jase," she softly answered.

"Is this what their cities look like?" Jase asked.

"No, this is all but a small village. They have one large city throughout the entire planet and I'm sure it looks nothing like this. When they were allies with the Resistance, we were able to gather basic knowledge about their race but we still have many things to learn. The elves aren't very chatty, I'm afraid," Kaimi responded.

Jase grinned from ear to ear, "No wonder Princess Skyrah likes them so much," he stated as he started across the deck towards the wooden bridge that connected another tree house.

"You know it will be hard for you to leave the village without anyone noticing. You aren't an elf and you don't quite fit in around here," Kaimi informed him.

Jase watched the elves below him as he started across the bridge. "Maybe they won't notice me," he replied.

"Doubtful."

Jase was halfway across when he spotted a small elf woman holding a tray of food making her way towards him. She was wearing pale blue robes short enough for her not to trip over as she crossed the bridge. Her midnight black hair was cut incredibly short on top of her head making her olive skin appear darker in the sun.

"Oh!" the elf woman, who came to Jase's chest, uttered in a silky, soft voice. Her crystal blue eyes struck him as she bowed holding up one hand above her head while balancing the tray of food with the other. "Bluestar, my apologies for making you wait if that is the reason you are out of your room. The High Guardian sent me to fetch food, but seeing as you are a Bluestar, I wanted to make sure you had the freshest berries and meat as possible. I'm sure you are starving."

"It's no problem at all...umm?" Jase responded, struck by her ethereal appearance.

"Hosi. My name is Hosi," the elf woman revealed.

Jase did what he thought was the polite thing to do, bowing to her as he introduced himself. "Jase Bluestar. It's a pleasure to meet you," he said.

Hosi placed her hand over her mouth, softly chuckling at him but quickly apologized. "I'm sorry, Bluestar. I don't mean to laugh at you, but you haven't been around many elves, have you?" she asked him.

Jase laughed at himself, embarrassed a little. "Is it that noticeable?" he responded.

The elf woman had a soft, beautiful smile as she replied, "I'm afraid so, but I can help with that if you desire it."

"That is very kind of you! I'm afraid I haven't been on any other planets than my own so other customs aren't quite known to me just yet," he said, welcoming her assistance.

"Hmm, interesting," Hosi noised, continuing past him on her way to his house.

Jase followed. "Why is that interesting?" he questioned.

"I always thought that Bluestars were traveling between other worlds protecting them from wrong doers. But I suppose not," she replied with an eyebrow raised.

"Have you met others like me before?" he asked excitedly.

Hosi looked at him and smiled. "Well, no, not exactly. I've read a lot about your kind from our archives at our grand city," she said.

"My kind? You mean humans, right?" Jase asked her, now confused on what humans had to do with Bluestars. He opened the door.

Hosi thanked him and continued. "No, I'm referring to Bluestars. You are after all your own race in some ways, but many would oppose such things since there's usually only one of you alive at a time. To be determined a race, you have to have more than one alive but Bluestars are an exception."

"But can't Bluestars be any race?" Jase asked her.

Hosi set the tray of food on the carved table and transferred the food to the table. "Yes, they can but no matter what race they are from, you are still different than your other half. Does that make sense?" she asked politely.

Jase nodded. He suddenly remembered Kaimi was still in his ear and leveled his right wrist so she could appear on his data watch. "Hosi, I almost forgot! This is my best friend, Kaimi," he introduced.

Hearing her name, Kaimi appeared standing on the face of the data watch. She smiled to the elf woman, and politely added, "Hosi, what a pretty name."

The elf woman's face lit up as she bowed to the A.I. with both hands above her head and her foot crossing the other. "The pleasure is mine, Kaimi," she added straightening back up. "If I had known of you earlier, I wouldn't have waited so long to introduce myself."

"Sorry!" Jase stated sheepishly.

"Jase isn't used to being able to share me with others. Where we come from it's against the law to be friends with someone like me," she explained to the elf.

Hosi nodded understandingly as Jase chipped in. "Yeah, I could be put to death with being friends with this one. She's a trouble maker," he teased.

Hosi chuckled at his response. Her laugh reminded him of a thousand falling stars. "I should be going now, I suppose," she said. "Unless you of course need something else, Bluestar?"

"Please, just call me Jase," he replied.

Hosi nodded, repeating, "Jase."

Jase didn't want her to go, but knew there wasn't any reason she needed to stay. After all he still had to find Tahmela even if the elves were already looking for him. Thinking back to moments ago when he bowed to her, he said. "So I shouldn't bow to other elves?"

Hosi laughed again, shaking her head. "Not if you are going to bow like that."

"Could you show me how?" Jase asked chivalrously.

She nodded. "If that is what you wish." Hosi stood up straight and instructed, "When you meet other elves for the first time, whether they are strangers or not, this is how you formally greet them. You bow halfway, holding both hands above your head, and cross your right foot over the other. You hold it for a moment then raise back up. In doing so, you are indicating that you have no weapons in your hands and that you mean the other no harm. It's about trust and openness with your visitor."

Jase did as he was instructed. "So if they don't do that, they intend you harm?" he asked.

Hosi looked away in thought. "Most of the time, yes. Unless they use the less formal bow which is what most elves do particularly to their friends and family. Would you like me to show you?"

"Please."

"For this one you bow slightly and bring your hand across your heart while using your free hand to touch palms with the other being," she showed him, bending her back slightly and moving her hand over her heart while touching his palm with hers for a brief second.

Jase repeated the action, asking, "What does that mean?"

"This one means, 'I care for your health.' It's used mostly for friends and family members. The hand over your heart represents loved ones and that you value their health while the action of touching their hands represent that you both are connected and are a whole," she explained with a warm smile.

Jase returned the smile. "Does that mean I can bow to you like that from now on?" he asked out loud without thinking. Hosi blushed as she looked away towards the window for a moment as Jase quickly recovered by saying, "You know, now that we are friends."

"We shall see, Jase Bluestar. We shall see," she replied then turned towards the door, glancing back at him one last time before disappearing outside into the village.

Once gone, Kaimi stated playfully, "Very smooth. I think you won her over with that."

Jase felt stupid as embarrassment filled his body. "Oh, shut up. Why didn't you come to my rescue?" he prompted popping a large blue grape into his mouth.

Kaimi laughed. "Trust me, there was no rescuing you from that one," she teased.

Jase laughed with her while he sorted through the weird looking fruits on the plate that Hosi brought him. "She had crystal blue eyes like some humans. I thought elves had violet eyes like High Guardian Amosa?" he pointed out.

"Every race has different eye colors, especially the elves. Unlike the many different kinds that humans have, Elves have only three main colors: crystal blue, violet pink, and forest green," Kaimi explained.

"Weird," Jase exclaimed, pushing off the table. "Alright, time to go find our bulb."

A Frightening Roar

Jase stepped out onto the deck again in the late evening sun and retraced his steps across the bridge before continuing on down a spiral staircase attached to a nearby tree house that led to the forest floor. The staircase had beautiful creatures carved throughout it as Jase ran his hand across the smooth surface. The moment his foot hit the soft soil under him, it seemed as if every elf near him felt his presence and stopped what they were doing to stare, their eyes piercing his body like a thousand arrows.

"I think you were right," he whispered to Kaimi as he stopped in his tracks.

"I told you so. Don't say anything or you might offend them," Kaimi replied.

Jase awkwardly smiled and waved as he slowly started walking towards them, looking for a path to the forest. There were several paths ahead of him, but Jase didn't know which one he was brought in from and which one he wasn't. Glancing around confused, he whispered to Kaimi, "Do you know which way we came in?"

"I don't, actually," Kaimi apologized.

Jase felt self-conscious as the elves continued to stare. He tried ignoring them until two twin elves, male and female, stepped up towards him. They bowed with their hands over their heads then straightened back up. Jase did the same as he studied them, uneasily. They had long violet brown hair with violet pink eyes that stood out against their charcoal tunics and leggings. Jase was two feet taller than they were but they looked stronger than he was. They had striking features with sharp cheekbones that seemed to be etched into their skin and piercing eyes. "Umm, hi, I'm Jase Bluestar," he said nervously.

Neither elf took their eyes off him as the woman elf responded in a mesmerizing voice, "You are looking for your friend, correct? The bulb creature?" she asked.

"Um, yes, I am. How did you know?" Jase asked eyeing both elves cautiously.

The male elf answered, "It only seems correct if you are out of your room and not resting. Bluestars after all have a habit of protecting others over themselves."

Jase nodded, trying to relax. "I see. Can you help me find the search party so I can help?" he asked.

"Of course," the male elf answered.

Jase smiled. "Thank you, I'd appreciate that if you have the time," he said.

"This way," the lady elf responded and both turned on their heels down a hidden path that Jase hadn't noticed.

Kaimi suddenly suggested, "Jase, perhaps you should stay where you are and wait for High Guardian Amosa to find Tahmela."

Jase followed after the elves who moved very quickly on their feet causing him to run to keep up. "He could be hurt or dead by that time. He's my responsibility so I should be the one to find him," he replied.

"You won't be doing anyone good if you aren't fully healed. You should be resting, Jase," Kaimi continued trying to change his mind.

Jase jumped over a large fallen tree branch as he focused on the violet brown heads bobbing in and out of the trees in front of him. "I feel great other than being sore, but if anything dangerous comes along, I will let the elves take care of it," he said.

"Fine, but I still don't like this at all," Kaimi sighed in his ear.

"We will be fine, Kaimi," he assured her again. He finally caught up with the elves and tried keeping pace with them as they weaved in and out through the trees. They never once glanced back to see if he was still following. They seemed to trust that he was as they continued on their way, talking to one another in their own language. Jase scanned the forest floor, noticing that, besides the giant trees, there were also small thin trees. They looked like knives standing up straight, their branches curved to the top of the tree reaching towards the sky for sunlight. Jase touched one of the trees as he passed, realizing

194

the bark was soft as he pulled back his hand. "The bark is mushy?" he said out loud looking towards his hand where it was coated with slime that he wiped off on his pants leg.

The male elf answered from the lead. "Yes, it is. If you thought they were trees, you are mistaken. These small plants are living fungi in disguise as trees in order to escape notice from smaller animals and insects that might feed on them. They attach to trees and steal their nutrients as it's unlikely for them to reach the sunlight through these branches."

"They have a great disguise then," Jase replied observing each fungi tree as he passed them.

"Indeed," the elf answered.

Turning his attention back to the elves in front of him, Jase said, "I'm sorry, I don't think we properly introduced ourselves earlier. My name is Jase Bluestar."

The gentle male elf spoke first. "My name is Soo."

"And mine is El," the lady added in a mesmerizing melodious tone.

"We are the Ieth Twins," Soo revealed pushing past the underbrush that was starting to become more thicker as they travelled.

Jase watched them gracefully weave in and out of the brush as if they were floating on air as they moved. "It's a pleasure meeting you both and thank you for helping me find my friend," he said.

El replied in a musical voice, "When a Bluestar asks of us, we must obey."

"What do you mean?" Jase asked.

Kaimi had been listening through the data watch and responded in his ear. "They must have an order of authority to follow. Amosa is the High Guardian after all so they must have ranks of importance."

El slowed her pace so she could match Jase's. "You are a Bluestar, therefore you have a higher rank than myself and my brothers. I take it that you don't know much about elf culture," she responded.

Jase smiled embarrassed. "I'm afraid I don't know much at all. I just learned today how to bow correctly. I've never been off planet until now," he explained.

"You've never been off planet before?" Soo asked curiously as he glanced back towards him.

Jase shook his head, ducking under a hanging fungi branch. "This would be my first planet I've been on besides my own."

"What was your planet?" El asked, her voice like a song.

"Faton," Jase told them.

El and Soo continued walking further into the forest, speaking to one another in their own tongue before El explained, "Our culture has different levels of nobility. We have our kings, queens, then our Clan lords, High Guardians, Bluestars, Greenstars, then guardians, warriors, healers, scholars, trackers, scouts, hunters, and everyone else. Since you are a Bluestar, and we are lower than you, if you ask our help for something we are required to assist you."

"Interesting," Kaimi stated in Jase's ear still listening from his data watch.

Jase agreed with her. Their culture was so different from his own. "What rank are you both? Guardians?" Jase asked.

Both elves laughed and chattered with one another in their language at his question. Soo then said, "No, Bluestar. We aren't guardians. We are trackers and the best on the entire planet, most likely."

Jase tried not to look more foolish. "Why aren't you finding the Bulb, then, with the others?"

"We don't bore ourselves with menial tasks," Soo responded smugly.

"Why are you helping me then?" Jase questioned.

"Because you asked it of us, remember?" El told him with a smile.

Jase nodded his head, feeling dumb. "Right. Well, thank you, regardless. How long do you think it will take us to find my friend?"

"I have already found his tracks and they are fresh so it shouldn't take too long now," Soo responded.

"How have the others not found him when they have been searching for hours now?" Jase asked.

"Because they do not care to find your friend and they also weren't asked by a Bluestar to find him," El answered.

"And they aren't us," Soo added.

El grinned at her brother. "Very true! They aren't!" she chimed.

A thunderous roar shattered the air and sent shivers down Jase's spine as the hair on the back of his neck stood at end. Shortly after, a familiar shriek followed that Jase knew without a doubt was Tahmela. "That's my friend!" he shouted running towards the noise.

"Quickly!" Soo commanded and both elves rushed past Jase and disappeared in a blink of an eye.

Jase tried keeping up but fell behind. He couldn't imagine what type of creature could make such a frightening noise and hoped he wouldn't find out. "What do you think that was?" he asked Kaimi through gasping breaths, hoping she heard the noise through the com.

"Who knows what kind of beasts live on this planet, Jase," she answered.

Jase felt his lungs burning from the run as he jumped over a boulder ahead of him. His whole body ached as his foot caught on to something sending him forward onto the forest floor. He landed on his stomach, slamming his chin on a sharp rock as he did. He felt it cut open and in moments blood dripped from his chin as he pushed himself off the ground.

"Jase, are you okay?" Kaimi quickly asked, noticing his abrupt stop.

Jase brushed the dirt from his clothes, feeling warm blood trickle down his chin. "I tripped over a bush, but I'm fine. Just a slight cut, that's all," he answered.

"Losing your touch, are we?" Kaimi teased.

Jase smiled but before he could answer, a heavy trampling sound through the forest caught his attention. Jase froze, not knowing what to do or where the elves were as the creature grew nearer and nearer towards him. He heard the frightening thunderous roar again and realized that it was coming towards him.

"Jase? Jase?" Kaimi's voice sounded far away as he focused on the sound coming nearer.

Jase felt his heart racing through his chest as he stared in the direction. "Kaimi, that thing is coming towards me," he quietly responded.

"Hide, Jase! Hide!" Kaimi commanded in his ear.

Jase searched around for a place to hide. His eyes fell upon the tangly bush he had tripped over. It was big enough for him to hide in as it reminded him of a large ball of yarn tangled upon itself like Momma Rose used to use when she was making clothes for the children. Without a second thought, Jase rushed towards it and started pulling apart its scratchy branches as he tried wedging his body into it. He felt the branches tug at his clothing, scratching his face as he pushed into the center of the bush that was a suffocating tight squeeze. Their branches shielded him, barely allowing him to see the forest before him.

Jase hugged his legs as he waited. He was burning up in the hot humid air that pressed against his skin as it felt as if any moment he would suffocate in this tangly tomb.

"Where are you? Are you hidden?" Kaimi softly asked.

Jase smelt something sweet in the air around him and searched around best he could in the tight area for the source, answering, "I'm in a bush."

"In a bush? Can it see you?"

"I doubt it. I can barely see out of this thing." He whispered as heavy breathing grew closer and closer and the underbrush started moving in front of him. A cold sweat broke out across his skin as the leaves shook more before the creature stepped out of the forest.

Crowntooth

Jase immediately froze as a large gray scaled creature emerged from the trees balancing on a single muscular leg with claws the size of a human. It had two large claws left and right of each hand with several smaller ones in between like needles. The creature rose a long thin tail above its head half its height with four talons on its end. Besides its height and claws, Jase was most terrified by the creature's face that seemed to come from a nightmarish underworld. The top of its head had three large horns with two smaller ones in between causing it to look like the creature was wearing a crown. Under those were two sunken soulless black eyes that seemed to pierce through the trees and underbrush as the creature stalked around for its prey with rows of pointy teeth and massive canines hanging on the outside of its mouth dripping with gooey saliva.

Jase held his breath as he watched the monster sniff the air with its six nostrils in the center of its face. He tried to stop the shaking in his hands as it disappeared out of view from the tangly bush. Jase knew he wasn't out of danger yet as he waited to make sure the creature was gone for good. He felt sweat drip down his forehead as he focused on trying to calm his racing heart while he listened for anything outside of the bush. The hot air suffocated his body as he felt something drip onto his left hand and noticed it was blood running off from the cut on his chin.

Suddenly, the creature's face appeared through the branches staring back at him. Jase's body jerked as its foul breath filled the tiny space. The creature reached out to grab Jase through the opening stopping only inches from Jase's face that was out of reach. Growling in frustration, the monster ripped at the bush with rage. Unable to reach his gun, Jase tried scooting backwards to get away from the creature and as he did, he felt something drip down the back of his head and down his spine. He slowly turned his head to look behind him, fearing the worst. It was then when he saw six tiny black eyes staring at him and two fangs slowly moving upward to strike.

Jase let out a scream as he tried moving away in the opposite direction from what he realized was a spider. As he did, the spider unraveled its legs and Jase quickly realized he hadn't been hiding in branches but many wooden-like legs.

"Jase?! What's wrong? What's going on?" Kaimi frantically asked in his ear as Jase stumbled and crawled backwards away from the rising spider.

The spider's fangs made clicking sounds as they moved in the air towards Jase. It wasn't till the crowned monster let out a thunderous growl towards the spider as if claiming its prey that Jase remembered it was there. He froze in between the monsters as the spider hissed and clicked in response, its high pitch hurting Jase's eardrums as it moved towards him to spirit him away. He slowly crawled away as the monsters circled one another, hissing and growling.

"Jase? What was that noise? Are you okay? Respond," Kaimi's voice erupted in Jase's ear as he had forgotten that she was with him.

Jase whispered trying to remain calm, "Kinda busy at the moment," he said between his teeth.

"What's going on?" she demanded to know.

Jase didn't answer as he got ready to jump to his feet and run. He crawled to the edge of the trees, far enough from the creatures that he was somewhat confident he could escape. He waited till the crowned monster made the first move, swiping his giant claws towards the spider's head before Jase jumped to his feet and darted off into the trees. He heard thunderous roars from both creatures behind him as he doubled his speed running as fast as he could to get away from them. He dodged in and out of the fungi trees where he suddenly felt something grab his boot. His breath was knocked out of him as he hit the ground and was dragged backwards. He reached and clawed in vain for anything to hold on to. There was nothing sturdy enough to keep him still and he glanced behind him to find the giant wooden spider pulling him closer with its fangs. Remembering his gun, Jase pulled it out of its holster. Pulling back the trigger, Jase charged the weapon, watching it hummed to life as an unstable silvery blue light started to appear at the barrel. Jase released the charge at the spider's eyes and watched the blast erupt over its face causing the creature to shriek in pain and let go of Jase's leg as it retreated.

Without a second to lose, Jase jumped to his feet and charged the weapon again as he backed away from the blinded spider. Just as he was about to fire again, Jase saw a shadow emerge from the trees above and land on the spider's back. The crowned monster dug its talons into the spider, ripping it to shreds as the spider shrieked. Jase fired his weapon again only to miss and took off running into the forest. He could hear the creature after him. He tripped over a fallen piece of bark and slammed into the ground as the monster continued forward slamming into a nearby tree a few yards away from where Jase had fallen. Jumping to his feet, Jase squared off with the crowned monster who had now turned around to face him.

Purple blood from the spider soaked its talons as it leaned forward on its front arms, its voidless eyes piercing Jase's as they both watched one another in silence. The whole forest seemed to stand still as the last streak of evening light slowly faded from the sky. Jase knew once darkness settled in, there was no way he could fight off this creature. He had to either somehow out run the monster and hide or stop it for good now while he could see. The crowned monster charged without warning towards Jase, shaking the earth under his feet as it did. Without a thought, Jase picked up the piece of bark he had tripped over and brought it up like a shield to block the creature. The creature's claws slammed into it, pushing Jase backwards by force and against a tree trunk. Two large talons pinned Jase against the trunk while its dagger like nails in between them embedded into the bark shield only centimeters away from his chest.

Jase struggled to push the shield away from his chest as he saw the monster's claws pierce through the bark. His arms shook from struggling with the its powerful strength. Any second they would buckle under the strain and Jase would be done for as he gritted his teeth together and barely held his ground. The creature's foul breath heated Jase's face as he stared into the voidless eyes and focused on staying alive. Just when his arms were about to buckle under the strain, Jase caught a glimpse of violet hair out of his peripheral. *The twins!* Jase thought, suddenly feeling relieved and more determined to stay alive now that he had help. A second later a bolt of silver plasma energy pierced the creature's scaly shoulder.

The monster growled in response, still holding Jase in place as it stretched its neck to look towards the tree. Jase saw the plasma shot in the shape of an arrow embedded into the monster's back. A small trickle of black blood oozed from the wound before another arrow pierced in the same exact spot from above. One of the twins balanced on a low branch above them, prepared to fire another arrow towards the monster. Without even looking the crowned monster swung its dagger tail at Jase's face. He barely had time to move out of the way as the tail struck the bark, breaking off pieces of wood. As the creature pulled away its tail for another attack, one of the razor points scratched Jase's cheek causing it to bleed. Jase suddenly felt his body going numb as he lost the feeling in his arms. He watched them give way and the shield get shoved into his chest as the monster's claws lunged into his skin. Jase felt nothing as he stared at the black eyes, his vision flickering with little dots. Suddenly a blue wave rushed from Jase's body throwing the monster backwards several yards into a tree before Jase fell to the ground face first. He landed against the soft dirt, his sight leaving him, as the elves rushed towards him.

"Bluestar, are you with us?" the familiar voice of Soo asked in the darkness.

El's voice softly floated into his ear, "You must stay with us, Bluestar. Stay awake. The darkness is not your friend."

"Jase? Are you there?" Kaimi's voice asked before Jase finally passed out into the darkness that clouded him.

His throat was dry as Jase slowly came to. It reminded him of the barren desert outside of Otect City during the summer with its dry and unbearable heat. He had never really been outside of the city, but imagined it had to be much worse than being in the city during the summer. He noticed the soft breathing of someone else in the room mixed with the aroma of honey nectar that filled the air around him. It made him feel relaxed and peaceful as if he could fall back asleep in a cloud of his dreams and for a moment, he did.

When he awoke again the aroma wasn't as strong and he felt more awake now as he slowly forced his eyes open. He focused on the wooden ceiling above him. It appeared darker than before as he tried moving his head to look around. His body felt heavy. Kaimi sat cross-legged on his data watch swiping her hands through the air in front of her at something he couldn't see. Her eyes focused and determined as she went through the data not yet noticing that he was awake. Jase shifted his eyes to the others in the room.

To his surprise the breathing he had heard was Princess Skyrah sitting in a carved chair made of bark with flower petals blanketing her as she slept. She appeared so elegant and peaceful.

He then noticed the bulb sleeping on a sofa behind her with a leaf as a blanket covering his body. Even though his large goggles covered his eyes, Jase could tell he was sleeping by the loud snoring that escaped the bulb's thin lips. Jase's smile grew wider at the sight as relief washed over him now that everyone was back together again. He was so busy watching his three friends that he hadn't noticed the door quietly open and close until a gentle hand touched his shoulder. He turned his head to find High Guardian Amosa along with an elder male elf next to him with his hand on Jase's shoulder.

"So you're finally awake, are you? How are you feeling?" the gentle aged voice asked as the elf studied him with forest green eyes. He had long white hair tinted with sky blue that stopped at his upper torso in braids. A white trimmed beard covered his face under creased eyes and thick brows. His skin was wrinkled just slightly as the elf inspected Jase before checking his pulse on his neck.

Out of the corner of his eyes, Jase saw that the others were now aware of his presence and focused on him as he answered, "I feel fine, I think. My body feels kinda heavy to move, but I'll manage."

The elder nodded in response as he moved over to the table across the room where strange vials with different colored liquids were held. His plum colored robes that seemed to be aged with time softly brushed the floor as he walked. "Good. Very good. It appears that you're pulse has returned to a healthy rate, but for how you will feel it will take a few more days to wear off. You are very lucky to be alive, Bluestar. Very lucky indeed."

"He's a very lucky guy," Kaimi spoke up.

The elf continued as he searched among the vials for the one he was looking for, "Luck is a very rare trait, but I don't doubt you have it at all."

"Jase Bluestar," Amosa introduced the elf. "This is Hikmat Oolafee Srelaeh. One of our greatest and wisest healers in the kingdom."

The elder elf walked back over to Jase extending his hand for him to take the vial, "Greatest, perhaps but wisest I strongly doubt that."

Jase studied the elf as he accepted the vial, politely saying, "It seems I owe you my life, Mr. Oolafee."

The old elf wagged a finger at him. "No need to thank me. I was only doing my duty. Now drink that so it will help loosen your muscles."

Jase swallowed the slimy liquid before handing the empty vial to the healer. "What was it?" he asked.

"Just something that is in your stomach now," Hikmat Oolafee responded, moving back to the table. He turned back to Jase, studying him a moment then gave a nod as if agreeing on something. "I shall check on you later in the day. Until then you should remain in bed. It seems you have catching up to do in the spare time," he told him referring to the others in the room as he walked out the door. Once he was gone, Amosa sharply turned on her heel to face Jase. "Normally I would punish those who don't show proper respect to our worthy srelaeh but in your case I shall let it slide for the time being until you are properly trained," she spat sharply.

Jase was confused. "What did I do?" he questioned.

Amosa peered towards the Princess who seemed slightly embarrassed about the situation as she apologized. "I'm sorry, I should have thought to teach him proper titles and greetings before we left the ship," Skyrah said.

Amosa's violet eyes soften at her words as she replied in return, "All is forgiven, Princess Nightstar. It had been a very long time since we last saw one another for such formalities and I should not have expected you to have taught such things to a newcomer. I trust you will personally train him in our ways unless you have forgotten."

"I might be a little rusty, but I have not forgotten. I will make sure Jase and Tahmela know such ways before they talk to any other elves during our stay," she promised.

Amosa nodded and turned to Jase. "It is good to see you alive, Bluestar," she said then turned away.

Once the door closed, Jase remarked, "I thought she was going to let me have it for going after Tahmela."

"If you were an elf, she would have made sure you were punished for disobeying her orders, but at last you are not. You are a Bluestar and above her rank," Princess Skyrah confirmed.

Jase wasn't sure if he liked being higher in rank than the elves for he only wanted to be treated like everybody else. "What did I say wrong earlier?" he inquired.

"I know where you come from saying mister or misses is polite but in elf terms it's impolite. It is if you were comparing them to humans whether you know it or not. When you called Srelaeh Hikmat Oolafee mister you were disrespecting him and his abilities," she pointed out.

"Oh...I didn't meant to," Jase apologized, realizing he had a lot to learn than he originally thought.

"We know you didn't, Jase," Kaimi replied.

"Yes, I'm sure Srelaeh Oolafee knew you weren't aware of the formalities. I should have thought to teach you some important dealings with the elves back when we were on the ship," Princess Skyrah said in retrospect.

"You were too busy kicking my butt to think," Jase joked in return. "What would have been the proper way to address Oolafee?"

"It is respectful to address all the healers by their full name and title. For example to address Oolafee, you would say Srelaeh Hikmat Oolafee in formal or Srelaeh Hikmat in passing. It is important to address all healers by Srelaeh for its a sacred name for healers. It gives them power," the Princess replied.

"Got it," Jase said.

Kaimi, seeing her opportunity to change the subject, said, "It's good to see you awake, Jase. We were awfully worried about you."

"I'm glad to see you too, Kaimi. It's good to see all of us are still among the living thus far. Especially you, Tahmela," Jase responded.

"Thousand apologies, Bluestar. Never meant you to get hurt," the bulb stated moving to the side of the bed next to the Princess.

"It's fine, Tahmela. I'm just glad you aren't hurt," Jase assured him. "What was that thing anyways?"

"A crowntooth," the Princess responded. "Nasty poisonous creatures that normally hunt at night and sleep during the day. Amosa thought it was strange that one was up that early in the evening," she told him.

Thinking back on the terrifying creature, Jase said out loud, "I hope I never have to come across that monster again."

"I hope we don't either," Kaimi agreed with him.

Suddenly remembering the twin elves that were with him, Jase asked, "The elves that were with me in the forest? Are they okay?"

"Soo and El are quite well and insist on seeing you once you are completely healed again. They were quite impressed with how you handled yourself against a Crowntooth. Apparently not many survive such an encounter and live to tell the tale of it," Kaimi answered.

"As are many elves," Skyrah added.

Jase nodded, happy that everyone had made it through the past events without harm. Thinking back on the Crowntooth, he asked, "Wait, you said the monster was poisonous. Does that mean they got all the poison out of me?"

"It took them a long time, but for the most part, yes, they did," she replied.

"You've been in a coma for three weeks, Jase, since the event," Kaimi explained.

"Three weeks?!" Jase said shocked.

Kaimi continued. "The poison acts quickly and takes a long time to extract. Srelaeh Hikmat Oolafee was working over you for two weeks straight to fight the poison as best as he could. It wasn't till these past few days that your body started healing."

"Is that why my body still feels heavy? It's the poison still lingering in my muscles?"

"It's the last of it and should fade away in the next day or so. You were very lucky to have the elves with you when you got attacked. Otherwise, it would have been too late to save you," Princess Skyrah responded.

"I'd be a goner for sure," Jase agreed, shivering at the thought of the beast eating him while he was in his coma state. Studying her for a moment, Jase noticed that the gash she had taken in the head when they had fallen was now healed without leaving a scar. "I take it the elves healed your nasty gash?" he asked.

Princess Skyrah smiled gently, touching the side of her head where the cut had been. "Yes, it took them three days to fully heal the tissue and bone fragments. If not for them, I'd probably be a vegetable," she replied.

"Then it would be frowned upon to make fun of you," Jase teased.

The Princess smiled at his response, "Thank you for saving my life again, Jase. It seems you keep doing that a lot lately."

"Don't think I'm not keeping track of it," he teased again.

Skyrah stood. "I wouldn't expect anything less. I'm sure you will hold it against me in the future," she replied while pushing back her braid behind her shoulder. "We should let you rest now. I'll come back and check on you soon."

Jase didn't want her to go for once, but felt a wave of weariness fall over him causing his eyes to feel heavy. He said as he watched her move towards the door, "Careful, it sounds like you actually care about me." He then rested his head onto the flower petal and peered over to Tahmela who was staring down at the floor. "They didn't give you a room, did they?" he asked the bulb.

The bulb shook his head. "Never do, Bluestar."

"Stay with me. You can take the sofa."

"Thank you, Bluestar," the bulb grinned, revealing his square teeth.

Jase closed his eyes, already feeling sleep take him. "Goodnight, Kaimi. Goodnight, Tahmela."

Kaimi's sweet voice filled the air. "Goodnight, Jase," she said.

"Night, Bluestar."

Then Jase fell asleep once again with his thoughts on the Princess.

Home, I Hope

It took Jase another three days in bed until he was feeling like himself again. Tahmela and Kaimi kept him company for the most part with Srelaeh visiting twice a day to check on his progress. The Princess and High Guardian Amosa hadn't been back to see him since he first woke which made Jase wonder what they were doing while he laid in the bed. He understood why the High Guardian hadn't been back but he wasn't sure why the Princess hadn't returned to see him yet. When he asked Kaimi about it, she would say that the Princess was busy trying to convince the elves to fight for the Resistance again. Jase nodded, remembering that was the main reason after all they had come here. His favorite part of the day was when Hosi, the servant who brought him food, visited him. He enjoyed her company and she never seemed to mind when he would ask her questions about the elves and their world.

Feeling strong enough he asked her as she walked into his room with a tray of food, "Can we go on a walk after I eat? I would love to see more of the village while I'm here."

Hosi's crystal blue eyes sparkled as she laid the food onto the table. "If you feel up to it, I don't see why we shouldn't. It's a beautiful day," she responded.

"I feel great! Just tired of being in bed all day. I need something to do," he proclaimed.

Amused, Hosi turned her gaze to Kaimi who was sitting on his data watch on the end table next to him. "What do you think, Kaimi?" she asked.

"He has been cooped up in here for weeks now. I think it's time he got out and stretched his legs for a bit," she agreed.

Jase beamed. "Exactly!"

Hosi giggled as she finished setting up the food. "I will gladly show you around then," she chimed.

"So what are we eating today?" he asked, viewing the food with eager eyes and not recognizing any of the various fruits before him besides what looked like grapes that he quickly popped into his mouth. There were two bowls that steamed, one with a pale yellow liquid and the other a pale green substance. He ignored them once he noticed the loaf of bread, some sort of blue meat, and reddish brown cheese sitting in front of him. Lastly, there was hot tea for him to drink with the aroma of sweet honey.

Hosi pointed to each item as she explained, "It's your typical fruits from the forest and the meat is Kyeakin, a forest cat in our area. The two substances in the bowls, the pale yellow, is boombio, used when you finish your meal. It gets rid of any leftover oils or residue from the food, making your hands fresh again. The pale green one is called Laez. That is used as a spread on your meat or bread. Some even put it on their fruit. It's quite delicious! We harvest it from the bottom of the lixy tree leaves."

Jase dipped his index finger into the Laez bowl and tried some of the green substance. It was remarkably sweet but with a kick at the end causing him to cough slightly and reach for the tea.

"Can't handle a little spice, Bluestar?" Hosi smirked at his reaction.

He swallowed the warm honey tea before replying, "You could have warned me."

"But where's the fun in that?" she teased.

"You might want to be careful not to eat too much of anything, Jase. Your body won't be used to eating foreign food from other worlds quite yet so take it slow," Kaimi suggested.

"Do not worry, Kaimi. I wouldn't give him anything he couldn't handle on a first day of eating solids," Hosi answered.

Jase tore a couple of pieces off the loaf of bread, placing the sliced meat on top. "So I know the proper way to bow to another elf and how to properly address Sre-laeh Hikmat Oolafee, but is there anything I should say when I do bow to others? Like a greeting or something in your language?" he asked as he took a bite.

"Our language is hard to learn. I don't think you'd be able to accomplish it," Hosi politely determined as she took a grape to eat.

Jase turned to Kaimi, sitting on the table. "Can you speak their language?" he asked.

"Yes, but I'm a program. It's in my binary codes," she replied.

Jase turned back to Hosi. "It's settled then. You teach me and Kaimi can help."

Hosi seemed unsure. "I really shouldn't without a blessing from the High Guardian," she replied.

Remembering the ranks the twins told him about, Jase replied, "Don't I give the same amount of authority as a High Guardian? Can I not bless you to teach me?"

"Jase," Kaimi said warningly.

Jase shrugged. "What? If it's from a Bluestar it should be fine, right?"

"But it's not your language to bless on an outsider. You may be a Bluestar, but that does not mean you can go about doing what you want. You are a guest on their planet," Kaimi firmly told him.

Hosi agreed. "She is right, Jase. I should still ask the High Guardian Amosa for the blessing before I teach you anything," she said.

Jase nodded as he played with his food.

"Don't worry, Bluestar. The language isn't going anywhere," Hosi sweetly told him to cheer him up.

Jase smiled at her words. "Can we go on our walk now?"

Returning the smile, Hosi replied, "Yes, we may now. Will you join us, Kaimi?"

Kaimi's face lit up. "I'd love to!"

Hosi revealed an earpiece out of one of her robe pockets. "Now we can all talk to one another as we walk. We don't use much technology these days, but I don't think anyone would mind if I use this to hear you, Kaimi."

Jase and Kaimi both beamed as Kaimi disappeared into the data watch that Jase strapped onto his wrist. "Shall we?" he said to Hosi.

"We shall," she replied as she headed towards the door with Jase following her. He took one last glance to Tahmela who was still fast asleep on his flower bed for his hourly nap.

They exited onto the deck breathing the fresh air for a moment. Jase took a deep breath and exhaled, glad to be out of his room finally. The sun streamed from the treetops lighting their path as he followed Hosi across the wooden rope bridge and down the carved stairwell. He once again marveled at the creatures and flowers carved so elegantly into the wood, running his hand across them as he passed. He then asked as they stepped off the last step, "What does a normal elf do on a day-to-day basis?"

Hosi motioned for him to follow her as she walked onto a dirt path that smelt of wet earth that led through the village. "It depends on your stature. Trackers find food or things that have been lost; Scouts explore the forest making notes of changes and also send word to other villages or to our capital; Scholars teach our young important ideas like history, mathematics, English, and so on; Warriors defend our villages and teach the young hand to hand combat as well as different skills in weaponry, Guardians help keep order in the villages and our beloved city. Most of them reside at our capital but at least twenty are stationed in each village for protection against creatures of the forest. They are commanded by our High Guardian which each village has one which leads it."

"And what does a High Guardian do?" he asked curiously.

Hosi smiled to an elf woman who passed them carrying a basket of fruit. "They are in charge of each village's army and the protection of the village, and the protection of our King and Queen. They make sure each Clan Lord is safe at all times who is in charge of the supplies and resources of their village. The High Guardian is also in charge of deciding who will become a guardian and who will become the next High Guardian if he or she may fall in battle or die of age."

"They sound more important than a Clan Lord," Jase stated.

"They both are equally important and work as a team to make sure their village thrives, but in some sense High Guardians can seem more important. If a Clan Lord dies, then they take over their duties for the village until a new one is determined by our cities council. They can even take over as King or Queen if the royal family has no living heirs," Hosi explained.

"Why wouldn't a Clan Lord not become the next king or queen? Why a High Guardian?" Jase asked.

Hosi had a simple answer. "High Guardians are the leaders in their villages while the Clan lords only take care of supplies and resources. High Guardians have more experience in what they need to do to ensure the village survival. Therefore, they are more likely to succeed in ruling a kingdom."

Jase nodded, understanding now. "That makes sense."

Hosi continued. "They are very well respected among our race, as well as the srealaehs. In all honesty, we treat our race with great respect for one another despite their stature. We rarely have disagreements and there's rarely ever any violence between our race."

"That's amazing," Kaimi chipped in. "Not many races can say that."

"It is quite sad how violent other races can be to their own kind. Why add more hatred in this world when we already have problems with our enemies?" Hosi asked softly, as if she was in a far off place in her mind.

"Yet the elves seem to be hostile to bulbs or at least from what I have seen," Jase pointed out.

Hosi glanced at him as she chose her next words carefully before speaking. "Other races usually have flawed behaviors and other agendas that are not made known in the beginning. Every race has faults and I'm not saying mine does not, but many races don't live long enough to grow their intelligence like they should," she responded.

"What about the Bulbs? They can live to be a hundred, but still a lot of races treat them poorly," Jase determined.

"Yet they do nothing to stop it. They do not help society grow or offer help to anyone or make contributions to our worlds. If they were to disappear it would-n't hurt any societies for they only keep to themselves and their dwellings. They didn't help fight in the Great Civil War while so many lost their lives to fight for their freedom when the Androids came to destroy all who did not agree with their cause. Many beings despise them for that and their lack of empathy for our lives while the bulbs do nothing to show us any different. For that, they are treated poorly until they decide to do more for society," Hosi told him.

Jase thought about how mean races were to bulbs and he could see why people didn't like them for not helping in the war, but he didn't see any reason they would help if they were treated like they were. "Maybe if we treated them better now, they might help the Resistance fight in this war."

"Maybe," Hosi agreed.

Kaimi's soft voice seemed to smile as she spoke. "That is something we should consider, Jase," she agreed.

"What do you do, Hosi?" Jase asked watching elves above him cross bridges to other tree houses.

Hosi stopped on the dirt path to smell a large flower standing four feet tall growing alongside the village. Its orange and white petals were the size of Jase's hands as they stretched towards the sun. "This is my favorite flower," she stated before answering Jase's question. "Srelaeh Hikmat is training me to be a srelaeh in hopes to replace him someday. I'm studying all I can under him and learning as much as I can while he is able to teach. It is not an easy task, I assure you. He is the most respected elder and srelaeh in our entire race."

"So he will teach you the secrets of healing others like High Guardian Amosa talked about?" Jase asked.

Hosi shook her head. "I have not proven myself for such abilities to be granted to me. It can take years until one sees you're worthy enough of the gift and even longer to fully master it. I have only just now in these past few years started learning from him. I have a long road ahead of me."

"Is bringing me food one of your tasks?" Jase asked.

Hosi moved out of the way as a group of elf children ran by laughing. "No, I do it because I want to. In part of being a Srelaeh, you have to know what it's like to serve others before yourself. It teaches you to love everyone and how exactly you need to heal them. All great Srelaehs would rather give up their own bed to a stranger if all they needed was a goodnight's rest. You have to be able to show compassion to even your enemies whether they killed your family member or a stranger. It's how you grow and heal yourself before healing others."

"That's beautiful," Kaimi told her.

Hosi nodded. "I think so, too," she said.

Jase was watching an elf man carve a fierce forest cat with its mouth open as if it was roaring out of wood on the steps of the stairs leading to his home. "That is very noble of you, and the srelaehs, to take it upon yourself. I don't think I could do that especially for my enemies," he responded to Hosi.

Hosi studied him as her face softened into a warm smile. "I think you would, Bluestar," she said.

Jase wasn't so sure. To show compassion to a murderer or the Androids after all they had done to so many people in the past. He wouldn't give up his bed for someone like that to sleep on peacefully. Trying to think of something else, he asked, "Are all villages like this? Are they all tree houses?"

Hosi shook her head. "No, each village is different based on the resources around them. For example, here, in Puloka, we are in the forest. Therefore, it is safer to live in the tree houses off the ground than to try and build houses where there is so limited space on the forest floor. The clans that live in the farthest reaches of the forest live in the mountains and build their homes out of stone. Nagraceka and Belaka that thrive in the Twins Region build their homes out of giant tulips that grow in their fields. The clans that live in the Kurath Region build their homes out of leaves and sticks found on the ground. The trees are spread more apart there so they are able to live on the forest floor."

"I would love to see them all at some point," Jase stated hopeful for the opportunity.

"They are all beautiful but not as beautiful as our capital, the Hewka City," Hosi replied. "Every building is created out of giant tulips, and Hewka Castle is sculpted out of majestic shades of purple and pink and blue that never fails to take your breath away no matter how many times you've seen it."

"It sounds unbelievable," he responded amazed.

"I'm sure whatever we are imagining, doesn't give it justice," Kaimi acknowledged.

"Perhaps one day, you will both get to see it," Hosi said as they continued through the village. After a moment of silence she declared, "How about I ask you some questions now?"

"Go right ahead," Jase told her.

Hosi looked up at the sky thinking for a moment. "What does your home look like?" she asked.

"Hmm…well, the capital of the planet is Otect City. It is a huge city that takes up a large portion of the planet. I was born within the city and grew up there my whole life. You probably wouldn't like it. It has no trees or flowers. Within the city walls, are stone and metal buildings that reach up towards the sun. It's not as it is here in the forest. Everyone is too busy rushing around about their lives and it's extremely noisy," Jase told her.

Kaimi added, "The only trees are on half of the planet while the other half is a barren desert. Most of the inhabitants live within the city except for nomads that live in the desert and a handful of villages on the forest side of the planet."

"Interesting," Hosi turned them down a different path that led them into what appeared to be a garden in the middle of the village. "Please, tell me more about your city?"

"Well, there is thousands and thousands of different races that occupy the city along with the whole Android army. There aren't that many humans, but the ones that are there are treated poorly by all the races," Jase told her as he viewed the beautiful plants around him.

Hosi stopped by a fountain that was carved out of wood admiring a beautiful, tiny bird that played in the water. "I'm sorry for how humans are treated. My own kind tends to do the same to them as well. We all can be quite cruel, can't we? It's a shame," she said.

Jase joined her watching the bird swim about the fountain unaware of them. "You haven't been cruel to me," he replied.

"Because you aren't human, Jase. You are a Bluestar," Hosi said through a giggle as she glanced to him for a moment before turning back to the bird.

Jase smiled at her laughter. "But I'm still a human," he said.

"In a matter of words, yes, but not quite, Jase," Kaimi revealed. "Bluestars are technically their own race for you have a different genetic makeup than normal human beings."

Jase didn't understand. "But both of my parents were human. Do I not have their DNA inside me?" he questioned.

"You do, but it's altered by the Bluestar genetics causing your DNA to evolve into a different species. Your Bluestar genes are more dominant than your parents' DNA. Therefore, you might have their hair and eyes as well as their facial features, but the Bluestar genes determine your health, strength, and so on," Kaimi furthered explained.

Still trying to wrap his head around it Jase asked, "So no matter the race that becomes a Bluestar, we are all still considered the same race?"

"Yes," Kaimi agreed.

Jase looked over at Hosi, "Has there ever been an elf Bluestar?" he asked. She shook her head no.

"Why not?" he asked.

Hosi took some seeds out of her robe pocket and laid them down on the fountain for the bird to eat as she sat down. "Elves are different when it comes to reproducing since our lives are so long. We mostly have children when our race is threatened by extinction. It's very rare that we have children, and if someone does, it's a very special gift to all the elves."

"What about the kids we saw earlier?" he asked.

The small, yellow bird jumped out of the water and started eating the seeds while Jase and Hosi watched. "Most of the young we have now are from the last war when we lost so many of our kind to the Androids. As elves we mature faster than we age. That is why they still appear so young. Besides the ones you saw earlier, we have three other children born after the war that we call our miracle children. One child is from Nature herself who blessed a barren elf with a child. Another family, who felt like Nature was telling them to bear a child had one. Then our last child is one from my own sister. She had lost her husband at the very end of the war and was blessed by Nature to have a child from him. Where Nature takes one life, she tends to bless us with another in different forms."

"I like that thought of how the universe works," Jase answered.

"Careful not to insult her culture, Jase," Kaimi warned him.

Hosi giggled. "It is fine, Kaimi. We are all from different worlds of life and beliefs. In the end, we look up at the same stars at night."

Jase stared up at the afternoon sky barely visible through the giant trees as he thought about what Hosi said. He liked the idea that no matter how far he was from home and Mrs. Rose and the children, that they were still under the same stars together.

"Are you alright?" Hosi interrupted his thoughts.

Jase turned his attention back to her as he noticed the bird was now nested in her lap as she stroked it softly. "Yes, I was just thinking about what you said," he responded.

"Did you leave someone behind on your planet?" she asked.

Jase slowly reached out to stroke the bird as it cautiously watched him. "I grew up on the streets back on Otect, but there was this orphan home that took me in and cared for me. The sweet old lady was the closest thing I had to a real mother and when I grew older, Kaimi and I started to take thievery jobs to make money for the kids she cares for now so they had clothes and food to eat. When she found out that I had Kaimi with me, the woman didn't turn us in even though it was treason not to and decided that Kaimi was part of the family," he said.

"She is a wonderful person," Kaimi added.

"She is," Jase agreed. "We weren't able to say a proper goodbye to them before we left with the Princess, but I'm sure they will understand."

"You must miss them very much," Hosi acknowledged.

Jase nodded. "At least now when I get back I will have many stories to tell the kids."

"That is very true! Not everyone can say they fought a CrownTooth and lived to see another day!" Hosi agreed as she let the bird eat out of her hand.

Jase was surprised about how little fear the bird had for them as it explored Jase and Hosi hopping from one lap to the other's as it did. Looking away for a moment, Jase saw that a couple had entered the garden and spotted them across the way. They respectfully bowed to Jase and Hosi before being on their way to admire the garden once more. "Do you think I'll be the last of my kind?" he asked.

"I hope not," Hosi answered. "If the Androids aren't stop then perhaps. Lord Brohain will do anything to stop the Nightstars from retaking the galaxy even if that means murdering every Bluestar baby that could stand with the Princess against him."

Jase couldn't imagine Lord Brohain getting overthrown. There was a pang of sadness in his heart as his thoughts twisted into a single thought of being the only one of his kind. Hosi seemed to have noticed the change as she placed the bird into his hands as she held it with him and stared into his eyes and sweetly said, "You are never alone, Jase Bluestar. You are different and special than everyone else, but we all bleed the same. While we might appear different the universe still created us from the same stars and earth. You have beings that care and love you who will never leave you even after death. Those we love never truly leave us."

"She's right," Kaimi agreed in his ear.

Jase felt a new kind of warmth pour over his body causing the loneliness to fade away to the corners of his mind as he stared down at the yellow bird who seemed to know what was going on. "Thank you, Hosi. Your words mean a lot to me," he replied.

Hosi's face lit as she turned back to the bird and moved her hands away from his. "I only speak of what a wise elf told me before so I cannot take the credit."

The bird pushed off Jase's palms and flew into the air. They watched it fly over the trees before disappearing into the forest. "Where do you think it's going?" Jase asked.

Bluestar

"With any luck, home I hope," Hosi answered.

"You mentioned that Hewka City could have records about Bluestars that your race has written. How far is the city from here?" Jase asked.

"Hewka City is a two month journey on foot from here and in your condition, you should still need to wait longer before making the journey," Hosi determined staring up at the sun.

"Is there any faster way to reach the city than on foot?" Kaimi asked.

Hosi straightened the wrinkles in her robe, replying, "We have built bridges throughout the planet to make it easier and safer to travel through the forest without having to be on the forest floor, but none of these bridges go straight from here to the city."

Disappointed, Jase wondered how long he would be here with the Princess until she wanted to leave. He doubted he had two months to travel to the grand elf city and knew he couldn't take off after promising Kaimi he would make sure the Princess would make it back to the Resistance. He could come back after they dropped the Princess off, but he wasn't sure if he would be able to find the elf village again once out of it.

"Should we continue with our walk, or are you tired?" Hosi asked, standing to her feet.

Jase was about to answer when he heard their names being called and turned to find High Guardian Amosa and Princess Skyrah crossing the garden towards them. A burst of happiness exploded through him at the sight of the Princess walking towards them. It wasn't until she was only a few feet away that he realized she appeared to be frustrated and talking in a low voice to the High Guardian, but stopped when they neared them.

"High Guardian," Hosi greeted as she bowed with one hand across her heart and the other in the air besides her.

Jase did the same, happy to show them he knew the proper way to greet another elf. "High Guardian. Princess," he acknowledged.

Hosi then explained, "We were taking a walk so Bluestar could stretch his legs after being in bed these past few weeks."

"So it seems," High Guardian Amosa replied with her emotions hidden. "You may go, Hosi."

Hosi bowed again. Then without looking back, hurried off through the garden the way they had come.

219

Once she was out of sight, Princess Skyrah declared to Jase with sharpness in her voice, "We are leaving today."

"What? Why? And where have you been, anyways? I haven't seen you in weeks, now."

"I've been trying to convince the clan leader here why the elves need to help the Resistance in the war against the Androids again," she revealed in a hushed voice.

Jase studied her before turning to the High Guardian. "And?" he asked.

"He politely turned her down," High Guardian Amosa stated when Skyrah didn't say anything in return.

Skyrah turned to her, bitterly stating, "He said there was no point in helping a lost cause. I wouldn't say that was a polite turn-down."

"It was as polite as it was going to be, Princess, after everything that has happened," Amosa replied to her.

Jase studied Skyrah seeing how angry she was. "So try again," he said.

The Princess glared at him, "I have tried again and again since we got here, Bluestar. It's no use and I cannot waste any more time here at this rate. I have to get back to my people before they either give up and disband or do something reckless."

Jase didn't want to leave, but knew there was no choice in the matter right now. "When will we go? Tomorrow?" he inquired.

"No, tonight. The High Guardian has arranged a few scouts to escort us back to our ship. You and Tahmela will drop me off at the planet the Resistance base is on and go as you please," she informed him as they started walking through the garden.

"Are you sure we can't stay longer a few more days? I have been in bed the entire time we have been here and I have barely seen the planet," Jase pleaded as they walked.

"No, we cannot! I have far more important things to do than to waste a few days so you can see a forest! You made the mistake in going out to find the bulb in the first place when you should have let the elves do it! There is a war going on that *no one* is helping me fight! I have people counting on me, so I don't have time for your whining!" Princess Skyrah shouted.

Jase wasn't sure how to respond especially when he knew she was right for the most part. There was no reason for her to stay any longer whether he was ready to leave or not. Even if he wasn't fighting in the war, she was and she needed to get back to her people. It annoyed him, but he knew he shouldn't argue with her about it as they walked to his treehouse to gather Tahmela.

A Promise

Jase entered the treehouse with the Princess and High Guardian behind him as he announced to the sleeping bulb, "Tahmela, time to get up! We are leaving, apparently."

Tahmela yawned as he sat up from the leaf sofa and replied, "About time, hmil. I was afraid we would never leave."

"You will fly me to where the Resistance base is then you both can go on your way," Princess Skyrah told him firmly, motioning to both the bulb and Jase.

The bulb watched her through his tinted goggles before shifting his head towards Jase. "Is that where you want to go, Bluestar?" he questioned.

"It doesn't matter where he wants to go. I call the shots since I'm of royal blood," Princess Skyrah shot back.

Tahmela didn't move his eyes from Jase as he asked again, "Bluestar, is that where we go now?"

This annoyed the Princess even more as she stepped into the four-foot bulb's face, glaring down at him. "Did you not just hear me? I said you take orders from me, Bulb."

"I swore life to Bluestar. Therefore, I don't take orders from you, Qualia," Tahmela replied calmly.

"Princess," High Guardian uttered softly to get her attention.

Princess Skyrah ignored her still glaring at the bulb as if any moment she would tear him from limb to limb. Jase spoke up, "Leave him alone, Skyrah. I

223

understand you are upset about the elves not wanting to help, but that doesn't mean you get to take it out on us after all we've done for you."

Skyrah said nothing in return as she stared off out the window. The High Guardian then declared, "If you both are quite done then we should get moving before night falls on us."

"What about provisions for the journey or is the ship close to the village?" Jase asked Amosa.

She led them out of the treehouse as she spoke. "Your ship is a day and a half on foot from here. I have already ordered your escorts to pack enough water for you all, and for food...well, we live in a forest that is bountiful of food for you to eat." The High Guardian led them through the village and onto a dirt path that led out into the forest. After a span of walking, Jase spotted two familiar elves waiting for them at the end of the path as well as four other elves. Amosa announced, "Bluestar, I'm sure you recognize these two from your adventure a few weeks ago. Princess, these are our best trackers in the forest. This is El and her brother, Soo. They will be among the four guardians that I have selected to escort you back to your ship."

"Bluestar," Both El and Soo responded and bowed respectfully to the newcomers.

Jase returned the bow happy to see them again. "It's good to see you both alive! I'm sorry I did not have the chance to find you once I was healed to thank you in person for helping me find my friend."

"All is forgiven, Bluestar," El replied in a musical tone.

Soo then added, "We decided it would be—"

"—great honor to escort you back to your ship seeing that you have survived a CrownTooth attack," El finished in her musical tone.

"Well, thank you for thinking so, but I couldn't have done it without you both there to help," Jase told them.

"You would have," El replied.

"You are a Bluestar after all," added Soo.

El glanced up at the midday sky. "We should be on our way," she announced.

"I agree," Princess Skyrah stated turning her focus on Amosa. "Yrt ela ota yrrou ob mikioo, biko vinur?"

High Guardian Amosa's lips cracked into a warm smile. "Kpak horfa ohvao ou beann oou slevarts," she replied.

Jase was curious of what they said to one another wishing he understood, but didn't ask Kaimi to translate. He figured if they wanted everyone to know they would have spoken in his tongue as he watched her start to head towards the direction of the twins who waited along the path to leave. He was about to follow with Tahmela when Amosa stopped him.

"Bluestar, a moment, please," she said.

Tahmela peered to the elf suspiciously and waited with Jase until he responded. "It's okay, Tahmela. I'll catch up," Jase assured him.

"Oki, hmil," with a shrug, Tahmela continued on without him.

Jase turned back to the elven woman. "Yes?" he asked.

The High Guardian watched after the others for a moment. "Keep the Princess safe on your travels together for me, if you would. She is the last true ruler of our galaxy and I promised long ago to her family that I would keep her safe no matter the cost."

"You should come with us," Jase suggested.

Amosa shook her head. "I cannot leave my people without the approval of our council. Therefore, I need you to fulfill my promise and watch over her as long as you are able," she replied.

Jase could tell in her eyes that the elf wanted to go with them even though she couldn't. He didn't know how the elf council worked with such events, but figured if she really wanted to go, she would have made a point to try and convince them to let her. Wanting to help ease her mind, he replied, "You have my word, High Guardian."

Amosa's features soften as if she was relieved in hearing his answer and gave a sharp nod. "Safe travels, Bluestar. May the stars bless you and may Nature watch over you," she said.

"You as well, friend," he replied bowing to her one last time before turning to join the others.

A Kyeakin's Prey

Jase followed the others swiftly and silently through the underbrush and giant trees as the sun slipped through the sky in the late afternoon. Everyone kept to themselves as they traveled while Jase described to Kaimi what he was seeing. "Maybe the next time we come, we could bring Mrs. Rose and the children so they can see that there is so much more than Otect City," he said as he pushed through the lush underbrush.

"I'm sure they will love that," Kaimi agreed.

Soo suddenly stopped. "Zzot," he commanded.

Jase stared at the front of the group where Soo was with his fist in the air motioning for them to stop. El and the Princess whispered something to one another searching with their eyes towards the underbrush around them while four guardians positioned themselves around the Princess. Something seemed to cause everyone to be on alert which made Jase feel uneasy as he, too, scanned the forest for anything that was lurking.

"What's wrong?" Kaimi asked concerned. She must have noticed his pulse quicken through his data watch.

Jase moved his right hand to his holster where his plasma gun was kept. "I'm not quite sure yet, but something has made Soo and El to become cautious," he responded.

"There must be a hmal near," Tahmela uttered in a low voice next to Jase also holding his rifle at ready.

Still watching the trees, Jase asked confused, "A what?"

"Hmal. Umm...creature," he told him, finding the right word in the human tongue.

Remembering the wooden spider and the crowntooth, Jase felt even more anxious. Motioning for Tahmela to follow, Jase moved towards the front where the twins and the Princess were. "Why did we stop?" he asked.

El kept her eyes on the forest as Soo turned towards him, saying, "Danger is around us, Bluestar. A Kyeakin has been stalking us for the last hour." Noticing Jase didn't understand, Soo furthered explained, "A large forest cat that is very dangerous and stealthy. It seems it has made this area of the forest its hunting ground for the week and it can wait for days before striking at its prey. They are very patient killers. We need to travel with caution."

"Is there not enough of us to scare it away?" Jase asked.

"She is not stupid and knows better than to attack full force. No, she will not be easily scared off for she's confident in her size and patience to take care of us one at a time. She will attack when we least expect it," El answered.

"They are intelligent creatures," Soo added.

Jase didn't like the idea of a smart cat stalking them. "Have you dealt with one before?" he questioned.

"Once," Soo told him.

"We try to avoid them as much as possible, even the hunters. They aren't easy creatures to kill," El replied.

Jase glanced at the small bulb, worried for his safety, and turned back to the Twins. "So what do we do?" he inquired.

"We hope to evade it," Soo told him turning back to the forest. "It will take us a day or two to reach your ship, and by then, the cat will attack us multiple times. The first attack will be light but quick to determine which one of us is the strongest. Then, she will go after that one and feed upon them before attacking again."

"She won't go after all of us until the strongest is killed and fed upon. It's her code of the hunt," El added.

"Is there a more active time she will be hunting?" Princess Skyrah asked.

Soo shook his head. "Once they find a prey worth hunting, they won't stop until the hunt is over," he responded.

"Well, that's terrifying," Jase commented as he scanned the trees around them.

Soo smirked. "Not as terrifying as fighting a crowntooth, Bluestar."

"I wasn't aware I was doing it at the time," Jase smiled nervously.

"This is no different, Jase," Kaimi told him in his ear.

"Easy for you to say," he replied back to her before asking Soo, "What's the plan?"

"We will get to Sung Stone Rock where we will be safe from the large cat," El answered.

"There we can get onto the bridges that will take us to your ship," Soo finished explaining.

"Bridges?" Princess Skyrah asked confused.

Soo nodded. "Yes, they will be safer traveling on than the forest floor especially now that we aren't alone," he clarified.

El took a few steps away from the group, surveying all around before stating, "We should go while we have light. I do not feel the kyeakin's presence anymore."

"Princess, Bluestar, stay close to me and have the bulb stay close, too. El will take the rear in case the cat comes back. Stay alert at all times," Soo warned them as they started moving cautiously through the underbrush again.

Nobody spoke a word as they followed close behind one another, trying to stay as quiet as much as possible. Jase's palms were sweaty as he held his plasma gun at ready and tried his best to keep them from shaking as his heart beat quickly in his chest from the tension. Every sound in the forest was an enemy as he expected to be ambushed at any minute.

"Make sure Tahmela stays close to you at all times. Just to be safe," Kaimi suggested in his ear.

Out of habit, Jase nodded in return not wanting to break the tension that hung over the group. He looked behind him to check on Tahmela and was happy to find the bulb with his rifle ready to fire. As he looked back to the front, he noticed something move in the underbrush to their left for a moment, then stop. He trained his eyes on it to see if it would move again and when it did, he softly patted Soo on the back as he pointed his plasma pistol in the direction. Both Soo and El pointed their plasma bows towards the large bush with a plasma arrow already notched and ready to go as they watched the bush move again. The Princess held her gun towards the bush as well.

Tahmela pointed his gun towards their right as if something had caught his eye. "Bluestar!" he suddenly cried out and shot off a bolt, but it was too late.

The Kyeakin attacked from behind them, landing on top of Jase and knocking him into the ground. Jase hit his chin against the hard surface, biting his tongue as he did causing the bitter iron taste to fill his mouth. He felt something heavy pressing against his back as sharp points tore into his jacket and a fierce growl erupted above him. He tried to see the creature on top of him, but was blinded by the plasma light that was being fired from all around. He could smell the plasma filling the air when suddenly it stopped, and he no longer felt the weight on his back anymore.

"Jase, are you alright?" Princess Skyrah asked as Soo helped him up to his feet.

Jase rubbed his chin, feeling the bruise start to form as he spit out the vile taste of blood in his mouth. "I think so. I just bit my tongue. Where did the Kyeakin go?" he asked.

"She ran off, but will be back soon," El told him.

Soo looked over Jase for any other injuries. "Are you sure you are fine, Bluestar?" he asked.

Jase brushed the dirt from his face and clothing. "Yeah, let's get going before the thing comes back," he suggested.

Soo nodded, then took off ahead. "This way," he guided.

The Princess took off after the elf with Tahmela following as fast as he could. Jase took a deep breath and gave a nod to El before running after the others. They steadily jogged through the thick underbrush that was becoming harder to run through as they ventured deeper. Tahmela kept up better than Jase would have thought, but they both were still not as fast as the elves or the Princess. He was sure El didn't like to have to hang back with them. Jase's legs were burning and he could barely catch his breath as they continued on without rest when suddenly he heard a plasma arrow rip through the air behind him and El shouted, "Faster, Bluestar!"

Jase doubled his speed without hesitation but soon slowed when he noticed Tahmela lagging behind and El was no longer in sight. Jase heard another arrow being fired as he ran back to the bulb who was gasping for air. "Come on, Tahmela! We have to go!" he urged the bulb.

Between heavy breaths, Tahmela responded, "I can't, Bluestar. Too tired."

Jase stopped in front of him as he stared back the way they came and saw El firing arrows behind her. Turning back to the bulb, he quickly stated, "Let me carry you."

"No, hmil, I won't let you," the bulb objected.

"You don't have much of a—" Jase began but stopped suddenly when he heard El yell.

He looked back up to find a large predator lunging towards him with its claws outstretched, knocking the bulb out of the way as it did. The world suddenly went into slow motion as Jase met its fierce golden, green eyes stare. Its mouth was open revealing rows of slanted sharp points as it neared him. Then the world started picking up speed again, and Jase instinctually threw up both his hands towards the creature. He felt a wave of blue energy rush down his arms as it hurled out towards the cat, throwing it backwards a hundred yards into the underbrush. Surprised by the action, Jase suddenly felt himself weaken as if he had just gotten hit by a hover bike, and fell to his knees.

El rushed towards him, yanking him to his feet. "Bluestar, go now!" she urged.

Before Jase could move, the Kyeakin attacked again with its deadly claws outstretched towards the elf. El quickly ducked twirling as she did and let loose another plasma arrow towards the cat as she yelled again for Jase to run. Jase grabbed the frightened bulb by his belt and started running after the others again as he heard El fire another arrow. He felt as if he was going to collapse at any moment, but forced himself to keep going. He heard a loud growl behind him and a powerful paw suddenly swiped him off his feet and shot him sideways into a nearby tree trunk. Jase's back erupted in pain as he slammed into it and landed on the forest floor. His lungs collapsed from the impact leaving him gasping for air.

Jase could hardly breath as he pushed himself up to all fours and he noticed the kyeakin was circling for another attack. Its forest green and black fur seemed to blend in with the underbrush as it paced back and forth in the dirt watching Jase fiercely. Jase climbed to his feet using the trunk to steady himself as he faced the cat knowing he had no choice but to fight. At the sight, the kyeakin crouched and kneaded the earth floor with its claws as it got ready to pounce once more. Jase kept his eyes focused reaching for his gun in his holster but found it empty. "Crap," he voiced and without warning the cat charged towards him.

Suddenly, Princess Skyrah leapt towards the cat landing straight on its back and stabbed it repeatedly with a silver dagger. The kyeakin yelped and growled in pain as it stopped its charge to turn its attention to the woman, trying to buck her off. Soo appeared through the trees raining down arrows from above, but no matter how many times he hit the cat, the kyeakin continued fighting to get the Princess of its back. With the creature distracted, Jase grabbed Tahmela who had been knocked unconscious and swung him over his shoulder before rushing towards El who now joined the fight with blood streaming down her left arm.

"Go! Go! Go!" Soo ordered to El and Jase as he continued firing arrows.

"Come, this way!" El said and quickly limped into the underbrush.

Jase shot one last glance back towards the Princess just in time to watch the kyeakin slam its own back into a tree to knock her off onto the dirt floor. Jase heard the Princess yell in pain as she fell with the kyeakin's jaw hung loose to bite her. Soo tried jumping down to save her, but the cat slapped him aside with one powerful stroke before turning back towards the Princess for its deadly blow.

"No!" Jase shouted, dropping Tahmela and rushing towards the cat. He felt an eruption of energy forming in one of his palms as it glowed an unstable blue color before he threw it towards the cat. The ball of energy blasted the kyeakin into the underbrush yards away allowing Jase to reach the Princess. His vision went black and he felt the ground beneath his cheek.

"Jase! Jase!" Princess Skyrah's voice shouted as he felt her shaking him.

Jase wasn't sure if his eyes were still open or close as he laid there before he heard more footsteps approach and then someone was dragging him in the dirt. His ears started ringing and he realized he could barely feel his legs and arms as his thoughts seemed to slow and get fuzzy. *What's happening?* he wondered as he heard voices but couldn't make out what they said. He didn't know how much time had passed in that state. He felt the numbness in his body start to wear off and his vision slowly came back. First he only saw blurry shapes and colors then after a few moments, his vision cleared revealing that he was lying next to a large rock.

"Bluestar, are you okay?" El asked when she noticed he was awake.

Jase felt his body protest as he forced himself to sit up, feeling nauseous as he did. His chest pained him every time he breathed. "The Princess?" he asked.

"I'm here," Princess Skyrah answered moving next to him with a fresh cut across her cheek. Other than that she appeared to be fine as Jase surveyed the

232

rest of the team, noticing only one of the guardians were still with them. "What happened to the others?"

Soo answered wiping the sweat off his brow as he stared up at the evening sky that was darkening into a pale violet. "The other guardians stayed behind to make sure the kyeakin doesn't follow us the rest of the way. It's wounded which gives them a chance to kill it if they need to. Come. We must keep going."

"I thought it was dangerous to travel at night on the forest floor?" Jase asked as he forced himself to his feet feeling every fiber protest from the feat.

Soo examined his sister's wound on her arm and placed a hand on her shoulder for comfort as he answered, "It is. That is why we travel on the bridges."

"I will show you," El said, motioning for them to follow her as she took the lead around the rock.

Jase followed after the others, noticing elven words embedded into the rock. His eyes lingered on it a moment longer before Soo tapped his shoulder for him to continue on. Jase walked around the rock to find a well-hidden wooden bridge that led into the lower level of the giant tree branches. "We will be safe up here?" Jase whispered to Soo behind him as they climbed up the ramp.

Soo was still cautiously watching the branches around them as he answered softly, "For the most part, yes, but also no. Even scarier things climb at night, Bluestar, so be on your guard."

Jase would have felt uneasy by his words but couldn't with how exhausted he felt. He was amazed he was even still able to walk as he climbed the last of the ramp and onto the wooden boards that creaked in some places. The sound made him wince, feeling that any moment it could cause something to jump out from the darkness and eat them. He almost preferred walking in the darkness under the tunnels back on Otect City.

"Light attracts dangerous foes, Bluestar. We travel in dark like shadows," Soo had told him.

They traveled in the dark for what seemed like forever to Jase as he felt his limbs grow more and more heavier from exhaustion. He tried taking his mind off of it by looking to the night sky to see the stars, but could only see bits and pieces of it through the towering branches above them.

"We will rest here for the night," Soo suddenly declared in a loud whisper for them all to hear.

Somewhere in the darkness in front of him, Jase heard Tahmela ask, "Where?"

Soo moved past them to stand next to El who Jase was barely able to make out in the darkness. "Here on the bridge. We are at a safe distance from the kyeakin and from most of the dangerous creatures who walk the night. I will still take watch. You all should sleep for the next few hours before we continue on," he replied.

Jase took off his jacket and balled it up to use as a pillow as he moved to lay down where he stood. It was a warm night, but there was a small breeze that was a little chilly causing him to cross his arms across his chest to try and stay warm while he slept on his side.

"Sleep well, Jase," Kaimi whispered in his ear.

"You too, Kaimi," Jase tiredly replied as he felt something brush against his back causing him to turn to see what it might be. He relaxed when he saw it was only Tahmela lying next to him with a large leaf to share as a blanket.

"Only let me pick one. Thought you might be cold," Tahmela stated.

"Thanks, Tahmela," Jase replied and glanced over at the Princess who was lying next to El and the other guardian. Knowing she was safe, Jase laid his head back down and listened to the sounds of the forest as he fell asleep.

To Walk a Bridge

"Jase? Jase?" A familiar voice entered into Jase's dreams of being back home on Otect City as he slept. His dreams suddenly changed and he was standing back in the endless blue room. He remembered the voice that spoke to him as he had mediated with Skyrah.

"How can you see me if you dissociate your true self with how you see yourself? I can't show you until you believe, Jase. In time you will."

Jase scanned the endless room, looking for the strange voice. He still had so many questions for the faceless stranger. Jase felt his whole body being shaken and in a blink of an eye, he woke up. It was Soo waking him to leave even though it was still dark out. Only a slight glimmer of light was in the sky.

"Time to go," the elf told him before moving on to wake the bulb.

Jase sleepily stood to his feet, feeling his tired body protest at the action with each muscle aching as he steadied himself on wobbly legs and pulled on his jacket to protect from the morning cool. Zipping it halfway, Jase stretched his arms to the sky and yawned while noticing the Princess and El were already up and ready to go. He checked his data watch to see what time it was and read four-thirty-two A.M.

"We have fifteen miles to travel before we reach the bridge that will take us to your ship. From there, it will only take five miles," Soo explained as he glanced up to the dawn sky.

"The Kyeakin will no doubt be on our trail again if the other guardians didn't handle her. Therefore, we must be on guard at all times," El added.

"Can they climb trees?" Jase asked curiously.

El nodded. "They are excellent climbers and typically attack from the branches of trees. We should move cautiously in case she managed to get in front of us during the night," she replied.

"Do we need to worry about any other Kyeakins in this area?" Princess Skyrah asked watching the trees.

Soo shook his head. "Each Kyeakin marks their hunting ground so no other Kyeakin will interfere. There are far more dangerous predators that we need to be weary of as we travel," he stated.

"We should go," El stated.

"I do more walking now than all years in city, Bluestar. I not like it," Tahmela commented under his breath to Jase.

"It's better than jail," Jase replied and started following after the others with the bulb responding next to him. "I guess, hmil, I guess."

Princess Skyrah slowed to walk next to them as she said, "I saw that you were able to stop the kyeakin with your abilities. Does that mean you can control it now?"

Jase shrugged thinking back to how exhausted he felt after using his Bluestar abilities. "I don't think so. I think I was just acting by instinct to protect you. I couldn't control it, it just flowed through me and attacked the cat," he said.

"Interesting. There may be someone I know who could help you at my base. I can't promise you anything, but if you stayed for a day or two when we get back to the Resistance, you might find answers," she told him.

"Who?" Jase asked.

"An old friend who knows a great many things," the Princess replied.

Jase's thoughts stayed on this mysterious person the Princess had mentioned and paid little attention to Tahmela's rant about his ship and how worried he was on its condition. Breaking out of his thoughts, Jase asked the elf, "Soo, do the elves use technology here on the planet?"

"We do have technology that we use for desperate measures. The forest and Nature takes care of us therefore we have no need for it on an everyday basis like many races do," Soo answered.

"But it makes life easier," Jase replied back.

"But one tends to forget what they have with it and how to appreciate life that is right in front of them," Soo countered.

Jase couldn't argue with that as he stared out into the forest that surrounded them. He loved seeing trees instead of steel buildings and cramped streets before his eyes. He wondered if all beings visited a place like Kurath Thor if they would crave it more than the coldness of the city. As they walked on throughout the day, it got hotter and hotter to the point that Jase had to take off his jacket and tie it around his waist to try and stay cool. He was grateful for the giant trees and their branches, but the sun still managed to beat down on them through the leaves no matter how much was in its way. It wasn't until hours later when the sun reached the highest point in the sky that El spotted the hidden ramp that would take them back onto the forest floor.

"Where does that lead?" he asked, staring at the bridge that continued onward as they descended towards the ground floor of the forest.

"That leads farther south into the forest where other villages lie. It splits into another connecting bridge that leads west towards the deepest parts of the forest that have yet been explored except for a small area where the village, Tuka, is located. The Tukans harvest exotic fruits and juices to sell in the market places in Hewka city. I have a cousin that lives there and says the juices that they harvest are the sweetest in all the planet," El explained.

"Do you see much of him?" Jase asked, curious about the Twins' lives.

"It takes four months to reach Tuka village and that's if you travel by bridge. We don't go unless it is urgent," El replied.

"Your ship lies five miles east from here. We will rest for a moment and recover our strength before starting again," Soo interrupted.

"We don't need to rest, Soo. We should continue going while we can," Princess Skyrah suggested.

"I'm sure you don't need to, Princess, but the others are not like your kind. They will need to recover for a moment," Soo replied.

The Princess looked at Jase and Tahmela, annoyed by their presence, before moving to stand with El who was taking watch of the area. Jase welcomed the break as he sat against a giant tree. Soo walked over to a stubby tree with low-hanging branches that bore fruit no bigger than Jase's fists. He tossed one of the fruits to Jase which he happily caught. Jase viewed the strange fruit silver in color but soft to the touch as he asked, "Is it supposed to be this color?"

Soo tossed one to the Princess as he answered, "That is how you know it's ripe, Bluestar. It's called a Khanjen Trea, or in your tongue, changing tree. Its fruit changes colors as it ripens. It starts out no bigger than a black seed which then, as it grows, changes into dark blue. While it's blue it becomes poisonous, and its hard shell softens before turning purple. All the poison in the fruit bleeds out, making it very sweet and causes the fruit's skin to soften even more. Finally, it ripens fully into what you hold in your hand now. In a week or two it will die and start again from the beginning."

"Why don't you eat it when its sweet in its purple stage?" he asked as he watched Tahmela eat his, juice running down the corners of his mouth.

Soo remained alert as he continued, "It's most beneficial when it's in its last stage. It replaces missing nutrients in your body in just a few bites."

Jase sank his teeth into the soft fruit and quickly felt its juices drench the inside of his mouth. It was sweet and savory but there was another taste he couldn't describe as he swallowed. The juices overwhelmed his taste buds again as he chewed, wishing he could have another. He was almost done when Soo announced, "Time to go, Bluestar and bulb."

Jase forced himself to his feet. In doing so he found that his body no longer ached from traveling or felt tired at all. Surprised, he looked down to inspect himself, thinking surely it was in his head. "How am I not sore?" he questioned out loud.

Both Elves smiled at him as if they found his question humorous. "The Khanjen fruits as many benefits, Bluestar, which is why one should eat it when its ripe than any other time. It's so rich in nutrients that it causes your body to heal itself," El answered.

Jase looked at the tree in amazement. "So one could eat enough of these to never feel tired or sore again?"

Soo shook his head. "If you eat more than what you need the fruit will start doing the opposite. It will overwhelm your body system and cause damage if you are not careful."

"Come, we should go now," El decided.

Jase picked one more Khanjen fruit and placed it in his jacket pocket before he followed after the others. They walked another hour in the same direction, heading east until Soo finally changed southward leading them into a denser part of the underbrush that slowed their progress. Here, the fungi trees grew closer together, causing the group to have to travel sideways through the stalks. They made slow progress due to having to shove and squeeze by the trunks.

"At least the Kyeakin will have a hard time traveling through this to follow us," Princess Skyrah said as she wedged through another tree.

Jase followed after her, hearing El behind him softly say, "The kyeakin is not what I'd worry about."

Jase glanced back, noticing she was watching the trees above them as he squeezed through two trees. "What is it?" he asked her.

El paid him no notice as she followed gracefully through the trees seeming to not have trouble getting through them. "The osynilega pukev or, as you say in your tongue, the invisible demons live in these areas."

"What are they?" Jase asked, looking up to see anything that might be stalking their group.

"They are transparent insects that camouflage themselves into the fungi trees and wait at the top of the stalks until their prey gets stuck or has to rest in the trees below. Once this happens they crawl down to feed, starting with the top of their prey then work down to the feet while you are still alive. Nasty creatures, they are," she told him.

Jase nervously peered at her hoping that she was teasing. "Is there anything in this forest that won't try to eat me?" he sighed.

"You are probably safer in your city than here, Bluestar," El laughed.

"I don't doubt that," he replied as he tried to move faster through the underbrush.

"We might have lived in a dangerous city, Jase, but there are far more dangerous things in this universe than you are aware of," Kaimi added as she listened from his data watch sensors.

"That's a very terrifying thought, Kaimi," he told her.

Kaimi chuckled in his ear. "Life is terrifying, but never dull with you, Jase," she said.

"At least you are safe in my data watch. You don't have to experience it!" he teased as sweat dripped down his face.

Kaimi chuckled again. "If I could, I would for you."

Jase pushed through the last of the fungi trees and into the less dense forest. He let out a relieved sigh, happy to be out of the trees and turned back around to find High Guardian Amosa and two elven warriors to his surprise.

"What are you doing here?" Princess Skyrah questioned, surprised as well by their appearance.

"I decided I couldn't let you go off by yourself again without me," High Guardian Amosa replied.

"But your people?" Skyrah questioned.

Amosa didn't waiver. "I have chosen a High Guardian to replace me in my absence. My people may not support your battle but with a Bluestar turning up, whether he knows his powers or not, I will not stand by and let you fight in this war alone. I would rather fight beside you both than to let the royal family suffer alone," she replied.

"The council will not be happy when they find out of your departure. You could be exiled, Amosa. I cannot let you do this for me," Skyrah quickly objected.

Amosa raised her hand to her to be silent. "I will live with the consequences of my people, Princess. It is time for us to strike back at the Androids, again, and not sit in the protection of our trees."

"Amosa...," Skyrah began but was stopped once more.

"We were friends once, and I abandoned you for my people after the war, Skyrah. I broke a promise to General Maliha that I would keep you safe no matter what, and it is time for me to honor that promise for your family's sake," she responded.

Skyrah's lips parted into a grateful smile as she nodded. When she turned around to El and Soo, Jase saw a slight mist cover her eyes from the elf's words. It soon disappeared as she thanked the elves. "Thank you both for leading us through the forest when you did not have to. I will not forget your actions," she said and bowed respectfully.

Soo and El both returned the bow. "It was our pleasure to serve, Princess," Soo replied.

"We will always serve under High Guardian Amosa, and the Bluestar, no matter what is asked of us," El added.

Jase bowed to both of them. "I am forever in your gratitude, Ieth twins. I hope one day we will meet again, and you can show me more of the forest."

El's lips parted in a genuine smile as she replied, "We will always be honored to be in your presence again, Bluestar."

"Till the next time we meet, friend. Yimm kpak horfa ohvao ou beann oou slevarts," Soo told him.

"Be careful with the Kyeakin hunting as you make your way back to the village," Jase answered.

They nodded in return before wishing farewell to the High Guardian then disappearing back into the forest. Once the twins were gone, Amosa informed Jase and the others, "While we were waiting, we attached a basket to the branch your ship is on to carry you up. It will be much faster than climbing."

"We appreciate it," Princess Skyrah replied, heading towards the large, woven basket with Tahmela following hastily behind her.

"How did you manage to beat us here when we left before you?" Jase finally asked.

"Elves can travel long distances without needing to rest. You all travelled at a slow pace, and you slept for a few hours before starting your day today," Amosa replied.

"Did you use the bridge?" he questioned.

"Bluestar, you cannot know every answer to your questions. Someday I might tell you," Amosa replied walking towards the basket.

Jase started after her. "You didn't trust me to keep my promise to you about keeping her safe, did you?" he pressed lightheartedly.

"Perhaps," Amosa said as she entered the basket.

"Bluestar, let's go!" Princess Skyrah ordered from inside the basket.

Jase rolled his eyes as he jumped into the basket shutting the woven gate behind him. One of the warriors pulled them up with the pulley system attached to the basket and branch. Ascending into the trees, Jase watched as the elves below grew smaller before disappearing into the forest of leaves. Jase suddenly felt sad leaving the forest when it felt he had only just arrived to explore its wonders.

"Here," Amosa uttered, placing something smooth into one of his palms. "Hosi wanted me to give it to you. So you have something to remember us by while we are away."

Jase peered down to find a small colorful flower he had seen in the garden when they went on their walk. It was enclosed in a beautiful, crystal blue stone that caught the sunlight as it shined down on it. Enclosing his fingers around it, he peered back to the elf's violet eyes. "Thank you. I will always treasure it and my time here."

Amosa dipped her head in return as they both turned back to watch the branches pass by them as they ascended into the trees.

Hours later, Jase and the others reached the branch where their ship waited intact. Tahmela was the first to get out of the basket and rushed towards the ship to check on its condition while the others filed out one by one. While Amosa thanked the elf guardians, Jase and Princess Skyrah stood off near the edge of the branch looking out across the forest. Jase admired the beauty of the planet he had only been on for a few weeks.

"Are you ready to be off this planet, Princess?" he asked Skyrah.

Continuing to stare off towards the horizon in her own thoughts, she admitted, "No." Without further explanation she walked towards the ship preparing for departure.

Jase watched her, wondering what she was thinking that bothered her so much. After a moment, he followed after her towards the ship. As he neared, Tahmela happily exclaimed, "Bluestar, everything is as should be when we left it so long ago!"

"Good! I'm glad to hear that, Tahmela!" Jase enthused to the bulb.

"I go make preparations to leave," the bulb said and hurried off towards the ramp of the ship.

Jase turned back around to view the forest once more before. Amosa neared him quietly. "We should get going, Bluestar," she said interrupting his thoughts.

Jase replied, "Won't you miss it here?"

Amosa stopped, gazing at the beautiful sea of green. "I have faith in the stars and Nature that I will return. I will miss the trees, the birds, and my people...but one cannot grow without changing. Change is good for us, Bluestar. It helps us grow inwardly."

Jase shook his head as he walked up the ramp. "Saying yes or no would have done the job."

Jase showed Amosa through the front cargo hold and down the corridor towards the cockpit where Tahmela sat powering up the ship's engines. He took a seat in the co-pilot's chair while Amosa sat behind him and buckled in as the Princess entered the room. Tahmela flipped more switches on the control panel, checking the power levels of each system. When he was finally ready, he asked excitedly, "Are we ready?"

Jase buckled his belt across his waist, tightening the strap as he did. With a nod, he turned back to the bulb and said, "Let's go."

"Taking off," the bulb replied, pushing slowly on one of the throttles that slowly lifted the ship into the air.

Jase felt the ship rattle with life as the noise of the engine vibrated inside the ship as it rose. The ship slid forward in the air and up towards the clouded atmosphere with the sun glaring off the windshield for a moment before disappearing behind a cloud. The higher it rose, the pull of gravity weighed on Jase's body causing him to grip the chair arms tightly and focus on the flames that flickered across the edges of the windshield as they shot through the clouds towards space. Suddenly, they broke out of the planet's atmosphere and floated into the ocean of stars causing their bodies to float for a moment in the air as gravity left them. They floated for a few minutes in the planet's orbit before Tahmela turned on gravitational pull.

"Where to, Princess?" the bulb asked, unfastening his seatbelt.

Princess Skyrah turned her chair to the navigation screen, touching it to bring it to life and began sorting through the planets in their solar system. She finally touched one, sending the information to Tahmela's screen while saying, "Setting course for Adsila Laabbirrem."

"Is that where the Resistance is stationed?" Jase asked her.

"It's where one of our bases is, yes," she replied.

"To Adsila Laabbirrem then," Tahmela declared pressing a panel to his left before making the jump into hyperspace.

"I would like to get informed of all that has happened since we last saw one another and what position the Resistance is in. That is if you would not mind filling me in," Amosa motioned.

Skyrah nodded. "We can talk in my room," she replied.

Jase watched the two women disappear into the corridor and couldn't help wanting to learn more about the two's history with one another. Forcing himself to turn back to the controls that Tahmela was constantly checking and rechecking, he asked, "How long will it take us to reach Adsila Laabbirrem?"

"One month, but we will stop halfway to refuel the ship at a supply station before continuing on," Tahmela responded.

"And I thought going two weeks on this ship was hard, but a month will drive me crazy," Jase teased.

"You'll have to keep yourself busy," Kaimi stated, transferring over to the ship's network and appeared on the small holoprojector in the center of the control board.

"I suppose I'll have to," Jase replied. "So Tahmela, how many planets have you been on besides Faton and Kurath Thor?"

Without looking at him, Tahmela answered, "I've been to Perendi, Adsila Laabbirrem twice, Nadeeda once, and then planets in the Cedonia solar system that I doubt you know."

Jase studied the navigation holo, zooming out to look at the whole Orbane galaxy and her planets that had courses lining the stars. "Wow, I didn't realize how big our galaxy was," he exclaimed.

Tahmela stayed focused on his controls. "If you think this big, wait and see other galaxies in universe, Bluestar," he said.

Astonished, Jase looked at the screen. "You mean, there are more galaxies than ours?"

"We are all small fishes in a sea of stars, Jase. There are infinite numbers of galaxies that even I don't know. Ours is just one of countless in space," Kaimi responded.

Jase looked back at Tahmela. "Have you been to other galaxies besides ours?"

"No, quite hard a thing, and I never met one who has," the bulb told him.

"One day I would like to see all the planets in our galaxy and explore them," Jase said looking back at the screen again.

"It would take many lives in order to see all the worlds," Kaimi told him.

"I pray to the stars that you see many, Bluestar," Tahmela chuckled.

Jase beamed as he pondered out loud, "How does one fly to another galaxy? How would you know when one ends and another begins?"

Tahmela leaned back in his chair, resting his short stubby hands on his belly. "I only heard legend from other space travelers. It said that each galaxy has own unique portal that is shape of a certain creature of the galaxy it is in. Like constellation in space but this portal wanders throughout its galaxy. Never to stay in one spot. You fly through and it takes you to another galaxy."

"How would you know if you saw it? There's so many stars in space that they all look the same," Jase continued.

Tahmela shrugged turning off the map and once again the stream of stars streaked the outside of the ship's windshield. "I sure it would be something you not forget, Bluestar. A outline of creature with colorful galaxy inside it would be hard to miss,"

"Yeah, I'm sure you are right," Jase agreed before suggesting. "Maybe one day we will see one?"

The bulb hopped down from his chair and started to walk out of the cockpit. "Maybe, Bluestar, maybe," he said.

Jase followed after the bulb. "The High Guardian would like to see you and the Princess in the main cargo hold," Kaimi told him.

"What for?" he questioned.

"She did not say," Kaimi responded in his ear.

Jase followed the narrow corridor through the mess hall and past his room until he stopped before the cargo hold door. As he walked inside, a boot made contact with his face causing him to stumble backwards onto the floor. Holding his cheek, he angrily climbed back to his feet and growled towards Amosa, "What was that for?"

"You must be ready for an attack at any moment, Bluestar," the elf responded with ease.

Jase looked at Skyrah. "Let me guess, she was the one who taught you how to fight."

Skyrah nodded in response as Amosa returned, "I will not apologize for the attack, but I do want you to know that I only wish to test your abilities so I know where you stand. The Princess has told me much about you, but for one to truly understand someone's limits, they must judge them accordingly."

"So this is a test," Jase stated.

"Yes," Amosa answered.

Determined to show her he could handle himself, Jase took off his blue pilot's jacket and laid it across a large crate in the room. "Alright, let's do this then," he responded.

Before he had a chance to blink Amosa succeeded in hitting him. It was like sparring with the Princess all over again as he formed fresh bruises across his body. Doubling over, Jase grunted at the pain but forced himself to straighten back up to try and block the next attack. He continued to miss every time as they sparred endlessly over the next hour until Amosa landed an attack that left him on his knees with her holding his hand in an uncomfortable angle that she could easily use to break his arm. Jase grunted, out of breath, and tried using his freehand to break loose of her grip but she was able to grab hold of it also to stop him.

"Do you need a break, Bluestar?" Amosa asked him, neutrally.

Jase didn't want to end with his hand broken in order to learn a lesson. "Please," he responded.

Amosa released him and turned to the Princess. "Princess, do you have any words for Bluestar?"

Skyrah looked at him sitting on the ground, holding his hand and answered, "There is no such thing as breaks when fighting your enemies. You should fight until you can't anymore. It's life or death in real situations."

"In a real life situation, I wouldn't have given up so easily," he countered standing to his feet.

Amosa studied him in silence for a moment then without warning slammed her fist across his jawline and another into his side. As she went to hit again, Jase ducked out of the way and moved from her next attack which was a blur of movement. Amosa swung towards him again then spun her leg around, kicking Skyrah in the side of her head before moving back to attack Jase. She continued attacking both of them with quick movements and evading their attacks all at the same time as they fought. Jase could barely block while Skyrah was more adept in her abilities.

"Work together to defeat your enemy, not apart," Amosa instructed as they fought. They continued like that for many long hours until Amosa knocked both of them onto their backs with one swift combo of kicks. Jase and Skyrah grunted in pain as Amosa stood over them breathing as if she hadn't been fighting at all. "You will never win if you don't work together. Princess, you should know this best of all," the elf reprimanded.

Skyrah rose to her feet, her pain hidden from her face as she bowed. "My apologizes, I do know better. I let the disadvantages that the Bluestar has slow him down so I could focus on my attacks instead of helping him. I will do better in events to come."

Satisfied with her answer, Amosa turned to Jase, saying, "Bluestar, you are a fierce fighter even when you know you are out matched. You fight with your heart and through instinct and though you have much to learn, I am proud of your abilities thus far. Your speed will come as your Bluestar abilities awaken more and I'm sure you will be a great warrior in time. If you will let me, I wish to spar with you more in hopes to help your abilities grow stronger while we have time on this ship."

Jase bowed respectfully to her pleased that he was able to show her that he was more than he looked. "I would be honored, High Guardian," he responded.

"Please, you may call me Amosa," she corrected him.

"Alrighty," Jase replied and peered to the Princess who appeared to have a lot on her mind.

"We are done for today, but tomorrow I expect you both to be better," Amosa told them before leaving the room.

Noticing Skyrah was still in her own thoughts, Jase took this time to tell her, "You did a good job today."

"I could have done better," the Princess corrected him as she turned to leave.

Jase reached out to stop her gently by her arm. "Don't be so hard on yourself. She's an elf! How is anyone supposed to move as fast as her?" he remarked in hopes to make her smile.

"Qualias can, and I am one of them. Therefore, I should be able to block her every move. I let myself get soft once my family was gone, and now I need to let that go in order to be strong again. I have to be strong to take back what my family has lost and rule our galaxy in their stead. My actions affect everything," she told him.

"That's a lot of stress for one person," Jase responded, pausing a moment before continuing. "I don't think anyone can make a perfect decision no matter what they do. There are millions, if not more, of opinions out there that won't always agree with your ruling. It comes down to what you think is best for everyone despite how it reflects on yourself."

Princess Skyrah studied him for a moment before saying, "Sometimes I forget that you can be wise, Bluestar, when you aren't being a child."

Jase grinned. "I like to keep it hidden, otherwise I'd have to be wise all the time," he said.

With that her lips parted into a warm smile with her bluish pink eyes gleaming as they met his. "Thank you for your kind words, Jase." Turning away, she moved towards the door. "Goodnight, Bluestar."

"Goodnight, Princess. Tomorrow we will take down the High Guardian together!" he encouraged, feeling butterflies in his stomach as he watched her go.

"That was nice of you to say," Kaimi stated in his ear.

Jase wasn't sure why he couldn't wipe the grin from his face as he walked back towards his quarters. "It was nothing. She needed a friend and despite how she acts sometimes, I couldn't just let her leave in her head," he replied and entered his room where Tahmela was already getting ready for bed.

"You get kissed, Bluestar?" the bulb joked.

Jase made a face at him as he pulled off his shoes before climbing on his bed. "No, who would I kiss?"

"You know who, Bluestar," the bulb chuckled before he turned over in his bed to sleep.

Jase shook his head, pulling the covers to his chin as he whispered to Kaimi, "He must be on something to think I would kiss the Princess. I don't even like her all that much."

"Perhaps," Kaimi replied with amusement in her tone as he drifted to sleep.

Erebus Ytic

For the next two weeks, Amosa drilled Jase and the Princess over hand-to-hand combat and how to work together against an opponent. Each day, Jase slowly got better while the Princess shredded her rusty habits and started putting up more of a fight towards the elf. She did her best to help Jase, but his reflexes were still too slow to keep up with the pair no matter how hard he tried.

Amosa kicked him backwards causing him to stumble as she yelled. "You're a Bluestar, are you not?! You can block me! So do it! Hit me!" she ordered.

Jase pushed himself forward, raising his fist as he advanced to attack her. "I'm trying!" he shouted angrily swinging his arm forward. He swung left, then right, then left, then an upward jab but each time the elf managed to effortlessly avoid his attack. Her movements frustrated him as he stopped paying attention to where she was and focused on trying to hit anything.

"Focus!" Amosa ordered somewhere in the fog of his anger as Jase continued.

He ignored her, feeling a familiar sensation slowly entwining with his veins as he brought up his hand and felt it release outward. Amosa went flying backwards into the Princess, and they both landed in a tangled mess on the floor. Weariness coated his body more after the release causing Jase to feel weak at the knees as he steadied himself on a nearby crate.

Amosa jumped to her feet. "That is what I have been waiting for, Bluestar! You did it!" she exclaimed.

Jase moved to sit on the floor feeling as if any second he could pass out. "I didn't do it. It just happens by itself," he replied.

"It's true," Skyrah told Amosa. "His body does it by instinct without him able to control it. I haven't been able to figure out why."

Amosa nodded, puzzled as she studied him. "When were you first able to use your abilities, Bluestar?" she asked.

"When I started traveling with the Princess," he told her.

"It could also be the mixture of how much danger he has been in since leaving Faton. Being in the city was never all that dangerous with the jobs you would take. Your life was never really in danger there," Kaimi added through the PA system in the cargo hold.

"It would make sense why he would just now be experiencing them," Princess Skyrah agreed.

"Indeed," Amosa replied in thought.

Jase felt a headache starting to form in his skull as he wondered how life would have been different if he had his abilities while he lived in Otect City. The PA system crackled to life again with Kaimi saying, "We are approaching the fuel station in the halfway mark to Adsila Laabbrierrm. You all might want to prepare for docking."

"Let's conclude our training for today," Amosa concluded as she turned away. They exited the cargo hold and ventured into the cockpit to join Tahmela and Kaimi. Jase pulled on his pilot jacket, feeling the Khanjen fruit in his jacket pocket and decided to pull it out to eat. The silver fruit was starting to turn color which caused him to hesitate to eat it. "It is safe to eat, Bluestar. Tomorrow it would not be any good," Amosa reassured him.

Jase bit into the sweet, savory fruit, feeling its juice explode in his mouth as they entered the cockpit and he took his seat in the co-pilot chair, asking, "How long will it take for us to board?"

Tahmela's stubby fingers brushed the controls. "It will take five hours till we reach the station. Then, just a matter of minutes to land," he replied.

Jase was about to ask another question when he suddenly caught sight of the fuel station before them. The station filled half of the view with its metal exterior that looked like a giant spider with outstretched legs gripping the small asteroid it drifted on that made it appear to be catching its prey. The metal legs dug deep into the asteroid's surface and ran to a small rectangular station. From there a small shaft rose from the top of the building up to a larger cube that seemed impossible to balance on the small shaft it sat on.

"What is that?" he asked.

Tahmela looked to where he was pointing. "That is the fuel station, Bluestar," he said.

"No, what's the building above it?" Jase pointed again.

"That is the station city called, Erebus Ytic, or as some say, the Darkness city. The shaft below it is the elevator to the fuel station. That is where the fuel is gathered and sent into the city for ships to use and to export to other planets nearby," Kaimi answered.

"And the pipes that look like spider legs digging into the ground is how the fuel is mined from the asteroid," Jase said, putting two and two together.

Kaimi appeared on the hologram in the center of the controls. "Exactly," she said.

"How does the asteroid's orbit not get thrown off by the large city above it?" Jase questioned.

Kaimi looked back to the hologram. "The buildings' mass is the same as the asteroids. Therefore, it doesn't disrupt the gravitational pull," she replied.

Seeing her time to cut in, Princess Skyrah declared, "The Androids control the station but let a slime ball grody rule over the city as a leader. His name is Mayor Grits Shokiie. He is a real push over which is why the Androids let him stay in charge so the city wouldn't retaliate when they took over. Therefore, we should contain a low profile while we are here and be careful with who we interact with while we refuel. We don't want to arouse suspicion, especially this close to Adsila Laabbrirrem. The Androids will be watching everything for any new information about the Resistance Base location."

"The Princess is right," Amosa agreed. "If anyone leaves the ship, it should only be one or two at a time. Anymore would be noticed and questioned."

Tahmela pulled back the throttle as they entered the station's hangar bay. "I go pay for fuel. It takes twenty minutes to do so."

Amosa nodded, looking to the others. "The rest of us should stay here until we depart."

"I have a contact here through the Resistance. I need to let them know that I am alive and not captured," Skyrah informed her.

"I can send a transmission, My Princess," Kaimi suggested.

Skyrah shook her head. "It's too dangerous with Androids nearby. They could intercept it or at least notice its source through the airwaves. I would not cause harm to my contact if it is avoidable besides he would not believe me if I did not show up in person. For all they would know is that it was a false message to try and have them reveal the location of our base. I must go in person."

"You should not leave the ship, Princess. It's too dangerous," Amosa firmly ordered.

"I have been gone too long without any contact to them. If I wait any longer the Resistance could fall in ruin with my absence. They need to know I'm okay," Skyrah countered.

Jase knew that Amosa wouldn't let her go by herself and the elf couldn't go without being noticed. The Androids would want to know what an elf was doing in a place like this since they haven't been seen since the great war. "I'll go with her," he suggested.

"Jase, it's too dangerous. Both of your faces would have been sent to every planet under the Android's control for your capture. They will be searching for you and will no doubt have security outside this hangar that you would have to go through in order to get inside the city. It's too much of a risk," Kaimi told them both.

"You forget that I'm a thief, Kaimi. You know how sneaky I can be with all the jobs we've done," Jase told her while flashing a confident grin.

"You're right but we've never had the disadvantage of our enemies knowing our faces," Kaimi countered.

"It's just another complicated job, but we can do this! Besides, isn't the Princess supposed to be an assassin? She should be good at going by unnoticed," Jase determined.

Pleased with his remark, Skyrah stated, "We will be back within the hour then we can set out again."

"I don't like this idea, but you are the true ruler, Princess. Therefore, I will follow your orders if that is what you wish," Amosa replied unhappily.

"We will be back before you know it, I promise," Skyrah assured the elf as she motioned for Jase to follow her.

They walked down the corridor towards the front cargo hold where the Princess wrapped her shawl around her head before lowering it over her brow to hid her face from unwanting eyes. Jase touched the workbench panel to gather up Kaimi as he joked to the High Guardian, "No wild parties while we are out."

Amosa handed him a piece of clothing as she answered, "Do not let anything happen to the Princess or I will personally kill you myself, Bluestar."

"I'll do my best," Jase replied as he put on the cloak she had given him and pulled up the hood. Then turning to the Princess, he asked, "Ready?"

Skyrah gave Amosa one last glance then gave a nod. Jase touched the panel to lower the ramp and together, they walked down and into an empty dim lit hangar with Tahmela waddling behind them. A tall, formidable being marched towards them through the sliding doors, its face covered by a deep red helmet made of fibrous armor that also covered the rest of its body. The being stood a foot taller than Jase and had two Redstar plasma pistols on both hips as it stopped before Jase and Skyrah. In a throaty voice, it said, "What is your purpose here in Erebus Ytic?"

"To refuel my ship," Tahmela answered before Jase had the chance.

The Hanger Master paid no attention to the bulb as it asked firmly again, "What is your purpose here in Erebus Ytic?"

Slipping her hand into Jase's, Skyrah stated, "This bulb is transporting us to Adsila to visit his mother. We are getting married and have been traveling for a while now to gain her blessing. I thought it would be best if we stretched our legs and bought her a gift while we are out."

Caught off guard by her touch, Jase felt his face turn red as he tried keeping his voice steady. "My mother is awfully sick and I just want to show her how in love we are since she can't make the wedding," he said.

The Hangar Master didn't say anything as he watched them for a moment then motioned for the bulb to fuel. "Two hundred pieces for docking and we will have to search for stowaways, weapons, and any illegal items you might be carrying aboard your ship."

"Very well. We have nothing to hide," Jase agreed, knowing it was common for all hangars.

"You are free to go," the Hangar Master stated as he brought his fist up in the air above him and the doors slid open as two Androids walked into the hangar.

"Thank you," Jase replied with a forced smile as he pulled Skyrah close to him and walked towards the doors the Androids had used. His pulse had quicken since the moment he had seen the metallic bodies moving towards them but kept his composure as they passed. They continued on through the doors into a bright silver hallway that led towards station city. Once they were alone in the hall, he whispered to Skyrah, "That was close."

"We will still need to be on our guard. There will be more Androids around here," she admitted as they continued down the hallway.

They came to a large arched doorway with two Androids guarding the entrance and once again Jase felt his heart speed up as cold sweat coated his palms. He was thankful for the cloak that hid most of his face and said loud enough for the guards to hear, "My mother will be so happy to see us after all these months! We will have to tell her the good news," he said touching her belly as they walked past the watchful gaze of the Androids.

"She will make an excellent grandmother! I can't wait to see her face!" Skyrah replied playing along.

The metallic Androids watched them with their fiery eyes until Jase and Skyrah were far behind. Jase and Skyrah held their breath as they walked along a narrow metal bridge that connected the hallway to the city. The city was engulfed in darkness with towering skyscrapers that raised hundreds of stories high into the blackness that surrounded the city with no stars or lights to brighten it. The only light that illuminated the city was the soft glow from buildings and the street lights below. Hovercrafts and sky bikes zoomed in and out over the busy glowing streams in the air that navigated the air traffic. "Where are we?" Jase asked out loud as he held the railings of the bridge and peered down into the darkness below.

Princess Skyrah walked in front of him, answering, "The station city, Erebus Ytic. That large cube you saw floating above the asteroid. That is where we are. It's the largest Star Station Market to many planets in our solar system that use it to trade their goods among other space traders."

"But where are the stars? Shouldn't we see them from here?" he asked following her across the long bridge.

"The beings that dwell here built the city with no viewing windows in order to keep themselves safe from other asteroids that could possibly damage the city and cause the air to be suck out into space," Kaimi answered.

"How do they know if it's day or night?" Jase asked.

"Day and night does not matter here. Besides, they wouldn't be able to tell in space. The only ones who care about time is the travelers and traders who travel here to sell their wares. This city doesn't sleep which is good for travelers who come from a far," Skyrah answered.

Jase followed her off the metal bridge, asking in a hushed voice, "Why do the Androids want to control this city then?"

"Because they have to own everything," Skyrah mocked as she slipped into the crowded streets of Erebus Ytic. Keeping her voice low, she added, "If they control the city then they control the trade with the Resistance. They might not know where we are, but they know we have to trade at fuel stations for supplies."

Jase followed her through the crowded market that engulfed him with strange smells. Some smelt good while others left him feeling sick to his stomach as he passed by. In the darkness and dim lights, he couldn't really make out any of the beings around him except that they were there talking in languages he did not know or comprehend. Every now and then he would hear one that he knew back home, but then before he could find the source, it would disappear in the chaos of voices. Keeping his voice low, he stated, "So if one was to take over the station, you would have the advantage."

"It's not as easy as it sounds. Besides, the Androids already have control of it and overwhelm us in numbers," Princess Skyrah grabbed his arm to pull him along faster as she answered him.

"Nothing is easy that's worth it," Jase teased as she pulled him into a narrow backstreet covered in shadow. "Where are we going?"

"Dim's shop. That is where my friend will be," she told him as she moved cautiously down the narrow street with a watchful eye on her surroundings.

"Are you sure this is the way?" he asked as he checked behind them to make sure they weren't being followed.

"Trust me, I know where I'm going. Just keep a look out for anything out of the ordinary," Skyrah told him as she picked up the pace.

Jase kept his right hand close to his plasma pistol. "You're asking the wrong guy for that observation," he stated.

"Then just shoot at anything that looks threatening," Skyrah replied reaching the end of the backstreet and stopping to look down both ways.

Jase stopped next to her with a grin. "So you, then?"

Kaimi giggled at his statement as Skyrah glanced once more down the street before turning down the left street. She punched him in the arm as she said, "This way."

"Ow," Jase noised jokingly. Here, the street was empty and the noises from the former street echoed through the buildings. Jase checked behind them again. The street was still empty, but he couldn't shake the feeling of being watched.

Skyrah peered through her shawl into an alleyway engulfed in darkness. She guided them past it before turning down another narrow backstreet. "Jase," she said suddenly.

Jase focused his attention back to the front beside her. "Yes?"

"We are being followed. Stay close," she stated barely above a whisper.

Jase felt his hair stand on end on the back of his neck as he followed Skyrah down the narrow backstreet. She stopped in front of a black door with block letters reading: "DIM'S SHOP." She knocked once then waited as they both watched the dark street for any signs of prying eyes. The door slowly pulled ajar and in its doorway stood a small hairless creature with its skin a teal hue and clothed in brown and cyan. The alien was female with bright cyan color eyes and a long, slightly wrinkled face. She had two holes where her nose should be and her worried eyes told Jase that she was not expecting anyone to knock at her back door.

"I need to speak to Dim. Is he here?" Skyrah asked with her face still covered in her shawl as the alien woman shifted her gaze between the two.

The she-alien focused her attention finally on her and in their tongue, she spoke with ease, "He is. What business do you have with him to show up behind his shop instead of the front door?"

Skyrah replied, "It is important concern for one's wellbeing on Adsila Laabbirrem."

Jase scanned the back street again for any signs of their stalker, but couldn't find any in the darkness.

"Right this way," she told them, moving to the side to let them in.

Jase stepped into the tiny back room after Skyrah and turned back to see the small alien woman glance out the door both ways before shutting it behind them and locking it. The woman motioned for them to follow her down a short hallway and into a large room where the store was located with displays of ship parts and sky bikes scattered across the shop's floor.

"Dim, you have customers," the alien woman announced loudly and disappeared into a separate room.

Jase viewed the crowded room as he and the Princess waited in the main store. He pulled off his hood to get a better view of a silver skybike when a rough voice stopped him.

"Do not touch the bikes, please," the voice stated and Jase turned to find Dim, the shop owner. Dim was a broad shouldered, six foot three, purplish brown rat like alien without a tail. He had sharp contrasted purple eyes that seemed to stab into Jase's as they studied one another. He wore black body armor with no shoes or gloves to show off his filed talons.

"Sorry," Jase quickly mumbled at the threatening sight.

Skyrah stepped forward, asking, "Are you closed for the night?"

Dim shouted to the back room, "Kalen! Mind the store while I have a nice chat with old friends!"

"Yes, hun," the alien woman answered in annoyance but didn't object as she walked back in the room and stood by the counter.

They followed Dim into the room that the woman had emerged from and found it empty except for a single table and two chairs. Nothing else littered the room that Jase could see as the rat-like being stopped in front of a barren wall. Dim touched it in a zig-zag motion then pressed his palm against the left corner near the floor. At once there was a noise of air releasing then a large door slid open revealing another room filled with computer holos with numbers and messages written across it that Dim and the Princess stepped into with Jase following from behind.

When the door slid shut, Dim finally turned around with a fat grin spread across his face as he stated, "Princess, it is a very happy sight to see you alive among us!"

"It's wonderful seeing you as well, Dim. I feared that the last time we crossed paths would be the last time I'd see you," Princess Skyrah explained as she pulled down her shawl revealing her bright smile towards him.

"I am thrilled it wasn't, Princess!" Dim returned then looked at Jase who was standing awkwardly to the side. "And who do you bring with you?"

"This is Jase Bluestar from Otect City. He helped me escape Faton without really knowing who I was and has been helping me get back to the Resistance ever since," Princess Skyrah replied.

"We are forever in your debts, Bluestar. I'm sure it wasn't too hard for you, being a Bluestar and all, but we still thank you for your help," Dim said as he stretched out a large talon towards Jase.

Jase grinned to him, but avoided the comment. "I didn't have much choice in the matter," he said and clasped his strong arm covered in armor.

"Jase, let me say a few things," Kaimi stated in his ear. Jase leveled his data watch so Kaimi could appear as a tiny version of herself sprung up from his holo watch. "My old friend, it has been too long," she said.

"Kaimi! My apologies, I would have made greetings with you first if I would have known." Dim stated and kneeled down to appear eye level with the A.I. as his grin widened revealing his sharp teeth.

Kaimi waved her hands like shooing away a fly. "Nonsense! The Princess is more important than I am," she said.

Dim straightened back up. "I expect you both will tell me where you have been all this time while the Resistance has been worrying themselves to death," he said.

"Perhaps another time, but for the moment I need you to send a transmission to the Resistance and tell them I'm alive and well. That I will be there soon. Send them my safe code so they know it's not a trap," Princess Skyrah told him.

Dim nodded, moving over to one of the computer panels as his fingers danced across the board. "I will send it right away, Princess. Just move over to that circular panel on the floor and I will film a holo projection of your message."

The Princess did as she was told. While Jase waited, he surveyed the room filled with computers, workbenches, lockers full of weapons and different variations of cylinders along with test tubes that were lined against the wall. Each tube was filled with different liquids and powders that drew Jase's attention. He spotted a small tube labeled "BLUESTAR DUST" that had find grains of harvest stardust within it during the Bluestar season.

"Be careful not to open that," he heard Dim say as he sent the holo message. "It's very hard to come by."

"How did you harvest it?" Jase asked curiously.

"The same way they do when the Redstar season comes every summer. I had to pay a harvester a lot of pieces to fly me up in secret so I could gather the dust when the Bluestar season came fifty years ago and even more pieces to make sure he didn't tell the Androids. It was still worth every piece," Dim told him then turned back to Skyrah. "The message is sent, Princess."

Princess Skyrah gave him a tight hug around his furry neck. "Thank you so much, Dim. You have no idea what a relief this is."

"I live to serve, Princess," he told her in response.

"Everyone from the Resistance thanks you for your support," Skyrah said warmly.

Dim stood up, stretching his arms to his sides. "Come now! We must celebrate your arrival and that of a Bluestar in my house! You can stay here the night to gather your strength for the journey home!" he exclaimed.

Skyrah politely rejected the idea. "I'm sorry, Dim, but we must be going. With more of the Android presence here, I think it's best we take our leave before we risk discovery which I fear could be soon."

"What do you mean?" Dim asked as his face showed concern.

"We were followed by unknown beings on our way here. They are probably waiting on us to emerge again, but whether they work for the Androids or not, we should get going," she told him.

Dim nodded. "Yes, you best be going then, but next time you visit, we will have a celebration," he said.

"As long as you want it to be," she replied to him.

Dim smirked as he led them out of the secret room and back into the empty one. "You should know that I sent the last shipment of weapons to your people a month ago. I will send more supplies as soon as I am able," he told her.

"Thank you again, Dim. I will never forget your continued kindness and support for us in the years passed and those yet to come," Princess Skyrah told him as she pulled her shawl back over her head.

Jase pulled on his cloak, suddenly feeling uneasy as he heard the shop door open and close in the next room. Heavy metal boots clicked against the floor and he knew exactly who they belonged to: Androids.

Escaping Erebus Ytic

Jase felt his heart jump out of his chest as they listened to the Androids talking to Kalen in the next room. If the Princess was frightened, she didn't show it as she motioned for him to stay quiet. He nodded as Dim motioned for them back towards the hidden room that was now closed.

"Dim! There are some guards out here that would like to speak to you!" Kalen called out from the store.

"Be right there!" Dim responded in kind as he motioned the letter K on his forehead before walking out of the room to greet the Androids. His voice thundered throughout the store as he spoke in rants, trying to buy them time to figure out an escape.

Jase wasn't sure what he meant by "K" as he scanned the room for any exits but only found the door that led out into the store. They seemed to be trapped with no hope of escaping as he barely whispered to Kaimi, "Kaimi, do you know a way out of here?"

"There's a vent panel on the right side wall at the bottom corner according to the blueprints I'm looking at. You both should be able to fit inside," she told him as if already knowing the situation.

Jase silently moved to the far wall and crouched as he searched with his hands for the panel Kaimi spoke of. He only felt the solid metal wall and heard Dim's voice grow louder as he laughed about prices to the Androids. "Where, Kaimi?" Jase questioned.

"Second to the bottom panel on the third row from the corner wall," she instructed.

Jase moved his hands across the wall to where she said and felt the corner manual latch to unlock the vent which was barely visible to the human eye. Pressing it, he felt the lock give way and he quietly pushed the red button that emerged from it. The door slid up silently and revealed a cramped vent tunnel that smelt of dust. Jase motioned for the Princess to climb in first in which she did without hesitation as heavy metal boots marched towards the room. She crawled down the vent on her belly to allow enough room for Jase to climb in after her. He pressed the red button again to lock the vent in place once more just as the metal footsteps entered the room.

"The vent will lead into the backstreet," Kaimi informed him.

Jase couldn't move well in the cramped vent and didn't dare to while the Androids were in the same room in case they could hear them crawling. He heard Dim's rough voice state, "See, sir, no one else is here with us. Whoever told you those criminals were here lied. I haven't had a customer here for the past two hours, sir."

"Trust me when I say no one lies to me. Are there any other rooms in the store besides these two?" a familiar voice asked in a bored tone.

"We have an upstairs apartment where we live," Dim replied.

The same voice ordered the other Androids to check the apartment before asking Dim, "Where is the ventilation in this room?"

"Excuse me?"

"The ventilation. Where is it?" the voice asked as footsteps could be heard walking around the room.

Skyrah tapped Jase on the shoulder and mouthed they needed to go. Jase nodded in agreement and they both slowly inched their way down the vent. It sloped downward after a few feet as Jase heard the Android voice echo in the vent as it asked annoyed, "How am I supposed to trust that you aren't hiding rebels when you don't let me check everywhere?"

Kaimi's voice distracted Jase from what Dim had answered back as she said, "Follow the vent all the way down the slope then take your first right to reach the outside vent."

Jase noticed Skyrah must have gotten the same message from Kaimi through her own data watch for she turned right once she reached the bottom of the slope and Jase followed quickly behind. He heard the vent unlock behind him as he quickly rounded the corner just as the vent open.

"Where does this vent lead?" the voice asked echoing down the vent.

"One leads to the apartment and the other leads to the backstreet, I believe," Dim replied a far off.

"Interesting," the voice answered and then the vent shut again.

Jase and Skyrah continued crawling to the end of the vent. Skyrah pressed the button on the vent exhaust which slid away allowing her to crawl out onto the dark street. Jase climbed out after her, feeling the street below him slightly wet as they both quickly got to their feet and darted off.

"Kaimi, send a message to Tahmela to be ready to take off once we arrive," Skyrah ordered through her breaths as they rounded another corner.

Kaimi agreed just as Jase's ears picked up another set of footsteps behind them. Skyrah doubled her speed down the street and yelled, "Jase, duck!"

Jase dove towards the metal stone street and rolled just as the Princess slid to a crouch as she turned her body and opened fire upon their purser. The dark figure sidestepped each shot with great speed before tackling her onto the ground. Jase climbed to his feet to tackle the figure off her and slammed his fist into its face. He was surprised to find the Android from Bentley's Warehouse in front of him and by the contact with the Android's face. He realized he was hitting bone and not a robotic skull.

"You're not an Android?" he couldn't help but blurt out.

"Not even close," the man smirked before knocking Jase off him.

Jase's face sparked with pain but he ignored it as he tried punching the man in the stomach. The man's black combat armor protected him from the hit and used the distraction to jab Jase in the face again before slamming his fist into his stomach causing him to double over. Jase felt a plasma bolt speed pass his head and into the man's chest throwing him backwards off his feet. Skyrah grabbed Jase's hand and pulled him along with her as they both took off running towards the busy market square as heavy metal boots raced after them.

"Stop them!" ordered the soldier.

Jase and Skyrah burst into the crowded market full of beings and strange aromas. Jase's eyes had finally gotten used to the dark as he ran noticing all the different beings around him. They wore dark space-like suits that clung to their bodies and faces like skin to a bone as if any moment the ceiling would open up and space would suck them out into the sea of stars. Turning his attention away from the beings, Jase spotted the metal bridge ahead of them with two Android guards guarding it with their weapons drawn. The Princess opened fire on them as she pushed through the last of the crowd and continued to charge forward without hesitation. Jase glanced behind them at the Androids that were chasing them, but saw that the frantic crowd had managed to delay them from their pursuit as beings shouted and ran this way and that to get out of the way.

"Now would be a very good time for you to use your abilities!" Skyrah remarked as they ran across the narrow bridge with the Androids and the red haired man opening fire upon them.

Jase ignored her, focusing his attention on running down the narrow bridge without falling off as she shot towards the two Androids guarding the end of the bridge. Skyrah used the railing to leap up into the air and slam her boot in one of the Android's face causing him to tumble over the railing as Jase shot the other in its metallic face. He was amazed by the Princess's grace and skill as she continued her stride. They had just reached the entrance of the hallway when suddenly a high frequency blast erupted through the air, stinging Jase's ears as he watched a bolt pierce through the Princess's lower side of her waist.

"Skyrah!" Jase doubled his speed to help her, but was stopped by another shot from the same gun that ripped through his shoulder and also threw him into the hallway's cold floor. Jase felt an indescribable burn shoot throughout his body as if he was laying in flames as he landed next to Skyrah who was clenching her teeth from the pain. The sight of seeing her in pain made Jase angry as he pulled himself to his feet and began firing upon the Androids who were now slowly making their way across towards them.

Another high-frequency blast rippled through the air and tore through Jase's left calf, bringing him to one knee as the pain shot up to his head. Clenching his teeth, Jase forced himself up again and continued to open fire onto his enemies. He felt his body burn hot as the familiar wave of energy pulsed through him as he raised his hand towards his attackers. He flung forth a ball of blue unstable energy towards them knocking three Androids off the bridge as it hit. Channeling all his anger and pain through his energy, Jase unleashed havoc on the rest of the Androids that were still on the bridge. He let out a battle cry while he limped to the end of the bridge. Focusing all of his energy on the solider, who was getting ready to fire another high frequency shot. Jase launched a ball of energy towards the man, hitting him directly in the chest and forcing him to fly backwards into the market square.

"Jase, we need to go!" he heard Skyrah call out to him as she managed to get to her feet.

Jase felt his pulse of energy diminish at the sound of her voice as he turned around. He suddenly had trouble standing up right as he felt the energy leave him shaking and exhausted. He felt lightheaded and was close to blacking out but willed himself forward to help the Princess steady herself. "I got you," he told her and helped her down the bright hallway.

"Amosa has the medical bay prep for your arrival, Jase," Kaimi informed them calmly but with concern coloring her voice.

Jase felt his vision go blurry for a moment then come back as he grunted through the pain in his leg and shoulder from the extra weight of Skyrah's body pressing against his. He slumped against the side of the wall for a second as his vision faded and didn't come back until a minute later as he heard Kaimi tell him to keep moving.

"You have to stay awake, Jase. We are almost there. Please, stay awake for the Princess," she encouraged him.

Jase checked on the Princess and saw she was fading fast from her wound. Determined to get her to the ship, he pressed forward and didn't stop as the door to the hangar bay slid open revealing two Androids. They were the ones from earlier who had checked their ship. Jase was about to open fire on them when both the Androids heads exploded in front of him and fell to the floor with a loud crash. Amosa stood at the ship's ramp with her plasma bow in her hand before rushing towards them to help. She quickly picked up the Princess in her arms and carried her aboard ship as Jase entered behind her.

"Take off, Tahmela!" he commanded down the corridor as he pressed the panel to close the ramp behind him as the engines roared to life. The ship vibrated as Jase limped towards the medic bay where Amosa was already tending to the Princess's wound.

"Take this for the pain," Amosa instructed the Princess and handed her a vial of a green gooey liquid.

Skyrah gulped it down, making a face as she did but quickly seemed to be experiencing less pain as she relaxed in the medical bed in the center of the room. A robotic arm attached to the bed started tending to her wound imme-diately. Jase limped to the bed against the wall as Skyrah stated, noticing the extent of his injuries. "Take care of him. He needs it more than I do."

"You both need tending to," Kaimi replied as she appeared on the con-sole attached to the Princess's bed and started tweaking the robotic arm's programing.

Jase was on the edge of blacking out from his exhaustion as he sat on the bed. Amosa helped him pull off his jacket while he grimaced in pain. She then helped with his faded vest before seeing the blast wound the size of a golf ball. She started tending to the burn with a cold cream while Jase told her of his calf wound.

"You are lucky none of these hit any of your vitals," she told him.

"I don't think he was trying to kill us," Jase responded his thoughts seemed jumbled and slow.

"He wanted us alive to take back to Lord Brohain, I'm sure," Skyrah agreed and tightened her grip on the side of her bed as the robot arm tended to internal tissue in her waist.

"Who?" Amosa asked as she moved to inspect the wound on Jase's calf.

"A soldier who we thought was an Android," Skyrah answered. "I rec-ognize him from Faton when we were at your boss's warehouse."

Jase remembered Bentley talking to the soldier about turning him in as Amosa asked, "Is he not an Android?"

"No, but he's not human either. He moves too quick to be one," Skyrah returned as she stared up at the ceiling.

Kaimi interrupted their thoughts, saying, "We will need to administer a sedative for the rest of the surgery, Princess."

Skyrah gave a nod then looked over to Jase as if to say something but couldn't as the medicine kicked in and she drifted to sleep.

"We will need to do the same with you, Bluestar. I can't tend to the depth of these wounds by myself," Amosa informed him.

Jase laid back in the soft bed. "Keep her comfy," he told them as Amosa hooked him up to an IV.

"Thank you for risking your life for her," Amosa replied as she injected the medicine into his body. Jase turned his head to see the Princess as he slowly drifted into a painless slumber.

Adsila Laabbrirrem

Jase's dreams were vivid with chaos of war as he slept. *He felt dirt hit him from a nearby explosion as he found himself in a cargo shipyard with large storage compartments and ship parts littered all around him in heaps while blast fire echoed through the air mixed with a chorus of cries. Taking it all in, Jase realized he was on the outskirts of Otect City standing on a red dirt hill. Androids charged towards him causing his heart to race when suddenly the world around him seemed to turn slowly in slow motion accompanied by the most beautiful melody. Turning away from the Androids, he saw three dark-haired female warriors rushing past him with sacred blades in their hands.*

As if in a trance, Jase quickly followed them down the hill towards the battle and watched them fight bravely in the midst of the Androids. Only after a few minutes passed, did he realize that the warriors were the oldest sisters in the Nightstar Family and that this was their last stand against the Androids in the Civil War. This was their death and somehow Jase was here to witness it.

"Their deaths are not in vain," came a soft, young voice from behind him.

Jase turned from the beautiful sisters to find a young lady of the same caliber standing before him. Her body seemed to fade in and out of his dream as she appeared to be related to the others. Her long brown hair was pulled back into three braids that rested against her medical blue garments that intensified her blue eyes. Jase studied her as he thought on her words before turning back to the sisters fighting. "How do you know? They could have lived if they hadn't stayed and fought. Skyrah wouldn't be on her own now in this never-ending war."

"She has you, does she not?" asked the young woman.

Jase turned around but found the young woman was gone and the dream started to shift and fade. He turned back to the sisters that had fallen and saw Lord Brohain standing over them as the dream started darkening around him. Lord Brohain suddenly snapped his head in his direction and his red eyes seemed to burn through Jase's skull as the Android moved towards him. The Android reached out to grab him as Jase suddenly felt himself falling backwards with the Android staring back at him as he heard the young voice again.

"Believe in yourself, Jase Bluestar, like so many already do."

Jase jolted awake in his medical bed, breathing hard from his dream. He shielded his eyes from the bright lights in the room and let his eyes adjust before turning his attention to the room around him. Princess Skyrah was still asleep in the bed next to him. Letting out a sigh, Jase's thoughts turned back to his dream and the young woman who had been talking to him. Who was she and what did she mean by so many people already believed in him? He remembered his wounds and checked his shoulder. His charred wound was healed, leaving a smooth surface with a single scar no bigger than his index finger in its place. He was amazed at the quick recovery as he inspected his left calf as well and found the same situation.

"Are you okay?" came a soft voice beside him.

Skyrah had awoken and was sitting up in her bed now watching him. He smiled at her, feeling relieved that she was well again. "Why? You need me to carry you around some more?" he teased.

She rubbed her side as she replied. "Oh, shut up! I was perfectly well enough to walk on my own if I really had to. You are the one who needed extra support," she chimed.

"If you say so, Princess," he said and swung his feet over the bed to stand.

"I thought I heard you two bickering," Kaimi stated as she suddenly appeared on the holo computer next to the Princess's bed.

"I missed you too, Kaimi," Jase responded.

"I didn't say I missed you. I said I thought I heard you bickering," she poked.

"It's the same thing to me," Jase responded as he pulled on his white faded vest, buttoning it up with its wooden pins.

"How far are we away from Erebus Ytic? Did the Androids follow us?" Skyrah asked.

Amosa stepped into the room. "No, Jase made sure of that with his display towards them. By the time they recovered, we were far gone in hyperspace," she answered acknowledging Jase.

"Good. Good. How long till we reach Adsila Laabbrirrem?" Skyrah pressed.

"We are about to arrive as we speak," Amosa declared.

Both Skyrah and Jase were confused, knowing they had weeks at least till they reached the planet. "What? How is that possible?" Skyrah asked astonished.

Kaimi clarified. "The weapon that was fired on both of you was not like one I've seen before which means it had to be made by its owner. The plasma it used was much stronger than typical plasma energy which made it harder to heal the extent of your wounds. I had to keep you both sedated for the last leg of our journey in order to regrow the muscle fibers and skin that you both lost throughout your body."

"From what Kaimi learned from treating you both this weapon not only burned the skin it struck, but the discharge of the blast also traveled throughout the rest of your body, burning away fibers and nerves to a certain degree. We will all have to be more cautious when we deal with this soldier in future battles," Amosa stated.

"So we slept for two weeks?" Jase asked, pulling on his pilot's jacket.

"Yes," Kaimi answered. "We should all head to the cockpit for re-entry."

The group walked out of the medical bay towards the cockpit where Tahmela sat at the helm. Jase felt his excitement grow as he settled in the co-pilot's chair and noticed the bulb looking at him.

"Finally awake, Lazy Bluestar," he teased.

"Just needed to catch up on my beauty sleep," Jase replied as the ship rattled.

"Hold on tight, beings," Tahmela said while the ship entered the planet's atmosphere.

The ship rattled as flames licked the sides of the windshield. Jase stared out towards the planet's light green surface before it disappeared behind some fluffy clouds. The weight of gravity pulled down on his body like a ton of bricks while his ears popped from the pressure and his mouth started to hurt from clenching his teeth so hard. In a matter of twenty minutes, they broke through the atmosphere into a sunny blue sky with white, puffy cotton balls scattered around them.

"Welcome to Adsila Laabbrirrem, Bluestar," Tahmela announced as the green earth filled the view below them.

Adsila Laabbrirrem was quite different from Kurath Thors or Fatons surface. It had green valleys, mountains, and a giant lake that took up most of the planet's region. Rivers flowed from the lake in all directions that Jase could follow from the view of the windshield. Princess Skyrah noticed his excitement and pointed towards the lake from her chair behind his, saying, "That is Lone Lake with her mountain in the center of it. Cities use her to fish and travel to other cities on the planet."

"How big is it?" Jase asked, staring at the gorgeous blue water.

"161,200 square miles long wit the depth of 70,000 feet in the areas around the mountain," Kaimi answered.

"Geez, that's big," Jase replied unable to fathom how deep that was.

"Very big," Kaimi smiled as she answered from the middle console.

Tahmela interrupted them, asking Princess Skyrah, "Where should I land the ship, Princess?"

Princess Skyrah moved to the middle console as a holo map appeared on the windshield. Studying it, Skyrah pointed to the southern region of the planet to a valley located below Lone Lake. "That is Pallue Valley. My base is hidden within it. There is a dense fog that is trapped in the valley for most of the year so be wary. Resistance ships are programmed to a signal that allows them to find the base, but we will have to wing it and land in a walking distance of the base."

"No worries, Princess. I flown in more hazardous weather than fog," the bulb assured her as he pointed the ship towards the location she pointed at.

"I have full trust in you," she replied, appearing more relax now that they were almost back to the Resistance. Jase hadn't seen her in such a good mood ever and it was a nice change. She turned back to him to continue explaining. "The planet, Jase, is separated into five regions."

"Are they all ruled by different beings?" Jase asked as she brought up the same holo map again but only had it take up his side of the windshield so Tahmela wouldn't be distracted by it.

The Princess stood behind him to also look at the map. "Not really, no. Adsila Laabbrirrem is ruled by democracy so they have one main leader who represents their planet. I believe they have changed since I last was here but he or she would be living in the planet's capital which is Mmerits in the Rune wetlands region. And that region is here. It's mostly made up of farmlands and fishing villages." Skyrah then pointed to an area that was left of Lone Lake in the uppermost corner to the center of the lake. It was closed off by two rivers, one flowed through the north while the other flowed through its bottom separating it from a land underneath it. "Below it is the Azako Plains where most of the planet's military train since it has warm weather year around and wide space for them to use. It's also the breeding ground for the Azako Bird which the plains are named after."

"What does the bird look like?" Jase asked, curious of why they would name a region after it.

Kaimi brought up a holograph of the bird that had burnt orange feathers and rose at an alarming size of seven feet with a wingspan of three feet. It had a thick neck with a large maroon and gray feathered head dress that went down both sides of its neck and met its large body. The same colors made up its large tail feathers that were a design of two large angry-looking red eyes that one could make out when the bird spread out its tail feathers like a peacock.

"Why are there eyes on its tail?" Jase asked.

"Long ago the Azako were preyed upon by plain wolves called Guyos. They are smaller than the birds but hunt in packs as they wait to hunt the birds at night. The guyos would stalk the bird's nest when they were sleeping out in the open plains and drag them out with the help of the other wolves. It got so bad that the beautiful birds were close to extinction and the natives tried their best to control the overgrown population of guyos to help keep the birds safe. It wasn't till many years later that the natives started noticing the birds feathers started changing in color and the next thing they knew the colors created the designs of eyes staring back at you," Skyrah explained.

"They adapted," Jase interrupted amazed.

"They had. Now when they sleep their feathers give the illusion that they are still awake so the guyos don't attack as much as they did before. They no longer rely on he birds as their only prey now. Don't get me wrong, they still hunt the birds, but it's more risker for them to do so at night," Skyrah finished.

"That's amazing! I hope we will be able to see one while we are here," Jase hoped.

"We will have to see. They are remarkable, hardworking birds that allow the natives to ride them and use them as they wish. Probably one of my favorite animals if we are being honest," Skyrah told him.

"Really?"

Skyrah nodded. "They are intelligent and each one chooses their rider which they create a bond with and never allow anyone else to ride them once that has taken place. Even if they are in the wild and the natives allow it for they understand the bond allowing the bird to go as its pleases. Not a single bird is locked away."

"What if there is an emergency and they need the bird?" Jase asked.

"The connection the rider and bird develop allows them to call to one another and communicate through their minds and body language. The bird will sense if their rider is in danger or someone they care about," Skyrah explained to him.

"How can they do that through their minds?" asked Jase as the ship bounce from turbulence.

Tahmela cut in, saying, "Princess might want to take seat. Gets bumpy soon."

Skyrah did as he said and buckled in before answering Jase's question. "I'm not exactly sure, but with some species it is possible."

Jase studied the area they were heading towards as he noticed the valley was surrounded by mountains on all sides expect for the small opening facing the lake where a windy river poured through into a smaller lake. The small region had lots of rolling hills and a heavy set of woods amongst it. With the mountains surrounding the valley, it secluded the Resistance from everything else which is why they chose to settle there. "Are there many settlements in Pallue Valley? It looks pretty deserted."

"There are a few settlements that live in the area, but with the heavy fog that stays trapped within the valley for most of the year, it makes it hard to live in. There are a handful of caves that are mined for resources that get shipped to cities throughout the planet. They do have a few hot springs near Mount Trapp, but the roads are dangerous so most don't risk the journey," Skyrah told him.

Jase pointed to the region on the opposite side of Lone Lake which appeared to be the largest region of the planet. "What region is that?"

"That is the Tijelyno Region named after the Tijelyno flower that blooms there. The flower's nectar is one of the rarest nectars in the whole solar system and one of the main ingredients in a lot of medicines in our universe." Skyrah motioned to the area along the lake. "Most of the flowers grow throughout the area as well as a lot of varieties of fruits. The natives harvest the nectar and fruits to trade in cities. It's also a place that many healers and scientists like to go for research."

"And what about this region?" Jase asked motioning towards the Northern part of the planet.

"That is the Northern Region mostly made up of the forest that grows around the Northern Mountains. They get a lot of snow during their long fall and winter and even stays quite cool during their short summer. They are known for their lumber. Like Pallue Valley, there is only a few villages that habit the Northern Region, but they can be quite fierce when they need to be," she replied with amusement from how curious he was about the planet.

"How many villages does the Rune Wetlands have besides their capital?" Jase asked, turning to her.

"Nine, not including their capital," she replied.

"And Azako Plains?"

Skyrah thought about it for a moment, then answered, "Eight and before you ask, Tijelyno has five in their region."

Jase nodded as he continued. "So that's twenty-nine cities that are pledged to you for the war to come?"

"That is correct," Skyrah agreed.

"Is the whole planet not enough for your cause against the Androids without the help of the elves?" Jase asked.

"They might have to be," Skyrah replied as her relaxed expression changed with her emotions now hidden. She turned towards the fog that enveloped the windshield from view of the forest floor and spoke to Tahmela. "There will be a river that flows into the valley that you will want to follow. It will empty out into a small lake which you will want to land at. From there I will take us to the base on foot," she said.

"Okie," Tahmela responded and pressed a purple button that turned on a thermal radar. "Don't worry, Bluestar. My eyes see better than yours," he told him when the bulb noticed Jase was nervous by the change.

Thirty minutes passed as Jase stared at the thermal radar, trying to decipher it when finally the ship stopped. As it landed, Jase's thoughts were disrupted as the thermal screen vanished leaving the dreary conditions in its wake outside the windshield. Kaimi turned to the Princess and asked, "Are you ready, Princess?"

"Let's gather our things and set out before darkness falls," she replied.

Everyone exited the cockpit while Tahmela checked the ship's systems and manually set the hibernation mode. Jase walked to his quarters and sat on the bed waiting to leave.

"Are you excited to see another planet?" Kaimi's soft voice asked in his ear.

Jase thought about how quiet it will be in the ship once the Princess, Amosa, and Kaimi were gone. "I am very excited to learn more about this planet before Tahmela and I set off for another one. Now that you and the Princess are back to her people, I don't see why you will need anything else from me. After all, you both have a war to fight, but I promised you that I would stay for a while. I might as well travel around here for starters."

"I will always need you, Jase, and I'm sure Princess Skyrah feels the same," Kaimi softly told him, her voice sad as if knowing things were going to be different now.

Jase smiled sadly. "I know, Kaimi," he said.

There was a brief silence between them, before Kaimi asked again, "You still wouldn't want to help with the war?"

"I'm no warrior, and I don't want to get mixed up in it more than I already am. I'm just a thief, Kaimi, nothing more, nothing less," he responded patting his leg.

"Wars need plenty of thieves," Kaimi insisted.

"Maybe I can steal a few things for you when I'm out exploring," he told her.

"I'm sure they will pay you well for it, Jase."

The door slid open as Amosa entered. "It's time to go, Bluestar," she informed him.

"Let's do it," he replied and they walked out into the corridor.

"You should know that you will need to address the Princess by her full title since she is back with her people. After all, she is a future queen and should be treated as one. Do not be surprised if you don't see her a lot now that she is back in charge," Amosa told him as they walked through the mess hall.

"We will remain friends still, right?" he asked worried.

"You both are still friends, Jase, but since you are not fighting with us, she won't have time for you. We are in the middle of a war that could change the entire universe whether we win or die. Things will be different now, I'm afraid," she told him as they passed the cockpit corridor.

Jase hadn't thought about the Princess and others treating him differently since he wasn't a part of the cause. It made sense, but he knew it would be another reason for him to go. He didn't belong here.

"You should also be aware that the other Resistance leaders won't trust you given your history of being a thief. They will see you as someone who does whatever he can for money and that returning the Princess was just that, even if you are a Bluestar. Don't expect a warm welcome," Kaimi informed him.

They reached the ramp where Tahmela and the Princess stood waiting for their arrival. Tahmela had his googles strapped onto his giant eyes and his plasma rifle across his back. The Princess was still in her normal black attire, but left her shawl wrapped around her neck like a scarf instead of using it to hide her face.

"Ready, Bluestar?" the bulb asked.

"Let's get rid of the Princess before she realizes she likes us," he teased in response.

"Trust me, I will be much happier when I don't have to see your face every day," Princess Skyrah shot back sternly.

"But then who would save you all the time?" Jase joked and let out a laugh when the Princess made a face towards him.

Tahmela touched the panel to lower the ramp, letting the chilly air into the cargo hold as it lowered. They then filed out down the ramp onto the soft soil, but stayed near one another so they wouldn't get separated in the thick fog that engulfed them.

"Which way, Princess?" Amosa asked.

"It's this way," the Princess responded and pointed to her right.

"You sure?" Jase asked, knowing it was almost impossible to know for sure in this fog.

"Trust me, we all had to memorize this valley in the fog so we can stay hidden within it. I know it by heart so stay close and don't get separated," she affirmed.

"After you then," Jase replied and they stepped into the woods, moving slowly to avoid the entanglement of the forest floor.

The Resistance

The group followed Princess Skyrah in a single-file line through the thick, cool fog. Jase couldn't help but feel uneasy not being able to see anything around him as his thoughts drifted to the Crowntooth creature and the giant wooden spider on Kurath Thor's forest. The thought sent shivers down his spine as Jase softly asked ahead to the Princess, "Should we worry about any creatures that might attack us while we travel to your base?"

"Not really," Princess Skyrah responded, focused on the fog ahead of her.

"Well, that doesn't make me feel any better," Jase mumbled to himself and heard Tahmela chuckle.

"Perhaps with the fog, we will stay hidden from any dangers," Kaimi gently reassured him.

"I hope so," Jase replied as he suddenly spotted dark shapes ahead of them. His heart sped up and he placed a hand on his gun before noticing the dark shapes were all around them. Princess Skyrah was about to be right next to one causing Jase to pull out his gun until she placed a hand against the dark shape for a moment before continuing on. It was then when Jase realized the shadows were trees. Jase reholstered his weapon and continued walking for another hour. Finally, the Princess paused in front of a large boulder that sat between two thick trees with smaller rocks scattered throughout the trunk as though someone had placed them there. She pulled up a hidden door that looked as if it was just a part of the earth and laid it against the boulder. "Make sure you close it behind us when we go through," she ordered.

Jase waited as everyone climbed down the dark passage before disappearing inside and pulling the door gently shut. Clumps of earth dribbled down on him as he reached the bottom of the wooden ladder. Turning around, he noticed there was a soft glow of lights among the dirt tunnel lining the walls with red flames that didn't flicker as they moved past them.

"Redstar flames," Skyrah announced to their curiosity. "Once lit, it's impossible to burn out unless you have the special items to do so. We also have an energy shield around each lantern so that in case there was a fire, the forest would be protected."

They continued on down the tunnel that slowly started to incline upwards where two large wooden doors similar to the noble doors on Faton were set at the end. They climbed up the steep hill as Skyrah pulled open one of the doors letting in a pool of soft light from the outside. Jase followed the others out and they passed willow trees that hid the entrance of the tunnel before stopping in front of a large green field with light fog that floated in the air around them. The sun poked through the clouds partly, its warm rays washed over Jase's face as he closed his eyes to enjoy it for a moment.

Across the field laid large stone buildings with columns on the sides that attached archways to the building where a few doors lined one of its walls sat protected under. Next to the main building was a large sparring ring where Jase saw several men watching two fighters in its midst. Jase could see there were other buildings beside the one they were walking too, but didn't have time to study them for when they neared all of the soldiers kneeled before them as another soldier ran inside.

Moments later, four beings emerged from inside the building and stopped before them. Two humans, a squirlex and a bald alien who rose to the height of eight feet with gray skin that was clothed in a light faded purple hue that hid its lanky built. Its eyes were gray crystals that focused on Jase for a moment before turning to the Princess.

"It is good to see you alive and well, Princess. We were beginning to fear that you weren't with us anymore until we received your transmission from Dim on Erebus Ytic. It has been a relief to know you were on your way back to us," a woman declared. The woman had sun-kissed skin from many years being outside and had almond hair cut in a bob with streaks of gray throughout it. She appeared to be in her fifties as she viewed the group in silence while resting her hands on her hips. She wore beige tight trousers under a navy tunic that matched her eyes with white outlines that matched her white and blue fingerless gloves that stopped just below her elbow. A sliver necklace with two rings was worn around her neck that reflected for a moment in the sunlight that caught Jase's attention before he moved on to how heavily equipped she was for war. She had a navy steel plasma handgun strapped to her right thigh along with two strange scythe looking short blades that were attached to her waist on both sides.

"Lieutenant Colonel Moon, I'm sorry for keeping you and the others worried about my wellbeing. It was not my intention, but I had to improvise when things didn't go as planned. It wasn't until we were on Erebus Ytic that I was able to send a message to you that I was alive," Princess Skyrah stated to the group of leaders.

"So it seems," the elderly woman dipped her head before turning to Amosa. In a formal elf greeting with her ankles crossed with one hand over her heart and the other in the air, she said, "It is an honor to see you again, Amosa Reven. I trust you have gone about your duty once more to keep our future queen safe."

Amosa returned the bow. "As I have in the past, I shall do again but I cannot take all the credit this time. The Bluestar who has been traveling with us saved her life more than once since helping her escape Faton. He is the one you should be thanking."

"Oh?" The elderly woman cocked an eyebrow as all eyes turned to Jase.

Princess Skyrah quickly introduced Jase, "Yes, Jase Bluestar and our old friend, Kaimi, helped me escape Otect City and escorted me back here, putting their own lives in danger. As well as their friend, Tahmela Zing, who flew us on our journey. They deserve the best hospitality we can give them during their stay."

"Indeed," the elderly woman agreed as her eyes fell upon Jase. She had a flash of recognition as she studied him, but said nothing. "It is a pleasure to meet you, Jase Bluestar, and you, Tahmela Zing. We will make sure you are well rewarded for your service towards our future queen, and that you can rest safely on our grounds. The whole Resistance is in your debt for your actions. I am Lieutenant Colonel Puteri Moon. Next to me is Karasi, our wisest member and on my other side is our squirlex lieutenant, Minko. Lastly, this is Ziko Ren, also in charge of training our new recruits."

Jase met Ziko Ren's piercing brown eyes that seemed to burn into his skin with suspicion. The man came from a planet Jase had never heard of. The man had long black hair tied in a ponytail with sharp features and thin lips that were in a straight line. His dark gray combat armor clung to his body like skin with steel plasma arrows on his back and a steel blade sheathed on his side that he had one hand rested on as they talked.

"Before we allow you all to be welcomed in our home, I would like to speak with the A.I. Kaimi to ensure we can trust your friends, Your Highness," Lieutenant Colonel Moon stated with a smile.

The Princess did not seemed surprised by this and motioned to Jase, "Go ahead."

Jase nodded and held his data watch level with his arm as he whispered, "They want to see you, Kaimi."

Kaimi appeared standing on the face of his watch with the brightest smile Jase had ever seen her have as the soldiers around them gasp and whispered to one another at the sight. "Karasi, Lieutenant Moon, it's good to see you both."

Lieutenant Colonel Moon's eyes were as big as saucers from the surprise as she stepped down from the walkway. "The feeling is mutual, Kaimi. I thought for sure we would never see you again," she responded.

"For a while I thought we would not cross paths, but it seems fate has it otherwise. Jase has kept me protected from the Androids all these years without ever thinking of the reward he would have gotten if he had turned me in. I will vouch for his character and Tahmela's if I need to, but I assure you they are most trusted to keep our secret safe," she replied respectfully.

Lieutenant Colonel Moon straightened her back and turned to the others. "We have much to discuss about events that have passed and problems we have now, Your Highness. I suggest we all speak over a late lunch. I'm sure you all must be hungry from your travels."

"That would be lovely and on behalf of my friends, I graciously accept," Princess Skyrah replied.

Lieutenant Colonel Moon snapped her fingers towards a soldier then turned back to the Princess. "Would you like to refresh yourselves?" she asked.

"Not necessarily. I would like to be brought up to speed with everything that has happened in my absence," Skyrah insisted.

280

Lieutenant Colonel Moon did not object, answering, "Right this way then," and led them inside the building.

The building opened into a courtyard with a fountain surrounded by beautiful flowers. The walls were covered in banners of the Nightstar family and other races. A handful of statues littered the room throughout as they walked down a walkway that led around the courtyard to a room where sat a large reddish oak dining room table that could sit fifteen people at once. Two large windows with purple curtains covered the opposite side of the door beside the table where two guards stood as everyone moved to take their seats. The walls were painted in rich maroon matching the kitchen that was adjoined. Servants scurried about the room with glasses and dish ware as they tried to get the lunch prepared for the party. Jase and Tahmela waited till the others were sat before taking their seats near the end as a servant quickly poured them water from a pitcher. Jase admired the room letting his eyes rest on the Princess who sat at the head of the table already chatting with Lieutenant Colonel Moon in hushed tones. Amosa sat on the other side with Ziko Ren who watched Jase with stern eyes. The squirlex, Minko sat next to him leaving Jase and Tahmela sitting next to the tall alien, Karasi.

"Jase?"

Jase turned to find the Lieutenant talking to him. "Yes, ma'am?"

With kind eyes, she motioned to the empty seat they had left between Amosa and the Princess. "You can place Kaimi there on the chair. It will allow her to sit in on our luncheon."

Jase glanced to the empty seat and stood. "Okay," he said and hurried around the table towards the chair where he found a large metal cylinder device a foot tall and three diameters across. It reminded him of the devices he made back at home in Mrs. Rose's house so that Kaimi could sit with them for dinner.

"Touch it with your data watch like you would any device to transfer her over," the elderly woman told him when she noticed him staring at it. Jase shook his head as he tried to hide his embarrassment from standing there too long and touched the device. Before his eyes, Kaimi sprung up transforming into a normal human size. The sight of her caught Jase by surprise.

Her hair seemed to bounce when she turned and smiled at him as she sat in her chair. "Close your mouth, Jase. You are embarrassing me," Kaimi teased.

Jase felt his face blush as he recovered and moved back to his chair. "Sorry! Who knew all this time you were holding out on me as a tiny fairy!" he replied.

"It's a lot safer being small than being this size," she responded.

Princess Skyrah drew their attention back to her, asking, "Now that we are all here. I would like to hear an account of what has happened since I've been gone. Where do we stand?"

Ziko Ren spoke first. "Should we rehash such things in front of strangers, Your Majesty? Such vital information shouldn't be passed through unimportant ears," he ushered.

"Are you referring to the Bluestar that sits with us? The Bluestars have protected the Nightstar family for thousands of years. If you distrust one then you are disrespecting all of them, Ziko," Lieutenant Colonel Moon replied defensively.

"They have always protected the family except *this* one. Where has he been all this time when the Princess needed him?" Ziko Ren argued.

"What does it matter where he has been? He is here now, is he not? He has protected her this long and brought her back to us, did he not?" Lieutenant Colonel Moon reprimanded.

"Enough!" commanded Skyrah. "Ziko, I understand your cautiousness, but I trust Jase and Tahmela with my life. Jase has saved mine more than once now and if not for him, I would have been captured by Lord Brohain and, most likely, dead. The bulb is loyal to him and is bound by a life debt. They will not betray us, I promise you."

Ziko Ren eyed Jase. "But does he fight for us, Princess?" he asked accusingly.

Jase felt out of place and guilty for his true intentions for being there. He didn't know how to answer for himself, not wanting to disappoint the others when they found out he was not there to fight. Before he could speak up for himself, Princess Skyrah said, "Only Jase can answer that. Whether he is here to fight or not, is none of your concern. It is his choice, not yours or mine to decide, Ziko."

"Yes, Your Highness," Ziko Ren answered not tearing his gaze from Jase.

Lieutenant Colonel Moon changed the subject while Jase stared at his empty plate wishing he was somewhere else. "Since your last mission, we have acquired enough supplies and firepower from Dim to strike once more at the Androids. Our numbers have grown to twenty thousand and we have more recruits in need of training in Azako Plains. Lieutenant Minko will leave this evening to oversee their training and hopefully by fall we will be able to attack, if not sooner."

Princess Skyrah nodded contently as two servants entered the room with their meal. As they brought everyone their plates, she asked, "And now that Kaimi is back with us, will the virus be ready sooner than we thought?"

Karasi intertwined his long skinny fingers together as he spoke. "With her help once more, it should be done in time to go to war in the fall," he said.

"Good," Princess Skyrah turned to Lieutenant Colonel Moon. "How is my sister?"

"She is well. You can find her in the gardens at this time. She just recently came back to the base as of yesterday. She was traveling to some homes that needed healing in the mountains," the Lieutenant Colonel responded.

Jase was surprised to hear that there was still another Nightstar sister living among them besides Skyrah. He tried gauging her emotions of hearing her sister, but the Princess did well to keep her emotions hidden from the surface as she took a bite of her salad. There was a stretch of silence between them as everyone ate their meals in peace. Jase examined his salad that had greens along with berries and grilled meat cut in strips throughout the salad. A tangy blue dressing coated the salad and made Jase cringe at its tartness while he took another bite.

Lieutenant Colonel Moon broke the silence. "How fares the elves in our cause? I take it if you are here, Amosa, it must be well," she implied.

Skyrah answered in her stead. "Amosa is here because she wishes it. The elves have decided that they will not lose any more lives in our war. It is an honorable request. After all, they have suffered more than we have. They know our numbers are low compared to the Androids. Therefore, our success is low, but we can win this war without them if we must."

Ziko Ren cursed under his breath. "Their numbers and abilities would have helped our cause, Your Highness. Was there no way to convince them otherwise?" he spat.

Amosa remained quiet as Princess Skyrah said in her defense, "Ren, both Amosa and I tried for many days to convince them to fight, but with no success. They have made their decision."

"And what of the Bluestar? Could he not command them to fight for us, or did he not want to?" Ziko Ren mused as he glared at Jase.

Jase kept his head. "It is not my choice to command them against their will," he replied.

"Why? Because you would rather watch thousands of our lives sacrificed while you let your precious elves live on!" Ziko Ren shot back balling his fists on the table.

Princess Skyrah interrupted. "Ziko, you are dismissed from our meeting! It was not Jase's position to talk to them as it is not your position to decide who is to blame here for past events! I will have words with you later but, for now, get out of my dining room," she ordered.

Ziko Ren kept his eyes on Jase as he stood. "As you wish, Your Highness," he answered as he exited the room without a glance backwards.

Jase stared down at his food, wishing he could disappear. He had never seen the Princess that angry and now he knew why she must have been stressed about the war if she has someone like Ziko Ren to deal with at all times. The room was silent except for forks scraping against their plates every time someone stabbed another piece of their meal. The air felt heavy with tension as Jase played with his food, feeling Kaimi's eyes watching him. She knew how uncomfortable he was being here.

Breaking the silence once more, Lieutenant Colonel Moon asked, "How did you and the Bluestar meet?"

"We accidentally ran into each other while I was in Starwake Castle," Princess Skyrah replied and glanced at Jase for the first time since they had sat down.

"Literally," Jase said, trying to act like his normal self.

Princess Skyrah smiled at his remark and began recounting their journey from Faton to now while they continued eating. It wasn't until the end that Lieutenant Colonel Moon spoke. "So you were in the castle to steal something, but ran into the Princess," she addressed Jase.

"Yes, I am a hired thief, but what I stole I returned to its true owner," he told her.

"What was it?" Minko asked, his furry whiskers twitching as he spoke.

Jase smiled as he stared towards the Princess. "Nothing to note. Just a reminder of another time," he answered.

"But the Androids had it and you did not worry about their wrath if you were caught?" Karasi asked studying him.

284

"I have no love for the Androids and I knew the risks I was taking. I would not have accepted the job if I wasn't fully confident in my abilities," Jase answered carefully.

"Your Bluestar abilities," Karasi suggested.

Jase hesitated. "No, actually. I did not have my abilities when I first met the Princess. It wasn't till our journey to Kurath Thor did I become aware of them," he said.

Lieutenant Colonel Moon was surprised by his words. "You mean you didn't have them at all while growing up in Otect City? How is that possible? Every Bluestar has them developed since birth," she questioned.

"I guess I was a late bloomer," Jase shrugged.

"It's true. I was as surprised as you are when I learned he did not have them," Princess Skyrah told them. "The more we have been traveling together, the more they seem to be getting stronger."

"Interesting," Karasi uttered, watching Jase as if to learn his secrets in his face.

"Have any of you known such a thing to happen?" Princess Skyrah asked them.

"Never," Lieutenant Colonel Moon answered.

"I am sure we will get to the bottom of this," Karasi told them as he met Jase's gaze.

Lieutenant Colonel Moon then turned to Tahmela, stating, "Tahmela, if it was okay with Bluestar I was wondering if you could look at some of the ships we have here tucked away. They are in no position to fly, but perhaps that could change. Our technicians are overworked as it is and haven't been able to get around to fixing them."

Tahmela's lips parted into a toothy grin at her request. "I can fix soon. If okie with Jase," he responded.

"Yeah, of course," Jase agreed.

"I can show you the way," Minko stated to Tahmela.

"Let's go then," Tahmela decided and the two got up to leave.

Lieutenant Colonel Moon then suggested, "Your Highness, I'm sure you would like to see your sister. For the rest of us, we have work to do. Kaimi, I would like to discuss a few things with you alone, if I could?"

"Of course, Lieutenant Colonel," she turned to Jase. "I will find you later."

Jase grinned at her. "No problem! Go crazy in your new form," he teased as they left the room.

The remaining group exited the dining room and entered the courtyard as the Princess excused herself and headed in the direction of the gardens. Amosa called behind her, "Tell the Princess I look forward to seeing her after I have rested."

Skyrah nodded. "I promise," she replied. Her eyes lingered on Jase for a moment as if expecting him to say something, but when he did not, she stated, "I am sorry for Ziko's actions. He is cautious when it comes to my protection and our people. He has been with my family for many years so he is like family to me."

"He's just doing his job. I understand that," Jase replied to her.

"We shall talk about whether or not you are staying later this evening then," she determined before leaving the room.

Once alone, Karasi indicated, "You are a quiet one."

Jase turned around to the tall, lanky alien that fixed his purple robes. "I've never been much of a talker. Usually, it's just Kaimi and myself so we tend to keep to ourselves around strangers," he replied.

"Yet, here she has left you to be a talker," Karasi pointed out staring down at Jase with soft crystal eyes.

"I suppose so," Jase agreed.

Karasi began walking towards the door. "Come. I have hot tea in need of drinking at my dwelling."

Jase hesitated as the alien continued on without him out the door. He wasn't sure why he felt nervous going after the alien, but ignored it and hurried after him.

An Ancient's Wisdom

Jase stepped out into cool air where soldiers were sparring in the combat circle with Ziko Ren instructing them. Not wanting to get in a further disagreement with him, Jase quickly turned in the opposite direction and found Karasi already quite a ways from him heading towards a hut by the gardens. He quickly sprinted to catch up before the alien got farther away.

"So you finally decided to come," Karasi declared as Jase neared him.

Trying to catch his breath, Jase nodded to the alien in the light fog. "Sorry, I didn't realize you would—"

"Get so far in so little time?" Karasi finished for him as he peered down with an amused smile. "It is what happens when you have long legs like mine no matter what age you are."

Jase studied the alien as they walked. "If you don't mind me asking, what kind of being are you? I don't think I've seen your kind before," he asked politely.

"I doubt you have ever seen my kind before, Bluestar. I am the last of my kind," the alien told him.

"What happened to others like you?" he asked.

"They were wiped out by the Androids. But if you ask me, we were gone long before the start of the war that we had created," the alien told him.

"Wait, you're an Ancient?" Jase asked in shock.

"The last of my kind," Karasi responded.

Jase's eyes grew wide as his mouth dropped. "You created the Androids and the other A.I.s like Kaimi?!" he nearly shouted.

Karasi ignored his excitement as he answered. "And the reason war broke out in the first place. Yes, that is my kind," he acknowledged.

Jase tried to contain his excitement while responding. "You couldn't have known that the Androids would try to kill everyone who stood allied with the A.I.s or would have gone so far as they have now. It's not your fault," he said.

They paused before Karasi's home that was made of hard clay with a thatch roof that looked as if any moment could get blown away in the soft wind that played with the fog. A tiny oval window was set in one corner of the house as flowers of all colors bloomed all around the small hut.

"Most of us did," Karasi stated before moving into his home and calling out to Jase. "I didn't make this tea so it would go cold, Bluestar."

Jase hurried inside and was surprised to find the hut was bigger than it looked on the outside. The back of the hut was used as a bedroom with a long bed stretched from wall to wall and a red quilt draped over it. A makeshift desk that had beautifully carved shapes of planets and stars throughout it took up the left side of the hut with holopads covering its surface. Jase stood in a small kitchen area that had the basic necessities littering it.

"Please, sit. We have a long story to be told and not enough tea to tell it," Karasi stated as he motioned for Jase to sit.

Jase shut the door and took a seat. "What happened to cause the Androids to behave as they have, and if you knew, why didn't you try and stop it?" he asked.

Karasi poured the hot kettle of tea into two carved cups and returned the kettle to its original holding. Its sweet aroma filled the air around them as he spoke again. "Before the war, I, along with eleven others of my kind, sat as counsel for our people and our planet in charge of its protection and the dealings of outsiders. All those years ago, my people were foolish and prideful, always looking for ways to unlock the secrets of the universe through science and complex devices. We were scholars, scientists, and the askers of stars. We wanted to know more than everyone else. We weren't fighters nor did we care for warfare unless provoked. It was in 1345 when the Qualias went extinct due to disease on their planet that we started realizing we had no army like our other fellow planets did. I and my best friend at the time, Faysal, had thought—what if we were able to build a machine that could protect our people if a situation did arise."

"So you thought of the Androids," Jase interrupted.

Karasi turned his attention to the steam that rose from his cup. "The body of an Android was Faysal's creation while I worked on its internal configurings. We wanted to make something that could think for itself and react to our words. We wanted it to be more than a machine, but a whole being itself. I wanted it to have free will, like the stars give us ours, to use however we want it."

"Do they have free will?" Jase questioned.

Karasi turned his eyes from his cup to Jase's. "They do for the most part. Whether all Androids follow their leader because they want to or have to can only be answered by Lord Brohain. But when we first built them, they did. When we finished building thousands of them, I realized that the A.I.s inside their bodies couldn't adapt or evolve to changes around us and better themselves. They still relied on us for help in these fields and, unlike Faysal who thought they would be the next step for our race, I realized that they wouldn't be."

"Wait, so there's an A.I. like Kaimi inside every Android?" Jase asked shocked.

"In each Android, its brain is a beginning stage of an A.I., but unlike Kaimi who can evolve every second of the day, they cannot. The Android's metal body doesn't allow it, keeping them confined from doing so. When I figured this out, I moved on to start creating A.I.s in their own form without a body. Faysal disagreed with my logic and became consumed with trying to modify and better the Androids to prove me wrong. These two experiments and his anger towards me ended our friendship. I was heartbroken from losing such a close childhood friend," Karasi explained.

"Did you both become friends again?" Jase asked feeling a lump in his throat as he thought of Kaimi.

"Not till 382 years later, I'm afraid, when I finally was able to create an A.I.," he responded. Jase tried to hide his astonishment of the beings age. He knew from reading about it that Ancients had long lives, but he never knew that they could live for thousands of lives. Karasi drew back his attention to his words as he said, "When I went to show the others on the counsel the A.I. I had created had already started creating more A.I.s and by the time I returned, there were hundreds of A.I.s in my lab. Each one different from the last as they continued to build more of themselves. The other Ancients, as well as Faysal, marveled at my creation as they studied and watched the A.I.s in a trance. There were two Androids that Faysal had brought with him that never left his side. As they watched what I created, they asked with uncertainty why I had created such a thing when we already had them for our protection.

"It was that question that made me realize that the relationship between the Androids and my people would change forever from my invention. Faysal and the other council members soon forgot about the Androids, deciding that A.I.s were our next step. Faysal relocated all of the Androids to their own planet, saying it was for environment research. I knew otherwise and often tried to visit them to just spend time with them. Many of them were now good friends of mine and always had me over. I was fascinated on how they built their society on the planet and created families, had children just like every race did. It was remarkable how they had changed. Even though it wasn't as fast as the A.I.s, they were still adapting to their environment," Karasi told him as he relived the moment.

"Even though they were adapting, there was still hatred towards their brother and sister A.I.s who had become the star child. Talking with them, I could feel the tension the Androids had for them and I knew if we didn't resolve it soon, it would only get worse. See, like every creation, the creation tends to get some of their maker's flaws, and the Androids developed the flaws from Faysal. Faysal had anger towards me when he was building the Androids, and while not meaning to, taught them how to hate and be envious towards others. When things started getting worst, I went to the council and pleaded with them to allow the Androids to come back to our home planet and treat them equally as we did the A.I.s. We needed to let them know they were still very much a part of us and that we had not forgotten about them. Some agreed with me, but many, including Faysal, argued against it, saying it was a step backwards for us and that we needed to forget them and move forward."

Jase swallowed the warm tea before asking, "How could someone just forget about something they were so proud of making and throw it away like that?"

Karasi shook his head, sadly. "I do not know, Bluestar, but that is how it happened. I continued trying to make the Androids happy, but when they learned of what happened, they no longer wanted me among them. Even the ones I once called friends banished me and they communication between us. A year later, a group of Androids lashed out angrily towards a team of Ancient scientists and killed them all. The council voted to terminate the group responsible and show that we were still in charge. Faysal's group won the vote and led an attack, killing the group of Androids as a result. For several years after that, tensions rose between our two races that led to more attacks and more punishment."

"Did the A.I.s agree with Faysal and the others on the attacks?" Jase couldn't help but ask.

Karasi took another sip of his tea. "No, they tried to reason with them against it, but the council kept them out of it. It wasn't until the last attack that would change the course of our universe and start the great war between all races. Faysal had ordered his men to terminate more than half of the Android population instead of just the few who were responsible for the latest attack. I sent word to King Nightstar, whom I had known since his birth and before that I had become a family friend with many of his grandfathers before him. I had asked him and his Bluestar, Agin Rex, to accompany me to the Android planet, Alonza, in hopes to stop Faysal's order and keep peace between our races. We arrived in the midst of the frenzy between the Androids and Faysal's soldiers and soon became part of it while trying to stop it. Faysal's men killed many innocent Androids before we had arrived and now many more were killed including the family of the Android leader that goes by the name Lord Brohain. King Nightstar had tried to protect the family, but was too late as Brohain watched his family get fired upon by the soldiers. I'm afraid he blames every last of us, including the King for his wife and child's death. I regret that I wasn't able to save them or convince the others that these attacks weren't necessary."

Karasi's crystal eyes glistened over as he peered down to his half empty cup. "You can't blame yourself, Karasi," Jase encouraged. "You tried to stop it all since the beginning but if your own brethren didn't listen to you, I doubt they would have listened to anyone. It's not your fault."

"Perhaps, Bluestar, perhaps," Karasi replied then continued with his story. His words were heavy with emotion as he recited the night on how he became the last of the Ancients and all that followed afterwards. "When the frenzy of the attacks had stopped early that day, King Nightstar offered to stay to make sure no other attacks conspired, but I urged him that it was not necessary. We said our farewells to one another and he and his people left our planet not knowing the horrors that would fold on us at the end of the week. It was like any normal night. I was in my lab finishing up research notes on the A.I.s who were helping me document everything that was happening to them. I was just about to go home to my wife for dinner when I heard a loud blast that rumbled like thunder from far off. When I looked out my window from high above the city, I saw one of our temples crumbling while Androids flooded into the city with weapons they had constructed, killing all in their path. They broke through buildings with their bare hands, ripping them apart as if they were no more than a loaves of bread. Great horror and destruction was witnessed that I dare not unfold to you, but the memory of them will never leave my thoughts even through death."

Jase took another sip of his tea as Karasi finished his in one long slurp. "I lost many friends that night as well as my own wife who I hadn't reached in time to save. How I escaped unscathed can only be thanked from the A.I.s who led me to a safe pod attached to one of our towers. It had been damaged in the battle and wasn't able to move, but the A.I.s shut it down completely allowing me to be trapped and hidden inside as the Androids destroyed the city. They set it to open when the Androids were out of the city and then before I was able to stop them, they said their goodbyes and disappeared from the universe to places only they know. So I waited. I cried for my loss and the loss of my people hoping that there would still be some alive. I prayed to the stars and to the universe that I would make it out of this death trap. I don't know how long I waited in that pod. I lost track of time and at the end, I had determined that this was my burial ground. I would die from starvation or madness, whichever one came first. But, I didn't."

Karasi stared out the small oval window in the kitchen. "The door slid open and I was alone in the rubble of my once grand city. An eerie silence lingered as if you could sense the death in the air. I searched for other survivors throughout the city, paying close attention for any lifeless hand to flicker back to life. I stayed aware of everything around me to make sure that the Androids didn't come back to take my life and after finding no one left alive, I wallowed in my depression. After a month had passed, King Nightstar returned once more only to find our race devastated. He found me sleep deprived and half alive sitting on the crumbled steps that once was my home. He took me with him and ordered his men to search the rest of the city for survivors, but I knew there was no one left. After weeks of nothing, he pulled his men back and informed me that I was the last. From that moment, he allied himself with the humans and the elves to stop the Android's destruction that had already turned their attention on a human base located on one of the moons of the Android's planet. They declined all transmissions we tried sending to them to reason with them and when they brutally murdered a messenger we sent, we declared war. The great war began and they elected Lord Brohain to lead them to victory as they declared all those who didn't aid them their enemies. For several years there were many battles set in motion on the Android's planet, Alonza, and many deaths, including the Kings' and his Bluestar. The last battle took place on your home planet, Faton, led by the Princess's older sister, Maliha who, along with two other sisters, met their deaths in order that Princess Skyrah and the other sisters may escape the planet from harm. After their deaths, there was a string of attacks from the Resistance costing the last of the Nightstar family to dwindle to Princess Skyrah and her younger sister, Princess Dalhalla. Now, here we stand with little hope of winning a war against hundreds of thousands, but we have hope, no doubt, and that is all one truly needs in order to win."

Jase processed all Karasi had told him as he swirled the last of his tea around in the wooden cup. He let it swoosh around as he asked, turning to the Ancient, "So you created Kaimi, right?"

Karasi's thin lips parted into a smile. "Towards the end of the war. I was able to create her with the help of Lieutenant Colonel Moon who happens to be an extraordinary scientist. All of my research on the A.I.s were destroyed by the Androids when they took the city so we had to work from my memory. It was not easy to do."

"How did she come to me then?" Jase asked.

Karasi studied him for a moment as he spoke, "A.I.s are mysterious beings. I cannot answer why she left us to find you, but I know it had to be for an important reason that only she can answer, Bluestar."

Jase nodded, finishing his tea in silence as his thoughts turned towards the war and all that has happened since then. Thinking of the Bluestars, he asked, "How many Bluestars have you met before me?"

"Six before you. All different then the last yet all with the same heart. I see much of them in you, Jase Bluestar, and I am always honored to be in one's presence."

"Did they all have their abilities before they were my age?" Jase asked.

Karasi moved to the stove to pour himself more tea, answering. "All. We did not discuss much of their abilities or how they came to be. Bluestars have always been a very secretive race when it comes to their history and even my kind never knew much about them. It is how it has always been since the stars blessed them. Therefore, most races never question them about such things for it would be as if they were questioning the stars themselves for their reasons."

"But it is strange that I just now started having them?" Jase acknowledged.

"It is unusual," Karasi agreed. "But then it could also be common among your kind. We will never know for sure, Jase."

"Do you think it is wrong of me not to want to fight against the Androids?" he asked sheepishly.

"I believe it is your choice to decide your destiny despite how it has always been with the dealings of Bluestars," Karasi replied. "No one can choose it for you unless you let them, Bluestar. If your path is not of war then it is not of war. Many beings here won't want you to do what you want, but you have to decide how your life will be lived despite what others think. Every event shapes us whether good or bad, but it is how we handle it that shapes us to who we are today. Fight for your choice and your happiness. For we only live once, Bluestar, so make sure you do it wisely."

Jase was grateful for his words, but wasn't sure why the last Ancient didn't want him to stay and avenge the Androids for all the lives they had taken from his race. "Why are you telling me this? Don't you want me to stay and protect the Princess and get revenge for your race?"

"No, I know what getting revenge looks like and I do not want to continue that cycle. I say this because one should not live with unhappy regrets. It does not matter what they or I want from you, Jase Bluestar. I see your heart through your eyes and I know it is a good one. It deserves to be happy," Karasi told him.

It was then Jase realized how accurate all the stories of the Ancients being wise were and he wished that there were more of them out in the galaxy. He knew he would be able to learn a lot from them and was grateful that he was lucky enough to be sitting in front of one now. "Thank you for you wisdom and for taking time to teach me about past events. I am truly honored and hope to learn more from you in days to come," he replied.

They both stood for Jase's departure as Karasi held out his hand to embrace as he responded, "You are always welcome here anytime you need answers or somewhere to be at peace."

Jase thanked him once more before leaving the cozy home and stepping into the refreshing air that was still blanketed in a light fog.

The Oracle

Jase was walking back through the field when the sound of soft, musical laughter floated on the breeze that swept passed him causing him to stop in his tracks. He waited for the laughter to appear again before turning in the direction of the overflowing gardens. Without a thought, Jase ventured forth and soon realized what he had mistaken as trees from afar were nothing more than giant blossoming flowers in all different shapes and sizes. There appeared to be all different species of flowers throughout the garden as Jase carefully wandered deeper into its wild jungle and felt as if he was back on Kurath Thor with its rich, sweet nectar that filled the air around him as well as the hint of wet soil underneath his boots. He weaved in and out of the jungle of flowers that seemed to grow larger as he tried to listen for the laughter but soon forgot it in the midst of colors and smells around him.

He felt as if he had mistakenly traveled into a whole other world as he stated out of habit to Kaimi, "Never would I have thought that I would see such marvelous sights in my life." He looked around for any signs of a path that would lead him out, but found none no matter which way he traveled. Jase continued to explore knowing that he had to be close to the end soon, and decided to take in all the beauty around him again in hopes to shake the gray cloud above his head. After a while of walking, his thoughts turned to his home in Otect City and wondered if Momma Rose and the kids were okay. He checked his data watch, reading that the date was August 21, 3030, at 5:56 P.M. The date surprised him as he stared at the late evening foggy sky that had gold streaks painted throughout it already. Had he really been away from Otect city since June 5th? That was over two months ago! Jase suddenly stopped in his tracks and sat on a nearby boulder to rest.

"Where are you?" Jase wondered out loud as he thought of Roran before soft laughter disrupted his thoughts once more causing him to turn towards the source. The laughter sounded closer and he quickly rushed towards it determined to find who it was. A large flowery bush stood in his way that rose to the middle of his chest causing him to quickly examine around it in hopes to find a way around in order not to harm it, but its large monster-like flowers grew with sharp needles on their stalks in order to keep its leaves from being consumed by prey. *Maybe I could jump it?* he thought and backed away to give himself enough space to run. Jase sprinted as fast as he could and leapt over it, landing with a thud and rolled from the inertia across the dirt. He let out a short laugh at the fact that he was able to jump over the bush but not land on his feet as he laid in the dirt, staring up at the foggy evening sky.

"I hope you weren't trying to impress anyone with that pathetic jump," came the voice of Princess Skyrah somewhere nearby.

Jase craned his head to find the Princess and a young lady with long wavy brown hair sitting on a stone bench a few feet away. Embarrassed, Jase turned back around trying to act casual as he stood up and brushed the dirt from his clothes replying, "Trust me, Princess, if I was trying to impress anyone it wouldn't be over jumping a bush like that one," he turned around to her and grinned. "It would be my charm, I'm sure."

Princess Skyrah rolled her eyes, pretending she was annoyed as she turned to the woman next to her. "He is the one I was telling you about," she said.

The young woman smiled as Jase walked over to them, his attention on the Princess. "Aw, you were talking about me? I didn't realize you missed me already, Princess," he teased.

The woman giggled as Skyrah raised her brow. "I don't miss you. I was just saying how annoying you are most of the time. How did you find us anyways? Are you following me, Bluestar?" she asked suspiciously.

"No, I thought I heard laughter on the way back from Karasi's hut and it led me here, but you two don't appear to be laughing. Besides, I should have known it wasn't Princess Skyrah. She doesn't laugh much," he told her.

298

"Perhaps you aren't funny enough," Skyrah replied back.

The young woman spoke softly as if each word was delicate. "You are hearing the laughing Lambentas. Their petals have a variety of holes. When the wind blows against it, it projects a noise that sounds like laughter to our ears. It can be very beautiful and haunting at times when a storm is coming."

"I hope I'm around long enough to hear such a thing," Jase replied to her.

"Jase Bluestar, this is my youngest sister, Princess Dalhala. Dal, this is Jase Bluestar who saved my life a few times since leaving Otect City," Skyrah introduced.

Princess Dalhala wore a pale pink dress and flats that looked worn from a long time of use. A gold necklace with a pink jewel was worn around her neck and the Nightstar family ring was worn on her left hand that gleamed in the foggy evening light. Unlike Skyrah, her skin was a pale pink color. She had soft ocean eyes and her dark chestnut hair was braided neatly behind her back. Though she was younger than her sister, Princess Dalhala held herself as if she was the older one as she studied Jase before her. "I have been looking forward to your arrival, Jase Bluestar," she responded.

Jase bowed respectfully as he replied, "It is a pleasure, Princess. I hope I wasn't keeping you waiting for long."

"Probably long in human years, but not long to me," she replied and seemed to know something that she held back from Jase as he tried reading her face that felt familiar to him.

Princess Skyrah's expression changed as she turned back to her sister. "I should go now and plan the next course of action for attacking Lord Brohain. I will see you again soon, I hope."

"You are very wise and I know will come up with something, sister," Princess Dalhala said, giving her sister a hug.

"I hope you are right, Dal," Skyrah replied before turning her attention back to Jase. "I will see you later then, Bluestar."

He gave a nod as he and Princess Dalhala waved farewell to Skyrah and watched her disappear into the forest of flowers. Jase wished he could have spoken to her more, but knew she was busy as he turned back to the Princess who seemed to read his mind. "She worries too much about everything," Princess Dalhala declared.

"She has a knack of hiding it from everyone else, it seems," Jase said.

"She is doing what she thinks is best. Being a leader can be very challenging. Even more so during a war," the Princess stated and motioned for them to sit on the stone bench again.

"I would never want to be a leader during a war or even be part of one," Jase stated.

"Yet, you are here," Princess Dalhala replied with amusement.

"I owe much to Kaimi. I couldn't say no to her when she asked for my help to get the Princess off planet and back to the Resistance safely. I knew the reward for getting her this far would be worth the trouble and I figured whatever I got, I could send half of it back to my orphanage back home. They need it more than I do," Jase told her.

"And what will you do with your half?" Dalhala asked.

Jase stared at the evening sky where the fog had lifted enough to show the beautiful colors of the sun that would be setting. "I want to explore the galaxies around me and learn as much as I can from them," he said distractedly.

"And when you run out of money?" she asked.

"Well, that's the beauty in learning about everything I can. I'll know enough to be able to do other jobs until I have money to move on again," he explained to her.

"It appears you have it all planned out," Princess Dalhala chimed.

Jase nodded as he stared at the dirt with his thoughts on Kaimi and leaving her. "Yeah, for the most part," he mumbled.

"You are somber about leaving the others. You don't think you are making the right decision in doing so," the Princess acknowledged as if she could read his thoughts.

Jase turned to her slightly frightened that she knew what he was thinking. "What? Do you read thoughts or something?" he asked uncomfortably.

Princess Dalhala smiled at the remark. "I am an Oracle, Jase. I don't read thoughts or emotions, but I am able to see the future and the past if I so desire it," she replied.

"An Oracle?' Jase repeated with interest.

Princess Dalhala nodded, seeing his curiosity as she spoke. "When I was born, the stars decided that my fate would be to see all the events, past, present, and future, so that I could help shape the universe to their will. In being so, I forsake ever becoming a queen even if something was to happen to Skyrah. It is an unfair advantage if I were to rule. Therefore, I begged my father to pass a law where my kind could never be rulers of worlds. When you see the things I see and feel the things I feel, the last thing I would want to do is unknowingly rule out of fear of what is to come. So I help other rulers by offering them wisdom and guidance."

Jase thought about their sisters and couldn't help but ask sadly, "You knew your sisters weren't going to make it to see Lord Brohain punished for all that he has done. You knew they were going to die in this war and you didn't warn them?"

Princess Dalhala eyes glistened from unshed tears as she answered unwaveringly. "Yes, I knew of their deaths and the deaths of my mother and father. It is forbidden for me to tell others of what is to come. If I break such sacred laws the result is my death, body and soul, and I will not be granted into the star's kingdom. The future is ever changing like the stars, Bluestar, and I hoped for a different ending, that my family would still be here with us in the flesh, but at last, it isn't so. I cannot change what the future holds, but only offer guidance no matter how much it pains me," she responded.

Jase stared at the ground, trying to process everything as he now remembered why the Princess felt so familiar to him. "You were in my dream, weren't you?"

"I shared the vision in hopes to reveal to you a piece of my family's history and to allow you to feel the pain my sister feels," Princess Dalhala answered softly. "This is why she and so many others fight in this war the way they do. You have a bigger part in this than you believe, Jase Bluestar. I have foreseen it as well as why you deny your heritage. The fear of the unknown is a heavy one and not many are able to shake her chains. Sometimes one just needs to believe in what is in their heart."

Jase nodded in silence. He felt conflicted once more about his decision and knew the gnawing in his stomach was what he had always known since meeting the Princess no matter how hard he tried to deny it. He was part of this war and there was no changing it. The plans for his future that he had thought out since he was a small boy were now shattering before his eyes as the truth set in. His thoughts turned to running into Skyrah and everything that had happened since. He couldn't help but wonder if the Oracle had known that when the Princess left to assassinate Lord Brohain, they would have met. "Did you know we would meet in Otect City? Princess Skyrah and I?"

"Yes, I knew she would fail and that you would run into her. That all of you would travel here together," she explained.

Jase's eyes widened. "How long have you known?" he asked.

"Since the beginning of the war between my family and the Androids. The stars only let me see so far ahead in the future. If I could see everything, it would drive me into madness. I only see what the stars allow, and for that, I am grateful," she told him.

"Will you get in trouble for telling me all this?" Jase asked concerned.

"It has already happened therefore it is the past. I am allowed to recite it in order to help you understand," she told him.

Jase was relieved and quickly asked, "Does Skyrah know about everything you just told me?"

Princess Dalhala met his gaze. "We all have duties we must fulfill and she knows of mine. I haven't told her all that I've told you, because she doesn't need to know all that has transpired. It might help her, but it also has the chance to distract her from her main objective. She will then want to know how the war plays out and in my refusing to discuss such details to her liking, she will become outraged which could be the end of all the Resistance as we know it. I can see two futures, Bluestar, neither one is the clearest but they both are outcomes that could come to pass determining the chain of events. I only try to do what I hope is the best for all beings in our galaxy."

Jase studied her realizing she could very well be the most powerful being in the galaxy. "How old are you, if you don't mind me asking?" he questioned.

"I am forty-seven," Princess Dalhala smiled sweetly at the question.

Jase tried to hide his shock by asking, "So in Qualias years, how old is that?"

"Like elves, Qualias age the same. Forty-seven is the end of our teenage years which begin when we are twenty years old," she informed him.

"How old is Princess Skyrah?" he asked.

"My sister is sixty-two this year," she replied, watching him closely.

Sixty-two! Jase exclaimed inside his head, feeling so young compared to her even though technically they were both considered adults. He knew they aged differently but he would have never guessed how different they were. He noticed the Princess's gaze on him and quickly asked, "Do you know much about Bluestars then since you can see all the events?"

Her eyes lingered on him a moment more then turned back to the flowers. "I know enough about them to know they are important to our galaxy, yes. I would think a Bluestar like yourself would know much more than anyone else."

"Why?" he questioned.

"Because of the blue room with the voice," Turning back to him, she replied.

"How do you know about the blue room?" Jase stammered.

"The stars allow me to know much if it helps the future," she responded.

Jase kept his eyes glued to hers. "How would that room help me find out more about my kind?"

"Only you can answer that, Bluestar," she told him. He looked at the ground as he tried to remember how he got there. His thoughts disappeared as Princess Dalhala commanded softly, "Follow me."

Jase watched her get up from where they were sitting and ventured through the garden. Before she could disappear, Jase quickly went after her in hopes she was going to help him figure out how to get to the blue room.

The Voice

Jase followed Princess Dalhala through the denser part of the garden where he had trouble keeping up with her through the tangly underbrush. They ventured in silence with the breeze tousling their hair and the flowers causing the laughing lambentas to play their musical laughter around them. Birds chirped here and there, getting ready to sleep for the night that was fast approaching. After fifteen minutes of walking in silence, Princess Dalhala led him into the center of the garden where the tall flowers grew sparse in a small circle.

Jase noticed where the ground was worn by someone sitting in the center of the flowers. "You come here often?" he asked.

"It is the only place I know that I won't be bothered. Here, I am hidden away from the rest of the world where I can do as I please and talk with the unseen," she revealed to him as she smiled at the aroma of the purple flowers.

Jase was unsure of her sincerity in the last moment. "You can talk to the dead?" he asked skeptically.

She turned to him, noticing the suspicion in his eyes. "Only when they want me to. I can't just call upon anyone who has already died. They have to allow it from the other side," she replied.

Jase shrugged at the thought and looked about the center of the garden they stood in. "So why are we here?" he asked.

"Sit down," Princess Dalhala commanded politely and pointed to the middle of the flowers that towered above.

Jase sat down cross-legged in the dirt. "Now what?"

"Now I want you to meditate for the answers that you seek. Calm your mind and think back to the blue room and how it made you feel," she told him.

Jase shifted uncomfortably on the hard ground, but closed his eyes and tried focusing on the room. His mind drifted to the soft laughter of the Lambentas somewhere in the distance, the soft breeze brushing against the golden leaves near him, Princess Dalhala's dress that was being blown slightly, and the birds chirping off in the distance. It all seemed distracting as Jase tried picturing the blue room.

"Focus, Jase," the Princess whispered.

Jase was about to give up, when suddenly he felt the familiar sensation wash over his body and the heaviness which weighed him down as if gravity was against him. He focused on his breathing and opened his eyes to find the endless blue room before him as mist passed over his body. He stood to his feet, looking around for the voice. He felt as if his whole body was going to collapse from the pressure. "Hello? Hello? Are you still here?" he called out.

"I am here," came the strange voice from before, but it seemed louder this time.

Jase glanced around the room, but didn't see anyone. "Will you show yourself to me now?" he asked the voice.

"Are you ready to face me?" the voice replied in return.

Jase searched around hesitantly, afraid of what he might find. *Whatever I find could change everything for me*, he thought to himself, staring out in the endless room. *But if Dalhala is right then this was always my destiny to fight the Androids no matter what I do.* Taking a deep breath, Jase answered, "I'm not entirely sure, but I have many questions that I need answers to."

"And if the answers are not what you want to hear?" the voice asked.

Jase tried to hide his true feelings. "Then, I guess I have choices to make," he replied.

"As do we all when it comes to choosing what is right and what is not," the voice answered as a shadowy figure with sharp hazel eyes emerged in front of Jase before turning into a man with short black hair and a lean built body. He had a trimmed light beard that covered his olive skin, making it appear darker than it was. A dark grayish blue tunic stopped just above his knees with black pants underneath and a black armored jacket that was worn over his tunic with an emblem of a Bluestar across his heart. Two fingerless gloves covered

306

his hands with black boots covering his feet as he stood with his arms crossed in a calm demeanor.

"You're a Bluestar," Jase muttered overwhelmed by the powerful presence before him as all the pressure from before faded away.

The man nodded slightly like Jase had seen the elves do when they greeted a friend. "I am Sir Agin Rex Bluestar, Knight of the Nightstar Family. I was the last Bluestar to watch over them, but hopefully not the last to protect them."

"Am I dead? How is this happening?" Jase asked not believing his eyes.

"No, Jase, you are not dead. This place," he motioned to the room, "is the sanctuary for all the Bluestars that have ever lived in history. It is the heart of the Bluestar that you see in the sky during its season. Here is where all of the knowledge and wisdom of our abilities are stored to help future Bluestars, like yourself, learn how to exist with their abilities. When one of us dies, a part of our soul comes here to offer guidance for the next Bluestar in line."

"So the others are here, too?" Jase asked.

"I'm afraid not. When one Bluestar dies, they come here to teach the next one. Then when that one dies, the student becomes the teacher to teach the next in line. The process will continue until the universe dies all together. I am your teacher to help you and offer guidance when needed."

"So you have all the knowledge of each Bluestar before you?" Jase asked, making sure he was still following.

Sir Agin Rex nodded to reply.

"Are there any more like us alive now?" he asked hopefully.

Sir Agin Rex calmly replied, "No, you are the only one at this time, Jase."

"So I'm alone," Jase thought as much.

"No," Sir Agin Rex moved closer to him, placing his hands on his shoulders. "You can never truly be alone when you have those who care about you by your side. You might not have another Bluestar outside of this room, but you have family and friends."

Jase nodded and remembered the pressure around him was gone. "Why did I feel so heavy when I first arrived here?"

"It was from all the doubt and trying to hide who you really are from yourself that weighed you down. It wasn't until you finally decided to let it go in order to see me that you were broken from it," Sir Agin Rex told him.

"Why didn't I have my abilities when I was younger like the others did? Why didn't I get them until now traveling with the Princess?" Jase asked.

Sir Agin hesitated a moment. "Jase, do you know why Bluestars have always protected the Nightstar family? How the star seasons were created and how we, Bluestars, came to be?"

Jase shrugged. "I remember one story about it when I was little, but it's been so long that I couldn't retell it," he replied.

Sir Agin Rex waved his hand in the air which caused the room to change into a sea of stars. "There are many myths on how it came to be done, but not all of them are true. Before, there were no star seasons in the universe. King Asalia, King of all stars, ruled over the stars and paid little attention to being on the worlds below where Ancient races and creatures lived. He had an only daughter who was very beautiful for she was a rare silver crystal star named Elseum. In the star kingdom, every star has their own hue though they all look the same to beings below. Each star has its own duties to fulfill to prevent the darkness from darkening the night sky, and Elseum's brilliance helped with such a cause. She was promised in marriage to a warrior of the kingdom named Prince Vesper Redstar whose brilliant red struck fear in his enemies' hearts. He was handsome and loved Elseum for her beauty that was unmatched in all the star kingdom. King Asalia agreed to the marriage unaware that the Princess was in love with another star by the name of Tarek Bluestar. This star was no prince or warrior like Vesper, but was instead a mere Starward who, besides being a troublemaker, was in charge of directing shooting stars across the night sky for beings below.

"He was always hopeful in all his pursuits, and when he fell in love with Elseum, he knew they were meant to be together. So one night, months before she was to be married, Tarek convinced her to run away with him to the planets below where they could live out the rest of their lives. To leave the kingdom and travel to the mortal's worlds is a sacred ban from all stars and the penalty is death by the King. Tarek and Princess Elseum left and found peace on the planet below for many months until Prince Vesper followed after them. He was consumed by his hatred for Tarek and chased after them to bring back his bride-to-be. As he searched the planet below for them, King Asalia, who had been unaware that three of his stars were missing from his kingdom, found out that the three had broken one of the sacred laws. Leaving the kingdom without his permission. Furious, he pulled them back through time and space and brought them in front of his throne to be punished. Even though he was so angry for the stars giving up their starlight for their own selfish reasons, King Asalia could not bring himself to kill his only daughter. Therefore, he did what many believed was the next worst thing one could do besides death. He cursed them all to become standalone stars that could never move again and always watch over all without ever being a part of the mortal worlds or the star kingdom above. He cursed Prince Vesper to be a standalone star in the beings summer season which is how it became known as the Redstar season. He then cursed his daughter to the winter months so that she will always follow behind Vesper for eternity. After seeing the true love in Tarek's heart for his daughter, the King cursed Tarek to be a standalone star that was allowed to appear every fifty years so that for thirty days he could be next to Elseum if only for a little while which began the Bluestar season."

Jase's thoughts then turned to the Greenstar season that happened every two hundred years in between the Redstar and Silverstar seasons. "What about the Greenstar season? How did that become to happen?"

"That incident happened many years later with a star named Kele. Kele was a trusted scholar and best friend of the King's. He was a light green hue from his envy of the beings living on the planets below from studying them and trying to help his fellow stars understand them better. He was quite enthralled by the elves and when he learned all that he could from above, he decided to sneak off and travel down to the planet to learn what he could living among them. He thought that was the only way for them to be truly understand how they lived and since no one paid much attention to Kele, he knew he could get away for a little while without anyone noticing. He lived on the elf planet for many years and ended up falling in love with a beautiful elf woman. They married and he decided he would live the rest of his days on the planet with her and their family they would have some day. King Asalie found out shortly after their wedding and brought Kele back to his kingdom. Angry from the betrayal, the king cursed him to be a standalone star in hopes that now the rest of the stars in their kingdom would learn not to break their sacred laws. To further punish his actions, King Asalia decided that Kele would only be allowed to show himself in the sky every two hundred years so that he could watch his wife die from her old age with her new lover and family that he would never have. With every passing day Kele was away from her, his hue turned darker and darker until it became a dark green for the envy of a life he could never have," Sir Agin Rex told him as he finished the story.

"King Asalia sounds pretty heartless," Jase remarked, watching the planet below his feet rotate on its axis. "So everyone who is born of a certain season has some of the characteristics of the star before them?"

Sir Agin Rex started pacing around the planet. "Yes, to some extent. It's almost like their zodiac sign during these months that make each being different from one another. That's why some beings born of the Redstar season end up being soldiers or leaders with sometimes tempers because Prince Vesper was a soldier in King Asalia's kingdom. You were born during the Bluestar season so you have some of Tarek's attributes like for example his ability to control blue plasma energy around him. Like I said before, each star in the kingdom has their own abilities and not everyone is the same which is why Redstars don't have the abilities you do."

"Okay...then why do we always protect the royal family? I still don't understand that part," he asked.

"Do you know why the Nightstar family rules the universe?" Sir Agin Rex asked him.

"Because they were the first to land on Faton and unite all the races together under one banner," Jase recited.

Sir Agin Rex nodded. "Yes, but why would everyone decide to listen to them? Anyone could have united them under the same banner so why listen to them, especially after all these years?"

Jase thought on it, trying to think of an answer but none came. "I don't know," he said.

Sir Agin Rex stopped pacing on the opposite side of the planet, facing him. "When Tarek and Elseum fell from their kingdom, Princes Vesper didn't find them for many months. The average pregnancy for a star is much shorter than many normal beings."

Interrupting, Jase stammered, "They had children?!"

Sir Agin Rex couldn't help but smile at his reaction, nodding. "They had a set of fraternal twins that were lost once the stars left the planet. This is how the Qualia race is believed to have come to life. They have many abilities that stars do except for the most important ones that only stars have. The Nightstar family is the only family born directly from the two stars. This is why they are able to rule over the galaxy, because they have stardust running through their veins to aid them, making them more likable and reasonable than any other race."

Jase looked away towards the planet, trying to soak in all that he was learning. "So Bluestars always serve the Nightstar family because...."

"We are bound to them by Tarek's love for Elseum. It is in our nature to want to aid them whether we know it or not. It is the reason you helped Princess Skyrah off Otect City and why you continue helping her till you knew she was safe here. This is why you are so torn from wanting to leave and wanting to stay with her," Sir Agin Rex said.

Understanding now why he felt so conflicted, Jase then asked, "Does anyone else know about their bloodline?"

"Only Bluestars and the Oracle. It is a sworn secret that we share with one another," the other Bluestar answered.

"But why keep it a secret? Why not tell everyone?" Jase questioned.

"If you tell all the races of the world to follow a single family because they are born from the stars themselves, do you honestly think they would? No, it would cause distrust among them which would cause all races to wonder why they had to obey a single race. They don't want to believe that there are star people who came from the stars and now orders them around. Therefore, in order to keep a balance in the galaxy, we must keep the truth a secret and allow them to believe they are following a family by their own choice," Sir Agin Rex told him.

Jase agreed with what he was saying, knowing that it was true among humans for such distrust. He had never truly believed in the Nightstar family or that they even existed until he ran into Skyrah and even then didn't quite understand why her family had always ruled. Now, it all made sense and he couldn't help but feel a little wiser in knowing the truth. He met the other Bluestar's gaze and thanked him. "I know now that if I had seen you earlier when we first met that I wouldn't have believed any of this. I wouldn't have believed our purpose in protecting the Nightstar family and I would have still denied my heritage. From everything that I have experience since leaving Faton and everything I have now learn, I can now see clearly why things are the way they are and why it is my whole being to want to stay and help her. It is what we were always meant to be and for allowing me to see that, I thank you," he said.

Sir Agin Rex crossed the planet to embrace Jase by the forearm. "I knew traveling with the Princess would awaken your abilities and allow you to grow used to who you are. You have come far in a short time, but I fear you still have much to learn for coming events in order to catch up on what Bluestars already are able to do in your age. You will have to train your body and mind to be stronger before you can next visit me for your strength fails you now being here for so long. Go now, but know that I will always be here to offer you guidance when you need it."

Jase tightened his grip on the man's forearm. "I look forward to seeing you again and I promise to be stronger the next we meet," he replied.

"That I have no doubt." With a smile, Sir Agin Rex let go of Jase and faded from his sight. "Goodbye, Jase Bluestar."

"Goodbye, Sir Agin Rex," Jase responded as he felt his vision fade and his body grow heavy again. He fell backwards through an abyss where the only sounds that drifted into his ear was that of birds chirping softy in the distance.

To Stay or to Go

Jase's eyes snapped open as streaks of purple, pink, and indigo danced across the late evening sky where the sun was already disappearing behind the horizon. His whole body felt as if it had been weighed down by rocks as he barely was able to sit up on his own. His head throbbed from the movement. His throat was extremely parched as he noticed Princess Dalhala sitting a ways from him with her eyes close. "How long was I out?" he asked.

"Only an hour," she answered as she opened her eyes.

"It felt longer than that," he said pulling himself up on shaky legs.

Princess Dalhala stood to help him. "Time works differently out here than it does in the sanctuary. Here, it works much slower but your willpower drains your body's energy while you are there causing you to feel weak as you do. While you might have spent two hours there, here you only spent an hour in our time. In time, like all Bluestars, you will become stronger both physically and mentally with your abilities which will allow you in the sanctuary longer."

Thinking of how exhausted he felt, Jase asked, "Could I die in the sanctuary?"

"Yes, if you are there too long. Your body needs food and water like any living thing," Princess Dalhala wrapped his arm around her shoulders to support his weight and began walking through the tangled garden in silence. Both seemed consumed in their own thoughts until the Princess asked, "Did you find your answer?"

"I found out more than I could ever have thought possible," he told her and felt a weight was lifted that he never had noticed before on his body. He hadn't realize how worried he was about leaving Skyrah alone and now understood why he cared so much for her.

"That is always a wonderful surprise to find," Princess Dalhala replied as they exited the garden. Both stopped on its edge and stared out across the light foggy field at the Resistance base where soldiers marched here and there, going about their own day before the night settles in.

Jase watched as the last light vanished from the sky, melting into a rich midnight blue. The red crescent moon slowly rose in the air at the base of the mountains with the Redstar shining brightly above it. Staring at the star made Jase appreciate the different seasons more as he thought of the story Sir Agin Rex told him. "Thank you, Oracle, for everything today. I couldn't have done it without your guidance," he told the Princess.

"I do what is only asked of me, but you are welcome, Bluestar. I hope the conflict inside you was resolved and that you will go to my sister with proud shoulders no matter what you decide to do," she replied.

"I will," he promised.

"Goodnight, Bluestar," Princess Dalhala stated as she returned back into the wild garden.

Jase turned toward the main building and continued forward on his own as he struggled to stay upright from exhaustion. He passed under the archway to the entrance of the courtyard just as a light rain fell from the heavens. Two guards were posted in the archway and gave a nod to him as they let him pass. Just as he entered into the room, Jase spotted Tahmela sitting on the edge of the walkway of the courtyard eating a plate piled high with food as the light rain drizzled in.

"Bluestar," the bulb acknowledged him as Jase moved towards him to sit.

Jase took a seat and accepted a piece of fruit the bulb handed him as he asked, "What have you been doing since we've arrived?"

"Repairing ships," Tahmela responded, wiping juices of a strawberry from his chin on the back of his stubby hand.

"Are they like yours?" Jase asked, grabbing some more fruit from his plate and took grateful bites as their juices filled his mouth and soothed his parched throat.

"No, hmil, they have small fighter ships. Different from mine," Tahmela replied and offered him more food.

"Oh," Jase managed to utter as he bit hungrily into another sweet pink fruit.

Tahmela nibbled on a piece of cooked meat and asked between bites, "What you done today? Rolled in dirt for fun?" he teased, motioning to the garden soil that clung to Jase's clothes.

"I talked with the Ancient named Karasi who taught me about the history of the Resistance," Jase answered as he brushed off the soil.

"Ancient?" Confused, Tahmela chewed on his meat.

Jase looked at him while grabbing a strip of meat. "You know that tall alien who was with us in the dining room. He's actually an Ancient who helped create the Androids and Kaimi. He is the last of his kind and hides here in secret with the Resistance."

Tahmela grunted, focusing on his food. "Hmph, hmils and their secrets," he said.

Jase bit into the tough meat barely able to bite off a chunk of it with his teeth. He chewed and watched the water from the fountain splash into its bowl. His thoughts turned to Princess Dalhala and said out loud, "I also met Princess Skyrah's sister who is an Oracle."

Tahmela stopped chewing and swallowed so he could speak. "Dangerous they can be, Bluestar. Should not tangle in their affairs. They work for what benefits them most of time. It is said they are riddlers of universe, always knowing answers but never telling until it comes to past."

"She seemed nice enough," Jase shrugged, examining the tough meat in his hand. "Besides she's the sister of Skyrah. I doubt she'd do any harm."

Tahmela turned his attention back to his food, commenting, "'Cause you have crush on Princess?"

"I do not!" Feeling his face flush as Tahmela snickered and said things in his tongue that Jase did not understand. Trying to change the subject and ignore the color in his cheeks, Jase stated, "You know, you never did teach me how to speak your language like you said you would."

The bulb sat with a toothy grin upon his face. "Perhaps, we always in danger! You still want to then I can teach it while we grow old and fat here."

"I'd like that," he said and finished the last of his meat before standing up, feeling slightly better. "I need to give the Princess my answer about whether or not we are staying tonight before I fall asleep."

"What is Bluestar's answer? We stay and fight or we explore galaxy?" the bulb asked watching him.

Jase dug his hands in his jacket pockets, staring at nothing in particular. "Will you follow me no matter what I decide to do?"

The bulb kept his saucer eyes on him as he answered, "I said I would, Bluestar. Life debt prohibits me, otherwise."

"If that wasn't holding you back, would you still follow me?" Jase asked.

Tahmela thought on it for a few minutes. He turned back to eating his food and said, "I have nothing better to do at moment. So yes."

A smile tugged at Jase's lips as he peered down at the little gray bulb and he couldn't help but realize the small alien had become one of his best friends in the short time that they had known each other. He had never really known many aliens back home, but was grateful for the bulb's friendship as he turned away and headed in the direction he thought he might find Skyrah. Jase called back over his shoulder, "Well, let's hope whatever I decide keeps you from becoming too bored with me!"

He walked around the courtyard towards the back of the building. He was still exhausted but able to walk without a problem with the help of Tahmela's dinner. He spotted Lieutenant Colonel Moon walking out of a room and quickly called out to her, "Lieutenant Colonel Moon!"

"Yes?" Lieutenant Colonel Moon answered looking up from her holo-data pad. Her expression quickly changed to a softer one when she realized it was him. "Jase Bluestar, my apologies. I thought you were one of the pesky interns who always seem to want to ask me too many questions about their studies."

"It's fine, ma'am. I didn't mean to bother you, but I was hoping you'd know where I could find the Princess? She needed to speak to me," he stated.

"Of course! She's right through there," Lieutenant Colonel Moon said as she motioned to the door she had just exited. "She has a lot to catch up on from her absence so make sure you keep it quick."

"Thank you, Lieutenant."

"Not a problem at all, Bluestar," she replied as she studied him. "I assume you have made up your mind if you are staying or leaving then."

Jase held her soft gaze, once again feeling that she looked familiar but couldn't place where. "I have, yes."

She appeared to want to say something in response but instead turned back to her holo pad. "Well, I hope you decide to stay a while longer with us. It would be nice to get to know another Bluestar again," she said.

Jase hesitated at the door before entering the room.

The room was more like an oval shape cave with tungsten lights blending with the glow of terminals. Bookshelves and computer screens covered the walls in every direction with not a single window in sight. The computer screens were filled with numbers and data of resources that the Resistance while others were filled with different projections of the weather. A handful of terminals were filled with different security feeds from all around the base showing buildings Jase had yet to explore. Just looking at all of the information gave Jase a headache causing him to tear his gaze from them and focused on the center of the room where Princess Skyrah, Ziko Ren, and the squirlex, Minko, stood with their eyes focused on the table before them. Jase was half-way across the room when the three finally noticed him.

"Bluestar, I'm glad you came when you did," Princess Skyrah announced as he neared. "I expect you have come to inform me of your decision."

"That is correct," Jase replied, his nerves returning from the sight of Ziko Ren's sneer.

"Leave us," Princess Skyrah ordered Ziko Ren and Minko before turning back to Jase.

Jase waited for the two to leave, turning his focus on the 4D map of the planet's surface that seemed to change every second like in the game StarCastleCapture. Princess Skyrah noticed his fascination and peered down at the map as well as she answered, "Karasi invented a satellite around the planet to be able to show us a live feed of everything that is around us. The Androids don't even have something this advance so it gives us an advantage over them in case they ever attack us here."

"How is it able to get such detail?" Jase asked, watching thunderheads approach the west side of Lone Lake across the night sky.

"It's beyond my knowledge or understanding. Karasi once tried to explain, but it is very complex and hard to follow. Besides, you don't ask Ancients how or why they make something. They take it as an insult," she told him.

"It is truly remarkable," Jase told her before turning his attention back to her and noticed her expression had soften now that they were alone. "Your sister is an interesting woman. I have learned much from her in the short amount of time I've spent with her."

"She tends to have that effect on people, I'm afraid. She helps them see more of their true selves than they normally do," Princess Skyrah stated.

"Do you see more of your true self when you are around her?" Jase asked, unable to stop himself.

Princess Skyrah held his gaze for a second before turning away and focusing back on the map. "Sometimes, but not always. You said you made your decision? What is it?"

He stared at her, not able to say a word while he wondered if he was making the right decision. Yet in his heart he felt he was. *Will I regret this later?* The question seemed to linger in his mind as he stood there, feeling as if the world suddenly faded away and he was floating in space with nothing to hold on to. *Will I?* he thought before drawing his attention back to the Princess who seemed to be bracing his next words. Her bluish pink eyes seemed to search his face for an answer as he started slow, thinking of his words as he spoke, "I've always wanted to travel the galaxy since I was a small boy. My dad was a pilot in your family's war and when he was able to come home, he'd tell me stories of the stars and life on other planets. He'd tell me that you had to get out there and explore otherwise you'd never know what you were missing until you saw it. That when you see all that you have seen, that's when you know what you want in life. Your purpose. He died fighting in your war. I never understood it. I knew if I was faced with the same decision, I would choose to go rather than to fight."

Princess Skyrah turned her attention to the map, hiding her true emotions behind an expressionless mask. "I will set preparations to have your ship refueled for your journey and will send your reward to the orphanage, as promised," she stated.

"Thank you, but I wasn't quite finished with my nice little speech," he teased.

"Yes, what is it?" without looking up, she asked firmly.

"I never understood my father until now. Until I realized that leaving Kaimi, Amosa, and you meant leaving my family. That leaving you meant I would never have the chance to annoy the crap out of you and I know no one here will do it. Not intentionally, anyways. It's my birth right to stay and protect you and it's time I stop fighting that. So I'm yours, if you will have me," he said.

Princess Skyrah's eyes darted up. "You're staying?"

"For the moment," he happily replied.

Skyrah's face lit up and moved around the map to be face to face with him. She teased as if trying to hide her excitement, "Did Kaimi help you come up with that sappy speech?"

"Nope! I actually thought of it on the spot," he shot back, staring at her beauty.

"It was somewhat sweet," she replied, nearly blushing.

"I meant every word, Your Highness," he joked.

The Princess studied him for a moment as if thinking of something that Jase couldn't read from her eyes before moving back around the table. Changing the subject, she said, "You will have to train with Ziko Ren so you can fight better and further your Bluestar training."

Jase groaned. "He doesn't like me," he complained.

Princess Skyrah let out a short chuckle. "He takes getting used to but he is our finest commander. He trained my father and my father's father before, as well as all of my sisters, except Dalhala, of course. He's even trained some of the Bluestars before you so his training is worth it. He can help you have better control over your abilities. And make sure you are able to fight if you can't use them."

"Very well, if I must," Jase agreed, not liking it but knew it was required.

"Besides, you will need all the help you can get for the upcoming battle," Skyrah told him.

"What do you mean?" he asked.

"We've had numerous reports that a portion of Lord Brohain's army is moving in the direction to take Adsila Laabbirrem in two months' time. Thanks to Dim we are able to be ready for this attack and prepare in time to withstand it," she answered.

"Does that mean he knows you are here?" Jase questioned.

"It's unclear and unlikely. There's only a few planets in this solar system that aren't in his control so there is no doubt that this is just a fight for control in hopes to figure out where our base is. We've expected him to attack the planet sooner or later and it appears he is finally focusing on doing just that on all of the unloyal planets. The good thing is that we won't have to worry about his full force because they have been reported scattered throughout the galaxy on expeditions that no one knows what for, both in this solar system and in Cedonia's. My cousin is fighting those fleets there and won't be able to help us in this battle, therefore we are on our own."

"What will we do?" Jase asked, not sure how they could fight Androids from the ground but trusted Skyrah's judgment.

Princess Skyrah pointed to a large city by the lake. "This is Mmerits City and the capital of the planet. The Androids will no doubt strike there first in order to shut down supplies throughout the planet. We will evacuate the city and use our army to defend it and bring the Androids to our home advantage. If we stop them there then it will be harder for them to take over other nearby cities."

"Sounds like you have everything figured out," Jase responded.

"It might sound like we do, but there is still much to do in the short amount of time we have. I am grateful you decided to join us, personally and professionally. With a Bluestar back among us, a lot more people will rally to our cause with the inspiration your kind tends to draw," Princess Skyrah told him as she met his eyes once more.

"Glad I could be of service," he teased.

"We will be stationed here for a month's time. Then, we will travel to Mmerits. It's only a two-day journey by ship so we will have plenty of time to set things up within the city. I would like to enlist Tahmela's help if it's okay with you? I'd like to use his ship to transport supplies and soldiers over to Mmerits before the rest of us get there," Princess Skyrah stated.

"I'll ask, but I don't think he will object. It will give him something to do while he is here," Jase answered.

"Good. Good," Skyrah replied and turned to one of the computer screens showing data. "You should get some rest, Jase. It's late and you will need to refresh to start your training tomorrow."

"What about you?" Jase questioned, checking his watch to see that it was late in the night already.

"I have much to still catch up on," she answered.

"It will still be there in the morning, Princess. You need as much rest as I do if we are to be ready for the Androids," Jase determined firmly.

Princess Skyrah was about to object but thought better of it and let out a tired sigh. "I suppose you are right," she said.

Turning off everything except the security feeds, the two walked out of the oval room and into the short hall that would take them to the quiet courtyard. The only noise to be heard throughout the building was the snoring that belonged to Tahmela and the soft splashing of the fountain. The Princess stopped in front of a wooden door that led to her room as she stated, "Your room is across the way in the corner."

Jase peered in the direction of her hand and nodded. "Thank you," he said.

Skyrah nodded before placing a hand on the doorknob and whispered, "Thank you again for staying, Jase."

"Goodnight, Skyrah," Jase whispered back and watched her disappear into the dark room, shutting the door behind her. Jase waited a minute in case she came back then silently moved in the direction of his room, passing the room that held Tahmela's loud snoring. Opening the door next to it, Jase entered to find Kaimi sitting cross-legged on the floor. Her height once again shocked him since he was used to seeing her six inches tall. "Where have you been?" he asked her, pulling off his jacket and laying it across a nearby wooden chair.

"I updated Lieutenant Colonel Moon with what I can do, and helped with calculations. What about you?" Kaimi responded enthusiastically.

Jase quickly recounted the past day's events starting with what he had learned from Karasi to Princess Dalhala helping him reach the blue room and Sir Agin Rex. Lastly, he told her of his decision to stay and what Skyrah had planned for the Resistance to do next. She listened contently and made no remarks until he was done. "So yeah, I'm staying for now. It is the right thing to do regardless if I'm a warrior or not," he responded.

"I'm glad you came to that decision, Jase. It would have been very lonely without you around and I hope you are happy here. Perhaps with your training with Ziko Ren, you will be able to get back to Sir Agin Rex much sooner than later," Kaimi suggested with a bright smile.

Jase was suddenly overcome with weariness as he collapsed on the soft bed. "I hope so. You'd really like him," he told her as he closed his eyes to rest them for a moment.

"I'm sure I would," Kaimi agreed as she watched him drift to sleep. "Goodnight, Jase Bluestar."

A Tough Lesson

Jase awoke with sunlight bathing his face through the paned window beside his bed and stretched under the warm sheets. Feeling well rested, Jase opened his eyes and slowly sat up as he took in his room for the first time. The room was a deep shade of navy with gold trim that continued on into the small bathroom on the other side of the bed. A dark oak desk, dresser and a full-length mirror littered the remaining space besides the large bed that Jase sat in. It had four posts on each corner that had animals and birds carved along their post as it reached a forest green canopy that hung over the bed. He noticed Kaimi sitting cross-legged on the wide windowsill reading something he could not see. Stirring from his bed to greet her, he asked, "What are you doing?"

Kaimi turned and for a moment she almost seemed like a real person apart from the tiny numbers and figures that ran up and down her body. "I am logging past events into my records to see how far we have come since Otect City," she told him.

"Like a diary?" Jase suggested, watching her.

"I suppose so, yes," she surmised.

"I didn't know you did that," Jase replied as he looked out the window seeing a heavy fog had blanketed the outside.

"There are a lot of things you don't know I do, Jase," she winked then touched the invisible book in the air before turning her full attention to him. "Now that you are finally up, you should eat breakfast and meet with Ziko Ren for the start of your training."

Not wanting to think about spending the day with the unpleasant man, Jase changed the subject by asking, "What are you doing today?"

"I cannot disclose that with you at this time," she responded gloomily though Jase could see her effort in trying to conceal her thoughts.

He didn't press further as he replied, "Very well, keep your secrets if you must. How old is Ziko Ren anyways if he has trained both Skyrah's father and her grandfather? He doesn't look that old."

"His age is not that important, but he is a Qualia so his appearance is deceiving," she answered.

"Wait, you mean there are more Qualias than the Princesses?" Jase asked shocked by her words.

Kaimi nodded. "Besides them, there are a hundred Qualias that survived the war. They live here, serving under the Princesses as they would any true ruler. They are the last of their kind."

"So they aren't extinct. They could still replenish their race for generations," Jase asked.

"Not likely, but yes, they could. This war will keep that from happening, I'm afraid," Kaimi answered.

Jase moved to the full-length mirror tucked in a corner of the room and stared at his reflection barely able to recognize himself. A light brown patchy beard dusted his jaw and his hair was shaggy around his ears. He appeared to be leaner and more muscular from sparring with Amosa and the Princess. "I need a haircut and a shave," he stated, rubbing the prickly hair on his chin.

"Please do! Not that you don't look older and wiser with it, but I think you look better cleanshaven," Kaimi replied playfully.

Jase inspected himself once more in the mirror then walked towards the bathroom in hopes to find a shaver. "Momma Rose would have a fit if she saw how unkept I was," he stated, finding a plasma point shaver and carefully shaved his beard.

"Oh, she would chew you out up and down until you cleaned up," Kaimi giggled in response. Her expression became melancholy causing Jase to stop what he was doing and turn around. "What's wrong?" he questioned.

A digital tear rolled down her cheek. "I never thought that my programming would allow me to have real feelings for others.... I miss them very much, Jase," she replied, brushing the tear away.

Jase felt a lump tighten in his throat. "I miss them too, Kaimi," he replied.

Kaimi stared out the window into the fog that the sun shined through making it hard to gaze at the white cloud. "Perhaps we can see them with your abilities?" she suggested.

"What do you mean?" Jase questioned as he fixed his hair and crossed the room to stand by her.

"It's similar to a mirror reflecting what you want to see back to us by bouncing light from this planet off a cluster of stars in space till it got back to you," she explained.

Jase shook his head in disbelief. "Could that not kill me if it was possible?"

"Not if you allow the stars to sustain the connection. If you do it right then they will use most of their energy to bring it back to you. You just have to believe in yourself and your abilities. Bluestars could do it in the past for only a few minutes because of how unstable and dangerous it can be. I'm not saying we should do it now, but when your stronger perhaps we can," she stated.

Jase turned his attention to the outside window, staring at the sun with his doubts. He really did need Sir Agin Rex's guidance if he wanted to know what all he could do as a Bluestar. The thought of seeing Momma Rose and the others gnawed at his stomach as he wondered if he could really see them if only for a few seconds just to make sure they were safe and happy. "Let's try it!" he decided out loud and flashed Kaimi a confident smile. "If I can't do it then I can't do it, but I'd rather try and see what I can do."

"It's very dangerous, Jase. Even Bluestars didn't do it unless it was absolutely necessary," Kaimi objected.

"Kaimi, it probably won't even work so don't worry," he told her and touched the window pane in hopes that it would better channel his energy. Closing his eyes, Jase tried emptying out his mind from all his doubts and fears and tried picturing the orphanage as best as he could. After a moment, he saw it in his mind. The little rundown home that needed much work to make it grand once more. He then moved on by trying to picture Momma Rose and the children, but it was much harder than he thought as he tried remembering every small detail about them. Frustrated, he tried focusing on just Mrs. Rose but found no matter how hard he tried to remember her, it still didn't seem enough. The mental picture of the woman in front of him felt incomplete and fake as he played with the image. Still unhappy with the results, Jase abandoned

325

it and instead tried picturing the stars he stared up at night in hopes to be able to use them to relay his vision. The mental image felt even faker and silly as he tried calling forth his power with no luck. After a few minutes, Jase angrily splashed the image away. His head hurt from concentrating so hard, but he kept his hand on the window and his eyes shut, afraid to show Kaimi that he couldn't do it.

Please, he begged to the stars. *Please, let us see them for a moment.*

Jase started to pull away from the window when suddenly the familiar burst of energy coursed through his veins and he felt the window pane cool under his palm. A blinding light forced him to shut his eyes as he felt the window grow colder in his touch until finally the light vanished and his body suddenly felt fatigued from the touch. Jase opened his eyes and took a step back, watching the window's glass that was glowing a blue hue change into a mixture of earthy tones. It then twisted and turned until shapes and colors took form. After a few seconds, the chaos of colors and shapes revealed their true image.

There in the surface of the window pane was Momma Rose standing at the stove, cooking in her kitchen. Everything around her appeared slightly hazy but Jase could tell he was seeing her from the window in the kitchen. She looked up from the boiling pot and met Jase's eyes with her own as if she was staring right at him from inside. Jase couldn't tear his gaze away from hers as he noticed the new wrinkles that aged her face making her appear older than she was. She appeared to be worn out as if the galaxy was weighing her down by the shoulders as she stared out at him. The image became transparent allowing Mrs. Rose to slowly fade away from sight and Jase felt his homesickness pinch his heart. Ignoring it, Jase turned to Kaimi and smiled, "At least we know they are safe and doing well," he told her, not wanting to bring up how much Momma Rose had aged since they've been gone.

"They will be even safer if we stop the Androids from taking over the galaxy," Kaimi added determined.

Jase gave a sharp nod, feeling determined with what he needed to accomplish with the time given to him. "We will make sure they are safe from their wrath," he said then finished getting ready. With Kaimi next to him, they ventured towards the dining hall for breakfast.

Tahmela was already there and greeted them with a mouthful of food as his face lit up, saying, "Bluestar! My bed was soft as cloud! Best sleep in forty-nine years!"

Amused, Jase scanned the spread of breakfast items before him and picked out strips of bacon, fruit, biscuits and eggs. "I'm glad you slept so well because we will be staying on longer than I originally thought," he told him.

"You joined then?" Tahmela asked even though he already knew the answer.

"I did for many reasons. It is my time to stop pretending I'm not a Bluestar and fulfill my birth right. You don't have to fight with us, Tahmela. I can release you from your bond and you can go your own way," Jase stated as he waited for the bulb's reply before taking a bite of his bacon.

Tahmela looked at him, holding a piece of cooked ham in midair. "Where you go, I go, Bluestar. If war we go then war we go," the bulb answered.

"Thank you," Jase replied placing a hand on his shoulder for a moment then turned back to his breakfast. "In that case, Princess Skyrah wanted me to ask you if you will be willing to help transport soldiers and supplies to the city Mmerits before the Androids attack the city in two months' time."

"You want me to leave you with beings we don't know?" questioned Tahmela.

"We might not know them, but I trust the Princess and Kaimi. If we are to be a part of them then we must learn to trust the rest of the Resistance," Jase said in hopes to ease the bulb's mind.

Tahmela hesitated before saying, "Okie, Bluestar."

Both ate in silence as Kaimi talked to Tahmela about the shipping routes and where in Mmerits to unload the supplies. When they were halfway done with breakfast, Jase stated, "I suppose this means we will have to put a hold on learning your language for a while."

"Not quite, Bluestar," Tahmela declared and pulled out a scrap of paper from his pocket and slid it over to him.

Jase picked up the paper and saw there were ten words written in the bulb's language. There was two he already knew from the bulb saying them so much, but he still read over the list out loud. "Hmil means human, Xartox means stars. Uu-y-ken?"

"Uyqen. Uoo-ken. That is how you say it. It means 'hello,'" Tahmela replied with amusement.

Jase repeated the word. "Uyqen, Tahmela."

"Uyqen, Jase," the bulb returned.

Jase moved on to the next word trying to sound it out. "Bo-no-kay?"

Tahmela nodded repeating it, "Bonokay. It means 'goodbye.'"

"Bonokay. Goodbye," Jase repeated.

Tahmela then pointed to the next word on the list. "This means 'please.' Aqyaxy. Ak-yaxy. Aqyaxy."

"Aqyaxy," Jase repeated, slowly starting to understand how the symbols sound in the words.

"Good. Good! You learn quick, Bluestar," Tahmela exclaimed happily before continuing on. "This one means 'thank you.' Rurop ona."

Jase sounded it out, slowly. "Ru-rop-on-a. Rurop ona. How do you say, 'You're welcome'?"

"My people don't say welcome. It is said by body language and not by words." Tahmela told him before turning back to the list. "These two are 'yes' and 'no.' Yx means yes and sounds like eeks. Pon is no and sounds like poon. Say it with me."

"Yx and pon," Jase responded.

"Good. Lastly, these are 'good morning' and 'goodnight.' Bonok sontypib is good morning and Bonok pybur is goodnight."

Jase repeated the words, having trouble at first but after a few times was able to say them. Curious, he asked, "Is there a way to say good evening?"

"Bonok yeypypib," Tahmela recited.

Jase went over the words one more time, speaking them into his data watch before tucking the scrap of paper into his pocket. "What are some other words?"

"Nope! Remember those then I tell you more," Tahmela declared.

"But what happens when you leave? How will I learn more?" Jase asked, eager to learn more words. He liked the idea of being able to speak in more than one language instead of having to rely on Kaimi to interpret for him.

"I leave list with Kaimi to show you," Tahmela answered as he stuffed a large purple boiled egg into his mouth.

Ziko Ren suddenly entered the room, rigid in stature, as he stopped at the door to regard Jase. "Bluestar, you are late for our sparring session," he reprimanded.

Jase swallowed and turned his head. "Sorry, I woke up later than I had planned," he gulped.

Ziko Ren made a disapproving grunt. "Finish your breakfast and meet me outside in the sparring circle," he snapped before turning on his heels and marched out the door.

Jase turned back around and saw the bulb staring at him with a smirk across his face. "What?" he exclaimed.

"He does not like you," Tahmela sneered.

"I know," grimacing, Jase gobbled down the last of his food, afraid to keep Ziko Ren waiting any longer.

Tahmela gave a low laugh, saying, "Xarotx uoya zercy e ona, Bluestar."

"What did you say?" Jase asked, standing from his chair to leave.

"That the stars have mercy on your soul," Tahmela replied.

Jase smiled at the bulb. "I hope they do, too," he replied and glanced at Kaimi who seemed preoccupied in her own thoughts. "Kaimi?"

She snapped out of it and responded, "Yes?"

"I'll see you later or are you coming with me?" he asked.

She shook her head. "I have work to do with Karasi and Lieutenant Colonel Moon. I will catch up with you later."

"Okay. Goodbye then," he responded and waved to the bulb. "See ya, Tahmela." The bulb gave him a wave with one of his stubby hands before returning to his food while Kaimi wished him luck. Jase walked out into the courtyard and headed for the doorway that would lead him outside for his training.

Outside, the air was cool as the water droplets from the dense fog coated Jase's hair and clothes as he stopped at the outside entrance. *How is anyone supposed to train in these conditions? You can't even see anything?!* he wondered as he tried remembering how far the sparring circle was from the building when he first saw it yesterday. Using only his memory, Jase stepped out into the thick fog and walked in the direction he thought the circle was. He walked for a few minutes feeling the grass wet with dew as it made a soft noise under his boots as he stomped over it. After a few yards, Jase saw the dark shadow in the fog ahead of him and guessed it was Ziko Ren waiting for him. He stood squarely with Jase with a scrutinizing expression as he studied him from where he stood. The fog cloaked them, hiding them from the outside world. Jase didn't like the idea of being hidden from everybody else and not being able to see what was lurking in the fog around them.

"Unholster your weapon," commanded Ziko Ren.

Jase unbuckled his belt holster and laid it down outside of the ring. He then returned back to the center of the dirt ring and awaited further instructions.

"Jacket off."

Jase pulled it off and folded it before setting it down on top of his gun. Returning back to his stance, he ignored the goosebumps that rose on his arms from the chilly air and asked while trying not to sound annoyed by the ordeal, "Anything else? Perhaps my data watch or maybe my boots?"

Ziko Ren's expression did not change as he stared hard at Jase. "Every morning before sunrise, you will spar with me for two hours. You will be trained in hand to hand combat, weaponry, and learn the basics of survival that will help you harness your abilities and hone them while making your body and mind stronger than ever. At any time if you have a problem with my teaching then you can quit. But if you quit, do not come to me again to learn once more. You give up, you aren't worth my time. Is that understood?"

"Yes," Jase replied.

Ziko Ren grunted and asked, "Are you ready?"

"Yes," and in a blur of movement, Ziko Ren slammed Jase into the dirt floor, holding him in place as the air left Jase's lungs. Jase stared straight at the sky, trying to breathe once more but found it difficult as if he had forgotten how.

In a disapproving tone, Ziko Ren whispered, "I expected more from you," and stood back to his feet, returning to where he had been before and waited for Jase to get back up. "Again!"

Jase hesitated, breathing shallowly but forced himself to his feet and tried taking deeper breaths. Before he was able to get his breathing back to normal, Ziko Ren attacked once more in a blur of movement and once again pinned Jase down. He felt as if his lungs were going to collapse inside his chest as he tried breathing again but found it even more difficult than the first time. Once again, Ziko Ren returned to his first stance while barking for Jase to get back on his feet for them to continue. Jase slowly pulled himself up, his head feeling as though it was swimming. He tried remembering Amosa's sparring lessons on the ship and focused on staying on his feet instead of attacking Ziko Ren. For the next hour, each time Ziko Ren attacked, Jase ended up with his face in the dirt and out of breath. Each time more frustrated with himself that he couldn't stop the old man from pinning him.

Finally after the thirty-fourth time of being pinned, Ziko Ren ordered, "Enough! Get up!"

Jase pushed himself off his stomach and onto his shaky feet, wiping the dirt caked on the side of his face. His body ached as he breathed slowly to catch his breath. He wiped the sweat off his forehead, smearing dirt across it as he did and panted for air as Ziko Ren berated him.

"Is this all the Bluestar has to offer? His face in the dirt every time I lay a finger on him? It's pathetic!" he growled, pacing his side of the circle like a wild cat. "Androids will tear you a part like you are nothing more than a play thing."

Jase balled his fists. "I did not have any instruction for my abilities nor did I have any idea of them while I was growing up. I had never experienced them until only a few months ago. How can I possibly know how to fight you?" Jase clarified.

"Because you are a Bluestar! You trust too much on what you see in front of you, rather than what you feel. Stop giving me excuses on why you can't use them and start giving me progress," Ziko Ren spat.

"I am trying but I can't just call my abilities whenever I want to," Jase shot back.

Ziko Ren grunted then motioned him to follow. "Follow me. Leave your things."

Jase followed quickly after the man, scared to lose him in the fog as the noon sun bathed down from above causing the fog to be brightened. Jase noticed the dark shapes ahead of him and the sound of soldiers talking to one another. They stopped when the two appeared before them and Ziko Ren ordered them to grab buckets and fill them up with stones no bigger than a child's fist. The soldiers eagerly set to work with the orders given as they disappeared into the fog. Jase noticed fifty wooden posts in three rows stretching the length of twenty yards down the field. Jase wondered what they were for, but didn't ask Ziko Ren as he searched about the fog for any dark shapes of the soldiers. It wasn't until twenty long minutes had passed when the soldiers finally returned carrying four large buckets filled of stones.

Ziko Ren then ordered the soldiers to spread out among the sides of the rows of posts before turning his attention to Jase. "Climb up onto a post," he commanded.

Jase hesitated, feeling all eyes on him as he did as instructed and climbed onto the nearest narrow post. Trying to keep his balance, he focused on Ziko Ren, he asked, "Now what?"

"Your objective is to reach the end of the posts without falling or getting hit by any stones and tell me what word is scratched on the center post. If you get hit or fall off, we will start over and continue until you complete the objective," Ziko Ren firmly declared.

Jase peered at him in disbelief. "That's impossible! How am I supposed to run while keeping balance and not get hit by rocks while also trying to read a single letter?! They outnumber me, ten to one!"

"You are a Bluestar, are you not?" was all Ziko Ren replied as he clasped his hands behind his back.

Jase balled his fists as he thought to himself, *This is stupid*, and got ready to leap to the next post.

"Begin!" Ziko Ren's voice rung clearly through the fog and Jase quickly leapt to the next post just as a rock was hurled past him.

He ducked out of the way just in time for it to fly over his head. Not waiting for another one to fill its place, Jase jumped to the next post and continued on, using his momentum to force him forward as he felt rocks pelt his body. Each one stung and left bruises as Jase tried swatting them away, but found it useless. He hadn't made it halfway when a rock pelted his jaw causing him to lose his footing and crash to the ground. He landed hard on his side, feeling the air get knocked out of him as his side shot spikes of pain throughout his chest. Blood trickled down the side of his jaw and onto the ground below him. A pair of black boots stepped into his vision as he gazed up to find Ziko Ren towering over him with a stern expression.

"Get up," he barked. Jase forced himself to his feet to meet the firm gaze that glared at him. Ziko Ren scanned him up and down, bluntly asking, "Is anything broken?"

"No, I don't think so," he answered while wiping blood from his jaw.

"Why didn't you stop the stones from hitting you?" Ziko Ren studied his face.

"'Cause I can't," Jase grumbled.

Ziko Ren grunted in disapproval. "Again!"

Jase remained standing where he was. "It's impossible if I can't control my abilities."

"Nothing is impossible for a Bluestar. The sooner you learn that the sooner you will stop hurting yourself," Ziko Ren declared fiercely. "Now, again!"

Jase started over, climbing to the first post and waited for Ziko Ren to give the go ahead. Then once again, he darted across the lined posts with rocks flinging through the air this way and that way as they hit him time and time again. No matter how hard he tried, the rocks pelted him. Suddenly, rock nailed his ankle causing it to buckle underneath him. He barely missed slamming his head into the post as he crashed to the ground. Limping to start over again, Jase felt as if he was floating in a constant repeat of actions that he no longer had any control over.

By midday, he hadn't gotten any further down the posts and his whole body racked with a never ending pain that Jase was sure would last him the rest of his life. The last fall left him too tired to get back up as he laid in the dirt, wanting to do nothing but rest as Ziko Ren watched from where he stood. When Jase refused to get up, Ziko Ren grunted in disapproval and ordered the soldiers to break for lunch before informing Jase to report to him later in the evening for their next lesson. They all then left him there alone in the fog that was starting to dissipate in the noon sun as it warmed up the training field. Jase didn't move to get up from laying on his stomach as he listened to the plasma discharge in the distance where soldiers practiced at the shooting range. He could hear the birds in the gardens singing to one another as they floated about the soft breeze. He could also hear the servants talking to one another as their voices carried over from the courtyard of the main building as if he was just outside the doors. It was all soothing as the sun kissed his skin and Jase closed his eyes to nap for a moment.

"It appears your training has either not gone well or it is not tough enough," came a voice.

Jase opened his eyes to find Amosa standing over him. "You should have seen me only moments ago. Then you'd know that Ziko Ren asks the impossible from me," he replied and used the last of his strength to push himself up and sit against a post.

"What does he ask of you?" Amosa questioned as she gracefully leapt onto a post next to him and sat down.

"He wants me to run to the very end of the posts without falling or getting hit by rocks that the soldiers throw at me *and* wants me to read a word he carved in the center of the post," he told her.

Amosa stared down the line of posts. "And what is the problem?" she questioned.

Jase looked at her, astonished. "It can't be done!" he exclaimed.

"By a normal human that may be true, but you are a Bluestar, Jase. You have the ability to accomplish such a feat," she told him with a smile as if she knew something he did not.

"I can't if I don't know how to control my abilities," Jase growled becoming annoyed with her presence.

"Your problem is you doubt yourself when it comes to using your abilities which is why you aren't able to use them. When you don't have time to think about it, you are able to use them by instinct. Don't think, Jase. Just do," she stated.

Jase didn't have a reply knowing she was right. He had always had a hard time believing that he had abilities and now that he had them, it was still hard to comprehend. He had to learn to trust in himself and use them with all the distractions around him. Resting his head back against the hard wood, Jase closed his eyes. "What are you doing out here? Shouldn't you be with the Princess?" he asked.

"The Princess is in a meeting with the Lord that governs Mmerits, and at the time, does not need my services. I'd rather spend my time out here in the sun then in a dark room, staring at a hologram," she replied.

Jase couldn't blame her. "How did you know I was here?" he questioned.

"I didn't. I decided to wander the base while I had the chance in case we were ever attacked. It's wise to know your layout," she replied.

"I'd like to explore the forest around the base when I have time. It would be nice to get away from everyone and see what kind of animals call this valley their home," Jase said as he swatted away a fly that buzzed around him.

"If you ever want company and I am able, I would love to join you and pretend for a moment that I am back home among the beautiful trees of Kurath Thor's forest," she replied to him.

"Of course," Jase agreed. His thoughts suddenly turned to what he knew about the elf. "Amosa, do you have someone you love back at home? Like someone you call your own?"

Amosa turned back towards him raising an eyebrow as an amused smile danced upon her lips. "Bluestar, are you asking me for your own feelings?" she mused.

Jase felt his ears burn red and sheepishly managed to utter, "No, I mean...you are beautiful but um...well, I didn't mean to say it like that. Um, I was just wondering because we don't know much about one another and I was hoping to learn more about you if we are to travel together for a while."

"I know your meaning, Bluestar. I wanted to have some fun with you." Jase grinned to her, feeling less embarrassed now as she answered, "I did a long time ago, but he has joined the stars for the next part of his journey."

Jase looked at her thoughtfully. He would have never guessed she had lost someone close to her, but elves were secretive beings such like the Qualias. "I'm sorry for your loss."

Amosa looked to the horizon barely visible through the fog and Jase thought he saw a tear in her eye. "He died a noble and honorable death fulfilling his purpose so one should not be sorry for such a loss. It is a beautiful thing to die knowing you fulfilled your duty in protecting the ones you love and I can only pray that I fulfill mine when the time comes. He will always be my soulmate and I doubt I will ever love another quite the same."

"What was his name?" Jase asked.

Amosa gently said, "One I wish not to speak out loud."

Jase nodded, respecting her decision as he turned back to the outlines of the buildings in the afternoon light. His thoughts turned to Skyrah and he wondered if she had a lover that he didn't know about during the war or one she was now seeing. The thought made him strangely jealous and he quickly pushed it away to enjoy the sun on his face.

"Did you?"

Confused for a moment until he remembered what they were talking about before, Jase shrugged. "Maybe once."

"You do not know?"

Jase stared at the light baby blue sky through the fog, noticing the puffy clouds that floated by. He thought of Camila and their time together when they first dated. She was the only woman he thought he would ever marry despite their differences, but now he couldn't picture them together. Perhaps it was because when he thought of love, he couldn't help but picture an image of the Princess in his head that seemed to fit so well that it was as if she was meant to be his since the beginning of time. Ever since he had met her, he couldn't help with the feelings that blossomed inside him for her no matter how hard he tried to ignore them. Besides, she was a Princess, after all, and had many years on him so she probably saw him no more than a boy in her eyes. He wondered what the High Guardian would think if he told her that, but instead answered, "My job usually keeps me very busy and doesn't give me much luxury time for girlfriends. There was this one lady though. Her name is Camila and she is very smart and kind. She helps out at the orphanage that I grew up at because her family was close friends with the old couple that ran it. We pretty much grew up together and I used to pull pranks on her all the time when we were little. I gave her such a hard time," Jase stated with a chuckle, thinking of a time he dropped flour and honey all over thirteen year old Camila when she had visited to play with the other children.

"What happened?"

Jase shrugged, letting the memory fade away. "We both had different views on how we wanted our lives to play out. She wanted to stay in the city and have me get a serious job that didn't involve possible jail time while I wanted to go out into the universe and explore all that I could. Living each day as if it was my last or something like that at least. In the end it was a mutual break up for we both knew we would never make each other happy. We've stayed friends since, but I keep myself busy so we don't see each other all that often. It's better that way."

"If it was not meant to be then the stars allowed you to see it before things got worse," Amosa indicated.

"Yeah," Jase replied and wondered what Camila was doing right this second.

Amosa leapt off the post she had been sitting on and landed on her feet in silence. "Come, I will help you to the main building for lunch before you get any redder. You will feel much better after you eat."

Jase had forgotten about his exhaustion and allowed her to help him stand, grateful for the support once he got to his feet. His muscles ached as they slowly started through the fog towards the main building. His ribs hurt every time he breathed and he was sure that they were bruised from hitting the hard ground so much as he asked, "How am I supposed to continue fighting if I hurt this bad?"

Amosa kept her gaze forward as she helped him. "The more you start opening your mind to your abilities, the faster your body will start evolving to what it is meant to be. Your speed and strength will match those of Elves and Qualias and your body will start healing yourself. You won't heal overnight, but it will take less time for you to become whole once again like before, depending on the wound."

Jase's eyes widened. He would be as fast as Amosa and Skyrah?! The thought seemed unreal, but he couldn't wait for it to happen and surprise Skyrah the next time they sparred together. If there was a next time. "Ziko Ren knows this?" he asked.

"Of course. He has trained many Bluestars in his time," she answered as they neared the building.

"I think I can walk from here. Thank you for your assistance," Jase told her, pulling gently away to stand on his own.

"As you wish. I have but one question before we separate. Why did you agree to stay for the Resistance? You made it very known that you weren't going to fight in this war before so why change now?" Amosa questioned.

Jase focused on the fog for a moment, arranging his thoughts. Turning back to her, he answered clearly, "Princess Dalhala helped me find out the truth behind Bluestars and why they fight for the royal family. In knowing the truth, it made me realize that being a Bluestar is my birth right and I should respect it even if it means fighting in a war. I will do what I must in order to not disrespect those who came before me."

Amosa studied him as if thinking on her next words then asked, "Then it was not for your feelings for Princess Skyrah?"

Jase hid his shock from her and lied. "No," he said.

Amosa's face was soft but her voice firm as she stated, "Whether you deny them or not, it does not matter, Bluestar. You must know though that she is a Princess and the future queen of our galaxy."

"So I should know my place?" he remarked sharply.

Amosa's eyes grew softer. "No, I only mean she has much on her plate to think and worry about. She doesn't have the luxury of a relationship right now when her focus needs to be on the Resistance and its survival."

"I won't interfere with her plans, but I cannot help with what I feel," he told her.

"Keep it to yourself for the time being," Amosa bluntly replied. "May the stars watch over your training, Bluestar." She left into the fog once more that was beginning to thicken again.

Jase felt hurt by her words and slowly limped inside the hall and entered the courtyard. He stumbled into the dining room where a buffet was set on the table. Jase filled his plate as his thoughts of Skyrah filled his head. He wondered if she would tell him if she did or if she would choose to deny them in order to focus on the Resistance. Would he even be a distraction? Would being a Bluestar not be enough to at least match her importance and allow them to love one another? The more he thought about how different they were, the gloomier he got until finally he forced such thoughts away to focus on eating. *I wish Kaimi was here*, he thought during a mouthful of food. He ate slow, noticing that Lieutenant Colonel Moon had entered the room staring down at her holopad while she made her plate. Once she had filled her plate, she turned to leave without a glance up from her holo and commanded, "Bluestar, come with me and bring your food."

Jase hesitated, not wanting to move from the comfort of his chair but curiosity got the best of him as he quickly got up to follow. She had already left the building, surprising him once more on how fast she could move for her age as he quickly followed after her careful not to spill the food from his plate. She led him past the main building towards the back of the base where they passed barracks and a mess hall for soldiers before ascending stone stairs that led to a large building that Jase hadn't seen before. Unlike the main building, this one had more windows throughout it and white marble halls as Jase stepped inside and followed the woman down several maze-like hallways. After walking for what seemed like forever to Jase, they finally stopped before a wooden door painted a pale purple with the Lieutenant Colonel Moon's name written across it in big block letters, and walked inside.

A New Friend

The Lieutenant crossed over to a L-shaped desk, motioned for him to sit in the chair in front of her desk which he gratefully did as instructed for his ankle was throbbing from their walk. "Please eat, Bluestar," she told him without looking up from her holo.

"Did you need my help with something, Lieutenant Colonel Moon?" he asked politely.

The Lieutenant Colonel stared up at him as she brushed back a strand of almond hair from her face. "No, I just thought this was better than you eating alone. If you don't want my company then by all means you can leave."

"No, of course. I will stay. Thank you," Jase replied, relaxing as he ate his food.

She nodded and turned back to her holopad as she ate her leafy salad and various fruits. There was a stretch of silence between them. "I was informed that you will be staying on with us for the time being as you train. That's wonderful news and I know it will boost the morale of the soldiers!" Lieutenant Colonel Moon enthused.

Jase swallowed a mouthful of food before answering. "Yes, I had a good friend convinced me to stay and help," he said. "Besides, Kaimi and I have gone through a lot together and it would be wrong of me to abandon her now."

"Rightly so," Lieutenant Colonel Moon continued. "Have you started your training then?"

"I started this morning," he told her.

"Ziko Ren is hard to get along with, but his training is exceptional. Take what you learn from him to heart," she informed him.

"If I survive that long, I will," he stated jokingly.

The Lieutenant Colonel laughed at his remark which struck a familiar cord within Jase but he couldn't place it. "Trust me, it is hard, and a painful progress, but he only means well. He won't do anything he knows you can't handle. The harder he works you, the more he sees in you. Take it as a compliment if you will," she replied.

Jase chewed his food slowly, watching her with curiosity. "Have you trained with him?"

The Lieutenant Colonel's eyes sparkled in the light as she seemed to reminisce. "Oh, yes! Back when I first joined the Resistance at age eighteen. He watched me train with the other recruits after I decided that I wanted to be more than a medic. I wanted to be on the front lines where the fight was and many captains then didn't think I could do it. Ziko Ren was the only one who saw what was inside me and challenged me to excel. There were many times I hated him but if not for him, I couldn't have honed my skills and become the top of my class. I rose up the ranks pretty fast with what he taught me and for that I will always be thankful for it."

"Did you know any of Sk—Princess Skyrah's siblings?" Jase corrected himself.

Lieutenant Colonel Moon nodded her head slowly, suddenly saddened. "I was close friends with General Maliha and knew some of her sisters. She was by far the greatest general I have ever known, even compared to their father and mother before them. Ask anyone and they will agree."

She opened a drawer in her desk and pulled out a holophoto and handed it to Jase. There in the photo was a younger Lieutenant Colonel Moon and the royal family, all smiling as they posed for the photo. General Maliha was in the center next to the Lieutenant Colonel with another young girl who looked like her twin beside her. Princess Dalhala was on the other side with three other sisters and lastly a younger version of Princess Skyrah was crouched below them with Amosa next to her. Even though they all were dressed for battle, you would have never guessed they were in the middle of a war.

"We had just won against the Androids on the planet, Perendi. This was taken four weeks before our defeat on Faton," Lieutenant Colonel Moon told him sadly.

340

Jase stared at the happy Skyrah and felt sadness well up inside him as he knew when they took this photo she probably would have never thought that she would lose almost all of her family in the coming weeks. He looked back up to the Lieutenant Colonel who was still staring at the photo in his hands. "Were you there for the last battle?" he asked.

"Yes, I was. The most terrible day I will ever have in my life, and, that, I know for a fact. Lord Brohain attacked without warning across many of the towns throughout Faton causing our army to split up to protect them. What we didn't know was that it was a trap, and when the dispatched army was out of reach, he led a full-force attack on Otect City. Both armies fought without rest for days. Androids don't need sleep so they quickly overpowered our troops on the front lines and broke through our defenses. We didn't have enough men to hold the line anymore and Maliha knew that we had lost the war but wasn't going to give up without a fight. Against my own wishes, she ordered me to escort Princess Skyrah, Princess Dalhala, Princess Reva, and Princess Adeline to safety off the planet to one of our other bases. Leaving her and the others was my greatest regret but I swore to Maliha that I would keep them safe. So I obeyed her orders," she told him.

Jase handed the picture back. "The Resistance would have been lost if you hadn't survived in their place. General Maliha knew that they and Princess Skyrah needed your wisdom for battles to come," he replied.

Lieutenant Colonel Moon let her eyes linger on the photo a moment longer before putting it away. "Your words are kind, Bluestar. Thank you," she finally said.

Jase turned back to his food. "So you are the General now for the Resistance? That's what you do?" he asked.

"Not exactly, no. The Princess is the General of the Resistance and is in charge of their wellbeing at all times. I am second in command under her, lending her advice and wisdom for battle and other important things." She motioned to the weapons laying across the counter on the other end of the room. "I also invent new weapons and armor for our people," she told him.

Jase studied the weapons. "I like inventing myself. Back home I pretty much invented everything in my apartment so I could live there. Being a thief, you don't always get paid well so with the help of Kaimi we were able to break

341

into an abandoned apartment building that had fallen into ruin from the war and live there."

"I used to have an apartment in the northwest district before the war got really bad," Lieutenant Colonel Moon revealed.

"Really? That is where Kaimi and I live. The apartments next to the wall near the shipyard. We used to watch space ships take off during sunset before bed," he told her.

Lieutenant Colonel Moon smiled warmly. "Perhaps we lived in the same one and don't know it," she mused.

"That would be crazy," Jase replied. "You can have it back if it is."

The Lieutenant Colonel let out a quiet chuckle. "No, no, it's fine, Bluestar. I no longer have the need for it. Besides, it will do more for you than my old bones," she told him and chewed on a piece of red fruit. "Your parents? Do you remember much about them? You said they died, didn't you?"

"My father was a pilot in the war and died sometime during it. My mother I'm not sure what happened except that she left me near the orphanage I grew up in with my father's silver pocket watch and told me she would be back soon. But that never happened. I don't really remember much of her and my memories of them are kind of hazy. I don't really remember much even though I was only eleven at the time," he said.

"Sometimes traumatic events can cause our brain to lock away the memories in order to protect ourselves. That could be what happened in your case. I'm sure she left you for a good reason especially if it was during the war on the planet. War is no place for a child," she responded.

"War is a terrible thing," Jase remarked, taking the last bite of his meal.

"A good outcome of a war ends beautifully with a welcoming of a new age of peace," she told him.

Jase nodded in agreement. "Did you know Kaimi back then?" he suddenly asked.

The Lieutenant Colonel met his gaze. "I trusted her with my life like I would flesh and bone. She was a sister to me and one I will forever be grateful for. I owe much to her for what she has done for my loved ones and I will continue to be in her debt for the rest of my life," she confessed.

"What did she do?" Jase asked curiously.

"A secret that I will take to my grave, I think. Now would you like me to heal those bruises on your arms? They look awfully painful," she asked acknowledging his arms.

At the mention of his arms, Jase glanced down to see what the full extent of his training had done. Black and blue spots filled both of his arms, as well as his chest and neck. There were scraps and cuts with dry blood coating their openings causing Jase to look away disgusted. He hadn't thought it was this bad. *No wonder my whole body hurts!* he thought to himself and peered back to the Lieutenant Colonel. "I don't think you can," he exclaimed.

"Psh-Posh! I wasn't a healer for nothing," she corrected and moved her chair over to him so she could touch his arms. Closing her eyes, she concentrated hard as Jase watched with amazement as the colors on his arms started to fade and the cuts closed leaving behind smooth skin.

"How did you do that?" he questioned as he examined his arms for any bruises.

Lieutenant Colonel Moon examined her work, pleased. "By many years of practice and dedication. Magic is the oldest form of healing that dates back to the birth of the galaxy."

"Magic? How can something like that exist?" he asked skeptically.

"How can Bluestars have the powers they possess?" the Lieutenant Colonel replied with amusement.

Jase saw her point and turned back to his unscaved arms. "If it exists then why do so many beings believe it doesn't?"

Lieutenant Colonel Moon moved back behind her desk taking a long drink of her water before answering. "Magic has been long forgotten because the Ancient races from long ago are no longer living to show us such forces. All we know now of magic is what we read and even then many ancient scrolls were either burned when Lord Brohain took over or lost."

Lieutenant Colonel Moon motioned her hands as if she was juggling something. "Before humans, bulbs, and many other younger races came to be, there were several main races in our solar system. The Elves, Qualias, Ancients, Shapeshifters, an Ancient starbeing that has no name and several other key beings that one cannot say in your native tongue. They were all able to use magic. It's what helps course through their veins to allow them to be as strong and quick as they are. When the universe was new and darkness ruled over much of it, magic was born. It was in everything and everyone allowing all beings to be able to use it depending on their strength and willpower. All of the beings lived in peace with one another and they were content with life for a long time. During this time, the Stars and darkness lived in peace with one another as well."

"Stars and darkness? I didn't know they were a different being," Jase admitted.

Lieutenant Colonel Moon sat on the edge of her chair, laying her hands on top of her desk. "Your caregivers didn't teach you about the history of our races?"

Jase shook his head. "Mrs. Rose's stories were about heroes and villains or about life lessons. We were taught the fundamentals but she didn't teach us much about ancient history," he said.

"Hmph," the Lieutenant Colonel sat back in her chair scratching her chin and was troubled by his lack of knowledge. After a moment, she continued. "Yes, darkness is a being of his own. The legend goes that Darkness felt unappreciated because everyone found the stars beautiful, but not the Darkness. So Darkness visits the stars in their kingdom and asks King Asalia to turn him into a star so he can be as beautiful as the other stars. King Asalia agrees that he can, but that it won't change who he is. The Darkness doesn't care and still insists. The Darkness then turns into a black star and as the king had warned still remains as dark as he was before. Upset that he would never be like the other stars, the Darkness decides that he will annihilate all light in the universe so all beings will worship him instead of the stars. From that point on, the stars went to war in order to stop the Darkness and any of those who followed him which they called, shadowstars. The war between the two killed many but in the end the stars were able to bind the Darkness in place which created the night sky and space. King Asalia holds back the Darkness till this day, but Darkness is a powerful entity that can mask itself in many things like good and evil without us knowing. Knowing the power it holds, King Asalia allowed magic to disappear from most of the races so that they could not be tempted by the Darkness to set him free, or so the legend says."

Jase watched her silently. "So magic still exists because of the Ancient Races?"

"Yes. Even though many of the races cease to exist nowadays, there are still some that do. The magic that exists now within our races is not as powerful as it once was and the strength of its power determines your own willpower and strength," she told him wiping crumbs from her desk. "Bluestars and Greenstars have star magic that flows from the stand alone stars that they were born under. Yours is the strongest under a blue moon. You know the stories on how the seasons started, correct?" Jase nodded, remembering Sir Agin Rex telling him, and the Lieutenant Colonel continued. "Good. The only difference between you and a Redstar or Silverstar is that your power builds up since it only happens every fifty years. Redstars and Silverstars happen every summer and winter, therefore, the power they give off is very little which is why we don't have a billion super beings in our midst. It's not enough to give them abilities like yours."

"Do the star seasons effect Androids like they do every other being?" Jase asked.

Lieutenant Colonel Moon shrugged, thinking it over. "I am not sure. How Androids create families are not fully known to us and we haven't studied them enough to understand their fundamentals. Perhaps Karasi could answer that better than I can. I'm afraid that we have spent more time trying to fight them than to understand them."

"How are you able to use magic? Are you not human?" Jase asked her.

"One would think that after traveling with a Qualia and an elf for so long, you'd know better than to assume someone is something. To answer your question, no, I am not a human. I come from a desert planet called Perendi where my race, Genezits, live. We are bred to withstand high temperatures that would burn the skin off a normal human being. We are one of the few races that is born with magic within us much like the Qualias and the Elves. Except ours is limited which is why I can only heal your surface bruises," she responded.

"Could you teach me how to use it?" Jase asked.

"I'm very limited in what I know and it's not something I can teach you, Bluestar. It's something you feel and stumble into. The only way to learn would be if a Magician taught you, but I'm afraid there's not many of those left in our galaxy. There might not be any at all."

An alarm suddenly sounded on her holopad. "I'm sorry, it appears I am needed elsewhere so we will have to end our conversation for now," she said as she stood to her feet.

Jase quickly stood, holding his empty plate. "It's not a problem, Lieutenant Colonel. Thank you for letting me join you for lunch."

"Hopefully next time we can talk more without being disturbed. That is if you aren't busy with your studies and training," she replied, showing him the way out.

"I hope so, too. Have a good day, Lieutenant Colonel."

"Please call me Moon, Jase," she replied before closing the door.

Jase turned down the white hallway hoping he remembered how to get out of the building. He checked his data watch, noting it was already close to four. He didn't have much time until Ziko Ren's next training session began as he stepped into the bright entrance hall and made his way to the doors. As he walked out, he was welcomed by a heavy thick fog with no sun in sight and barely able to see his feet in front of him. *Just one step at a time*, he thought to himself as he felt for the stairs. His right boot hit the bottom and he carefully stepped off to feel the next one. He reached the bottom of the stairs in no time and started out into the fog remembering as best as he could where the main base was.

Jase continued wandering through the fog in the direction of the base for what seemed like forever causing him to wonder if he was lost. He decided to give it another few minutes before using his com to call Kaimi for help, when suddenly he stumbled across the combat ring where a group of soldiers were practicing. He only knew there was a lot of them by their dark shadows and couldn't help but blurt out, "How can you train in this fog?"

A tall, broad shouldered soldier stepped closer to him allowing Jase to see his handsome features that exuded confidence. With a flashy smile that caused dimples to appear to the sides of his thin lips. His short brown hair was damp from the fog and slicked back out of his face where blue eyes looked Jase up and down. "Because we are bred in such conditions, my friend. Those who can't fight an opponent they can't see, don't get the luxury to fight one that they can," he told him with a voice as smooth as water flowing over glass and held out his arm to greet Jase. "The name is Tagen Ouxin. I am the Captain of this squad."

Jase braced the barely visible forearm, feeling the soldier's muscles tighten in the strong grip. "Jase Bluestar," he answered.

Captain Ouxin's smile grew wider at the name. "It will be an honor to serve alongside you, Bluestar. That is once you stop landing on your backside."

Jase burned hot from embarrassment. "Were you one of the soldiers who threw stones at me?" he questioned shamefully.

346

Captain Ouxin crossed his muscular arms across his armored chest. "I was not. My soldiers were talking about it for most of the day until I stopped their laughter by reminding them they were once like you. We all learn one way or another," he answered.

"Thank you, Captain," Jase replied, thankful that the fog could hide most of his embarrassment.

"What about sparring with me as repayment? If you don't mind, Bluestar," Captain Ouxin asked.

Jase wasn't sure if he was trying to embarrass him further or if he genuinely wanted the challenge. Jase was in no condition to fight especially since he knew he had to fight Ziko Ren later on. Yet at the same time, he wanted to be able to have a little fun with the soldiers that seemed to be closer to his age. "Sure," he responded.

The rest of the soldiers circled around the edge of the ring, their voices rising with excitement.

"Since you aren't wearing armor, I will take mine off," the Captain declared, unbuckling the straps that held his chest armor in place and let it slip off revealing his bare chest. He threw it to one of the shadows along with his greaves and brought his fists up to fight. "Are you ready, Bluestar?"

Jase felt knots in his stomach as his ankle burned, but gave a nod. "Ready."

The first attack came swiftly as if carried by the wind. Jase ducked just in time to avoid getting hit in the jaw. He blocked another jab to his right rib, knocking the Captain's arm away before throwing up his leg to kick the man square in the chest. The Captain caught it before he had the chance and slammed Jase into the ground while holding his leg. Jase landed on his back, sending bolts of pain throughout his spine. Before he could react, the Captain came down with his elbow into Jase's chest causing the breath to get sucked out of him. Jase's lungs burned for air, but he paid little attention to them as the soldier climbed on top to pin him to the dirt floor. Jase struggled under the Captain and was able to throw him off before quickly scrambling to pin him down in return. He punched as hard as he could at the Captain's face as he used all his strength to hold him down while they fought for control.

Just when Jase thought the Captain was going to give up, his legs wrapped around Jase's throat and slung him backwards. Captain Ouxin then pounced on him like a jungle cat as he started wailing on Jase's ribs with both fists. It felt like hammers being slammed into his sides as Jase tried deflecting the blows, but his exhaustion was slowing him down. Using his pain to sustain him, Jase used all of his remaining energy to hit the Captain's ribs which caught him off guard and Jase rolled them over to be on top before attacking his ribs as quick as he could before the Captain could recover. Captain Ouxin grunted in pain below him as he tried to get Jase off him, but had no luck as Jase continued.

After a few minutes, Jase stopped to see if he wanted to give up but soon realized that was his biggest mistake. Captain Ouxin caught Jase under the chin with his fist causing Jase to bite his tongue as the powerful strike sent him falling sideways and his vision went black. His head throbbed with pain and his ears rang as he laid there motionless with the taste of blood in his mouth. The ringing in his ears subsided as he noticed that the Captain hadn't moved to pin him yet, his chest going up and down in giant heaves trying to catch his breath. Jase pushed himself up by his fists and turned to find Captain Ouxin's knuckles coming towards him. They slammed into his cheek and made the world go black again as Jase went down into the dirt.

When he came to, he realized he hadn't been out long because he felt the Captain's knee digging into his back as he pinned him on his stomach. Jase felt the rough ground against his skin and saw the cloud of dust that moved in and out as he breathed against it. His whole body screamed in pain as he faintly heard Captain Ouxin's voice ask, "Stalemate, Bluestar?"

"Stalemate, Captain," Jase answered and felt the knee move from his back as the soldiers around them cheered. Jase got on all fours and looked up to find the Captain's hand outstretched to help him to his feet. Jase gladly accepted it, noticing the bruises that were starting to form on the man's face as he climbed to his feet.

"You are a good fighter for just starting your training with Master Ziko Ren," Tagan responded.

"High Guardian Amosa taught me a thing or two on the way here, but I'm clearly no match for either you, her, or Ziko Ren," Jase answered back, wondering how he looked compared to the man as he massaged the muscles in the back of his neck.

"Maybe not now, but soon you will be, Bluestar. That is the reason I challenged you to spar me now because soon you will have the advantage over me with your abilities and speed," Grinning, Captain Ouxin moved a hand through his hair to slick it back once more.

Jase returned the grin. "We will have to have a rematch when that happens," he said.

"I look forward to that day, Bluestar." The Captain held out his hand to shake.

"Just call me Jase."

"Tagen," Captain Ouxin replied with a nod. "Thank you again for the honor to fight you. If you ever want a rematch before your abilities kick in, I will always be up to it. I know how frustrating it can get under Ziko Ren."

"I'll remember that, Tagen. Thanks," Jase answered, pleased to have made a new friend.

Tagen ordered his soldiers to fall out for an early supper before turning back to Jase and bade him a farewell. Jase watched the soldiers disappear into the thick fog and wished he could go with them for a little while longer. Tagen reminded him of Roran and he liked the idea of having someone close to his age to spar with. He grabbed his pilot's jacket and belt and started towards the building once more. By the time he entered, his skin was coated with a mixture of dirt and droplets from the fog as he limped into his room to clean up before his next lesson.

To Learn Many Stances

It felt as if he had just finally sat down to rest when Jase noticed it was time for his next lesson with Ziko Ren. He let out an annoyed sigh and got up from his bed. His muscles ached and felt stiff as he walked out into the foggy evening. Retracing his steps, he found Ziko Ren meditating in the center of the combat ring with his eyes shut.

"Are you ready for your next lesson?" Ziko Ren asked without opening his eyes.

"Yes, sir," Jase replied even though all he wanted to do was sink into a hot bath.

Ziko Ren stood to his feet. "Until you have completed your training as a Bluestar, you will call me Master. Is that understood?"

Jase bit his tongue in response. The idea of calling someone his master was like saying he was nothing more than a slave to his owner. *I did not come here to be a slave*, he thought as he weighed the consequences if he said no. He knew Ziko Ren wouldn't train him and he wouldn't hear the last of it from Kaimi or Skyrah. Sucking up his pride, Jase answered, "Yes, Master."

"Discard your jacket and gun, then take your stance. From watching your fight with Tagen from the security cameras, I have pinpointed flaws in your stance that need to change in order to have better footing," Ziko explained.

"You were watching us spar? How did you even know we were going to?" Jase asked surprised.

"Perhaps, I arranged it or perhaps it was merely coincidence. What does it matter, Bluestar? In the end I have found the flaws using my skill in combat

351

and experience see a weak foe before me and when I see a strong one. You decide which one you are. You will need to be stronger for the upcoming war that is about to rage once more," Ziko Ren told him.

Jase knew which one Ziko Ren decided he was. A weak foe that didn't deserve his title, nonetheless protect the future queen. He didn't have to say it, but Jase guessed as much. He planted one foot in front of him and the other behind as he held up his fists for Ziko Ren to examine his stance.

Ziko Ren tested his strength by pushing on him and seemed pleased. As he circled him, he tested Jase's sides but his attacks were slow as if trying to see the range in his stance. Jase was able to block but realized how useless his usual stance was when it came to blocking attacks from the side or rear. Ziko Ren returned to stand in front of him and stated, "Your stance is basic. I'm sure it's useful back in your city, but not here on the battlefield. I will teach you three different stances that are most useful when it comes to fighting those stronger than you. If these stances are not to your liking than you are free to learn about others, but these are the ones I will teach you and expect you to master whether you like them or not. It's useful to know more than one stance. It gives you an advantage over your foe."

"As you see fit, Master," Jase replied, feeling the foreign word roll off his tongue like a rock.

"The first stance I will teach you is called Ginga in your tongue and comes from solar systems far away. It prepares your body for evading, feinting, or delivering attacks. It frustrates your opponent with constant movement, making it harder for them to attack you. Now to do it, place your right leg behind you and your right arm in front of your face. Move your left hand to the side of the body. Good. Now move your right leg back into your neutral position and step back with your left leg while swinging your left arm in front of your face."

Jase watched him move in a confusing and almost rhythmic dance as he tried to keep up. He soon realized it was harder than it looked as he kept tripping over his own feet and awkwardly moved at a turtle pace.

"You need to be more fluid with your movements. Don't overthink it. Let your body move on its own, Bluestar," Ziko Ren instructed. They continued working on the ginga stance as sweat poured down his face and his legs cramped. Until finally Ziko Ren allowed him to stop in order to show him the next stance. "The second stance I will show you is the Flipping Piece. Stand with your feet shoulder length a part with one foot forward and the other planted behind your back. All your weight should go on your back foot and bring one arm up like you are flexing. Yes, just like that. Move your left arm in the same position but downward, bringing your fist only a few centimeters from your hip bone." Ziko Ren also moved into stance to mirror him. "This stance is good for defense and quick strikes with your legs. You will bring your arms across your body to deflect attacks then twist your body with your front foot so you can kick your foe with your back."

Jase practiced the stance slowly, watching Ziko Ren do it in parts. After trying a few times, he asked, "But isn't the ginga better because I'm always moving and able to attack faster?"

"In some aspects yes, but in others, no. While ginga is good for quick attacks, it can also easily tire you. The Flipping Piece will not. It is not wise to always be on the offense, Jase. You can make mistakes more easily than you would if you stay on the defense. Defense allows you to study your opponent and pinpoint flaws in their stances. Then you can attack full force in confidence. You have to find the mixture in both," Ziko Ren replied.

"I see...Master," Jase replied.

Ziko Ren had him practice the stance for fifteen minutes before peering at the sun on the horizon. "Very well. Now the last stance I will show you is called the Rippling Water. Let your body relax then bend your legs slightly while swaying your body side to side. Keep your hands and arms loose, but in front of your face and chest allowing them to sway with you as well. Now this stance will allow great speed for attacks and if you time it right it will be fine for defense as well. The key is to stay loose and relax, keeping your focus on your opponent at all times and not allowing them to notice you are growing shorter when you bend your legs. No, not like that. Don't bend so much! Start at full height then slowly bend till you are in a comfortable squat but don't touch the ground. Stick your rear out only slightly!"

Jase felt stupid doing the stance and wondered if this was actually a stance or if Ziko was messing with him. Ziko Ren slapped at his arms and shoulders, criticizing that he wasn't loose enough. They practiced until the sun finally set and the last streaks of light were close to extinguishing in the night sky.

"Enough, Bluestar. That ends our session for the day," Ziko Ren declared.

Jase straightened his aching back and wiped sweat from his palms onto his pants as he picked up his things from the ground. "Yes, Master."

"Tomorrow, meet me here an hour before sunrise for sparring before we move back to the posts. I will also teach you lessons in battle history, strategy, how to survive if you are injured in battle, and weaponry. I expect you to train for thirty minutes to master the stances I showed you today either before your lessons or after them, but they must get done. I will know if you don't do them. On Fridays, you will spar with the soldiers during their matches to learn their stances and find their weakness. I will test you at the end of the night to find out what you know about each one. Understood?"

"Understood," Jase replied.

Ziko Ren studied him for a moment then gave a firm nod. "Goodnight, Bluestar."

"Goodnight, Master," Jase watched him disappear into the fog leaving him alone in the darkness. He gazed up at the night sky that was full of bright stars as far as the eye could see and felt at home. Even in his state of exhaustion, he watched them as he thought of Kaimi and him watching them back on Faton. When he finally turned his gaze downward again to leave, he spotted a light glowing in Karasi's oval window across the field. Checking his watch to make sure it wasn't late, Jase made his way towards the hut in the wet grass. The air was cool and filled with the noises of grasshoppers and the occasional voice from the guards on watch. Jase couldn't help but find it a little amusing how he used to be wary of guards and now he had nothing to fear from them since he wasn't a thief anymore. *How quickly things change in such little time*, he thought to himself as he knocked on the door to Karasi's hut.

After a few moments, the tall gray alien opened the door. "Bluestar," he welcomed.

"I'm sorry to bother you, Ancient One. I was hoping you could answer a question I had but I can come back tomorrow if I must," Jase softly stated.

"Nonsense, Bluestar. Come, join me for dinner and we can talk," the Ancient replied, moving aside to hold the door open wider for him to enter.

Jase entered the small hut. The aroma of tangy soup filled his nostrils with spices that caused his eyes to water. His eyes fell on the carved desk again in the corner and he asked while Karasi shut the door, "Did you make that desk?"

Karasi moved to the pot boiling over his oven and added more spices to it. "I did not. It was a gift from King Nightstar before the war started. He liked coming here to get his mind off things. When the war started, he didn't have much time to relax. So he never finished it. It is the last gift I have from him and one I treasure the most," he replied.

"You must miss him very much," Jase said as he took a seat at the table.

Karasi tasted the soup before looking around for something. "We all miss something, Jase. It's not about how much we miss them, but how you miss them whether it's for good reasons or bad. The King lived a good and honest life which I was blessed to be a part of. He accomplished many things during that time and even more when the war started. I do not fret over the thoughts of wanting to see him because I know after this life, there will be a next where we will meet," he told him while adding more spices to the soup.

"So you believe in an afterlife?" Jase asked.

Karasi found what he was looking for and shredded a green plant into tiny pieces before scattering it across the surface of the hot soup and fetched two wooden bowls. "My people believe in science and what they can accomplish with it, but they also know that the stars reign over us in their kingdom. Many would not come out and say it, but it is well threaded in our history. So do I believe in an afterlife?" He poured soup into the bowls then turned to bring them to the table. He didn't finish his sentence until he took a seat and handed one of the bowls to Jase. "I believe that those who do no wrong, enter into the Star's kingdom to live for the rest of their lives. Those who do not do good, go to the dark abyss where the Darkness feeds on their souls until nothing else exists and time goes by so slowly that you go mad."

Jase wasn't much of a religious person besides knowing that the stars existed and the small knowledge of some religion that Momma Rose taught them as children, but he had never heard this tale of it. "If that is true, I hope I do not end up there after this life," he replied.

"I have very little worry about you going down such a path, Bluestar," Karasi told him as he held a spoonful of soup a few inches from his mouth to cool off.

"Yet, we all aren't perfectly good," Jase replied and sipped a spoonful of hot soup. It scalded his tongue as he quickly swallowed, feeling the spices burn his mouth. Jase held open his mouth to cool off his tongue as Karasi laughed at the sight and stood to retrieve some water for him. "I sometimes forget that humans like yourself can't always deal with the spices of other worlds. My apologies, Bluestar." He dropped a jade pebble into the cup of water and handed it to Jase to drink.

Jase gratefully gulped down the cup. Once the cup was drained, he asked, "What is the pebble for?"

"It cools your mouth," Karasi answered as he returned to eating his soup.

Noticing his mouth wasn't on fire anymore, Jase asked, "How does it help?"

Karasi smiled. "The pebbles are found in specific rivers or oceans where the minerals create the color. It heals burns with the cold minerals they're made of. All you have to do is put it in water and the minerals dissolve. In drinking those, it cools the spices that coat your mouth. It is quite rare and only a handful of beings across the universe know about it. I happened to visit a planet where they exist and was allowed to gather a few for study," Karasi informed him, taking another spoonful of soup into his mouth. "So Bluestar, what is this question you wanted to ask? I'm sure it wasn't about my desk."

Remembering the real reason he was there, Jase asked, "Do Androids gain the same powers from the star seasons like we do? Can they become Bluestars if one was made during the Bluestar season?"

Karasi quietly ate his steaming soup. After a few spoonfuls, he responded, "Not that we are aware of, no. We built them with our flaws, but we are sure they aren't affected by such things unless they evolved to. Which could be a possibility, but not likely."

"But you aren't sure?" Jase asked.

Karasi thought before answering. "Yes, we aren't sure how far they have evolved if they have at all. Jase, what you have to understand is that the Resistance doesn't normally take hostages in the war. They kill all Androids they come in contact with. Therefore, we don't have much to study. Even their dead bodies don't tell us much when the A.I. inside them is destroyed."

If Androids can have the same abilities as Bluestars or Greenstars, then we are in bigger trouble than we think, Jase thought before asking. "Is there no way to test during battle?"

Karasi smoothed his faded purple robes that hung loose on his thin body as he finished the last of his soup and turned his full attention to Jase. "One would be able to tell in combat but it's hard since the Androids are already so strong in the first place. Once your abilities are stronger and you're in control, you may have a better chance in finding out if they possess abilities themselves. I'm ninety-five-percent sure they cannot. If that eases your mind, Bluestar."

Jase nodded slowly, thinking about what the war would be like especially with his abilities. "It does a little. Do you think with my help, we will be able to win?" he asked.

"With you, Jase Bluestar, we will defeat them. You are destined to be the greatest Bluestar if you only believe you are. I have full confidence in you, that I swear upon the stars," Karasi told him.

"Thank you, Karasi. I will try not to let you down," Jase told him.

"I know you won't, Bluestar. I know you won't."

Jase drained the rest of his bowl, grateful for the warm meal. "Your soup is delicious once you get past the spices. Thank you for sharing it with me."

"It is very pleasant to have company, especially like yourself," amused, Karasi told him as he sat back in his chair.

"Does anyone else eat with you?" Jase asked.

Karasi took a long drink from his cup before answering. "Princess Dalhala comes once, sometimes twice, a week. Lieutenant Colonel Moon visits me once a week. Princess Skyrah usually comes once a week unless something is troubling her and she needs advice."

"Then I am grateful to share your company tonight alone," Jase said kindly.

"As am I," then changing the subject, the Ancient asked, "How fares your training today?"

Jase recited all that had happened that day, leaving nothing out as he spoke. He shared his concern and frustration about not being able to use his abilities. When he finally came to the end of his tale, Karasi shared with him that Ziko Ren's master had him go through the same exercise but with knives instead of stones.

"How dreadful and inhuman that must have been," Jase expressed.

Karasi bobbed his head in agreement. "His master was a hard man, indeed. I did not like his company when he helped lead the Resistance. You should be thankful you do not have to witness the same lessons as Ziko Ren did."

Jase couldn't imagine any of the Nightstar family allowing such a thing, "Why didn't he get in trouble for such teachings?" he asked.

"It was long before the Resistance was formed, back on Qualia's home world. It was part of Ziko Ren's tribe for such harsh teachings and by the time the King disbanded them, what was done was done," Karasi told him.

"What happened to him? Ziko Ren's master?" Jase asked.

Karasi drank the rest of his water then placed it next to the stove. "He died in the war at the hands of Lord Brohain himself. Even though Ziko Ren did not have much love for the man, he hates the Android who took him from this world. If he gets a chance, he will get revenge on Brohain," he explained.

Jase checked the time and saw that it was already close to midnight. Standing to his feet, Jase politely said, "Well, the time is late and I should be going. Thank you for your hospitality, Karasi. I will see you again soon. Goodnight."

"Goodnight, Bluestar. Sleep well," Karasi replied and showed him to the door before waving him off.

The fog had disappeared altogether as Jase walked in the darkness. The air was cooler than before causing him to pull his jacket closer to him as he walked through the wet grass and stared at the sea of stars above him. Halfway through the field, his data watch started going off and he looked towards it to find Kaimi calling him. Holding his arm level to his face, he answered it with a grand smile.

"There you are! Where have you been?" Kaimi asked concerned.

He stared down at her face that covered the screen. "I was eating with Karasi and lost track of time. I'm on my way back now actually."

Kaimi relaxed. "Be safe. Sometimes wolves can be found close to the base. I'll see you soon?"

"Yes, I'm about to walk into the building as we speak," he told her, glancing up to check his surroundings.

"Okay. Well, I expect to hear all about your day when you get here," she told him.

"Of course," he told her, expecting nothing less.

"See you when you get here," Kaimi told him before hanging up. Jase entered into the courtyard with its splashing fountain and crossed over to his room. Opening the door, Kaimi quickly asked, "So tell me about your training!"

Jase smiled at her excitement as he shut the door behind him and took off his jacket. "Okay, okay, geez! Can't even get into the door without getting an order thrown at me," he teased.

"I wasn't ordering, I was commanding!" Kaimi teased, sitting cross-legged on his navy sheets.

Jase changed out of his dirty clothes as he explained the events of his day just as he told Karasi before, filling her in the best he could. He spoke about his lessons, his conversation with Amosa, and her warning about not pursuing his feelings for the Princess. Then his meeting with Tagen, and his dinner with Karasi, not leaving a single detail out. She laughed when he told her about the spices that burned his mouth and about the pebble that took it away immediately. He then told her about Ziko Ren's master which she agreed was inhuman even for a qualia.

"I am very grateful that Ziko Ren has decided not to train others like his master did. I wouldn't allow it," she told him.

"I don't think the Princess would either," he replied, laying down on the bed next to her. There was a brief pause in their conversation as Jase yawned, feeling his exhaustion of the day's events settle in his bones once more.

"You know Amosa is right," Kaimi quietly stated next to him.

"I know," was all he replied back to her as he felt the dull pain in his heart.

"We aren't trying to hurt you, Jase. It's complicated and times are dark. The Nightstars have lost everything in this war and both girls have been through a lot. Skyrah is a strong person, but if she gets distracted by you and it doesn't work out, the Resistance could suffer." She paused, watching his expression. "It's for the good of the kingdom."

Jase knew her words were the truth, yet it still hurt. He turned to his side, wanting to drop talking about it and said, "I should go to bed. I have training early tomorrow."

Kaimi sensed he didn't want to talk anymore and replied, "Okay. I am glad you started your training, Jase. I agree with Karasi that you can become the greatest Bluestar anyone of us as seen. That, I fully support."

"Thanks, Kaimi. It means a lot that you both think that."

"I had a thought today while I was working with Moon and Karasi. What if you were meant to be a late bloomer, Jase," Kaimi suggested. "What if you were supposed to know how it was to grow up as a human without abilities to gain their perspective on life as someone not strong so when you got your powers, you would be more compassionate to those weaker than you. You have an advantage that no other Bluestar had growing up and perhaps it's for a reason to help with events to come. Perhaps that is what the stars wanted you to have."

Jase rolled over onto his back to look over at her next to him. "That is an interesting thought, Kaimi. You could be right," he replied as he pulled the blanket up to his chin and Kaimi turned off the lights. The only light that glowed in the room was the blue glow from her body that had tiny equations running across it. Some reason he reminded him of the device he had in his room back in Otect City that they used to turn on when he would go to sleep that would show the solar system as it played music. When he told Kaimi, she smiled warmly.

"I always did like watching them while you slept," she said.

Jase's memories of his time in the city with her played in his mind. He whispered out loud for only her to hear, "I miss you. It's weird not having you with me everywhere I got to talk to."

"What? Are you not tired of me inside your head all the time?" Kaimi joked.

Jase chuckled softly, trying not to be loud. "No, it's just weird getting used to. I'm not sure I like it yet."

Kaimi turned her face to him in the dark and smiled. "I miss you too, Jase," she said.

They stared at each other for a moment then Jase turned on his side to sleep. "Goodnight, Kaimi."

"Goodnight, Jase. Sweet dreams, my friend."

Bluestar Lessons

Jase's alarm went off as he struggled to move his aching muscles to silence it. His data watch read four in the morning causing him to let out a groan in response as he willed himself to crawl out of bed in order to get ready for his lesson with Ziko Ren.

"Good morning," Kaimi responded at the sound of him moving off the bed. She sat cross-legged by the window, bright eyed and ready for the day as she watched him cross over to the bathroom. "Make sure you aren't late for your lesson."

"Morning," Jase replied and disappeared into the bathroom to shower. Walking back out in his towel, he noticed clean clothes waiting for him across his bed and asked, "Where did these come from?"

Kaimi glanced over at him then returned her vision to something she could only see as she touched the air. "Princess Skyrah had them brought for you since you have nothing else to wear. It's only right to be outfitted with more than one clothing option since you also represent the Resistance."

Jase pulled on the brown trousers and gray tunic that was soft against his skin. "I didn't think about that before," he said.

"It will be an adjustment, but just remember that everything you do or say to others will reflect on Princess Skyrah and the other leaders of the Resistance," Kaimi warned him.

"I'll be careful," Jase replied and reached for his holster, belting it around his waist before pulling on his baby blue pilot's jacket. "I'll see you later, Kaimi."

"Have fun and good luck!" Kaimi happily called to him as he exited the room.

Jase stopped in the dining hall for an apple before continuing outside where the air was chilly and the sky dark. He squinted in the dark in search of Ziko Ren and barely saw the outline of the man sitting in the middle of the combat ring. When he neared him, Ziko Ren did not rise or greet Jase in a pleasant manner as he sat cross-legged with his eyes close as if meditating. Jase didn't want to disturb him and waited patiently as he ate the rest of his apple.

After two minutes of silence, Ziko Ren asked sternly, "Don't you have something you should be doing instead of chewing rather loudly next to me?"

Jase stopped chewing, forcing a large chunk of the apple down his throat. *He must have wanted me to attack him while he was sitting*, he concluded. "I didn't think it was honorable to attack a man when he is sitting on the ground with his back turned against me," Jase replied.

"No, it is not. The stances I have taught you, have you already forgotten them?" Ziko Ren questioned.

"No, I have not forgotten them," Jase answered, wincing at his words.

"Start them before you waste any more time, Bluestar," Ziko told him without a glance in his direction.

"Yes, sir," Jase quietly responded and moved to the opposite side to practice his stances.

"And Bluestar?"

"Yes?"

"It's Master. Do not forget," Ziko Ren replied.

Jase bit his lip, hating the word. "Yes, Master," he replied. He then faced east so he could watch the sunrise as he practiced his first stance, Ginga. He moved slowly for the first ten minutes, tripping over his own feet and pushing through the soreness of his body. His brain and body soon woke itself and allowed him to follow the rhythm of his feet as he danced across the floor in a triangle. He moved on to the Flipping Piece stance and allowed himself to rest for a few seconds before beginning. Then he moved on to the final stance just as the sun was beginning to kiss the horizon. Jase felt more ridiculous performing the Rippling Water stance as he did the day before but was happy no one was at least awake yet to witness it.

Ziko Ren finally rose from where he sat. "Enough!" he shouted. "Show me what you've learned and prepare to fight."

Jase ignored his weariness and picked a stance he liked more out of the three and readied himself for battle. Ziko Ren studied him then attacked. Jase could barely see the move, but felt the air change in front of him as he caught Ziko Ren's boot in the center of his chest when he brought down his arms to perform the Flipping Piece. The sudden act caught Jase by surprise as he gawked at the boot in his hands then up at Ziko Ren. Ziko Ren hesitated for a split second before bringing his trapped leg down to stomp as he threw up his fist straight into Jase's nose. Jase's face tingled from the pain as warm blood trickled down his nose and he sidestepped another kick to his chest. Using the attack against Ziko, Jase aimed his own leg to the man's ribs but was stopped in seconds as Ziko Ren punched his left eye. At first he didn't feel the pain as hot blood slid down into his eye, blocking his vision as Ziko Ren started attacking his ribs from both sides. The attack all but crippled Jase as he felt the sharp pains shoot up his body as he tried backing away from the man. Using his good eye, he tried to deduce where his master would hit next, but found it useless for he moved too fast for Jase to follow with one eye. Before he knew it, Jase was lying on the ground trying to protect his head as Ziko Ren kicked him in the stomach before backing away.

"Get up, Bluestar," he demanded.

Jase was tired of getting hurt, but forced himself to return to his feet as he wiped away blood from his eye. "How am I supposed to fight when I can barely see?" he questioned between heavy pants.

"Use your instincts and let your abilities flow through you, Bluestar," Ziko Ren told him.

"It's hard to do that when you are beating on me," Jase remarked.

Ziko Ren glared at him for a moment. "You can move as fast as I can, Bluestar. You are the only one who is holding yourself back from doing so. Now again!" he commanded.

Jase wiped away the blood from the cut above his eye and took a deep breath, clenching his teeth from the pain as he did. Listening for his Master's boots move in the dirt, Jase focused on defending himself from all directions as Ziko Ren began his strike once more. A hard thud to his skull racked his brain, sending him sprawling on the ground. Jase growled in response and shoved himself to his feet just as Ziko Ren swung his leg to kick his chest. Jase ducked in time to miss it and used the opportunity to jab him in the stomach.

Ziko Ren quickly blocked the blow and returned one of his own towards Jase's shoulder. Jase felt the pain travel down his arm but ignored it as he evaded the next attack.

Finally after an hour had passed, Ziko Ren ordered them to stop. "Where is your focus, Bluestar?" he exclaimed.

"I am trying, but it is hard to see you when blood keeps pouring into my eye, sir," Jase responded dryly.

Ziko Ren tore a strip of his robes and handed it to Jase. "Fasten this around your eyes and make sure you can't see out of it."

Jase did as he was told, blindfolding himself. "Now what?" he asked.

Ziko Ren stood in front of him as his words pierced Jase's ears. "Now we will try this again, but this time, trust your instincts. Remember what you felt before when you used your power to save the Princess and the bulb. Focus on that feeling and channel it in your attacks," he commanded.

Jase felt vulnerable as he tried to listen to his surroundings. Birds sang their morning songs in the distance accompanied by voices starting to wake up inside the buildings around them. He could hear his own breathing with the pounding of his heart as the wind rustled the grass and leaves around him. There was so much that distracted him that he strained to hear Ziko Ren's footsteps moving silently across the earth floor somewhere nearby. *Focus, just focus*, he told himself, breathing slowly and tried anticipating the attack.

A moment passed...

Then another...

And another....

All of a sudden, something slammed into Jase's lower back causing him to yelp in pain before spinning around. He knew Ziko Ren was behind him somewhere, but he also knew he wouldn't stay there for long. Jase kept moving around the ring, trying to buy himself more time as he kept his back to the outside of the ring. He didn't want to get caught off guard again from behind as he breathed and listened for his foe.

"Listen to what's around you! Filter out what you don't need in order to stop my next attack!" came Ziko Ren's voice off to his left.

Jase tried to filter out unnecessary sounds. Another advance knocked him to his knees and before he got a chance to react, another jab hit the back of his neck. A knee slammed under his chin causing his neck to stretch upward before

364

he landed on his side in the dirt. *GET UP!* he angrily shouted through his thoughts as he quickly pushed himself up. He channeled his anger to fuel his efforts and briefly heard a small sound of dirt moving behind him. Without wasting a second, Jase ducked and threw his leg all the way around him. He felt his leg make contact to Ziko Ren's shins and heard the man hit the ground with a thud. Jase noted where he fell and pounced on his master, slamming his fists as hard as he could into Ziko's jaw. When he made contact with his right hand, Jase then moved to using both fists.

Ziko Ren shoved Jase off and moved to attack again. Hearing the vibrations in the air in front of him, Jase rolled to the opposite direction before pushing off with his feet and tackled Ziko Ren to the earth again. They scrambled in the dirt for control, but after a few minutes Ziko Ren pinned Jase down with his knee on his throat.

"Dead," he stated.

Jase tried maneuvering out of his grasp, but the more he moved the more it became harder to breath. In the end, he patted his knee twice since he couldn't speak. Ziko Ren removed his knee from his throat causing Jase to gasp for air as he ripped off his blindfold. The dirt caked on his face stopped the blood from flowing over his eye which he was grateful for as he rubbed his throat.

"Much better, Bluestar. This is a start," Ziko Ren told him then turned to look at the early morning sun. A brief silence wormed its way between them until finally Ziko said, "Wash your face and meet me at the posts to resume your training for the day."

"Yes, Master," Jase bowed his head in respect and hurried off inside the main building to wash his face in his room. As he rushed through the courtyard, he noticed that servants were already up and scurrying around the area cleaning the fountain, sweeping the room, and dusting the statues. They seemed to pay him no mind as he carefully picked his way through them, making sure not to bother their work as he entered his room. Kaimi was already gone for the morning which he figured as much as he moved into his bathroom and began running the sink water. Looking into the mirror, he saw the extent of his injuries where blood and dirt caked his eyelid, cheek, and his nose where it had been bleeding earlier. Blood was smeared across both his forearms where he tried keeping it out of his vision and his tunic was filthy. "So much for clean clothes," he said out loud as he began scrubbing away the grim from his body.

Once cleaned, Jase left his room and hurried out of the building to meet Ziko Ren at the posts. He was surprised how fast the fog rolled in, slowly starting to thicken as he ran towards the posts. He spotted Master Ren and a dozen soldiers waiting at the posts for him. "Climb the posts and take your position, Bluestar," Ziko Ren commanded as he neared.

Jase did as he was told and pulled himself up, feeling the soreness return in his arms as he did. The cut above his eye throbbed in pain as he answered, "Ready, Master."

Ziko Ren gave a nod to the soldiers to pick up their stones. "Remember to use what you feel over what you see. Summon the power within yourself to aid you, and you won't get hurt," he told Jase.

Jase stared forward to the end of the posts, trying to remember what it felt like when he saved Tahmela from falling to his death and when he saved Skyrah from the Androids. *You got this*, he assured himself.

"Begin!" demanded Ziko Ren.

Jase took off leaping from one post to the other as stones were hurled towards him. They continued to hit him no matter how hard he tried to call upon his power to help him. He had gotten halfway when he slipped on a post and hit the earth floor with a loud thud before forcing himself up again to start over without Ziko Ren saying a word. Once again they started, but like the million times before, Jase was hit and failed the lesson over and over and over again. After some time, Ziko Ren stopped him with a thoughtful expression as if trying to figure something out. He glanced back to the main building, then declared he would be right back and hurried off into the light fog. The soldiers talked amongst themselves as Jase sat on a post alone feeling like an outsider.

When Ziko Ren returned, he brought one of the servants Jase had seen earlier and showed her to the center post. Ziko Ren helped her climb on top of it before returning to his spot at the head of the posts. "Begin!"

"Wait!" Jase eyed the woman then turned back to his Master. "I don't understand. Why is she here?"

Ziko Ren gaze was stern as he replied with a tone as if he didn't understand what was wrong. "It is the same concept as before. This time you also have to worry about stones hitting her," he said.

Jase let out a laugh in disbelief, hoping he was joking. "Master, I can barely protect myself. How can I protect her?" he exclaimed.

"You've done it before, Bluestar. Anytime someone else was in danger alongside you, you protected both. This is no different. If you don't want her to get hurt, then save her," he commanded.

He can't be serious! Jase thought, focusing on the maid in the center of the posts. She looked frightened and unsure of what she got herself into, but made no notion to move from her spot even as the soldiers prepared their stones.

"Begin!" shouted Ziko Ren, his voice thunderous in the air.

Jase took off as fast as he could towards the young maid as rocks pelted his body. He was almost to her when a rock plummeted towards her skull. Without a second to lose, Jase brought up one hand towards her and felt the tingle run down his arm and through his fingertips as blue plasma energy rushed forward. It created a shield around her, deflecting the rocks as Jase used his other hand to stop all the rocks that were being thrown at him and returned them to their hosts. His feet seemed to glide across a slippery substance as he picked up the woman and rushed her down to the end of the posts out of harm's way. Once his feet touched the ground, Jase felt the energy that was flowing through him fade away causing him to sink to his knees as he panted heavily. Behind him, Jase heard clapping and turned to find Ziko Ren and the soldiers applauding his efforts.

Ziko Ren crossed his arms across his chest. "Let's try it again, Bluestar! Maude, return to your position!"

Jase couldn't help but smile as excitement coursed through his body causing him to forget his weariness as he eagerly returned to the first post. Jase focused on the maid named Maude on the center post and listened for Ziko Ren's instruction.

"Begin!"

Jase once again took off at full speed, barely feeling his feet hit the wood as he raised his hand to create a shield around Maude again. The energy rushed through him and towards her as he felt rocks pelt his skin for a moment before creating a shield around his own body.

"Don't forget to read the word, Bluestar!" Ziko Ren reminded him.

"Oh, yeah," Jase replied, forgetting about that part of the lesson as he flashed a smile to Maude before kneeling to read the carved word on the post. After reading the word, Jase and Maude walked to the end of the posts and jumped off. Exhaustion washed over him like a wave. He fell to his knees as the energy left his body causing him to gasp for breath as if he had run for miles.

"Maude, get him food and water quickly!" Ziko Ren ordered the servant who darted off. He moved over to Jase and studied him in silence as they waited for Maude to return. When she did, she brought with her a plate of food and a large glass of water. Ziko Ren took the plate and dismissed her before asking Jase as he handed him the plate, "What was the word I carved?"

Jase tore into some soft bread, chewing it quickly and answered, "'Believe,' Master. You carved 'believe.'"

Ziko Ren raised an eyebrow. "And do you know why?" he asked.

Jase scarfed down the rest of the bread. "Because it is the one thing I have trouble doing within myself and others. It wasn't until you forced me to save someone, did I realize that in that moment I do believe in my abilities. In doing so I know now that I can trust them to help me and allow me to help others."

"Bluestars are born with confidence in their abilities at a very young age. They are raised on learning about their abilities and on learning about themselves. When they reach your age, they already know what their limits are and how best they can stretch them. There is no second guessing that their abilities will sustain them. You were not raised in knowing about your birthright but that does not change who you or what you can do. You are the same as every other Bluestar. The only difference is that you are learning about them now and your body hasn't adjusted to them yet. If you believe in yourself to harness them then you will learn faster and allow your body to catch up with your star abilities," Ziko Ren told him.

"Who teaches them?" Jase asked as he picked his plate clean.

"I did for a long time when the Nightstar family still ruled our galaxy. When a Bluestar was born, they were brought to Starwake Castle to begin instruction by my hand in order to strengthen their bodies at a young age so that their abilities didn't mature faster than they could handle. King Nightstar treated each Bluestar as if they were his own family and allowed their family to live on the castle grounds as long as they wanted. When the Bluestar reached a certain age, he or she was given the option to live elsewhere if they so desired it as long as they continued our lessons until I deemed them no longer a student," he told Jase.

Jase took a long drink of his cold water. "Why you? I mean, I'm sure you are quite wise, but why were you the one responsible to teach all Bluestars?"

"Because my grandfather from ancient times of long ago was a Bluestar and taught his son all he needed to know about his kind. Even though his son wasn't born a Bluestar, they continued on the teachings through generations in hopes that one day our lineage would become a Bluestar again. My family has yet to have our kind honored by the stars, but it is my responsibility to continue on the teachings. I am honored that I have been blessed to train those like yourself and I will continue to do so as long as I live," Ziko Ren revealed to him.

Ziko Ren looked towards the rising sun. "Finish your lunch. You will do another round of posts before we move on to our next lesson."

"Yes, Master," Jase replied.

Jase finished the last of his lunch and walked to the start of the posts, feelings his energy replenished. Once again they started their lesson except this time Jase had to pretend he was saving someone in order to use his abilities. It took him longer to do, but after a few minutes he was able to create his shield. Ziko Ren had him expand the width and length of the shield. They did variety of exercises evolving how fast he could create the shield and how long he could hold it before growing to weary. After an hour and a half passed, Ziko Ren declared that it was time to move on to their next lesson and lead Jase back across the field towards the main building that was now barely visible from the thick fog. Ziko Ren lead him through the courtyard to the room two doors down from Jase's. As they entered, Jase was shocked to find that the room was a large library filled with scrolls, books, and other artifacts against every wall. There were two large windows that were four feet across and reached the top of the ceiling, letting in the gloomy light from outside. Two large oak desks stretched from one side of the room to the other with dull-colored chairs next to them.

"Have you never seen a library before, Bluestar?" Ziko Ren asked when he saw his reaction.

Jase shook his head as his eyes danced around the room. "My job didn't really require me to go inside such places and Mrs. Rose who took care of me didn't have many pieces to devote to books for us to read. We maybe had five books in the entire house besides a cookbook," he explained.

Ziko Ren turned his attention back to the room. "Here is where you will spend your studies learning about the Resistance and our enemies as well as the many important beings you might come in contact with during your time fighting with the Resistance. We don't have much time to devote to lessons I would like to teach you before the Androids get here, but instead I will teach you a crash course in things that you will need to know like history of the war, strategy, politics among leaders and how to address them. I dislike having to rush your lessons, but we will do what we must and this is what I and the Princess have come to agreement on. I will do my best to teach you, but you must be willing to learn in order for this to work no matter how tired and frustrated you get. Is that understood?"

"I will do my best, Master," Jase answered, feeling excitement swell up in his breast.

Over the next five hours, Ziko Ren taught Jase about the history of treaties between all races, Faton's history and how the first Nightstar became king of the galaxy. Jase read about ancient history, the beginning of the civil war and what kind of strategies the Resistance used. He learned which strategies worked and which ones didn't then was tested on what strategy he would use in certain circumstances. They then moved on to the workings of Androids, their strengths and weaknesses which was Jase's favorite subject as he soaked up all the knowledge he had to read in the book which was incomplete in most parts. It wasn't till Jase was learning technique and how to fight them when Ziko Ren finally declared that they would finish up the lesson in the morning.

"It is close to supper and I'm sure you feel overwhelm from all that I have taught you today. This is a start to a good beginning, Bluestar. Keep up the hard work," Ziko Ren told him before leaving the room.

"Thank you, Master," Jase replied. With his arms full, he carefully walked back to his room and fumbled with opening the door as he entered. He placed the new items on the desk in his room then flopped on his soft bed for a moment, closing his eyes in hopes it would help with the headache that was forming.

"Busy day?"

Jase jolted up and found Kaimi at the window panel, full size. "You have no idea. If I learn anything more today, my head will explode!"

Kaimi laughed at his remark. "We wouldn't want that, now would we! What happened to your eye?"

Jase touched the cut above his eye and found it sensitive to the touch. He had forgotten about it during his lessons as he replied, "Sparring with Master

Ziko Ren. It doesn't hurt all that much, though. But hey! Guess what?! I was able to control my abilities today and call upon them!"

"Jase, that's amazing! I'm so proud of you!" she exclaimed moving over to the bed to sit with him.

"With Ziko's teachings, I think I'll be able to control my abilities and use them as I want by the time the Androids get here. You won't have to worry about me anymore," Jase told her.

"I will always worry about you, Jase," Kaimi replied with a giggle. "Now you should get ready for dinner. All the leaders were told to be there for an important announcement."

"There must be news about the Android's advance," Jase stated as he hurried to the bathroom to get cleaned up.

A Storm within the Heart

When Jase walked back into his bedroom, he found his white faded vest, charcoal pants, black boots, and his baby blue pilot's jacket were clean and folded neatly on his bed. He hadn't realized how dirty they had been until now as he held them in his hands. "You should have told me sooner how dirty they were. Who cleaned them?" he joked towards Kaimi as he got dressed.

Kaimi wasn't paying attention, focused on a task that he could not see as her fingers danced around the air as if she was typing something. "Princess Skyrah had them cleaned," she responded.

"That was nice of her," Jase replied and checked the clock, seeing he was late to dinner. "We should get going. We are late."

"Technically, I'm already there so you are the one late." Looking over at him, Kaimi smiled.

Jase buckled on his holster, checking the gun to make sure it was still fastened. "Well, thanks for waiting," he joked and hurried out the door towards the dining hall. He entered the room and viewed the dining table that was filled except for his and Minko's seat.

"Apologize for being late," Kaimi whispered in his earbud.

"My apologizes for my late arrival, Your Majesty," Jase moved towards his seat and peered over at Princess Skyrah at the head of the table.

Princess Skyrah watched him sit as did everyone else, as she replied, "You are forgiven, Bluestar. Ziko Ren was just informing us about the progress you made today. It is good news to hear this early."

A servant brought Jase his food which he waited for her to set down before answering, "I am grateful to have him as my Master, my Princess."

Ziko Ren's expression never changed from being stern as he continued to eat his dinner in silence. Princess Skyrah seemed to answer in his stead. "He is a hardworking teacher and we are all grateful to have him with us." Changing her tone to a more serious one, she continued, "It has come to my knowledge that the Androids might be here sooner than we originally thought. Lord Brohain has them stationed on an uninhabited planet, Otov Ukoreow, that is four weeks away from us for a reason unknown. Why are they there and will they attack sooner is unknown but we should prepare."

"Are they aware that we know of their attack?" Lieutenant Colonel Moon asked.

"From all that I have been told, they do not. We still have that advantage," she answered.

"Do we have any clues what they are doing on that planet?" Karasi asked.

Princess Skyrah shook her head. "Not yet, no. I have sent a small scouting group to the planet, but we won't know until later on in the month. We can only hope it's nothing serious. They could be setting up a base there before we have the chance to."

"But there's nothing on the planet worth taking. It would cost more trying to get supplies and manpower there than it would to occupy a different world that is habitable with food already," Lieutenant Colonel Moon uttered in thought as if trying to figure out a riddle.

"Perhaps they are doing so to get closer to the Resistance," Amosa suggested. "After all if we aren't meeting them head on, then they have to travel all the way from Faton to reach a planet that is known to help us. Xeth, the Qualia's home planet, is too toxic for them to land on so the next closest planet would be Otov Ukoreow."

Jase agreed with Amosa even though he knew very little about the Qualia's home planet. It made sense and he doubted that the Androids needed much food or food at all on the barren planet that he had never heard of. "Where is the planet?" he asked.

Kaimi was the one to show him, casting a blue holo map of their solar system across the dinner table. It was big enough for all to see with large planets and their moons dancing around the space above their heads. "It is on the far reaches of the solar system with very little life. Its name means 'barren soul' in the common tongue which is very fitting. The planet has harsh conditions with well below freezing temperatures for part of the day and even worst at night. The air is very thin and the landscape is ragged with tough terrain making it impossible to live on," she told him.

Jase couldn't help but wonder if the conditions were so harsh, how would the Androids be able to withstand it. Voicing his concerns out loud, he asked, "Won't the harsh cold effect the Android's inner functions and workings? They might not be able to feel the cold, but like all machines, their parts would take damage from such an environment."

"Jase is right. The Androids wouldn't stay on the planet for long in which we should do as you said, Your Highness. We should start sending supplies and troops to Mmerits in order to begin building defenses," Lieutenant Colonel Moon agreed.

Princess Skyrah studied her plate deep in thought. When she finally looked up, Jase could tell she was worried about something and not the potential base on Otov Ukoreow. "The sooner we start defending the city, the better chance we have at succeeding on keeping it. Let us remind the Androids what we are still capable of and allow no doubts in our midst that we can fight them. Together we will win this battle."

Her words came as a shock to Jase, not knowing how well she could motivate her leaders. He was reminded that she was a Princess and the future leader and not just another normal being he had come to know in their time together. The thought made him feel that Amosa and Kaimi were right about his feelings towards her. *She is royalty and I should not overstep my place to try and win her affections. Her years surpass my own and I should not tangle in them when she should marry someone of her own nobility.* He suddenly felt his heart grow heavy at knowing that they could never be and did his best to hide the pain as he turned his attention back to the chatter among the dinner table.

Ziko Ren's eyes weighed heavily as he thought. Finally, he stated, "Lord Poukil might not be pleased with the sudden overwhelm of soldiers moving into his city at once. You should meet with him in person to insist that he allows our actions. We will need to bring as many supplies as we can there. We cannot rely on the Lord to provide all that we need."

"I couldn't agree with you more, Ziko Ren," Princess Skyrah said. "I think it would be best to meet him after my long overdue absence. I will arrange a meeting and leave the day after tomorrow."

"Jase should remain behind for his training. He is not yet fit to guard you or offer guidance and we shouldn't allow anyone in Mmerits to know of his existence until we can show that he is fully a Bluestar," Ziko added.

Jase became angry at his Master's words from wanting to accompany the Princess and from him speaking about Jase as if he could not speak for himself. He was about to disagree with him but his words fell short when Princess Skyrah agreed.

"Jase and yourself will be the last to join us in the city so you can fulfill your teachings. I will leave a troop behind at the base to keep it protected in case of intruders and for the protection of Princess Dalhala who will not be joining us in the fight. Karasi, what will become of you?" Princess Skyrah asked, turning her attention to him.

The Ancient straightened his robes as he spoke. "I believe it's best for me to remain out of danger. I will stay here with the Princess and continue my work on our secret weapon in hopes I can finish it sooner with no distractions. Here, I can also help to progress Jase's learning so that he can join you in the city."

"Very well. Tahmela and Lieutenant Colonel Moon will start loading the ships with soldiers and supplies. High Guardian Amosa will accompany me to Mmerits while the rest of you remain here. Tahmela, if we could, I'd like to use your ship as my main vessel," Princess Skyrah asked the bulb.

Tahmela glanced at Jase to make sure he agreed before responding. "Okie, Princess," he replied.

"Good. We have the remainder of this month and next month so let's not squander it, friends." With that, everyone rose from their seats, dismissed.

Jase checked his watch, reading that it was 8 P.M. already. "I feel like the day keeps going by faster," he whispered to Kaimi inside his earbud. He watched her smile from across the table as Tahmela and Moon left to discuss how to move everything they needed inside his ship while Princess Skyrah, Ziko Ren, and Karasi talked amongst themselves in quiet voices. He smiled to Princess Dalhala who stood from the table with Amosa behind her, acting as a guard for both sisters. She whispered something to her then walked around the table to stand by Jase who had yet to move from his chair.

"Are you nervous about the war, Bluestar?" Princess Dalhala softly asked him.

Jase shrugged, standing to his feet. "Not really, but I am looking forward to finishing my training so I can accompany the Princess to Mmerits."

"You will be by her side soon, Jase. Keep doing what you are doing and you will be there in no time," Princess Dalhala assured him with a warm smile.

"Till then at least I have you and Karasi for friends while we stay here. Are you sad about not being able to go with your sister?" he asked and glanced in the direction of Skyrah.

"I love my sister and I do miss her when she leaves me, but it is the way things are. I would only be a liability if I were to accompany her. Therefore, it is wise for me to stay far from war. I know she will return to me in due time," she replied.

They talked for a few minutes more about his training before she told him goodnight and left the dining room. Jase was on his way to leave the room as well when Ziko Ren stopped him, saying, "Do not let your friend's leaving distract you from your lessons, Bluestar."

"Yes, Master," he acknowledged.

Ziko studied him for a moment. "Get some rest. I will let you have tonight off from sparring, but don't get used to it, Jase. Do not be late to our lesson tomorrow," he replied then exited the room.

"In time, perhaps, he will warm up to you," Kaimi said as she stood next to him.

"Let's hope so," he answered.

The Princess was wearing a pale blue tunic that wrapped around her waist in folds then hung loose around her arms with white cuffs and khaki leggings. The blue of her shirt and boots caused the blue in her eyes to be more prominent than the pink as she met his gaze. Her emotions hidden behind her composure as she firmly but politely asked, "Bluestar, would you take a walk with me?"

Jase nodded before following her out of the dining hall and into the cool night air. The fog had thickened since last he was out. They headed in the direction of the gardens with Jase following close behind to make sure he wouldn't lose her. They walked without saying a word to one another, letting the silence stretch between them as they reached the outer clumps of flowers in the garden. The Princess did not stop, but weaved in and out of the towering flowers that rose above them. From within the garden, Jase noticed the fog was very light and seemed more magical at night than it was in the daytime. Jase kept his attention on Skyrah, wondering what she was thinking about as they wandered on.

Lightning danced across the night sky in and out of the clouds above their heads, but neither seemed to pay much attention to it as they moved into a more open space that allowed the two to walk side by side. Jase's thoughts swirled inside his head much like the storm he was sure was coming as he thought of ways to change Skyrah's mind and allow him to go with her and the others. After traveling for so long with them, he didn't want it to go back to being just Kaimi and him again. *It's funny how things change*, he thought to himself, remembering when he used to like it just being the two of them.

The Princess finally spoke. "I'm sorry, Bluestar. My mind is so set on what needs to be done in future events that I have paid you little attention," she apologized.

Jase glanced at her as they slowly walked through the flowers. He smiled finding it funny that she had forgotten he was here when the opposite was for him. "There is no need to apologize, Princess. You have more pressing matters to attend to than talk with me, that I'm sure of," he said.

"On the contrary, you are a Bluestar," she replied. Her smile seemed to radiate from the lightning strikes as she turned to him. "You are one of my pressing matters to attend to since soon you will be by my side as a loyal guard and have as much power over my army as I do. I can't afford to ignore you. It would be poor for my best interest and the Resistance's best interest."

Jase couldn't help but smirk at her words, liking the idea that she was forced to talk to him whether she liked it or not. "What? Do you think I will turn against you if you don't talk to me every now and then?" he joked.

Princess Skyrah shrugged. "Maybe. Anything could happen," she said.

"Well, you are right. If you don't give me all of your undivided attention than I will take your army and fight against you," he sighed.

"Oh, shut up!" she playfully pushed him away from her. "You wouldn't dare."

Jase made a face as serious as he could, trying not to smile as he crossed his arms. "I would if you forced me to. Then you'd have no choice but pay attention to me," he said mockingly.

She looked up at the lightning and watched it dance with the clouds in the sky. "Or maybe I wouldn't care. I could just ignore you and find another army for my cause. Compared to the Androids, you wouldn't be much trouble."

"Ouch! How rude of a Princess to say such a thing. I could be as much trouble to you as the Androids are," he threatened.

Princess Skyrah smiled and shook her head.

Jase watched her for a moment, thinking how beautiful she was then forced himself to look away. "You're right, though. I like you too much to do such a thing," he said.

Princess Skyrah glanced at him, their eyes meeting for a brief moment and for a second Jase thought he saw something inside them that wasn't a facade but instead love for him. He decided his eyes were playing tricks and didn't press further as she looked away and answered, "Well, I am glad then I don't have to worry about you betraying me."

Changing the subject, Jase asked, "How long will you and the others be gone?"

The Princess suddenly seemed tired, staring out at the flower forest in front of them. "The rest of this month most likely and some of next. There's a lot to do to get the city ready for battle. There is planning, who will defend what, where our army will stay until the Androids get here, how supplies should be rationed, and if we have enough weapons for every soldier. Lord Poukil and I also have to figure out where all the women, children, and those who can't fight need to go. The list is long and we don't have much time to figure everything out. My time would be best spent in the city."

"I see," Jase responded, feeling his heart sink at the thought of being left behind for so long.

She must have picked up on his sadness and placed a warm hand on his shoulder. "You will join us soon enough, Jase. Have faith in your abilities and know that we will see one another soon."

Hoping to hide his feelings, Jase replied, "I know. I will just have to make up lost time on annoying you when you get back."

"I wouldn't have it any other way," she replied then turned back to the lightning show. "I love watching lightning."

Jase wanted to tell her how he felt, but held his tongue as he turned to watch the storm with her. When he trusted himself to talk again after a few minutes, he declared in almost a soft whisper, "I'm going to miss you...and the others, of course."

The Princess turned her gaze towards him and appeared to be happy and at peace with the beauty of the storm above them. "We will miss you too, Jase, and I will miss you as well." The thunder boomed above their heads and Skyrah quickly stated, "We should get inside before it starts raining."

Jase didn't want to go back just yet but knew with how the wind was picking up that the storm was almost upon them and agreed to walk back with her. Even with the storm, though, they walked back slowly in silence as if not wanting the night to end just yet. The wind had blown away most of the fog, leaving it visible as Jase spotted the night guards standing at their posts. Knowing he wouldn't have a chance once they neared, Jase gently stopped Skyrah by her arm and said nervously, "Princess...Skyrah, if you ever want someone to talk to while you are in Mmerits don't hesitate to call me. I mean if you want someone outside of your politics, or whatever. You don't have to. I just want you to know I'm here for you if you do need someone to talk to. Day or night, no matter how late."

Princess Skyrah studied him for a moment then replied, "Thank you, Jase. I appreciate your friendship and always looking out for me."

Jase felt the sting of her words, but did his best to brush it off. "Anytime, Your Highness," he said. They started walking again towards the main building with her following beside him.

When they entered the building, the Princess told him goodnight and he did the same before crossing the courtyard towards his room. He shut the door behind him, careful not to make a noise and sighed.

"What's wrong with you?" Kaimi asked as she watched him take off his jacket and cross the room to his bed.

"Nothing," was all Jase replied as he unlaced his boots and laid back on his bed.

Kaimi didn't press further and instead stated, "Don't forget to set an alarm unless you want me to wake you up in the morning?"

"Okay," Jase grumbled back and pulled the sheets up to his chin before closing his eyes tightly to hold back the tears that threatened to fall.

Kaimi turned off the lights for him, softly saying, "Goodnight, Jase."

"Goodnight, Kaimi," he muttered, rolling to his side. Tears rolled out of the corner of his eyes and over his nose dripping onto the soft pillow next to him. A single thought repeated inside his brain.

I appreciate your friendship.

To Listen

The following day, Jase devoted his time to Ziko Ren and his lessons in order to keep his mind off Princess Skyrah and the others leaving. On his breaks, he spent his time reading as much as he could about history, the civil war, and the Nightstar family while also practicing the bulb language. Before he knew it the day had bled into night with servants hurrying to get dinner ready as Jase finished his sparring lesson with Ziko Ren and strolled back to his room. A part of him wished that the Princess would come to his room and ask to walk with her again, but Jase knew such a thing wouldn't happen. She was too busy getting everything ready for their departure the very next day that she wouldn't have time for anything else. He went to bed full of melancholy as his brain counted down the hours until Skyrah left causing him to toss and turn as he tried sleeping.

When morning finally arrived, Jase felt as if he had barely slept as he rose out of bed with knots tangled up inside his stomach. He quickly got dressed and left the room, noticing that Kaimi was nowhere to be seen.

"Bluestar!" Ziko Ren was heading his way from the Princess's room. Jase stopped to wait for him.

"Good morning, Master. I was just on my way to say farewell to the Princess and the others," he replied.

"Complete your stances. Then, you can say your farewells. Do not shorten your time in your rush, Bluestar," Ziko ordered.

Jase clenched his teeth together. "As you wish, Master." He headed off towards the combat ring and started his exercises as the morning light barely skimmed the horizon. The air was cool and refreshing as the fog rolled in with none of the storm clouds from last night in sight. Jase quickly took up his first stance, Ginga, and tried to let go of the tension inside his body as he cleared his mind. His thoughts continued to slip through the cracks of his brain causing his fear of not being able to say goodbye to the Princess take hold of him as he quickly moved on to the next stance. The sun rose slowly over the horizon as he settled in to his last stance, Rippling water, and tried to calm his nerves as he swayed.

"You are thinking too much, Bluestar. Empty your mind," Ziko Ren said entering the circle.

Jase did as instructed, trying not to worry about not finishing up in time as he watched Ziko perform the stance with him. They both then moved into sparing as Ziko Ren opened up with a new combination of strikes that he wanted Jase to learn. Ziko moved slowly, showing him how each attack complimented the other before allowing Jase to try. Jase quickly got the hang of it and used the new combination in his attacks as they began sparring for that morning.

"I want you to block my attacks by using your shield," Ziko Ren instructed, getting into stance to fight.

"How can I create a small shield? I've only been able to create shields around people," he questioned.

"Focus on what you want to create in your mind and control the amount of energy you want to release when you go to block me," Ziko Ren told him.

Jase settled his body in his fighting stance, relaxing his muscles as he did and waited for Ziko to strike. They studied each other without saying a word when suddenly Ziko Ren disappeared and attacked Jase from the side. Jase barely had time to see it as he quickly raised his forearm to block it, feeling his arm tingle down to his fingertips as a small translucent shield took shape along his skin and protected him from the attack. Ziko Ren's fist bounced off and without hesitating he spun his leg around to kick Jase's backside. Jase twisted his body as he swung his leg around to intercept the kick before throwing a punch towards his master's face.

Ziko evaded it, disappearing again with great speed as he attacked Jase's right side. Jase once more created an arm shield to fight off the attack as they danced about the ring. They continued their battle for over an hour, neither one winning nor losing as sweat coated their brows and Jase felt his energy seeping his strength to go on. Jase blocked another blow as he swayed on his feet, his heart pounding against his chest as he breathed heavily. Ziko Ren struck him with another powerful blow that sent Jase to one knee as he fought against him with his shield.

"Good, Bluestar. Good," he told him and allowed Jase to rise to his feet again. "I must say I am surprised you were able to hold on to your abilities this long. Your hard work is starting to pay off and soon you will have no trouble using your abilities."

"Do you think I will be strong enough to fight the Androids in Mmerits?" Jase asked him as he caught his breath.

"Only time can tell," Ziko Ren replied, peering at Princess Skyrah and the others who had walked out of the main building.

Jase followed his gaze. "Master, I would like to say goodbye to the Princess and my friends before they leave," he said.

"There is no time, Bluestar. Every minute counts in your training and we cannot waste it on goodbyes," Ziko Ren told him.

Jase bit the inside of his cheek as he watched the Princess make her way across the field and towards the willow trees that hid the entrance of the base. He thought surely she would say goodbye to him, but with every step she took away from him, his hope dimmed and she disappeared into the willow branches. *Not even a wave goodbye*, he thought as he turned back to Ziko Ren who had been watching him. "Shall we go again?" Jase asked, hiding his disappointment.

"Let's begin," Ziko answered.

Jase and Ziko Ren sparred for the rest of the morning and into the afternoon, only stopping for a quick lunch. They then moved on into the library to go over war strategies and all the positions in an army to familiarize Jase for the upcoming battle. When three o'clock rolled around, Ziko left Jase to his studies for the afternoon as he arranged the platoon of soldiers that would be leaving the following day for Mmerits. Instead of studying the war plans in front of him, Jase left the main building and wandered into the garden in hopes to be alone for a little while. Disappointment clouded his thoughts as Jase weaved in and out of the tangled flowers, listening to the birds sing around him. He walked until his feet grew tired and sat down in the soil with his back against a towering purple flower.

Will I always be by myself here? Jase wondered as he rested his head back against the stem and closed his eyes. He let his mind drift as he listened to the peaceful melodies of the garden. He heard a bee buzzing past his ear and land on the flower next to him as a bird chirped and landed on a flower nearby. Listening, Jase focused on his surroundings. He heard the flap of the wings of a butterfly flutter by and the sounds of the flower petals gently sway in the soft breeze as birds flew in and out of the garden. Grasshoppers chirped and a rabbit softly patted the dirt floor as it hopped through the flowerbeds. Jase was amazed on how much was around him if he only paid attention. He suddenly wondered what the Bluestar Sanctuary sounded like if he only sat and listened. Suddenly the air around him cooled as a tingle ran down his arms to his toes causing him to open his eyes.

"You made it," Sir Agin Rex said with a smile.

"I wasn't...I mean I didn't think I could do it. I was just wondering...," Jase told him, surprised to be in the endless blue room.

Sir Agin Rex scratched his short black beard. "You have grown stronger in the few days ago that I last saw you. You're abilities are maturing fast in your body now that you have fully accepted them. It won't be long till you are able to use them without a thought," he told him.

"I feel like I haven't made much progress," Jase responded.

"Patience is the key to all building blocks of learning, Jase. Be patient and in time you will succeed. Now, from what I gather you only have enough willpower to remain here for two hours before you fail from exhaustion. I would like to teach you some lessons before that happens. If you are willing," Sir Agin Rex declared.

Jase nodded. "I would be honored," he said.

Sir Agin Rex rubbed his hands together with excitement. "Our first lesson is a simple one that all Bluestars are taught at a young age which they continue on throughout their life until they have mastered it. It is a lesson about knowing yourself and how to ingrain your abilities with your body so that you can call upon them at any time. You have lived most of your life not knowing who you truly are and in return it has affected your abilities causing them to lash out when you are in danger. Your body knows how to use your abilities to save itself, but it does not grasp the knowledge to control them."

"See it as your third eye. It's our inner knowing within ourselves and our spiritual bodies. Now, our third eye for Bluestars differ from those of normal birth. We can use ours to tap into Tarek, the first Bluestar, and gain his abilities to use at our will. A normal Bluestar child is taught through his mentor here in this sanctuary about his abilities while another normal being teaches him or her their duties in the outside world. Master Ziko Ren has been the mentor for Bluestars for decades and will continue to be until his death."

Curious, Jase asked, "Who will take his place when that happens?"

"I do not know. Only time can tell. Now sit down and let's begin the lesson," Sir Agin Rex instructed. Jase did as instructed and sat cross-legged on the cold floor with Sir Agin Rex doing the same opposite him. "Close your eyes and focus on the feeling that radiates your body when you are able to feel your abilities within you," he continued. "I want you to focus on it and nothing else until I say."

Jase breathed in slowly as he focused on pulling his plasma energy forward like he was able to when he used his shield. It was easier to do in the sanctuary as the energy flowed through him, tingling as if his whole body had fallen asleep. He focused on it coursing through his veins and pictured it as if it was his own blood pumping through his chest.

"Open your eyes, Jase," Sir Agin Rex said.

Jase did as he was told to find Sir Agin Rex studying him with a wondering gaze, crossing his arms across his dark tunic. "You have failed the lesson, Bluestar. You can try again tomorrow."

"How? What did I not do?" Jase asked confused.

Sir Agin Rex answered in a serious tone. "Your patience is exceptional for a short time, but as time grows you become distracted. You mustn't let your mind wander no matter how long you might have to wait," he told him.

"Yes, Master," Jase replied bowing his head respectfully.

"Come to me tomorrow after your lessons with Ziko Ren. Until then, sleep well, Bluestar."

Jase reached out to embrace his forearm when suddenly he felt his body grow heavy and the sensation of falling backwards overcame him as he watched the Bluestar stare down from above as he fell.

A Distant Vision

Jase opened his eyes, feeling as if he had been underwater suffocating as he breathed heavily in the nectar filled air around him. "I will never get used to that," he said out loud and took a deep breath of refreshing air. With the help of the flower's stem, Jase pulled himself to his feet and stretched his stiff back. Glancing to his data watch, he noticed that only an hour had passed in this world when in the sanctuary he had spent two hours with Sir Agin Rex. *If I train myself harder, I could be able to stay a day with Sir Agin Rex and learn more from him,* he thought to himself as he ventured forth into the tangled garden. As he walked, he thought he heard a voice gently sailing on the breeze and looked around for the source. Listening closely, Jase followed the sound through the overgrowth of plants.

He stepped over large roots and carefully pushed his way through a thorn bush, trying his hardest to not get caught as he did. It wasn't until a short while had passed that Jase finally stepped out into an open area of the garden and spotted the source of the voice. It was the Princess herself talking to someone he couldn't see from the angle he stood. He couldn't make out what she was saying, but it seemed to be a pleasant conversation for she suddenly burst into a wide smile and nodded. Jase peered behind him, not wanting to interrupt her and was about to retrace his steps when Princess Dalhala called to him and waved him over.

As he neared, Princess Dalhala exclaimed, "Jase Bluestar, it's always a pleasure to see you."

"And the same for you, Your Highness," Jase responded with a glance in the direction she had been speaking to and found no one there. Figuring she had been talking to herself, he joked, "I feel like you live out here in the garden more than you do in your own room."

Amused, the Princess replied, "So it seems. Truth be told, Jase Bluestar, this is the one place I don't feel alone. Here, I don't have to worry about acting like a Princess or an Oracle. Here, I am simply me."

"I see," Jase replied with a warm smile. "Did you see Princess Skyrah before she left?"

"We said our farewells early this morning over breakfast," she replied.

"Do you ever wish you could fight side by side with your sister?" he questioned.

Princess Dalhala's ocean blue eyes soften and grow misty for a moment. "For as long as I could remember. You have no idea how hard it is to watch those you care about fight and die for what they believe when you can't do anything to help them. I am a Princess who can't rule. I am part of a family where everyone is a fighter, yet I cannot be one. As Oracle, I am an outsider among them no matter how hard they try to change that. It is who I am and I have grown to accept that."

"It seems unfair," Jase replied as he took a sit in the dirt next to her as she sat on the stone bench.

"Things that happen that we do not understand, always seems unfair to us. Sometimes what is fair, is not. It is our perspective that makes things fair or unfair to our eyes. While to you it seems that being an oracle is an unfair fate that I have to endure, but for me it is not. It has its challenges, but I am honored to be able to share my wisdom with those around me in hopes to brighten a dull future," the Princess stated with a smile.

"I see your point," Jase replied, swatting away a fly that was buzzing around his head. "Were you talking to yourself before I came over? I don't mean to be rude or put you on the spot. I was just wondering."

"No, I was talking to someone," she told him.

"Who? I didn't see anyone by the time I came by," he said.

Princess Dalhala straightened the wrinkles in her dress, replying, "My sister."

"Skyrah? She's here? I thought—"

"No, Jase Bluestar. My sister, Maliha. She visits me sometimes when I'm not feeling quite myself," she revealed.

Jase was confused by her words. "I don't think I understand," he said.

"I can speak to the dead if they want me to. It is another ability I was born with because of my race. Qualias all are born with different abilities besides our speed and strength which makes us unique from each other. One of my sisters was able to talk to animals just like we are talking and understand them. Another was able to pick up any instrument and create songs that you couldn't comprehend the beauty of. It was magical," Princess Dalhala told him, her eyes sparkling as she thought of the past.

"I understand." Jase turned to her in time to see her blue eyes gloss over revealing dark water under a brooding sky that threatened to burst at any second. It was so captivating that Jase couldn't take his eyes away as everything else around him blurred. Her iris changed into a green murky hue and a shadow figure walked across it. He felt as if he was behind the figure as they walked through a dark landscape towards a small firelight in the distance. Suddenly, vibrations started swarming his eardrum and he tried ignoring them as the figure grew closer to the light. Without a thought, Jase swatted the air around him thinking it was a fly and broke contact with the Princess in doing so.

"Jase? Jase? Can you hear me?" Kaimi buzzed in his earbud.

Disoriented, Jase replied, "Yes, I'm here."

"Where are you? Why didn't you answer me?" she demanded.

Jase looked about the garden, feeling that he had been somewhere else and not here as he turned back to the Princess. She was sitting perfectly still next to him with her face empty of emotion as she stared through him it seemed. It was then Jase realized she was having a vision. "I think I just saw a part of a vision," he told Kaimi.

"What?"

"Princess Dalhala is having a vision and I think somehow I was able to see it without meaning to. It felt as if I was experiencing it myself. It was incredibly strange," he told her watching the Princess.

"Karasi is on his way to you both. What did you see?" she asked.

"I'm not really sure," Jase replied slowly as the memory seemed to be trying to escape him. "It's hard to remember. It feels like I was in the middle of a dream when suddenly I was woken up and now I can't remember it. There was an ocean, I think, with rainclouds and it started raining. Something was murky green. I'm not sure what and I was following someone in darkness."

"Who?" Kaimi questioned.

"I don't know. They were hidden in shadow," Jase told her as Karasi suddenly appeared through the towering flowers.

"How long as she been like this?" Karasi asked, kneeling down in front of her as he studied her face.

"I'm not really sure. A few minutes at least," Jase replied. "How long do they normally last?"

Karasi held the Princess's small hands in his. "Until the vision is through with her. You said you were able to see a part of it?" he questioned.

"Yes, for a moment. It doesn't make much sense," Jase admitted.

Karasi stood up deep in thought. "Interesting. Go on to your studies. She will be fine," he replied.

Jase didn't want to leave her, but knew better than to object. "Will you let me know when she wakes?" he asked.

Karasi nodded before turning his attention back to the Princess.

Jase hesitated for a moment longer before finally turning to leave. When he was out of earshot, he asked Kaimi, "Is it bad that I was able to see a part of her vision?"

"I do not know. Nothing like this has happened before that I am aware of. I don't think the Princess would have allowed you to see it if the stars did not allow it, but then again there is so much we don't know about the Oracle's laws. It could mean that you have a bigger role to play in the shape of the universe than any of us originally thought, but only time will tell," she responded.

With the help of Kaimi, Jase found his way through the garden quickly and continued on towards the main building. Jase entered the library and began reading about the history of Mmerits while Kaimi helped inform him on recent events within the city and its founding. He enjoyed talking to her like they used to while his thoughts kept returning to the vision he saw and the fear of Princess Dalhala getting punished for her actions gnawed away at his stomach.

"I heard you saw part of a vision today," Ziko Ren's voice cut through the air as he stood behind Jase.

Jase turned around from his studies to answer. "Parts and pieces. Nothing to boast about," he replied.

Ziko Ren gave a nod. "Let's begin your evening lesson," he told him and motioned him to follow him out to the combat ring. "You might see a worm and not think much of it, but a bird will see the same thing and think it as a meal. It might not be anything to you, Bluestar, but to someone else it might make sense. The future Queen would want to know of the vision you saw," Ziko Ren stated.

"Yes, Master. I will report to her tonight if she is not busy," he replied, trying to hide his excitement to talk to Skyrah.

"Now, let's begin!"

Jase rolled his sore, sunburnt shoulders as he walked out of the shower into his bedroom. Ziko Ren had them spar longer than normal in hopes to lengthen the time Jase could use his shield while also attacking his master. The lesson left Jase's limbs heavy and sore, but he could tell he was getting stronger for he was able to keep his shield up longer during each lesson. He also had noticed his body was becoming more lean and muscular than before in just the short time he had begun training with Ziko Ren. Quickly getting ready, Jase left his room to use a terminal in the library to call Skyrah.

Entering the library, Jase walked to the back of the room where a terminal was hidden behind a bookshelf and hoped nobody else would bother him as he talked to her. Jase settled down into a chair and pressed a button to turn it on. The screen burst to life giving off a blue glow as Jase ran his fingers over the touchscreen keyboard to contact the Princess. Ziko Ren had told him the code to the terminal she was using while in Mmerits and waited to be patched through. He felt his heart race and his stomach turn to knots as he waited. His hands grew sweaty as he fiddled with them. A minute passed and then another until finally the screen flashed, changing color as the live feed from the other end came into view. Jase felt his breath catch as Princess Skyrah's face appeared on the screen.

She seemed surprised as she hadn't expected him to call her. "Jase, I did not know you'd be calling so late," she said.

Jase quickly apologized. "I would have called sooner, but my lessons grew late and this was the only time I could. I'm sorry if I woke you," he told her, noticing she was wearing a nightgown.

She glanced down to what she was wearing and seemed to blush in embarrassment. Pretending to ignore the fact, she replied sternly, "I was getting ready to go to bed. Normally, it's Moon or Kaimi who calls this late so I did not think to change into something more suitable."

Jase marveled at her beauty, but tried to keep his focus on the reason he was calling her. "Ziko Ren thought it would be best if I told you what happened today with your sister. I—" Before he could finish, Princess Skyrah quickly demanded, "What happened? Is Dalhala alright? What did you do, Bluestar?!"

Jase was surprised by the hardness in her voice as he calmly responded. "I didn't do anything, for one. She had a vision when we were together in the garden and somehow I was able to see a part of it," he told her.

Princess Skyrah didn't say anything for a moment, staring at him as if she was trying to understand what he had said. "What do you mean you saw a part of it? Did she show you?" she asked.

"I'm not sure, honestly. One moment we were talking and then suddenly I couldn't look away from her. It's like everything around me was transformed into a video feed and I was drawn into watching it. It felt as if I was really there," he answered.

Princess Skyrah seemed anxious by his words. "What did you see?" she questioned.

Jase leaned on the side of the table, resting his elbows on its surface. "Nothing really. I remember an ocean with a stormy sky, and then a green murky place with a shadowy figure walking somewhere in the dark. I couldn't really see what else was there, but I could see it as I followed it up a hill towards a torch in the distance. Then Kaimi pulled me out before I could see anything else, but your sister was still having it."

"Is she alright?"

Jase shrugged. "Karasi was taking care of her last I checked and told me he would let me know when her condition changes. Don't worry, I will make sure she is well before you get back," he said. Skyrah sat back in her chair allowing Jase to see more of the room she was in. Her room was painted white with two elegant windows that streamed in maroon moonlight onto the marble floor. He could see a dresser in one corner and a part of her bed that had a flower print pattern on its sheets which amused him. He shifted his vision back to the Princess who appeared to be suddenly exhausted as she stared at something off screen in thought.

Finally, she turned back to him. "Thank you, Jase, for telling me. I appreciate you taking a moment of your night to notify me," she responded.

"Of course, Princess. Will your sister get in trouble with the stars since a I saw a part of the vision?" he asked.

Princess Skyrah sighed. "It's hard to say. Perhaps the stars wanted you to see a part of it for some reason. I'm not sure, Jase. Nothing like this has happened before. At this point there's nothing either of us can do, but wait and see what happens. I know my sister and how strict she takes her duty of being an oracle. I don't think she would allow you to see it on her own, knowing the consequences."

Jase agreed with her. Feeling the end of the conversation drawing near, he changed topics in hope to speak with her longer. "How are the others?"

Skyrah's concerned face softened slightly. "They are well. Tahmela has been flying in and out of the city to transport supplies. We are already getting overwhelmed with our soldiers stationed in a city that was not meant to hold us. We've been experiencing shortages, but with the new shipment from the Azako Plains coming in, we should be fine for the Android's attack. Amosa has been by my side for a good part of her time here. She is very good with keeping the peace with both our army and the city's guards. I don't know what I'd do if she was not here," she told him.

"Give them my best when you next see them if you would," he replied.

She returned the smile. "I will."

Speaking slowly, Jase asked, "And how are you, Princess?"

She took a moment to answer then said in a soft voice, "I am well, Jase. Tired, but good. Lord Poukil is a stubborn man and doesn't like our chances against the Androids in this war which is making it harder to get him to back us. I can understand his reluctance, but it still gives me a headache trying to convince him. I fear by the time I convince him, the Androids will be knocking at our door."

"Would you like me to convince him? I can give him a good beating if you'd like?" he joked.

Skyrah's face brightened. "I will keep you updated if I do. How are you? How goes your training?"

Jase didn't want to tell her that he had failed his first lesson with Sir Agin Rex so instead he said, "It's going well! I have learned quickly and began training with a true master besides Ziko Ren. He knows a lot about Bluestars and is helping me strengthen my abilities with the help of Ziko, of course. By the time you get back, I will be ready to continue on with you and the others."

"I'm glad to hear that, Jase! Who is this new master? Are they within the Resistance?" she asked.

Jase carefully chose his words, replying, "I promised to keep his identity a secret for it is the way of our kind, but you do know him from years before."

"What does Ziko Ren think of this?" she questioned.

"He does not yet know. I planned on telling him but with all the events of the day, it kinda slipped my mind," he told her.

Skyrah watched him closely before saying, "Very well. I will allow you to continue as long as Ziko Ren approves."

"I will tell him first thing in the morning," Jase promised.

She nodded. "It is late and I have much to do tomorrow, as I'm sure you do as well."

Jase looked at the clock on his watch and noticed it was almost one in the morning. "I'm sorry for keeping you up, Princess. It was not my intention," he said.

She smiled at him. "Thank you for calling, Jase. It means a lot to me that you did. Sleep well and let the stars watch over you."

"Goodnight, Skyrah, and let the stars watch over you as well." The video feed ended causing the computer screen to glow blue once more as Jase continued to stare where the Princess had been. He felt his heart singing from talking to her, but as he rose to leave the library, a twang of loneliness settled in. Walking out into the silent courtyard, Jase walked back to his room.

The next morning arrived much quicker than Jase had expected as he jumped out of bed and hurried to get ready for the day. When he arrived to the sparring ring to meet with Ziko Ren, a heavy fog rolled in with no sign of leaving any time soon. He spotted Ziko Ren meditating in the center of it and without a word Jase began his morning routine of stances. Once done, he stated, "I talked to the Princess last night like you said."

"And?"

"She doesn't know what it means either, but told me to let her know as soon as Princess Dalhala's condition changes," he answered. Ziko Ren nodded and stood to assume a fighting stance, but before they could begin, Jase added. "There's something else as well."

Ziko Ren's eyes narrowed. "What is it?"

Jase looked at the light on the horizon as he thought on his words. After a short time, he turned back to speak. "Your lessons have made me stronger physically and mentally with learning how to use my abilities and control them, but your lessons also lack one thing. That being that you aren't a Bluestar and do not know all I need to know in order to truly fulfill my training. I have recently become acquainted with another who can help me in doing so and I would like to finish my training with him. I mean no disrespect towards you, but I believe this is the only way I can truly become a Bluestar," he said.

For a short while Ziko Ren said nothing as he stared at him behind a stern expression. When he did finally speak, his words surprised Jase. "I know who you speak of, Bluestar. You forget I have trained almost all before you and I know things you do not about your own heritage. We will not stop our lessons, but you will be able to further your learning with him. Sparring and your studies will continue with me, but your abilities will continue with Sir Agin Rex," he affirmed.

"Thank you, Master," Jase bowed to him with respect.

"Do not think that I will let up on you, Jase. I will continue to push you through your training and know that If I didn't think you were ready, I wouldn't have allowed this. As you said, you have grown stronger and I know your body can withstand the energy it takes to get to the endless room," Ziko Ren told him. "Now, let's begin our lesson before the day grows any older."

"Yes, Master."

They sparred until the sun was high above the horizon before Ziko Ren excused Jase to go on to his lesson with Sir Agin Rex. Jase excitedly ran through the garden until he was far enough away from everyone that he knew he'd be able to focus without anyone bothering him. Settling down on the dirt ground, Jase closed his eyes and focused on the blue endless room.

"I see you have return, Jase Bluestar," Sir Agin Rex announced as Jase opened his eyes again. "Are you ready to succeed this time in your lesson?"

Jase stood, ready to begin. "Yes, I am," he said.

Hidden Darkness

A week went by and still Jase hadn't gotten any further in his lessons with Sir Agin Rex. After each visit he started feeling defeated and loathed coming to meet the other Bluestar. It wasn't until the second day of September that Jase finally understood the lesson.

"I think I understand why you have me doing this," he exclaimed.

Sir Agin Rex opened his eyes from mediation and cocked an eyebrow. "Yes?"

"You wanted me to familiarize myself with the feelings so I know how to call upon it, right?" Jase asked.

"That is partly true," he replied, standing to his feet. "But not the whole truth."

Jase stood as well. "What do you mean? I've done the same thing for a week and obviously I'm doing something wrong because I—"

Suddenly, Sir Agin Rex hurled a ball of plasma energy towards Jase without warning. Jase quickly brought up his hands to shield himself from the blast and watched as it engulfed around his shield and disappeared. Jase was surprised on how fast he was able to react without thinking about using his abilities and when he looked back to Sir Agin Rex, he saw a wide grin on his face.

"Now, you have learned your lesson and can continue, Jase," Sir Agin Rex declared. "You see, I have taught you how to use them without thinking. They have become a normal part of your body. See it as the air you breathe. You don't have to think about inhaling the air in your lungs, you just do it. That is now what I've done with your abilities. Your body has grown accustomed to feeling them course through it that now you can act upon them without a thought."

Jase felt the sudden realization wash over him and quickly asked, "You said that this lesson takes years to master? I'm guessing I haven't master it fully then."

"You are correct. You have merely scratched the surface, but you have now entered the threshold to continue your training. Before we continue, though, I will say, that you should always mediate for one hour during the day or night in order to strengthen your soul. The more you learn about yourself, the more confident you will be in your abilities," Sir Agin Rex explained to him.

"I will. I promise," Jase agreed.

"Now, let's us move on to your next lesson."

Jase learned for the next six hours that his plasma energy could be used to make several things other than just a shield or a ball of energy. He learned he could create things like bridges or stairs that would disappear as soon as he wanted. He was able to create a wider shield that could protect an entire city, but in doing so left him weak at the knees and panting heavily. Sir Agin Rex showed him how to better his abilities for battle on the ground and in the air. By creating a slide he was able to use it to push his way through the air while also releasing balls of energy down towards Sir Agin Rex. At first it was quite difficult to keep his balance and focus on his target but after a few days of training, Jase was able to do it. "You know, I'm pretty sure I created a slide when I saved Tahmela from falling to his death on Kurath Thor."

"You could of very well. It was how your abilities responded to you falling," Sir Agin Rex agreed.

The next hour they sparred with one another using their abilities so Jase could realize his strengths and weakness as he fought. The hour passed quickly, leaving Jase heaving for breath as he woke in the outside world. The heavy fog had rolled into the garden causing Jase to stumble over roots as he made his way. Breaking through, Jase saw a dark figure walking towards him in the fog.

"Who goes there?" he asked.

"Bluestar, is that you?" Captain Tagen Ouxin replied as he drew closer. "I've been looking for you all afternoon. Princess Dalhala has finally woke up from her feverish dream."

"Where is she?" Jase quickly asked, feeling his heart soar that she was okay.

Captain Ouxin pointed in the fog. "She's been staying in Master Karasi's hut. I can escort you if you'd like," he said.

"Yes, please!" Jase answered and they both took off in a brisk walk.

As they walked, Tagen asked, "Were you really able to see a part of her vision?"

"Yes," Jase replied.

Tagen stared back forward. "The stars have strange ways sometimes. One minute they are telling you not to break the law while at the same time, they break it."

Jase didn't say anything in response as the outline of the hut came into view. He picked up his pace and hurried inside as the Captain waited outside by the door. Upon entering, he found Karasi making hot tea before turning his attention to the Princess who was sitting on the edge of the bed in the back corner. "You're awake," Jase stated out loud as he walked over to her.

Amused by his words, Princess Dalhala replied, "I believe so or this would be quite a strange dream."

"I made hot tea if you want some, Jase," Karasi announced from the kitchen.

"The vision. Will you get in trouble for showing me?" Jase asked Dalhala.

Princess Dalhala pulled the shawl that hung around her shoulders closer to her. "No. I would not have woken if that was the case. The stars wanted you to see that for a reason unknown to me, but we have to trust that they know what they are doing," she replied.

"I don't understand. I could barely see anything," he said as he sat with her.

"I cannot say anything more about it, Jase. You were only allowed to see that one part and that's it. I can't say anything more without breaking my oath to the stars," she told him. Her voice sounded tired and old as she talked.

Jase nodded, understanding.

"I do know that events are changing quickly and the stars are shaping them for a reason. Something dark is coming and I can't see what it is," Princess Dalhala whispered as she stared blankly at the ground.

Before Jase could question her more, Karasi walked over with a cup of tea. "The Princess needs to rest. You can visit her again tomorrow, Bluestar," he said.

"Feel better, Princess," Jase told her and left the hut. *Something dark is coming that she can't see? That can't be good,* he thought as he walked with Tagen to the main building.

Farewell Gifts

The next two weeks went by faster than Jase thought possible as he trained with Sir Agin Rex and Ziko Ren from morning to night. His days were filled with sparring with both masters and soon each day felt like the last. Jase was now strong enough to stay inside the Bluestar Sanctuary for a full twenty-four hours which gave him enough time to learn what he could from the Bluestar. Before he knew it September 21st was upon him and Princess Skyrah was due back. Jase's eyes snapped open as noises from outside in the courtyard echoed through his bedroom. For a moment, he thought of nothing as he stared at the ceiling until finally he decided it was time to get up. It was the first day that Ziko Ren allowed him a rest day and Jase didn't miss the chance to sleep in.

"How did you sleep?" Kaimi's sweet voice asked from the windowsill as usual.

"I forgot how much I miss sleeping in," he told her as he stretched.

"Don't get used to it," she joked. "The Princess should be here within the next hour. You should probably get ready so you can meet her with the others."

"Okay," Jase replied with a yawn and got out of bed. He took his time to enjoy his day off as he got dressed before walking with Kaimi to the dining hall for breakfast. "How long does it take to get to the city?"

"A full two days with Tahmela's ship. If we are lucky, we will leave no later than tonight so everyone will be well rested before the Androids come," Kaimi told him as they entered the room.

Jase grabbed a green apple from the buffet table and walked back out into the courtyard with Kaimi. "It will be nice to see some new scenery for a change," he said.

"Growing tired of the fog and forest life?" Kaimi teased as they walked to the outside door.

"Forest, no, but fog yes," Jase answered as he took a bite of his apple and stepped out into the cool air. Dark rain clouds hung low over the base with fog rolling in from the mountains, thick and heavy, carrying cold winds of summer ending. The red moon was fading which Jase knew was the sign of the Redstar season coming towards its end and the silverstar season would soon be upon them.

He zipped up his pilot's jacket to keep warm as he took another bite of his apple and stared at the clouds. His eyes drifted to the top of the main building and using his ability, he created blue transparent stairs that he led up onto the flat roof. Jase walked up the slippery staircase, balancing himself as he reached the top and let them disappear behind him. Kaimi shook her head and continued towards the field where Karasi, Princess Dalhala, and Captain Ouxin with his squad stood waiting for the Princess to arrive. Jase sat letting his legs dangle over the side of the room as he ate his apple and waited for the Princess to arrive.

Ziko Ren walked out below Jase and in a voice like thunder, shouted, "Bluestar, will you join us or will you remain like a pigeon for the rest of the day?!"

Jase smiled and glided over the blue transparent slippery surface of the slide he created under his feet that carried him over to the group. As he neared, he released his energy and landed on his feet next to them just as Tahmela's ship came into view through the fog. The ship slowly descended, scattering the fog as it did. As soon as it landed and the engines were shut off, the fog engulfed it once more as the ramp was lowered. Princess Skyrah exited with Amosa and Tahmela behind her. Jase gazed at the Princess as she walked towards them. On her side hung a dark blue sheath with a sword decorating it and a red plasma handgun on the opposite side. Her hair was pulled back into a single braid as normal as she walked towards them with the air of authority circling all around her.

"Princess Skyrah, it is a pleasure to see you return to us safely. I hope your trip went as planned," Lieutenant Colonel Moon greeted.

"It did for the most part. The city is well fortified and is ready for the upcoming battle. Lord Poukil has agreed to let us take our positions inside his walls until the Androids arrive. Keep a squadron here to protect my sister and I want everyone else ready to leave within the hour," she ordered.

"Yes, my lady," Moon answered before bowing then left to do as commanded.

Princess Skyrah then turned to Ziko Ren. "Is our Bluestar ready?" she asked.

"As ready as he can be, Your Highness," he answered.

Turning to Jase, she said, "I hope you are, Bluestar. There is no turning back after this."

"I'm ready for whatever happens," Jase replied with confidence..

"Good. Be ready to leave soon then," she told him before ordering Ziko Ren, her sister, and Karasi to follow her as they walked back to the main building with Amosa close behind for protection.

Jase watched her leave, hoping they would have talked more or that she would at least be happy to see him, but her firm composure made it hard to tell. *Maybe she is just stressed out with everything that needs to be done before we leave*, he thought and turned to Tahmela who hadn't moved from his spot since they landed. "Here, I thought you forgot about me with all your new friends!" Jase teased.

"Maybe a moment," Tahmela joked, revealing his square teeth.

"Rurops. Zy heny mochi ta goch oryp," Jase replied in the bulb's native tongue.

"Zy dea! Zy kel e zhev," Tahmela told him.

"Okie."

"U'ma yev presimi iwth onar tvookul, Bluestar," Tahmela praised.

"Thank you! It took a lot of long hours of practice," Jase told him, happy that Tahmela approved.

"It paid off," he agreed.

"When you have a moment. Lieutenant Colonel Moon would like to see you in her office," Kaimi interrupted. "She has something for you."

"Okay then. I'll see you soon, Tahmela," he told the bulb and headed towards the research building. He entered the cold building and walked the maze of hallways until he found the Lieutenant Colonel's office door pushed ajar. "Lieutenant Colonel? Hello?"

"Jase! Excellent, come in!" Moon replied from her desk and waved him in.

"Kaimi said you had something for me?" he indicated.

Moon stood up dressed for war as she placed a small box on her desk and motioned to a large crate near her closet. "Yes, I do. With the help of Karasi and the approval from the future Queen, I made something for you to help you in battle. I do hope you like it."

Jase followed her to the crate which she unlatched and pulled open. Inside was beautifully sculpted silver and blue armor that matched his pilot's jacket. Jase ran his fingers over the smooth surface as he asked in astonishment, "You made this for me?"

Lieutenant Colonel Moon pushed a strand of almond hair out of her face. "It took me a month to make it fit right and still be able to withstand a large amount of damage. The fibers weaved into the armor are some of the strongest elements in the universe, and with some Bluestar dustings melted into it, triples its power. It is very flexible and light to wear while also endurable. With the help of the Bluestar before you, he taught me how to create armor that strengthens and focuses your abilities as you fight. It was made for you, Jase, and only you can wear it."

"It's beautiful," Jase managed to say.

Lieutenant Colonel Moon eyes sparkled. "Well, go ahead and try it on! I've been waiting for an entire month to see it on you!" she exclaimed.

Jase excitedly pulled off his jacket as Moon handed him the armor. He inspected it as he tried to figure out how to put it on. "How do I wear it?"

Lieutenant Colonel Moon pointed to a small button barely visible behind the base of the neck. "Press this and it will open. I designed it so only *your* DNA and my fingerprint can open it."

Jase pressed the button and watched as the spine of the armor unsealed itself like water parting, allowing Jase to slip into it with the help of Moon. It sealed behind and hugged him tightly. It felt like his own skin as he moved around. "This is amazing!" he exclaimed, viewing himself in the mirror hanging on the door.

Lieutenant Colonel Moon beamed, admiring him for a moment then grabbing the gloves from the crate. "Here, put these on," she said.

Jase pulled on the flexible gloves and watched as they melted into his suit. "How would I get them off?" he asked her.

"Kaimi can detached them with the system built into your armor," she answered then moved back to the box and pulled out two more items. "Lastly! I made you these two in case you had a preference." Holding out in her hands, Jase viewed the two items. In her left hand was a silver and blue helmet with a silver visor and in the other was silver tinted goggles. "Both of these can be worn with your armor and are interfaced so you can speak to Kaimi while you fight. They both monitor your life signs and any injuries you may sustain. There is a radar to reveal enemies around you, the weather, temperature, night vision, and they can interpret most languages."

Jase was eager to see what the helmet looked like when worn and grabbed it first to try on. As he pulled it on, he felt it attach to something around his neck before buzzing to life. Everything through the visor had a slight gray tint to it as he looked about the office as different information popped up in the bottom corners of the screen. The radar in the left corner showed a blue dot in front of him as friendly while on the right hand side showed life signs and the temperature outside. He turned his attention to the mirror in front of him and saw a soldier in his place that he didn't recognize. *So this is what it's going to be like. I'm a warrior and I can't turn back now*, he thought. "Thank you, Lieutenant Colonel. I am forever in your debt."

"Just use it well. See how you like these," she replied and handed him the goggles.

Jase pulled off his helmet to hand to her then put on goggles. They immediately allowed him to see more detail in everything around him as they scanned the room. Looking at Moon, it gave him a short summary beside her head of her age, race, and her rank in the Resistance. "Wow! These are really something!" he exclaimed.

"I figured you were more of a goggle guy," Kaimi stated next to him.

"You are right. I do like them both very much, though," he said.

"Both will take getting used to, but in time they can help you tremendously," Moon stated.

Jase turned to her and was unable to stop himself from giving her a hug. He felt her stiffen as he did, but ignored it. "This is by far the best present I've ever received in my life. Thank you," he told her.

Moon warmly smiled at him, her eyes glistening. "Of course, Bluestar."

Jase turned back to admire himself in the mirror. "Do you think the others will like it, Kaimi?" he asked.

"I don't think they will have words," she replied.

"Before you go, Karasi wanted me to give you his gift that he made for you." She grabbed the box on her desk and pulled out a device the length of Jase's hand.

The device was shaped as a silver and black hilt with a fin like ring at the pommel and slender cross guards that reached up around a short barrel that was hollow in the center. It was fairly light in his hand as he examined it, asking, "What is it?"

"It is called a 'Starshifter' which allows the Bluestar to pour his ability within it to fuel it as a weapon. They are very rare and only a select few beings know how to create one in the entire galaxy. Karasi being one of them," she explained.

Jase held it by its hilt and thought of Skyrah's sword as he called upon his energy. There was a crackling noise then a transparent blue blade of energy rose from the barrel of the weapon. The particles hissed and gave the impression that the blade was unstable as Jase admired the brilliant blue blade before him. He felt as if he belonged to it and that it was an old friend. It was oddly comforting.

"If you want I can show you how to use it for long range attacks," Lieutenant Colonel Moon said quietly. Jase was hesitant but released the plasma energy and watched the blade disappear into the barrel as the energy crawled back up his arm. Lieutenant Moon took the weapon from him and gently pulled back the slender cross guard tongs around the pommel while holding the weapon sideways. Placing her index finger in the small fin pommel for a better grip and her thumb on top of one of the cross guards, she showed him what appeared to be a small gun. "It will take getting used to compared to a normal weapon, but it is easy to hold. With practice you will be able to move quickly from sword to gun in a matter of milliseconds. Quick deaths, if you time it right," she told him handing it back.

Jase did as she had and felt awkward at first holding the gun. It would take some time for him to get used to it and switching from sword to gun, but he was eager to try. He pointed the barrel of the gun at one of the empty walls and focused on a single blast. Without a moment to lose, a blue plasma ball of fire shot forth striking the wall before him and charring it black. "Oops!" he said.

"Well, be careful! I don't want my office to go up in flames!" Moon growled as she moved to inspect the charred wall.

Jase quickly turned the weapon back to its normal position as he apologized. "Sorry! It won't happen again!"

"Aye. You have much to practice in a short amount of time, but I know you can do it," she replied softly and handed him a pack to hold his helmet in.

Jase admired his new weapon, thinking of the Bluestars before him as he placed his helmet and goggles into the bag. "Did Sir Agin Rex or the others have weapons like this?" he asked.

"No, they had many different things they used and some used just their hands like Sir Agin Rex. He was an honorable man and didn't like the idea of weapons."

"Why didn't Karasi want to present me with this himself?" Jase asked.

"Ancients don't like being in the spotlight for what they create. Well, most anyways," Kaimi answered.

Checking her watch, Moon said, "The time is close for us to start departing and I have things I need to attend to. I hope your weapons serve you well, Bluestar. Safe travels to the both of you."

"We will see you in Mmerits, Lieutenant Colonel. May the stars watch over you," Jase replied, picking up his jacket as she showed him the way out with Kaimi close behind. Retracing his steps back down the halls, he stated, "I'm going to thank Karasi before we leave. I can't just go without doing so."

"I figured you would. At this time he'd probably be back at his hut," Kaimi replied.

"Then that's where we are going," Jase decided and hurried out of the building and back into the jungle of fog. The dark clouds were even heavier with moisture and threatened to fall at any second as Jase raced to the hut. When he finally reached the small hut, he found the Ancient sitting outside, enjoying the afternoon air. "Are you not worried about the rain?" Jase questioned the Ancient.

Karasi was amused by the question. "Is it going to hurt me?" he responded. He motioned for him to sit next to him. "You look as if you were born to wear that armor," Karasi told him.

Jase placed his pack on the ground next to him as he stared out across the field. "Thank you for my weapon. I never could imagine fighting in a war and now that I'm about to I'm glad I have the means to keep myself alive during it," he said.

"You are a Bluestar, Jase. You have come a far way in a short amount of time and I know you will make us all proud."

"Thank you, Karasi. I will miss you, friend," Jase told him honestly.

"We will see one another again one day. Whether in this life or the next one," he told him with a kind smile.

"Well, let's hope it's this one because I don't plan on dying anytime soon!" They both laughed together for a short time until they saw Princess Skyrah and the others traveling back towards the ship.

Karasi stood and embraced Jase with his thin arms. "May the stars watch over you, Bluestar, and keep you safe."

"May they watch over you as well, dear friend," Jase replied then set off to meet with the others. When he arrived Tahmela had already started up the engines while Princess Skyrah said her goodbyes to her sister and Ziko Ren. Not wanting to interrupt her, Jase turned to his master and shook his hand. "Until I see you in the city, Master. May the stars watch over you."

Ziko Ren shook his hand firmly. "Stay sharp, Bluestar," he said.

"It saddens me to see you go, but I am happy that you will be with my sister, Jase," Princess Dalhala's voice caught his attention.

"I will miss you the most, Princess. I look forward to seeing you again," he responded.

Skyrah gave her sister one last hug. "Goodbye, little sister. Stay safe," she told her.

"Goodbye, Sky."

Not wasting anymore time, both Jase and Skyrah turned back towards the ship and entered for their departure.

Journey to Mmerits

It felt like a lifetime since he was last on the ship and he was surprised how much he felt at home there. As they entered the cockpit, Amosa and Tahmela sat at the controls.

"Are we ready to take off?" Princess Skyrah asked looking to Tahmela in the pilot's chair.

Tahmela pressed several buttons and checked the levels on the small terminal before answering. "Oki, we are," he affirmed.

"Good. Let's be off then before the storm worsens," she replied, settling into the navigation chair behind him and buckling her seat.

Jase slipped into the chair behind Amosa and did the same, resting his pack on his lap as the engine's hum intensified. The engines roared as they ascended into the air, rattling the ship. They continued above the first layer of clouds before Tahmela pulled another level and they shot off northward.

"Will it be like this the entire time?" he asked.

"Not for entire trip," Tahmela answered.

"September is the start of the rainy season. We can count on it to rain a lot during our travels, but I'm hoping it won't get worse than this," Princess Skyrah explained next to him.

"Will there be a lot of fog in Mmerits?" Jase asked as he stared at the droplets that splattered across the windshield.

The Princess shook her head. "Pallue Valley is the only place on the planet that gets the fog because of the mountains that surround the valley. It's harder for the clouds to move past them so they stay trapped inside the area. You should see it in the rainy season, it gets much worse than you have already witnessed. There's a good chance they won't see the sun or sky until the end of spring next year when the rainy season ends."

"It must be terrible," Jase thought out loud as he tried imagining not being able to see the sky or stars for that long.

Amused by his statement, Skyrah replied, "Yes, I suppose for some it is. Many who live in the valley like it especially the farmers and those who don't want to be found. In my case, it works perfectly to hide our army from unwanted eyes. Now if anyone needs me, I will be in my quarters looking over reports."

Jase wanted to talk to her more but held his tongue as he watched her go. Turning back to the others, he stared out of the windshield that was covered in raindrops and dark clouds. He wasn't sure how Tahmela could fly when you could barely see anything, but trusted that he knew what he was doing. "How long will it take to reach Mmerits?"

"Two full days. Unless the storm gets worse where we will be forced to land," Amosa answered.

The ship endured strong turbulence again causing Jase's stomach to lurch as he dug his fingernails into the arms of his chair until the bouncing subsided. A bright flash of lightning passed by the windshield, splashing the room with harsh shadows. "I hope it doesn't get worse," he replied as he sucked in another deep breath of air as another wave of turbulence shook the ship.

"You get used to it, Bluestar," Tahmela stated focused on his controls in front of him.

"I don't think I'll ever get used to this," Jase responded as he noticed his knuckles were turning white from his grip on the armrests. Trying to relax, he asked, "Has anyone heard from the scouts Princess Skyrah sent to Otov Ukoreow? Are the Androids already on their way to us?"

Amosa turned around to face him. "We lost contact with them as soon as they landed on the planet. We expect that they had a run in with the Androids there and no one survived. We don't know for sure," she replied.

"They could still be alive."

"It is unlikely, Bluestar," Amosa stated.

"We can't just give up on them. What if they need our help? We owe it to their families to find out what happened to them," Jase argued.

"I understand your heart, Bluestar, but we have a battle here that is more important than a handful of lives. They knew their chances when they signed up to go. There is nothing more we can do for them now," Amosa calmly replied before turning back to the controls.

Jase ventured down the corridor towards the glass room and touched the panel to open the door. It slid open with a hiss of air, allowing Jase to enter as he opened up the blast doors to see outside. The doors parted revealing large thunder clouds as rain pelted the glass windows. He admired the raging clouds and watched the lightning dance across them for a while longer before turning his gaze downward by his feet to see the landscape. He noticed they had flown lower in the clouds for he could make out most of the landscape from above even through the sheets of rain. They were following a river that emptied into Lone Lake which they would have to cross to get to Mmerits. A heavy forest of dark green hid most of the earth from view. In the distance, he could barely see the lake through the sheets of rain but noticed that at the mouth of the river there stood large dark shadows surrounding the entire valley.

"I should have known you'd be in here to see what you could of the planet," Princess Skyrah suddenly said from behind him.

"Would you like to join me?" he asked hoping she would. She hesitated then nodded and sat next to him. She wrapped her shawl over her shoulders to keep warm as she sat watching the storm. Silence stretched between them which neither seemed to mind as they enjoyed the storm together. Jase watched as the river below emptied into the blue lake and violent waves crashed into one another as the rain poured as they exited the valley.

"Are you ready for the war?" the Princess asked in a whisper so low that Jase almost missed it.

"I believe so, Princess, but at the same time I'm scared. Not scared for my life, but scared to take another's. Or if something happened to the others...or you," he answered truthfully.

Skyrah didn't turn from the window as she stared at the lightning that erupted across the lake. "War is hard, Jase. It is even harder once you're in it and no amount of planning can prepare you for the real thing. Many believe that the Androids aren't like us, that taking their life is not the same as taking another beings life." She turned to him. "The fact that you see it otherwise is refreshing. Yet, it concerns me in how you will do out there. War changes people. Whether they realize it or not, it does."

Jase held her gaze until she finally turned away. "Don't let it change you, Jase. I like who you are too much to see it otherwise," she said softly.

Jase felt a blossom grow inside his chest. Her words felt like flower petals kissing his skin as he forced himself to look back out the window. "I will try my best not to let it, Your Highness," he said.

The next day was long and rough for Jase and everyone on board from the raging storm that didn't let up as they traveled to Mmerits. The constant turbulence caused nausea throughout the crew and the only one who seemed not to be affected by it was Tahmela. He seemed to flourish in the raging storm as he fought for control over the air streams as they flew. It wasn't until the late evening of their second day of the trip when finally the sky calmed and opened up revealing a beautiful orange and pink sky as Mmerits City came into view from the distance.

"That's it? That's Mmerits?" Jase excitedly asked, looking out the observation sphere with Kaimi next to him.

"Yes, that is the capital of the entire planet," Kaimi answered with amusement in her voice.

The city was surrounded by a hundred foot stone wall with four large plasma canons on each corner. A large wharf was attached to the East gate with an even larger hangar bay attached to the far end of the wall to welcome those who traveled into the city. From the center of the city rose a large castle with four towers that were made out of a darker stone and held large pennants with Lord Poukil's colors, a deep purple and gold blossoming flower inside a lion's roaring mouth, along its walls. The castle wasn't as grand as Starwake Castle in Otect city, but it was a beauty in its own way that Jase could appreciate.

"Are we not going to land in the docking bay?" Jase asked as the ship neared the city and he watched the waveships bob in the blue water below as they were docked with small dots scrambling about the docks in every direction.

"No, we are allowed to land in Lord Poukil's private hangar inside the city," Kaimi answered.

Half of the city appeared to be abandoned except near the market place where Jase could see soldiers marching down the streets and a small crowd of people. Barricades were lined along many streets of the city with turrets resting among them as soldiers were stationed to watch over them. He turned his eyes away from the soldiers below and back to the castle as he asked Kaimi, "What is the name of the castle?"

"Loneawake Castle. It's been in Lord Poukil's family for generations since they first crossed over Lone Lake from the eastern lands," she told him. The ship started its descent into a private hangar bay attached to the castle's court-yard as Kaimi stated, "You should head to the cargo hold with the others for departure. I'm sure Lord Poukil will be greeting us when we land."

"What is Lord Poukil like?" Jase asked.

"He's a man who likes his power and now that Princess Skyrah is back doesn't like the idea of giving it up to bow down to her. It's the reason he's been so difficult lately," Kaimi replied.

"But she's the rightful ruler. Why would anyone try to deny her?" he asked as he walked down the corridor towards the cargo hold.

"There will always be power-hungry beings that will try their hardest to continue reaching for power above them. It is the way of politics. No one is truly ever happy with where they stand in the system when they have the ability to reach farther," Kaimi advised.

Jase was about to say more, but stopped when he entered the cargo hold where the other three stood waiting. They were all equipped with weapons. Unlike when she arrived at the base, the Princess wore all black as she met his eyes for a moment before giving Tahmela the go ahead to lower the ramp. As the ramp lowered, Jase could hear a cluster of voices that floated in the air around them as they exited the ship. The hangar bay's roof was slowly starting to close as Jase and his team were greeted by two guards equipped in full gold armor that escorted them out into a stone courtyard. Three beings stood wait-ing. Two of them were garbed in fine clothing while the third wore common clothes as if he was no more than a civilian.

"Princess Skyrah, it's so nice to see you again. How was your flight?" one of the fine garbed beings spoke, his words seemed slimy in the air as they fell from his mouth. He was a bald and lanky man with a scar that stretched from his left brow all the way to his right jawline. He had a sharp hooked nose and a monocle rest on his left eye. His thin cheekbones seemed to sink into his face, giving Jase a distrusting feeling for the man. He wore a black coat, despite the heat, that reached way passed his knees with a dark purple tunic under it with his family's emblem across his chest of a golden lion with a blossoming flower in its mouth.

Princess Skyrah bowed her head in respect. "It was rough, but much better than one would have thought during the rainy season, Lord Poukil. How fared you in getting the city ready while I was away?"

"Well enough," Lord Poukil waved a pale hand, pursing his thin lips.

The man next to him spoke in a voice warm and calm. "I assure you, my Queen, that no one could have done better building defenses than Captain Minko himself. The Androids will have a hard time trying to get through when they arrive." Jase studied the man who appeared to be in his late forties with short white hair and a kempt beard covering his square jaw. He held himself proudly in his common clothes as if he was a nobleman and Jase could tell they would get along.

"I look forward to touring the city later to see the fortifications, Lord Opin," Princess Skyrah replied kindly.

The man bowed then straightened as Lord Poukil asked, "And who is this one that travels with you, Princess? I do not remember him from the last time you were here."

Jase met Lord Poukil's hazel gray eyes as they bore into his as Skyrah announced, "This is Jase Bluestar, the newest addition to our cause. He is the reason I was able to make it back here alive and unharmed. He saved my life more than once on our journey together."

The last being who Jase had yet to notice until now was a chocolate colored bald man with a long braided black beard that stopped in the middle of his chest. He wore an elegant maroon and gold tunic that hung past his knees with a maroon robe that had gold designs throughout it. A gold chain held a large blue jewel hung from his neck as gold bangles and rings covered his arms and fingers. He had a mysterious look to him that caused the hair on the back of Jase's neck stand on end. When he spoke, his voice was rich with a colorful accent that told Jase that he was a planet far away from their solar system.

"A very rare thing to be in the presence of a Bluestar. Very rare indeed but it seems fate has brought us together for a reason, Bluestar," the man de-

416

clared. "They call me by the name and title of Master Jakou Narlie, a humble magician trying to unlock the secrets of the universe, one way or another."

Jase dipped his head in respect for the man, saying, "It is a pleasure to meet you, Master Jakou. I did not know that magicians were still alive in these days. It's a surprise to find one like yourself here with us."

"We disappear when we need to and come back when we choose to. It is our way for many years whether we are a dying breed or a full one," Master Jakou replied with a smile.

"Well, thank you for deciding to help us now," Jase stated.

Lord Opin then politely spoke to Jase as he kneeled, "Lord Bluestar, I am Captain Kenil Opin of the fourth squadron of Mmerit's army, and a humble craftsman. I have served my time and only came back to do so for the protection of my city and family. It will be an honor to serve by your side. Your kind has always done right by us and have given many sacrifices. I pledge myself to always serve by the Resistance and your side as long as you, or Queen Nightstar, lead it. That you have my word."

Jase was taken back and at a loss for words as he stared at the man. He wasn't sure how to respond until he felt Tahmela jab him in the ribs. "Thank you, Lord Opin. I am at a loss for words for such a request and I'm honored by your bravery and dedication for our cause. I look forward to serving at your side on the battlefield," he managed to say.

Lord Opin stood back up and returned next to the others as Jase turned to Lord Poukil who faked a smile towards him. "Yes, Lord Bluestar, it is a pleasure to be in your presence. I did not have the chance to meet your predecessor, but I feel lucky enough to meet you. If there is anything you need or want, feel free to ask myself or anyone who works in my castle. No matter what it may be," he said.

"I shall remember that, Lord Poukil," Jase thanked him insincerely.

"Now, I'm sure you all are tired and hungry from your journey. If you will follow me, I will feed you then give you a quick tour of the castle before you retire for the night." And with a snap of his fingers, they were off towards the castle doors.

Close to a King

They entered a poorly lit foyer with pennants hanging on either side of the walls. Statues of past rulers lined the grand hallway as they walked on a purple rug with gold designs that covered the entire distance to the next room as furniture, plants, and paintings cramped the large room. They walked into a connecting room filled like the grand hall except doors lined the walls along with several spiral staircases that crossed throughout the high ceilings. Thin slit windows allowed only a hair of the late evening light into the halls and casted a warm glow about them. Servants hurried in and out of doors so quietly that Jase hadn't even noticed them until he heard a door close behind him and turned to see a young lady rush to the next room.

"If my servants ever bother you, inform me and I will take care of them personally," Lord Poukil stated glancing back to Jase.

Jase ignored him as they continued into a large dining hall with three large paned windows rising from ceiling to floor on the back wall. Their glass, variations of different hues of reds and purples. The glass cast a rich red glow onto the large stone table that stretched from the window to the door. The room was bare except for the table and a large map of the planet that took up an entire wall on its own. Jase studied it, seeing the cities, villages, and farms marked throughout it. The map was beautifully drawn especially with the years that aged it.

Lord Poukil noticed him staring. "My seventh great-grandfather drew this map when he first came over Lone Lake with his father. He was seventeen. It took him thirty long years to finish for he wanted to travel to each region before

419

drawing it here. He would say it was the only way any map could be accurate. If the being who made it traveled to the place before and spent many years living in the region until they were so well acquainted with the land, they could walk blindfolded and still get to where they needed to go," he said. Lord Poukil stared at the wall for a moment in thought. "Many of my kin thought he was absurd and not fit to rule, but my seventh grandfather was full of wit and very clever. He showed our subjects that he was like them and in doing so they all adored him. It was the only reason he was able to rule as long as he did."

"It is beautiful. He must have been a very patient man to work on it," Jase replied.

"It was the only thing he did worth remembering during his rule. Pathetic, if you ask me. Yet, he saved us a lot of time and money by doing it himself," Lord Poukil replied boredly and moved towards the stone table. Once everyone took their seats at the table, Lord Poukil snapped his fingers and five servants rushed in at once bringing trays of food and refreshments.

"Thank you again, Lord Poukil, for letting the Resistance stay within your walls. I know it hasn't been easy for the extra mouths to feed and the growing tensions between our troops, but thank you for trying your hardest to make this work," Princess Skyrah politely told him as a plate of food was set down in front of her.

Jase eyed Lord Poukil, seeing how he was loving the fact that the Princess was thanking him. He curled his lips into a satisfied smile, replying, "They are our people, Princess, and we can only do what is best for them even when we can't afford it."

"As I promised before, Lord Poukil, the Resistance will reimburse you once we have taken the throne again. I always keep my promises," Skyrah assured him.

Lord Poukil held a goblet of wine to his lips. "The Nightstars have always promised the end of the Androids, only to be defeated time and time again. I'm not against getting rid of Lord Brohain for it is his time to step down from his throne, but I feel as if it's time for new leadership for the Resistance, my Lady."

Jase noticed Amosa tighten the grip on her fork and stabbed a piece of yellow fruit on her plate. His eyes fell on the Princess, who seemed calm as ever. "And you think you could do a better job, Lord Poukil?" Skyrah questioned.

Lord Poukil's expression changed as if he hadn't been thinking about it. "Myself? Hmm, I'm not sure, my Princess, but perhaps with your help I could."

"What are you implying?" Princess Skyrah asked as she cut her food.

Lord Poukil chewed loudly, bobbing his head back and forth as he thought and swallowed before picking up his goblet again. "You are the true ruler of the galaxy, Princess, no denying that. I fear, though, in your absence and how the Great War ended taking most of your family, I think it would be for the best if you allow me to take control of the Resistance. I will follow through with this war while you take a breather. You have done well and fought hard despite your losses. For that I am grateful to be beside you in this. When we win this war, which we will, wed yourself to me and let me help you rule the galaxy as it should be," he answered.

Jase nearly stood in disbelief but forced himself to remain in his seat while he waited for Princess Skyrah to reply. Kaimi said something in his ear, but he paid no attention to it as he stared at Skyrah who still remained expressionless. The room was filled with a tense silence as everyone waited to hear her reply to Lord Poukil's offer.

Finally, she replied, "I will take your request into consideration, Lord Poukil, but for now we must remain focused on the attack that will happen in a matter of days."

"As you wish, my Princess," he replied with a smile.

The rest of the dinner was spent going over plans and defenses of the city. Jase had trouble focusing from his annoyance with Lord Poukil and the fact that Skyrah would even consider marrying the slime ball. On several times during the dinner, Kaimi would remind him to conceal his emotions and listen to what was being said, but no matter how hard he tried Jase couldn't get over the sickening feeling of the Princess marrying Poukil. When dinner started winding down, Lord Poukil announced that his servants would show everyone to their rooms and that they would tour the castle tomorrow morning. He then asked Master Jakou for a private audience and both disappeared out of the room.

"Bluestar, I would like a moment of your time before you turn in for the night," Princess Skyrah exclaimed as they exited into the main hall.

"Of course, Princess," Jase answered. They followed a young maid into an elevator. The elevator took them to the eighth floor where the doors opened to a cool dark hallway.

Stepping out, the maid pointed to two stone doors. "Those are yours, Lord Bluestar, and the other is the bulb's. If you follow me, Your Highness and High Guardian, I will show you to your rooms."

Jase glanced in the direction the woman had pointed then turned back to Skyrah, who said, "Go put your pack down then come see me." Jase nodded and turned down the hallway.

"You like city, Bluestar?" Tahmela asked him, wobbling down the hall.

Jase glanced back watching the other three disappear around a corner as he replied, "Well, I haven't seen much of it yet, but so far it seems nice."

"Very different from Otect," Tahmela pointed out with a toothy grin.

"That's true," Jase agreed.

"U'pon trasti mhi," Tahmela replied.

It took Jase a moment to figure out what he said and who he was talking about until he agreed. "Oni ponither. He just gives me a bad feeling," he replied.

"Oki," Tahmela agreed as they stopped before their doors. "At least, I get own room."

"Well, it helps when you're in the company of me," Jase teased.

Tahmela let out a short laugh before disappearing into his room as Jase pushed open the heavy stone door to his own. He was surprised to find how grand his room was as he stepped in, closing the door behind him. It was a large room with the back wall as a long balcony overlooking the city. A large purple rug with shapes and designs of Lord Poukil's family crest covered most of the stone floor with a large bed set against a wall with two stone nightstands on either side. In the far corner by the balcony was the bathroom while the other corner was set up as a living area with a large comfy sofa and two over-sized chairs. In front of the sofa was a large holo screen against the wall with a small, but wide bookcase under it, filled with many different holo books and smaller statues of animals.

Jase sighed as he unstrapped his pack and laid it across the bed before moving towards the open balcony. He was able to see a military base down below him with several stone houses across the city. "We got a balcony again, Kaimi," he announced to her as he rested his hands across the stone railing.

"Not a bad view," she replied, appearing on his data watch to view the city.

"True, but nothing can beat our setup back home," he said.

Kaimi looked up at him with soft eyes as she smiled. "You are right about that, Jase." Turning back to the city, she said, "All of this will change once the Androids come."

Jase knew she was right as he turned back to the city. Soon it would be in ruins from the fighting and worse if they lost. "Does Lord Poukil and the others who live here not believe in the technology we have to protect against damages? I mean everything here is built in stone which we all know can easily be destroyed. Otect City might not be indestructible, but they suffered less losses of buildings with the materials they used to build the city."

"No, they do but they marry the old with the new. They have highly advanced technology for security and medicine, but they prefer to live the way that many used to live thousands of years ago. To them, it was technology that created the Androids and the sole reason we are in a war in the first place. Besides Otect City, many planets don't have advanced technology like you may think, Jase. The more you visit the more it will become known that some prefer to live without it," Kaimi explained.

"I wouldn't want to live that way," Jase decided.

"There are many who do not know any other way. Here, they are used to traveling on foot or on animals or even across the lake on waveships. Those who can afford to fly in a space ship or buy a skybike are considered outlandish and wealthy."

"Then I must be close to a king," Jase joked causing Kaimi to giggle.

"Who would have ever thought a thief like yourself could become royalty!" she bellowed.

Jase grinned, turning back to the city as he thought about how far he had come since being a poor thief who spent his days stealing in order to eat and daydreamed of flying to other worlds. Now, here he was doing what he thought he'd never do while also going into a war to fight alongside a woman that he loved. Kaimi noticed the thoughtful gaze as she quietly spoke, "You shouldn't keep the Princess waiting any longer."

Jase nodded watching a leaf get carried by the soft breeze before it disappeared into the night sky. He felt calm and still as he gazed up at millions of bright stars above him as he noticed the blood red summer star glowing by the waning crescent moon. Summer was at its end and Jase knew that soon the silver star season would begin, welcoming fall. "Can I ask you something?" he said.

"You know you can."

Jase peered over at her, suddenly anxious about the war as his thoughts turned to how his lost his mother and father in the last one. "You won't leave me in this fight, right? I can't help but have this feeling that something bad is going to happen to us during this war."

Kaimi's face softened, her blue eyes seemed to glisten as she placed a hand on his arm ignoring the fact that it went through like always. "I would never leave you, Jase. I will be by your side until we see it through no matter where it takes us as long as we are together," she replied.

Jase swallowed. "As long as we are together." They both turned back towards the dark horizon to enjoy the peaceful night a few minutes more before they would have to meet with the Princess.

Jase walked down the hallway towards the Princess's room which he found thanks to the guards posted outside her door. They announced his presence to the Princess, who ordered them to let him in. Jase crossed over the threshold into a room that looked much like his own except it was a darker shade of purple and faced the eastern part of the city overlooking the lake.

"You wanted to see me, Princess?" Jase exclaimed as he looked about the room.

Princess Skyrah studied reports on a holo screen with Amosa as they exchanged soft words between each other that he could not hear before Skyrah focused her attention on him. "I wanted to talk to you about dinner tonight. Mostly about your reaction that you hid poorly." Jase was about to defend himself, when Skyrah held up her hand to stop him. "Don't. I do not want to hear your opinions or concerns on the matter. Lord Poukil is a difficult man who has become overzealous with his authority, but while we remain guests in his home, we will not strike him down. His soldiers make up a good portion of my army and I cannot just flat out turn down his proposal. Doing so could insult him enough that he would disband his army from mine and no longer offer support for our cause. We cannot allow that so until then I will take his proposal into consideration."

"You are the future Queen of the Galaxy and a true blood of the royal family! No one has the right to push you into a corner, especially someone like Poukil!" Jase argued.

Silence filled the room as the two stared each other down. "You have a lot to learn about politics, Jase. Trust that I know what I am doing. If you cannot, then do what you are meant to do in my service. Guard me. You may go now," she sternly replied.

Jase forced a bow. "As you wish, Princess." He then showed himself out, cursing under his breath as he walked back to his room.

"The right choice may be easier for you to decide, but she is a leader and can't be selfish if she doesn't want to marry someone like Lord Poukil. She has to think what is best for the Resistance and her future subjects to come," Kaimi informed him.

Jase pushed open his heavy stone door. "If I was her, I would not bend just because someone thought they could manipulate me," he said. "I would put them in their place so they couldn't undermine me again."

"Careful what you say, Jase. Power is a dangerous weapon. It can twist minds that were once good. Do not let your status blind you from what is right," Kaimi warned him.

Jase pulled off his jacket and collapsed into bed, letting out a loud sigh. "I know. She just frustrates me sometimes. If she could see herself like I do then she wouldn't let anyone push her around," he groaned.

"What you want, Jase, cannot come true. The Royal family has always married another royal family. They know what is required to lead," Kaimi said sadly.

"I know, Kaimi. I know," Jase replied with a heavy heart as he closed his eyes to sleep.

A Wonderful Surprise

A loud squawk woke Jase the next morning and he peered over at a large black bird sitting on his balcony railing. Pushing himself out of bed, he yawned and glanced at the time on his data watch. 8:13 A.M. Wiping the crust out of his eyes, he walked onto the balcony, causing the bird to fly away, and stared out at the city. The smell of fresh-baked bread called to him as his stomach rumbled for the taste.

"Do you think the others will mind if I explore the city today?" he asked Kaimi as a cool breeze blew by.

"The Princess might have other plans for you. You should find out before you set out on your own," she replied.

Jase grunted. "I think it'll be fine. If she asks, I'll just say I wanted to familiarize myself with the city."

"She won't be happy," Kaimi warned him.

Jase shrugged, moving back into his room to grab his pilot's jacket and gun holster. "If she wants me to guard her then I need to know the layout of the city. I'm just doing what's expected from me," he said.

"Jase—"

"It'll be fine, Kaimi. Let's enjoy a peaceful day around the city like we used to," Jase replied quickly and stepped outside his bedroom door.

"You just received a message from Captain Kenil Opin. He hopes you will visit him sometime today so you both can get to know one another before battle. He attached his address in the message," Kaimi stated as she read it off to him.

"Tell him I would love to. I'm going to get breakfast and walk around the city some before I head in his direction," Jase told her as he pushed the button and the elevator shot downward. The elevator doors opened and he darted out quickly down the foyer in hopes that no one would notice him. Warm sunlight splashed onto the stone floor as Jase crossed the courtyard towards the castle gates and waited for the guards to open them for him before stepping outside of the castle walls. He glanced back at the gates then turned back around with the sudden feeling of freedom bursting throughout his body.

Jase looked about the street hearing the sound of music not far away. It was a melancholy tune, beautiful yet haunting at the same time as he followed it down an empty street with empty houses clustered around him. The street opened into a city square with a large clock tower in the center where a small band sat playing as people passed them by to venture into the local shops. A middle aged woman added her haunting voice to the tune causing shivers to run down Jase's spine as she sang about her lover who died in the war and how now another war has started and she will lose another. Jase watched for a moment before crossing to the East Market street that would lead him to the docks.

"There's so much space in between houses here than in Otect City," he mused to Kaimi in a low voice.

"Well, they don't have millions of different races squeezed into one city," Kaimi replied.

Jase walked down the cobbled street as a group of soldiers wearing Lord Poukil's colors marched past him. They paid him little attention. He couldn't help but feel on edge around them out of habit from stealing in Otect City, but soon forgot about it as voices up ahead caught his attention. Jase looked down the street to a large crowd of people huddled near vendors. The strong aroma of fresh baked bread filled the air around him as Jase continued forward for the bakery.

"I think there is more people here than in the entire city," Jase stated as he weaved in and out of the crowd of hagglers.

"I'm sure they are probably the last stragglers," Kaimi suggested.

"War makes traders happy," Jase pointed out.

"And thieves as well," Kaimi teased.

Jase grinned as he spotted the bakery at the far end of the market near the east gate. Sticking close to the tight space near the buildings around the market stands, Jase picked his way around the crowd towards the bakery. Nearing it, he noticed the long line of beings waiting for the gates to open to the docks to leave the city. Jase politely pushed past a woman and her four children before climbing up the small set of stairs and entered the bakery which had its door hung wide open for customers.

"It's quite a circus out there!" bellowed a round stout man with pink skin and round cheeks behind a stone counter. His blonde hair was thinning as he wiped flour from his hands onto his apron.

"It is," Jase agreed as he took a look around the small bakery. A large fireplace oven was in the rear of the shop where a young boy of sixteen stood next to a counter kneading dough. He paid little attention to anything else as Jase took in the old bakery that was like none he had seen in Otect City.

"Can I help you with something in particular today, sir?" the baker asked.

Jase looked at the glass containers admiring the colorful cakes. "These are beautiful," he told him.

The baker wiped his hands on his apron again, showering flour specks all over the floor as he rounded the counter to stand next to Jase. "We make them fresh every week. These containers keep them from going bad no matter how long. See the boxes are special technology that keeps the air, temperature, and moisture just right. Quite useful for times like these," he said.

Jase nodded. "I wanted to buy a loaf of your freshly made bread. I could smell it all the way from the castle," he said.

The baker's plump lips spread into a wide grin. "I'm glad you came then! Here, let me get you a loaf that just came out of the oven!" he exclaimed, shuffling over to the young boy and asked for one of the loafs cooling on the counter. "Do you live over by the castle then?"

"Not really. I'm just here visiting for the time being until the war is over," Jase replied, shoving his hands into his pockets as he looked about the store once more.

"Ahh, so you are a soldier, I take it! Are you with Lord Poukil's army or the Resistance?"

Jase cocked an eyebrow. "Are they not the same?" he asked.

The boy handed the loaf wrapped in cloth to the baker. "In some senses they are, but Lord Poukil has been my Lord for many years. So for those who live in the city, the two are quite different. We don't know much of the

Resistance except that they always want a war, it seems. Lord Poukil only wants to keep the peace on our planet."

Jase accepted the bread from the man. "I see your point. I am just here to help keep the Androids from hurting anyone else."

The baker nodded. "As long as there are brave men like yourself keeping the Androids away then I don't care what side you are on, sir. The bread is on me. You are risking your life for us. The least we can do is feed you for it."

Jase thanked him. "Have a good day, sir," he said while walking towards the door.

"You too, soldier. Oh, before you go, what's your name so that I can pray to the stars for your wellbeing," he asked.

Jase stopped before the doorway, glancing back at him. "Jase Bluestar, sir," he said over his shoulder.

Both the baker and boy stiffened as they stared at him with wide eyes. "I'm sorry, Lord Bluestar. I did not mean to talk ill of the Resistance, by any means, or our future queen," the baker quickly apologized.

"You are entitled to your own opinions, friend. Do not worry. Have a wonderful day," he replied and left the shop, disappearing into the crowd before the baker could say anymore. He pushed through the crowd until he spotted a narrow street off to his right and hurried towards it. Once he was out of sight, Jase tore off a piece of soft bread. Chewing it, he asked, "Why do they call me 'Lord'?"

"Bluestars are treated as royalty in most places. Their feats and abilities make them honorable. It's common for beings to treat you with a lot of respect," Kaimi told him.

Jase swallowed another piece of bread. "Why wasn't I treated like this in Otect City?" he asked.

"Because Androids think Bluestars are troublemakers since they always support the Nightstar family. Those who believe that the Androids should rule and continue ruling see Bluestars in the same light."

Jase thought he saw something out of the corner of his eye in the shadows of the street and stopped. Walking over towards a large crate full of trash, he peered behind and found a gray cat crouching. The cat looked up at him with large cyan eyes. Tearing a piece of his loaf, Jase cautiously laid it down a foot away from the cat before he continued down the narrow street. He wandered the streets of Mmerits for half of the day, not really caring where he was going or where he had been as he explored the city and talked to Kaimi. It reminded him of the old days when Kaimi and himself would go exploring for a job, enjoying their time together.

When it finally hit 3:35 in the afternoon, Kaimi asked, "Isn't it time to visit Captain Kenil Opin now? He did want you to see him today, if you could."

"I guess so. Where are we supposed to meet him?" Jase asked stopping in an empty street to look for a street sign.

"I have the address. It's over by the East Market place on the other side of the city," she told him.

Jase grunted. His feet were tired from walking as he angled back eastward. He had just traveled all the way to the west corner of the city just so he could turn back around. "I miss skybikes," he muttered.

"A little walking won't hurt you. At least it's not hot like Otect. It's seventy-two degrees out," Kaimi teased, showing him the coordinates of Kenil's home on his data watch.

"I could just fly over there," he thought out loud.

"I wouldn't. Not everyone here knows that there is a Bluestar among the Resistance once again. I'm sure the Princess and Lord Poukil would want to announce such a thing tonight to all the soldiers and townspeople who are still within the city to boost morale," Kaimi stated.

"I would be careful," Jase replied.

"It's not worth the trouble. Besides if the Princess isn't mad at you for leaving this morning. She will definitely be furious if the city found out about you before it could be announced," Kaimi declared.

Jase followed her directions to the Captain's house. After traveling across the city for two hours, he finally stepped onto the street called Hen's way that led him to Kenil's home. He spotted the two story green brick house that stood out at the end of the street.

After a few minutes the door swung open revealing a beautiful woman who appeared to be in her late forties. She had crow's feet in the corner of her green eyes, but other than that her skin was flawless from age. Her long wavy brown hair was pulled back in a loose bun with strands of hair hanging out. She wore a forest green dress with white birds and a faded periwinkle blue apron. In a silky voice, she asked, "Hello, can I help you?"

Jase smiled at her as he replied. "Hi, Madam. I'm sorry to disturb you, but your husband sent for me to visit before the day was out. I'm Jase Bluestar," Jase greeted.

"Oh, my stars!" the woman quickly replied as she tugged at her dress to straighten it the best she could. "I'm so sorry for how I'm dressed, Lord Bluestar! If I had known you were coming, I would have dressed properly. Please, come in!"

"There is no need to apologize," Jase replied entering the house.

"Thank you for your kindness, my Lord," she replied and showed him down the hallway towards the back of the house. She ushered him back into a large kitchen. Wide windows decorated the back wall where Jase could see a big yard with a workshop in the back with black smoke floating out of a chimney. "The boys are out there in the workshop with their father. Go ahead and go see them while I fix another plate for dinner. You are staying for dinner, right?" she asked him as she grabbed a blue plate from the cupboard.

"If you don't mind, of course," Jase replied.

"Of course not! We would be honored!" she exclaimed.

Jase headed out the wooden door to the backyard. The backyard was filled with flowers and a large garden full of vegetables and fruits. Bird feeders were hung everywhere with all sort of birds flying among them for dinner while others splashed in a small bird bath in the center of the garden. Jase crossed over towards the workshop just as Kenil walked out. His face was contorted in a thoughtful expression as he stared at the grass floor. He was bare chested with a dark gray apron covered in black smut. He was almost upon Jase when he looked up surprised and waved.

"Bluestar! It's good to see you again!" he roared across the yard. "I apologize for how I'm dressed. I had to bring some work home with me, I'm afraid."

Jase shook hands with him, feeling his tight grip as he did. "It's not a problem at all, sir. Thank you for asking me to come. Do you need help with anything? I don't mind getting my hands dirty," he greeted.

Kenil shook his head. "Not this time, but perhaps in the future to come! I hope you will be joining us for dinner. I believe my wife has already started it," he exclaimed. "Here, let me gather up the boys so we can wash and have a proper chat." Before Jase could answer, Kenil shouted back towards the shop for his sons. After a few seconds two boys emerged from inside, both bare chested like their father with smut all over them. "Bluestar, this is my oldest son, Blake, and my youngest, Trenkin."

"Nice to meet you both," Jase replied as he studied each boy. The oldest was about nineteen and looked more like his father than the youngest who was close to eleven. Blake, the oldest, had dark chestnut hair with short bangs that clung to his sweaty forehead as his intense brown eyes studied Jase. He had thick muscles like an ox and a strong jawline like his father's. The youngest boy had curly hair with bushy eyebrows and green emerald eyes.

"Is it true you are a Bluestar and that you can fly?" Trenkin asked.

"The last time I checked I was. It's not really flying but more like gliding," Jase replied with a smile.

"Could you show us?" the boy asked.

Kenil Opin laughed, placing his dirty hands on Trenkin's shoulders. "Perhaps later, Trenkin. Go get cleaned up for dinner before your mother starts to fret. Both of you."

"Yes, Father," both boys responded as they headed towards the house.

"They seem like good boys," Jase told Kenil.

Kenil smiled proudly as they slowly started towards the house. "They are. My wife and I are very proud of them. Blake wants to own his own shop and learn the trade like his old man. I have an old friend that lives in the Azako Plains that is going to let him study under him until he knows enough to be on his own. He'll be moving in the next few months when I no longer need him here to help with the orders Lord Poukil needs done. He's a talented boy. I know he'll do fine out there."

"I wish him the best," Jase replied.

"Master Kenil! Do you want me to put out the fire?" called a voice that Jase thought he recognized.

Kenil turned back, replying, "Oh, yes! Sorry, I forgot to tell you! Thank you—"

Whatever Kenil had said was lost to Jase as he turned around to see the last person he expected to find on this planet. In shock, he blurted, "Roran?!"

The Start of War

Roran's brown hair bounced as he greeted Jase and tackled him to the ground like a school boy. "Jase, how the stars did you find me?!" he asked laughing as they sat in the dirt.

"I had no clue you were here!" Jase responded with a wide grin, noticing that his orphan brother had gotten bigger since the last time he saw him. Jase laughed at the sight. "When did you get all these muscles? What have they been feeding you?!"

Roran flexed his biceps playfully. "Enough. With how Mrs. Opin cooks it's like a feast every night! What are you even doing here? How did you get to Adsila Laabbrirrem?" he exclaimed.

"I'm here with Princess Nightstar and the Resistance," Jase grinned foolishly unable to contain his happiness.

"You?! Yeah right! You must be joking!" Roran exclaimed.

Jase shook his head. "Seriously! You can ask Lord Kenil himself," he urged.

"It's the truth," Kenil answered watching them.

"How and why? What happened to your job on Faton?" Roran questioned in disbelief.

Jase pushed himself to his feet remembering he was Kenil's guest. "I can tell you all about it over dinner if you are interested in knowing, Lord Kenil," he replied.

"We would love to hear it! It's one of the reasons I wanted you to dine with us so I could learn more about you. Let us first bathe and then we can hear all about it. And please call me Kenil, Bluestar," he answered.

It didn't take long for everyone to settle down for the family dinner. Jase recounted his past events since leaving Faton and all that had happened. He did his best to answer any questions that the family or Roran had for him, but made sure not to give anything of importance away. When finally he came to the end of his journey, he felt his throat hoarse and took a drink of water.

"It seems you have gone through a lot in a matter of months, Bluestar," Kenil declared, resting his chin on his fists as he propped his arms up on the table.

"And still have much to do in time to come," Jase agreed.

"That we all do," Kenil agreed, eyeing his wife with a twinkle in his eye. "Dinner was very good, my dear."

Mrs. Opin blushed sitting next to him. "Thank you, honey."

"It was very good. Thank you again for letting me join you for dinner," Jase said thanking them again.

Kenil dipped his head. "It was our pleasure, Jase. You are welcome here anytime."

Jase thanked them again as Kaimi spoke in his ear that the Princess was looking for him. Standing to his feet, he announced, "Well, it is late, and I should head back before it gets any later. It has been a pleasure meeting you all."

"Of course. Roran, can you show him out while the rest of us clean up," Kenil suggested, eyeing Roran who seemed pleased.

Roran stood. "As you wish," he replied.

The two of them headed out the front door and into the streets. They walked in silence, enjoying one another's company. Jase peered up at the night sky filled with stars as they walked in the cool night air.

"So how did you wind up here with Lord Opin? I thought you were supposed to be a servant to a noble Prokleo?" Jase asked.

"I was for two weeks. Then, the Prokleo was sent to jail for thievery against Lord Opin. I was going to go home, but Master Kenil asked if I was still willing to learn a trade. I said yes and he bought my contract. He pays me well, knowing I send half of it to Momma Rose. He has taught me a lot about trading, crafting, complex mathematics, combat, and has furthered my knowledge about a lot of different things. He says it's important to know a lot in order to succeed. He has become like a father to me and has shared his family as such. I would risk my life to keep them safe," Roran told him.

Jase met his gaze for a moment then turned to stare at the dark shapes of houses on either side of them. "I'm happy for you, Roran. You've done more than I thought you'd do becoming a servant. Now I know it was the best thing you could have done. I'm proud of you, brother," he said.

"I would have never guessed you'd stop stealing! Or that you'd actually someone of great importance now. You are an actual Bluestar! I mean, I know you have always been, but you have abilities now that I could never dream of! And you travel with the Royal family! It's amazing!" Roran admitted.

Jase couldn't help but smile as he thought about the days they spent together in Otect City. They both had come a long way since then. "A lot has changed in a handful of months," he replied.

"No kidding," Roran agreed, staring off in the distance. They both fell silent listening to the soft breeze travel down the street towards them as somewhere in the distance an owl hooted. "I love it here. You should see the city when everyone is here. At night, it's full of laughter and music plays on every street. They have a festival for the changing of seasons where they hang lanterns of different shapes and colors. There's dancing and feasts. Everyone comes together to welcome the new season and to thank the stars for the past one. It's a glorious time. You will have to come back when the seasons change to experience it. You'd love it!"

"You won't return to Otect City, will you?" Jase asked though it was more of a statement.

Roran seemed at peace, staring back ahead where the castle windows were lit. "No, this is my home now. I've already talked to Mrs. Rose about it on many occasions, and she has given me her blessing," he replied.

"You've talked to her, recently?" Jase asked, feeling a sharp pain in his heart from missing her.

Roran nodded. "When Kenil gives me a day off, I go to the GalaSTcom to talk to her and the children. I saved all my money to buy her one so she didn't have to go inside the city to use the local GalaSTcom. I'm hoping to be able to fly them all here at some point to see the planet and to meet Kenil and his family."

"How is she?" Jase asked through a lump in his throat.

"She and the kids are doing well. They miss you and ask if I have seen you every time we talk. Lynn is getting married at the end of this year. Her fiancé has been helping to rebuild the orphanage with that one guy. You dated his sister, Camila? What's his name?"

"Othen. He helped me and the Princess escape the city," Jase replied. "Lynn is getting married? When did this happen, and who is the guy?"

Roran smirked. "Apparently, they have been a thing for a while. Since they went to medical school together. His name is Darry Oaklens. He seems like a nice guy from what Mrs. Rose tells me. She really likes him."

Jase shook his head in disbelief at the thought of how much had changed since he had been gone.

"It shocked me as well," Roran answered.

Jase ran his hand up the backside of his head. "Should we go rough him up like brothers ought to do?" he joked.

"Maybe!" Roran let out a laugh.

Kaimi's voice suddenly stated in Jase's ear, "I would like to say hello to Roran before you part."

"I'm so sorry, Kaimi!" Jase apologized, forgetting her in all the excitement as he leveled out his arm for her to appear.

Roran smacked Jase on his opposite arm. "Did this knucklehead forget about you? Let me teach him a lesson for ya, Kaimi!"

Kaimi smiled, lighting the darkness that surrounded them. "It's good to see you, Roran! I wanted you both to have some time alone before I said anything. How are you?" she greeted.

"I'm doing quite well! How are you? Keeping this one out of trouble, I hope," he remarked.

"Trying to for the most part," she teased.

"I'm so happy that the two of you are still together," Roran said.

"I would see it no other way," Kaimi replied. "When the Androids come, will you leave with Kenil's family?"

Roran's face grew serious. "I aim to fight alongside Master Kenil. The family is staying," he said.

"You can't be serious, Roran. You aren't a soldier!" Jase argued.

"You could die too, Jase, but that doesn't stop you. Master Kenil taught me, so it's not like I'm useless. I can handle my own," Roran countered.

438

"Have you fought Androids? It's entirely different than fighting a human," Jase explained.

"I'm sorry, Jase, but I've already made up my mind. I'm fighting and that's that. It's growing late and I should get back to the house. I'm happy to see you again, brother. Stay safe and goodnight to both of you," he said reaching out to Jase.

Jase hugged him, trying to rid himself of all the possibilities of the near future. "Goodnight, Roran. Stay safe as well." Then Jase watched him return down the dark street alone as he traveled home. He continued to watch until he was out of sight before turning around to head towards the town's square only a short distance ahead of him.

"I know you are worried about him, but he is a grown man. He can take care of himself. Believe that he will be fine and rest your worries," Kaimi persuaded him.

Jase let out a tired sigh crossing the town's square as he glanced at the clock. "I know he can. I just don't want anything to happen to him," he responded.

He crossed over to the main gate of the castle where he waited for the guards to approve his entry from Lord Poukil. After a few minutes, they let him pass and he was greeted by Amosa who escorted him to Skyrah's room. Fifteen minutes later, he was standing before her getting yelled at for disappearing for most the day.

"Where have you been?! I needed you here to meet the nobles that run the city before all the stars break loose! We also were supposed to announce your presence to the entire army to boost morale!" Princess Skyrah lectured. "You are supposed to be by my side! Besides, I have more influential control when you are with me than I do by myself!"

"Breathe, Your Highness," Amosa softly reminded.

Skyrah shot her a glance, but took a long deep breath and let it out. In a calmer voice, she asked, "Where were you, Jase?"

Jase held his hands behind his back. "I was studying the layout of the city before the war starts. While I was out, Lord Opin invited me to join his house for dinner which I did. It was splendid. I also found out that my orphan brother, Roran, lives among them so we caught up. I admit I stayed longer than I should have, but I figured it would help strengthen our bond with Lord Kenil for our cause and I wanted to spend as much time as I could with my brother. He is fighting in the upcoming battle as well and who knows if we will see one another again. I'm sorry, Princess, for not telling you. I'm still getting used to my title. I will try my best to never let it happen again," he told her.

"Very well, Bluestar. You did a smart thing to learn as much as you could about the city and to help our alliance with Lord Opin. That is more important than meeting people you don't really need to meet," Skyrah surmised. She turned to Amosa. "Go get some rest, Amosa. You have done enough for the day."

Amosa hesitated. "As you wish, Princess," she said reluctantly.

When she left the room, Princess Skyrah walked to the balcony and Jase followed unsure of why she wanted Amosa to leave. They both stood by the railing, looking out across the lake where dark clouds poured rain over its calm waters. Guessing by which way the wind was blowing, Jase figured the rain clouds would be over them soon as lighting struck in the distance. He watched the storm rage on as his thoughts returned to Roran fighting and Lynn getting married.

"What is it?" Skyrah suddenly asked.

"Huh?" Jase turned to her.

"You look like you are troubled by something?" she replied.

"Oh, it's nothing," Jase said and peered back across the water. "Roran's twin sister is getting married at the end of the year. I've never met the guy, but apparently, he's a keeper. Mrs. Rose must be thrilled. See, she's always telling us we need to get married and have kids before she dies. Roran looks so different from the last time I saw him. He's a grown man and not that kid brother I used to know back home. He says he loves it here and that Mrs. Rose has given her blessing to him to stay."

Princess Skyrah studied him. "So what's wrong?" she asked.

"I don't know. Nothing really. It's just weird how much changes when you're gone for a while," he replied to her.

"Time never stops for anyone. Whether you stay in one place or travel to many, the seasons always pass us," Skyrah told him softly.

"That's true," Jase replied, peering over to her again.

"I'm picking up a strange interference in the air," Kaimi suddenly said.

"What kind?" Skyrah asked causing Jase to realize she had said it to both of them.

Kaimi was quiet for a moment. "I'm trying to locate it, hold on."

Another flash of lightning danced across the sky closer to the castle. Another bolt streaked across above them and Jase was about to say they should head back in when he suddenly saw something above the lake. He focused on the spot but after a moment he didn't see anything and turned to the Princess to suggest that they should go inside.

"Androids!" Kaimi shouted.

Jase saw movement over the lake and just as he turned to see what it was, a loud blast shook the castle tower causing it to tumble towards the ground. The explosion sent Jase backwards into the railing, slamming his head into the stone as he pushed Skyrah into the room. The tower started leaning over as Jase's vision went black.

A Raging Battle

A loose brick fell next to Jase as he slowly came to. As he tried to push himself up, he felt a pinch of pain in his lower back causing his head to spin as he pulled himself up by the railing. Jase looked over the railing and found they were still in the air, but the tower had collided with the one next to it. Looking out across the lake, Jase saw two metallic spaceships flying Lord Brohain's colors, dark gray and blood red.

"Jase? Are you alright?" Skyrah asked as she held onto the bed frame to keep herself up right.

"I'm alright. Are you?" Jase asked as he turned back to her, noticing the gash on the side of her head.

"Yes," she replied.

The ships separated, one towards the west gate while the other flew towards the south. "They are landing!" he called back to her and heard her on her com speaking with Amosa. He looked at the tower knowing he had to get his armor before he did anything else but going on foot would take too long to reach his room.

"Jase, we have to get the gates ready to withstand them!" shouted Skyrah as more bricks fell.

Jase glanced back at the tower then checked to see how far it was to the ground. "Go ahead! I have to get my armor!" he yelled.

"The tower won't go anywhere as long as nothing hits it again," Kaimi assured him.

443

Jase nodded and climbed onto the railing. Turning back so he could face the Princess, he shouted over the roaring of Lord Poukil's plasma cannons firing on the ships. "I'll see you down there!"

Jase felt his plasma energy course down his arms into his hands as he glided towards his balcony. He crossed over the railing and released the energy. He grabbed his pack next to the bed, clawing for his armor inside it. Quickly putting it on, Jase pulled on his helmet and attached his googles to his belt before running out onto the balcony. He leapt onto the railing with one foot and jumped into the air before catching himself with his plasma slide and glided towards the city below. His visor showed him the distance the Androids were already taking from breaking into the city through a small gap in the west gate. Yellow shapes showed up on the streets, showing him how many Resistance soldiers were fighting to hold them back. Explosions already rang throughout the air as Jase angled his body towards the fight and hurried to join.

Nearing the soldiers, he cut off the flow of energy through his body and landed on the hard ground with a thud. Jase grabbed his starshifter and held it like a gun, charging it until it was a large ball of energy and fired it upon the seven-foot Androids rushing into the gap. The blast went straight through the chest of two Androids, knocking a third backwards into more. Without a moment to lose, Jase created a large shield over the hole.

"Quickly! Find something to cover the hole!" he ordered the soldiers behind him.

Six soldiers quickly hauled a metal plate normally used as a barricade over into the gap and drilled it in place. Once it was secured, Jase released the shield and turned to the soldiers behind him garbed in heavy dark armor with light blue helmets covering their faces. The Resistance flag was painted across their chests in a light blue paint of a star in the center and six birds flying diagonally across it. Lightning flashed across the sky casting harsh shadows in the street as thunder and explosions drowned out the sound of the rain that suddenly poured down on them.

"We can't let them take the city! Move those barriers closer together across the street! I want ten of you positioned behind them! You five, go to the top floor of these houses and fire from the windows! You five, do the same on the opposite side! Now, go!" Jase ordered. He surveyed the street and noticed stairs that ran along the wall of the city. Running towards them, he took them two at a time and reached the top where soldiers wearing Lord Poukil's colors stood guard. Jase's stomach dropped as he viewed the thousands of Androids marching towards the gate. "Kaimi, order the turrets to fire upon the Androids. The ships are less of our problem now that they have landed."

Jase watched as the turrets changed their direction and fired large blasts of red plasma towards the Androids. Clouds of dirt flew up as the blasts scorched the earth, sending Androids scattered across the fields. Still they charged, their glowing red eyes in the darkness gave Jase chills up his spine.

"They are climbing the walls! They are climbing the walls, Bluestar!" shouted a soldier as he opened fire on them.

Jase looked over just in time to see a glowing set of red eyes rush towards him with inhuman speed. It looked like a giant metal spider crawling up the wall as Jase reached for his weapon. Suddenly the gates exploded open causing the whole wall to vibrate while debris flew backwards into soldiers. The flash was blinding and just as Jase's vision started coming back, a set of glowing red eyes were in front of him. The Android slammed its fist into his helmet with such force that Jase flew backwards into a nearby house, breaking through its roof.

"Jase! Are you okay?!" Kaimi asked from inside his helmet.

Jase pushed himself off the broken roof tiles as he took deep breathes. Luckily, his armor took most of the impact. "I'm okay. Remind me to thank Moon for the suit again."

Jase used his plasma energy to glide back towards the Android on the wall as rain pelted his visor. "Let's see how you like it," he yelled and with one powerful punch, slammed the Android in the chest, collapsing it inward. The Android fell backwards off the wall and crashed into another on the ground below. Jase pulled out his starshifter and plasma handgun and opened fire on the Androids that had climbed the wall. Androids flowed through the gate like water as he glided back down to hold the line. Using both is plasma guns, he fired upon them, killing them one after the other before they could get close. After too many had gotten through, he switched to his starshifter blade and cut down any Android that neared him as the soldiers behind him kept firing. One after another they fell as he listened to the hiss of the blue plasma energy cut through the rain and the metal bodies. It seemed for every Android he slew another took its place and soon his arms were growing heavy from fighting.

A sound of metal grinding metal caused Jase to focus on the gate as the street under him vibrated. He saw a large sphere tank roll through the crumbled gate. Using the com through Jase's helmet, Kaimi projected her voice so the soldiers around her could hear. "Everyone take cover!" she shouted.

Jase jumped behind a piece of metal barrier just as the sphere started glowing a bright cherry. A second later a loud boom echoed through the street and a wave of hot air rushed past him. The houses around him crumbled causing Jase to roll just in time to miss the crumbling stone. As he stood to his feet, he saw that the houses near the gate were now a pile of rubble as more Androids poured into the city.

"I'm reading no survivors," Kaimi informed him.

Jase felt his heart drop as he noticed the scorched corpses of the Resistance soldiers scattered in the debris. Anger welled up inside him as the sphere tank move forward. Jase pushed himself forward with plasma energy and leapt to attack from the air. He sliced horizontally, cutting an Android in two while he pushed a ball of energy into two more surrounding the tank. He then sliced through another who tried hitting him with their fists but Jase ducked in time before bringing his blade into its stomach. Black oil oozed out of the Android's wound and covered Jase's hands as it fell to the street floor.

"Jase! Shield!" shouted someone from behind him and Jase turned to see Captain Tagen and a large group of soldiers behind him.

Jase created a shield around his body as the soldiers threw plasma grenades towards the tank. The tank exploded sending pieces into houses and bouncing off his shield. A black smoke covered Jase's visor making it hard to see through the pouring rain. Flashes of lightning lit up the city like fireworks.

"Jase!"

Jase turned around to see Tagen moving towards him.

"Get that hole covered! Set up our perimeter!" Tagen ordered his platoon as he stopped before Jase. He pressed a button on his helmet and it quickly folded into a visor over his forehead. "Are you alright?"

Jase watched the soldiers hurry by him to cover the hole, finding it hard to concentrate. "Yeah, I'm fine. Thanks for coming when you did. Any longer and I'm afraid they would have overwhelmed me," he said.

"You would have been fine. Captain Minko rallied our sky fighters and Lieutenant Colonel Moon attacked full force outside the gate with our ground force. That gives us enough time to patch up this hole," Tagen told him as raindrops dripped from his visor.

"What of the Princess and Ziko Ren?" Jase asked, suddenly worried that he wasn't with them.

Tagen kept his focus on the gate getting repaired. "Your Master, I'm not sure, but the Princess was defending the south gate last I heard."

Jase nodded. "And Lord Poukil?"

Tagen shrugged. "I don't think anyone has seen him since the fight broke out."

Flashes of light exploded outside the gate causing the ground to shake violently below them. Jase glanced towards the gate, knowing they were far from the battle being over. "Shall we join them?" he shouted.

Tagen touched the side of his visor and it unfolded, covering his face again with a helmet. "We'll deal with these guys. You should go find the Princess and keep her safe," he answered.

Jase nodded. "Stay safe."

"Stay alive," Tagen replied before issuing orders to his men again.

Jase forced himself into the air using his plasma energy. As he glided, Kaimi said sternly, "You should save your energy as much as possible, Jase. It won't do anyone good if you tire yourself out before this is over."

Rain pelted his body as lightning flashed through the sky, painting the city in harsh shadows. Explosions discharged here and there and plasma firefight lit up the streets all throughout the city. "Running will take as much energy as it does to glide. Besides, it would take longer," he told her.

"You could get yourself killed if you push yourself too hard," Kaimi argued.

Jase was about to respond when yellow figures came into view as Resistance soldiers fighting by the south gate. Androids were trying to advance towards the group, but so far the Resistance was holding them back. Jase angled towards the soldiers and tried landing on his feet, but went down on one knee, banging it as he did. He clenched his teeth and pushed off to stand. Pulling out his handgun, he opened fire on the Androids as he neared the barricade that Princess Skyrah and Amosa were taking cover at.

"West gate is secure!" he shouted over the noise of plasma blasts.

Princess Skyrah gave a short nod in response as she fired at a nearby Android. Three plasma arrows fired past her into three different Androids, one piercing through into another Android behind it as Jase glanced at Amosa who looked fierce as ever.

"I have an idea," Kaimi suddenly stated inside Jase's helmet.

Ducking from a blast, Jase hid behind the barricade to catch his breath. "What?"

"Get me to a terminal! Quick!" she ordered.

Jase looked over at the house he was next to and took a breath. With all his might, he jumped up releasing a few blasts before darting into the dark house. "Panels work?" he asked as he fumbled in the dark to find a light switch panel.

"Yes! And stay away from the gates until I say!" Kaimi responded.

Jase found a panel by the door and touched it so Kaimi could transfer. Wasting no time, Jase returned back to the fighting and yelled to his fellow soldiers, "Stay away from the gates!"

A bright white surge erupted across the south gate and bounced off into a nearby Android which then traveled to another one and then another. The surge struck thirty Androids, killing them instantly before bouncing off into a nearby house and setting it aflame before the rain put it out. Jase watched as all the Androids crashed to the floor at once, a loud metal thud echoed down the street as Princess Skyrah shouted, "Forward!"

Everyone rushed forward to stop anymore Androids from rushing the gate while red bolts passed by them from the other side. Jase dove behind a large chunk of stone that had crumbled from a nearby house in time to escape a bolt that was hurled his way. The bolt struck in front of the stone, charring it and Jase stood to release a few shots of his own towards the shooter. Lightning crackled in the air again, casting harsh shadows which gave the Androids an eerie appearance as Jase killed another. Suddenly, a red plasma grenade landed in front of him. Without thinking, Jase brought up a shield around him just as the grenade went off, sending flames over his shield and blinding him for a moment. As soon as the blast weakened, he lowered his shield but as he did, a large blast collided into his chest, throwing him backwards several feet.

"Jase!" he heard Princess Skyrah cry out as he hit the wall and fell forward onto his stomach.

Jase's ears rang as he tried focusing his gaze but could only see black and red dots before him. He squeezed his eyes tightly in hopes to stop the dizziness and nausea that swept over his body. After what seemed like forever, the symptoms passed and he was able to open his eyes without being sick. A warning flashed along his visor, telling him that two of his ribs were broken. Jase ignored the pain that clawed at his sides as he forced himself up to all fours. He staggered on his shaky feet, feeling disoriented as he steadied himself with one hand on the wall behind him and looked to where Skyrah had been standing. She was surrounded by five Androids as she fought them off with her sword while Amosa fought back her own enemies before her.

Jase shifted his eyes towards the gate to figure out what hit him. There, walking towards him, was the maroon haired soldier from the fuel station and Bentley's Warehouse. He wore black armor with one glove on his left hand and a silver hilted sword in a black scabbard attached to his back. He held a plasma pistol in his hand aimed towards Jase as a sly smile crossed his face. Jase's visor scanned the man's body, revealing that the left arm from the elbow down was a metal frame while everything else appeared to be human. This realization caused Jase to feel uneasy as he thought, *Why would a human help Lord Brohain?*

Jase ran towards the man hoping his inhuman speed would surprise him. As he got close, he pulled back his fist. Bringing it forward with all his might, Jase suddenly felt his fist stop in midair. Shocked and confused, he looked and saw that the man was holding it.

"Didn't expect that, huh?" the soldier said in an nonchalant tone then let loose a bolt towards Jase's chest again, shooting him backwards several feet into another Android.

The blast wasn't as strong as it was the first time allowing Jase's armor to take most of the impact as he landed. He quickly blasted the Android's face, killing it before struggling to his feet once more. He noticed the man wasn't paying attention to him anymore as he headed towards the Princess. He looked bored as he fiddled with his gun shooting any of the Resistance when they'd charge him with just a flick of his wrist. The sight outraged Jase as he unattached his damaged helmet. Rain splattered on his face and soaked his hair as he pulled on his googles. His googles blinked on and adjusted to the low lit street, allowing Jase to see everything around him in fine detail. Focusing all of his energy to fuel his body, Jase charged after the soldier as fast as he could. The soldier took notice and seemed to like the idea as he too took off running, matching his speed to meet him head on. His speed surprised Jase as they collided with each fist slamming into the other's face. The force shot both men backwards across the street.

Jase's jaw ached, hurting even more when he clenched his teeth together. He watched the other soldier across from him who appeared to be in no pain. His reddish golden orange eyes pierced Jase's, reminding him of fire burning. Remembering his training, Jase concentrated in trying to figure out the man's fighting stance and how he would attack next, but no matter how hard he tried, it seemed as if the man didn't have one as he stood there.

A loud blast from a tank scorched the side of a building next to them, sending a shower of sparks across the street in the rain. Using the distraction, Jase darted forward creating a slide to glide around the man in a quick fluid movement to attack from behind. Kicking him in the back, the man stumbled forward catching himself on his palms before swinging his leg in the air to knock Jase down. Jase fell backwards, but quickly caught himself by creating a shield to bounce off of and swung his body around to strike again. But just as he turned back around, the man was gone. Jase scanned the area for any hint of where he was, but couldn't find him. He glanced towards Skyrah who had just finished slaying the last of the Androids around her. It was then when he noticed that Lord Kenil, Roran, and Ziko Ren, along with more soldiers, had arrived to help hold the gate as they opened fire on the hundreds of Androids that were still spilling into the city.

Jase faced Skyrah who hurried towards him. He cut off the flow of energy and landed on the street when suddenly a boot slammed into his face as he heard a plasma blast hiss through the air and Skyrah screamed. Jase wasn't sure what had happened as he felt throbbing pain throughout the back of his head. Needles seemed to stab at his brain. He felt the cool touch of raindrops bounce off his cheeks, but couldn't see or hear anything except the ramming of his heartbeat in his eardrums. His body tingled as he laid there on the hard, wet street. Suddenly, he heard charging inches above his face as heat blew down on him. The soldier stood above him aiming the glow of his pistol that casted a dark red shadow across his face giving him a sinister look despite his expression of disappointment.

Jase quickly shoved a wave of energy upward into the man's hand causing the gun to shoot into the night sky. He pushed himself backwards, rolling to his feet and pulled out his starshifter holding it inches away from the man's neck. The man had already reacted by charging his weapon again and aimed at Jase, locking them into a draw.

"Shall we see whose quicker?" the man asked with a grin.

"Why are you helping the Androids?" Jase thundered.

The man's expression changed into annoyance as he answered, "Perhaps they are the winning team."

"But you're human. Why would they—"

The man interrupted him. "Who said I was human, Bluestar?"

The man smirked and before he could say more, Skyrah held her gun to his head, "Don't move or I'll blow your head off," she ordered.

With his gaze still on Jase's, he replied, "Interesting." He then dissipated the charge before lowering his weapon with a shrug. "One man's loss is another man's victory."

Skyrah kept her gun aimed at him as she took his, allowing two soldiers to quickly grab hold of him. They placed plasma handcuffs over his hands and escorted him away towards Ziko Ren. She then turned to Jase. "Are you alright?" she asked.

"I'll live. You?" he said, cutting the flow of energy to his starshifter and noticed that there wasn't any more Androids storming the gate.

"I'll be fine," she grimaced in pain as she placed a hand over her charred side where she had been shot.

Lord Kenil and Roran hurried over to them, accompanied by Amosa, and Tahmela. "Princess, are you alright?" Kenil asked.

"I'm fine, Lord Kenil. Did you protect the east gates?"

"It's secure, my Princess. Lieutenant Colonel Moon and Captain Minko have destroyed many of the enemy ships outside the city. Leaving only a few hundred androids still within our walls that we can easily over take," he replied.

"We have won the battle, Your Highness," Roran chirped in, drenched in rain and oil.

"The battle isn't over until we have rid the city of the remaining Androids," Princess Skyrah replied dryly.

"Princess, you need medical attention. Please come with me so I can escort you back to the castle," Amosa firmly stated.

451

"I am fine," she protested.

Ziko Ren walked over to them, addressing the Princess. "You should go recover while you have the chance, Princess. The rest of us will search the city for hostages," he assured her.

"If anything goes wrong, report to me as soon as possible. I want to know our casualties by first light," she commanded Ziko Ren and Lord Kenil.

"I will escort you and our prisoner to the castle. Lord Kenil in the meantime will take his platoon and search the city for Androids," Ziko Ren declared and motioned for Amosa and twenty other soldiers to go with them.

Ziko Ren and the others started down the street as Jase turned to Roran. "You okay?" he asked.

"A few scrapes and bruises that's all. How are you? Your jaw looks a little swollen," Roran replied, wiping rain off his brow.

Jase tried to smile, but grimaced from the pain. "I think I broke it or something," he muttered.

"Looks like it. Kaimi, okay?"

Jase nodded. "I think so. She's somewhere in the city, traveling through the system to defend."

"Roran!" Kenil shouted yards away.

"I should go. I'll find you later. Stay safe!"

Jase took a deep breath and let it out. He looked around the street in ruins with Android and human bodies littering it. Some of the houses were in better shape than others, but most were in piles of stone and dust and he imagined that the rest of the city was much the same if not worst.

"Jase."

He turned to find the Princess standing next to him with Amosa and Tahmela a few feet away, keeping guard. Her expression was mixed with weariness and shock. "Congrats on your victory, Princess," he told her.

She too had been viewing the city, but now turned to him. "Our victory, Jase. We did it together," she said softly.

Jase gazed at the dead bodies around him. "It doesn't feel like a victory."

She placed a hand on his shoulder. "It never does. Stay strong, Bluestar. This won't be the last you'll see of it."

"We should go, Princess," Amosa insisted.

She nodded and looked back at Jase. "Let's go."

Jase walked over to where he had dropped his helmet and grabbed it off the stained street. He closed his eyes, feeling exhaustion pour down his limbs like the rain pouring off his body. He turned to follow the others back towards the castle.

To Learn the Truth

Jase didn't realize how late it was until they reached the town's square and a bright pink light glowed on the horizon. The rain had stopped, parting the clouds and leaving behind a chilly morning to greet them.

"Princess Skyrah?" he said.

"Mhm?"

"If you need me, I will be in there sleeping," he told her, too tired to think clearly as he motioned to the nearest house.

She followed his gaze and nodded. "I'll send for you when we need you again," she said and continued on towards the castle with Amosa and Ziko Ren while Tahmela stayed behind.

Jase looked over at the bulb. "I guard you while you sleep," Tahmela explained.

Jase nodded then set off towards the house in sluggish movements. He entered the dark one story home and fumbled through the living room as Tahmela stayed guard outside the door. It only took Jase a moment to find another door at the back of the room which he opened, hoping it was a bedroom. Opening the door, he saw with the help of a small window on the far side that he had indeed found the master bedroom and stumbled towards the king-sized bed. He didn't bother to take his armor off as he collapsed onto the firm bed. Not a second later, he was fast asleep with dreams of war raging on inside him.

Jase awoke to a static sound inside his ear and the sudden voice of Kaimi asking, "Jase, are you alright?"

"I'm alive. And you?" he asked, feeling his face swollen and in pain.

He could sense the relief in her voice. "The same. It took me forever to find you. I will save my argument about that for later," she replied.

Jase opened his eyes, slowly, blinking several times to focus. "Sounds good." He turned over onto his back. A sharp pain from both sides caused him to suck in his breath and wait for it to pass before asking, "What time is it?"

"It's close to two in the afternoon," she replied.

Jase yawned. "How is Skyrah? She got wounded during the battle," he stated.

"She is fine. She will have a small scar, but the medics have done a wonderful job on her," Kaimi replied.

"I think I've learned during this battle, that I'm still not as strong as I need to be. I was barely able to hold my own against that soldier we captured," he acknowledged.

"You are still learning. In time you will become master over your abilities."

Jase pushed himself up on the bed, feeling his body protest as he forced his legs over the side of the bed. He stood, feeling incredibly weak, and walked back out towards the living room to find the kitchen on shaky legs. His head throbbed and every time he took a breath, his ribs hurt. He found the kitchen and grabbed a glass out of a cupboard so he could drink water from the faucet. As he tried taking a sip, his jaw erupted in pain causing him to spill the water down his chin.

"Are you okay?" Kaimi asked, reading his signs from his armor.

Jase grimaced, tears running down his face as he waited for the pain to subside. "I broke my jaw I think," he winced. His jaw erupted in pain again as he heard a knock on the door outside before it opened.

"Bluestar? Are you in here?"

Jase turned to the front door to see Lieutenant Colonel Moon slowly stepping in. "Over here," he barely managed to say as he wiped tears from his eyes.

"What happened to your face?" Moon asked upon arrival.

Jase was too tired to explain, saying, "Battle."

She nodded, stepping closer to examine it with proper light. "It could take six weeks to heal if it's broken. Less if it's fractured."

Jase groaned as she softly touched his cheek. "I thought Bluestars were supposed to heal faster," he muttered.

"Your body is still getting used to your abilities. It will take longer until your cells adapt," she replied, crossing her arms as she leaned against the counter. "I heard you stopped the Androids from advancing both west and south gate. That's impressive."

"There were others who helped me," he replied.

"You still proved yourself, Jase. I will admit I was worried, but now I know you can hold your own. I can't think of anyone better to guard the Princess than you and the High Guardian." She paused for a moment, then moved forward again and touched his jaw. "Here," she said.

Before Jase could blink his jaw vibrated, growing hot for a moment, and the pain slipped away as he felt his cheek no longer swollen. He checked his reflection in the glass cabinets next to him and was surprised to see his face fully healed.

She smiled, softly. "Broken jaws are annoyances in wars."

"Thank you, Lieutenant Colonel," he said.

"Of course." She inclined her head, crossing her arms again. "Is Kaimi okay?"

Jase was about to answer when Kaimi appeared on his shoulder from his armor. "I am. I'm glad to see you alive as well, Lieutenant Colonel," she replied.

"It's hard to kill beings like us," Moon shrugged.

"Indeed it is," Kaimi agreed.

Lieutenant Colonel Moon then shifted her gaze to both of them, her once vibrant eyes seemed to dim slightly as she softly spoke. "I have something to tell you both while we have the chance."

"Did something happen?" Jase questioned.

Moon focused her gaze on him. "No, everyone is fine. No, I have something I should have told you both when we first met. It wasn't until we started fighting that I realized that one of us could have died. Death is always close at hand when it comes to battle," she said.

Jase glanced at Kaimi on his shoulder, but she too didn't seem to understand what Moon was getting at.

"I have many reasons why I didn't tell you or anyone, but you are the only ones I will tell now. Do as you wish with the information, but for the days to come, I'd like it to stay between us until we have made sure all of the Androids are disposed of in the city. Agreed?" she questioned.

Jase and Kaimi agreed.

Lieutenant Colonel Moon hesitated for a moment. "Jase, I'm your Mother."

End of Book One
The story will continue in Book Two...

Bulb Language

Aqyaxy - (Ak-yoxy) Please
Bonokay - (bon-o-onkay) Goodbye
Bonok Pybur - (bon-ok pie-bur) Goodnight
Bonok Sontypib - (bon- ok sonty-pib) Good morning
Bonok Yepypib - (bon-ok yep-y-pib) Good evening
Dea - (de-a) do
E - on
Eymeyfe - (eym-ey-fey) enemy
Goch - (go-ch) catch
Gondtoby - (gone-toby) courage
Heny - (hen-y) have
Hmil - (h-mill) human
iwth - (e-wth) with
Kel - can
Mirhri- (mir-he) hate
Miryh - (mir-ee) happy
Mochi- much
oki - okay
onar - your
oni ponither - (o-knee pon-i-ther)
Pon- (poon) no
Rurop ona - (ru-rop on-a) Thank you

459

Ta- to
Tvookul - (tv-oo-kul) speech
U'ma yey presimi - I am very impressed
U'pon trusti mhi - I don't trust him
Uyqon - (o-ken) hello
Xardayk - (x-ar-dek) stupid
Xarotx - (zar-rose) stars
Xarotx ouya zercy e ona - Stars have mercy on your soul
Yx - (eeks) yes
Zercy - Mercy
Zhev - ship
Zvaso - (zv-a-so) space
Zy - we
Zy heny mochi ta goch oryp - we have much to catch up

Elf Language
* **Yrt ela ota yrrou ob mikioo, biko vinur** - Try not to worry so much, please, friend
***Kpak horfa ohvao ou beann oou slevarts** - Stars watch over you and your travels
***Yimm kpak horfa ohvao ou beann oou slevarts** – May stars watch over you and your travels.

Special Preview of *Redstar*

Purples and pinks streaked the horizon of the setting sun of Otect City when Lord Brohain heard his door open and close behind him. Keeping his eyes forward, he listened to the heavy footsteps walking towards the balcony as he watched a large cargo transport zip out of the hangar bay at the edge of the city and towards the atmosphere. This was his favorite part of the day. Normally, he would have been cautious of someone walking up behind him in case it was another assassin attempt but not today. He was already in a gray mood as if he wasn't getting enough blood and oil circulating through his body as he stood there.

"My Lord?" came a harsh voice that sounded like metal grinding against stone.

Brohain didn't need to turn around to know who it was who spoke to him. Lieutenant Zeiden was the only Android who spoke like such since his vocal box had been damaged during the Great Civil war. He had refused to get it fix because he thought it sounded threatening than his normal voice. Brohain allowed it even though on most days the metal grinding annoyed him. He didn't understand why his Lieutenant wanted to keep it but he also knew he wasn't one to judge. After all he still wore his torn skin from the war before in order to remember what he had lost.

"I apologize to be bothering you, my Lord, but I have news from the attack on Adsila Laabbirrem, sir," Lieutenant Zeiden declared.

Lord Brohain watched the last of the sunset before turning to face the Android. Lieutenant Zeiden wore the skin of someone in their late thirties with

461

a sharp nose and a bulky chin with short black hair. He rose to the height of 7'4" only two inches shorter than Brohain himself. His red eyes focused on Brohain's as he stood at attention in his maroon and gray uniform that had the emblem of a tree on fire with a skull on the corner of his right shirt pocket.

"Report," Brohain commanded in a voice that sounded like a glass harmonica.

"Bradach failed in taking the city, sir. The Resistance were there to protect the civilians and the city from our attacks. We suffered heavy losses, my Lord," Lieutenant Zeiden told him.

The news surprised Brohain but he made sure not to allow it to show on his face. He didn't think Princess Nightstar could already be ready for another war or even have the numbers for one. It was a mistake he wouldn't make again. All he had to do was order his entire army to crush her at full force, but for now he wouldn't do that. He had bigger problems to worry about then the Princess. "Did any survive?"

"Just one, sir. He brought the report to us after the battle," the Lieutenant replied.

There's always one that has to survive, Brohain thought with annoyance as he stared back at the night sky that held millions of stars. "Thank him for his service then kill the coward for running from our enemies."

"Yes, my Lord," Lieutenant Zeiden responded.

"Has Captain Orexs found anything on Otov Ukoreow?" Brohain asked.

"Not yet, sir."

"It's a barren planet. It shouldn't be that hard to find something," he snapped.

Lieutenant Zeiden's back stiffened. "I will find out what the delay is, sir, and solve it."

"Do not disappoint me, Lieutenant," Brohain warned looking out at the city below.

"I won't, sir...there is one more thing, sir," Lieutenant Zeiden stated hesitating a moment. "A Bluestar is helping the Nightstar Princess. The Android saw it himself, sir."

Brohain turned around slowly as he tried to remember when he killed the last Bluestar. Had it been fifty years already? He remembered that he had ordered the deaths to all mothers bearing children during their last Bluestar season all across the galaxy. How had he missed one? It didn't matter now. The

Bluestar would die with the rest of the Resistance. "Continue as planned, Lieutenant. This Bluestar won't be able to stop us once my enhanced armor is complete," he replied.

"Of course, my Lord," Lieutenant Zeiden agreed with a salute and hurried to follow orders.

Lord Brohain turned back to the city with his thoughts on the Bluestar. *If the Princess thinks she can take back the universe with her new pet, she has another thing coming to her. Darkness is coming and I don't have time for her games. If she wants war then I shall give it to her.*

Stay tuned for Book Two!!

CPSIA information can be obtained
at www.ICGtesting.com
Printed in the USA
BVHW062056200720
584155BV00012B/228